DEATH IN TANGIER

"Look!" snapped Perez. "The crimson window!"

They saw Collier standing like an immense white slug against the crimson panes, frantically twisting the rusty brass handle of the window. He wrenched open the handle, kicking the window wide.

"Down!" yelled Perez. "Down on your faces, everybody!" Up went his hand, above his head, while he shouted an order to his men.

Rat tat tattattat, spurted the automatic rifles, their line of fire converging on the window.

Collier's very clothes seemed to flap and fly in the wind of bullets. In dying agony, he gave a terrific spring backward from the windowsill, and landed heavily, face up, on the carpet. His blood flowed out and over the design as he twitched once and forever lay still.

ZEBRA BOOKS
KENSINGTON PUBLISHING CORP.

ZEBRA BOOKS

are published by

Kensington Publishing Corp.
475 Park Avenue South
New York, NY 10016

First Zebra Books printing: March, 1989

Printed in the United States of America

CHAPTER ONE

The nine-thirty plane from Lisbon, due to arrive at Tangier two hours later, was on time; it swept in lower, broader circles above the airport. Most of the passengers, pressing their faces to the small windows of the small aircraft, were mystified or annoyed.

It was the first day in April. Below them they had expected to see Tangier, that lotus-city where you might do as you please, drowsing under a hot hard sunlight reflected from white houses, and the blue indentation of the Mediterranean where Cape Spartel marks the northernmost point in Africa. But, deplorable to relate, the weather was as bitterly cold as it might have been in London or New York. The plane bumped through tattered wreaths of mist through which such passengers caught glimpses only of dull green ground.

"Oh, dear!" inwardly groaned Miss Maureen Holmes.

It was only by accident that the slender, dark-haired American girl wore a fur coat. For some reason Maureen Holmes could not bring herself to leave it behind in New York. But dolefully she thought she spent as much on clothes—and light summer, almost tropical clothes—as the cost of the whole trip.

Suddenly, and apparently out of the air, Maureen was addressed by a bass voice whose owner seemed to think he was speaking in a hushed whisper.

"S-s-t!" hissed the voice. "Oi!"

The backs of these seats in the plane were very high. Also, electrically illumined signs in two languages above the door to the pilot's cabin announced that you must keep your seat belt fastened. Yet the very large, stout, barrel-shaped gentleman, occupying the seat in front of Maureen, had overcome these difficulties.

In some fashion he had turned round and kneeled to face Maureen. Over the seat peered a face which was large, round, and square-jawed, with a polished bald head and a pair of shell-rimmed spectacles pulled down on a broad nose. Though he meant only earnestness, he directed at Maureen a look of such horrible malignancy that the girl would have shied back if she had not recognized him.

"Now listen, my wench," he began, in what he imagined to be his most polished social manner. "I've got to explain a few things. Just between ourselves . . . sh-h, now! . . . my name is . . ."

Maureen knew what it was. Her green eyes, with the long black lashes, and broad mouth rather heavily made up against a pale complexion, held a certain anxiety as well as a secret admiration. Ever since the TWA airliner had left New York for Lisbon, she had half-hoped the old reprobate might speak to her.

"But you're the old man," she said simply. "You're Sir Henry Merrivale."

"Well . . . now," muttered H.M., not altogether displeased. *"Sh-h!"* he added, with a look so horrible that it would have paralyzed a Commando.

Against the blast of that personality, which seemed only a disembodied head glaring over the back of the seat, Maureen bristled a little. At home, at her work, she was cool and business-like and efficient, without losing any of her strong femininity. But now that she was abroad, her defenses were lowered, her true nature emerged; and she blurted out the words involuntarily.

"You're *awful!"* she said.

"What d'ye mean, I'm awful?" yelled H.M.

His powerful voice, against throttled motors as the plane circled down more softly through mist, caused shivering passengers to sit up and look. The Portuguese steward walked forward and indicated to H.M., more or less in English, that he was supposed to fasten his seat belt. H.M. handed the steward a ten-pound note and told him to sling his hook, which he did.

Maureen Holmes, already sorry for what she had said, tried to explain.

"I mean—according to the newspapers. When you first got to New York, you started a riot in the subway. Some people still say, in that Manning case, you . . . you . . ."

"Hocussed the evidence, hey?"

"If "hocussed' is the right word, yes. The police were after you in Washington, in Baltimore, in Philadelphia, in I don't know how many places! Including that little town near Charleston, where you persuaded the chief of police to arrest the mayor."

"Oh, my wench!" said H.M.

His big arm dismissed these small matters as mere peccadilloes. Sir Henry Merrivale, in fact, was puzzled as to why anyone should bother about them.

"When you got back to New York for the last time," persisted Maureen, "there was another riot and a murder in the Metropolitan Museum. Of course," Maureen glanced up from under her eyelashes, "the case was cracked by a Detective Lieutenant of the Homicide Squad. . . ."

"Uh-uh," grunted H.M., rolling up heavily innocent eyes. "Sure. Absolutely."

"But the Police Commissioner gave you a big banquet, and everything seemed wonderful. Everybody thought you were going back to England; not to Tangier. You sneaked out. You . . ."

Maureen paused. Lowering her head, so that her sleek black hair again contrasted with the beauty of the pale complexion, she tapped her gloved fingers irresolutely on her handbag.

"Oh, it's none of my business," she added softly, raising her green eyes, "but would you mind me telling you why, in a way, I hated the whole thing?"

"Lord love a duck, no."

"Aside from your—your horribly undignified conduct, and you an English nobleman, too . . ."

H.M.'s mouth fell open. "Undignified? *Me?*"

"Aside from that," insisted Maureen, "it was all those dreadful women! I'm sorry! And at your age, too!"

Now she had really produced a reaction from the man of dignity.

H.M.'s head, disembodied and slowly turning purple, moved from left to right like a saint's head on a platter.

"I am absolutely innercent!" he yelled, with passion and,

it must be conceded, a great deal of truth. "It's that newspaper crowd, so help me! They print what they like about me, 'cause they know I won't cut up rough about it. Burn me, I can't even speak to a good-looker without flash-gun pictures! If they could 'a made anybody swallow it, they'd have had me makin' passes at the Statue of Liberty."

"Then it really isn't true?"

"I'm misunderstood, my wench," said H.M., his face taking on the pathetic look of one who needs to be protected in this wicked world. "Honest! I'm the most misunderstood, clean-hearted ba—believer in good that ever walked. I stand there as good as gold, not botherin' anybody"—Sir Henry Merrivale really believed this—"and they up and mortify me. Look at me, my wench! Take a dekko at my dial! It's all right to call me Pop, which in America they mostly did. But am I an old rip?"

Despite her low spirits, mirth rose in the heart of Maureen Holmes. But her expression remained grave and sympathetic as she looked back at him.

"No, Sir Henry. I don't think you are."

"Good!" said H.M., his whole expression instantly changing. "Now we're going to land in a minute or so,"—here a heavy arm darted across the back of the seat, pointing its forefinger almost against the nose of the startled Maureen—"and you're goin' to answer me a few pretty intimate questions. Got that?"

"Well! I . . ."

"What's your name, my wench?"

Maureen told him.

"Are you here in Tangier on business, or is it a holiday?"

"It's just my vacation. Two weeks clear, with the addition of time for the plane trip back and forth."

"What's your job at home? If any?"

"I—I'm a receptionist for Jones, Howard, & Ramsbotham. You know—the big law firm. Three-eighty-six Fifth Avenue."

"Uh-huh. Where are you staying in Tangier?"

Maureen smiled wryly. It brought colour into her cheeks, making her face prettier and emphasizing the forthright yet reserved green eyes.

"At the Minzeh Hotel," she answered. "They said it was the best in Tangier; and I can't afford it, actually. But I just

. . . I just . . ." Ruefully she threw out her arms, and smiled again.

"Hah, better and better," declared H.M. "I booked reservations there, too. Now tell me. This Plushbottom law firm—what do they pay you—taking it by the week, say?"

Though her face grew more pink, Maureen told him.

"Uh-huh," said H.M. Again his forefinger pointed at her nose. "Then here's what I'll do. I'll triple that salary, and throw in two hundred as a bonus, it you'll pretend—only pretend—to be my secretary for a fortnight."

There was a silence, while Maureen looked back at him. Passengers, gabbling, were peering close to mist-stained windows in the near-silence of the plan. Then H.M. groaned.

"Oh, for the love of Esau!" he said, and smote his hands across his head. "No! It's not what you're thinkin'! It's not the evil old man creepin' up with evil propositions, which I'll prove." His martyred look returned. "I'm the poorest, most misunderstood . . ."

"But I don't think that!" protested Maureen. "Honestly!"

"Then . . ."

"I don't understand. Why do you want me to 'pretend' to be your secretary?"

"Sh-h!" hissed H.M., peering round conspiratorially. "Nobody knows I'm in Tangier. Not a soul! Oh, except the British Consulate; they're sending a young feller named Bentley to meet me; but they'll keep their mouths shut. What's more, nobody's goin' to know I'm here. I mean to sit back in a deck chair and sunglasses, doin' nothing, and recuperate from my holiday in America."

"But . . ."

"A while ago," H.M. sneered bitterly, "when you talked about the coppers chasing me practically from New York to San Francisco, I s'pose you thought I was having a good time? Well, I wasn't. 'Cause why? 'Cause those same coppers dragged me into the case to help 'em. Then, burn me if I know why, they got annoyed because I pinched the exhibits or flummoxed the evidence."

Here H.M. stuck his unmentionable face over the back of the seat, even his spectacles seeming larger.

"And what was every single one of those cases, my wench? Cor! I'll tell you. It was an impossible situation, that's what!"

"But," Maureen hesitated, "isn't that supposed to be your specialty?"

H.M.'s tortured expression was that of a reformed drunkard who sees before him a fine, noble bottle of whisky, with the top off and nobody in sight.

"I can't resist 'em," he said plaintively. "Supposin' I hear of a bloke shot to death in a locked room, or strangled on the sand at the seaside with no footprints except his own. Oh, my wench! Bright, burnin' flames of curiosity begin to shoot up round my collar; I can't rest, I can't sleep until I explain it."

"Yes; well?"

"It's got me, that's all. In London there's a snake named Masters: I couldn't understand why he went off his rocker, but I understand now." Again H.M. became all pathos. "I'm an old man, whatever they think. I can't stand the gaff. If anybody as much as says 'impossible' to me, "I'll bat him over the head with a soda siphon. Mind! I don't expect anything like that in Tangier; but I want to be smacking well certain I don't get involved. . . . That's where you come in."

"Where I come in? How?"

"Looky here," urged H.M. "You don't even have to be with me. When you go out of the hotel, just leave a note sayin' you've gone out with me; but you don't know where we're going or when we'll come back. If I'm in the hotel when you're there, you answer the phone. You say I'm paralyzed drunk—that's a good 'un!—or that I've got some awful infectious disease, or anything that'll keep 'em away. I'm dead serious, my wench. Will you do it?"

Maureen bit at her underlip. Her gaze roved over the quivering cabin, everywhere except at H.M. She threw back her fur coat, revealing a slender, supple figure in a dark-green frock with metal buttons.

"Sir Henry," she said wretchedly, "I can't."

With a soft bump and jar, the plane wheels struck the runway, hopped a little, and steadied. The steward bawled out in Portuguese that passengers must still retain their seats. The motors chuttered again, for some complicated maneuvering to bring the door of the plane, portside rear, opposite the airport station.

The romantic-minded Maureen stretched out a hand to touch the back of the seat under H.M.'s head.

"I'm terribly sorry," she almost pleaded, "but I can't!" She hesitated. "You see, these two weeks are complete freedom from—well, from what you just said. They can't get you, no matter how they try. You can stick out your tongue at a ringing telephone. You haven't any responsibility towards anybody or anything."

Maureen drew a deep breath.

"It's glorious!" she added in her low, fine voice. "If you'd ever worked for years in an office, and got to the point of thinking, 'I must remember this, I must remember that,' until you wanted to scream out loud, then I think you'd understand."

There was another pause, while Maureen lowered her eyes.

Then Maureen was astonished that H.M.'s big voice could be so gentle.

"I'm sorry too, my wench," he said, glaring at the floor. "And I'm the bloke who ought to apologize." Desperately he scratched on his head for hair that wasn't there. "Maybe the old man understands a lot more things than you think. But I say: you'll keep my secret, won't you?"

"Of course I will!" breathed Maureen. "All the secrets! Although . . ."

"Sh-h! Although what?"

"If we're staying at the same hotel, we're bound to run into each other. You must have made your reservation under a fake name. What name do I call you by?"

"Herbert Morrison," H.M. returned promptly. "Now don't get a funny look on your face, as if you'd heard it somewhere before! The initials are the same, ain't they? I'm good old Herbie Morrison. Sh-h!"

With a metallic sigh, the plane slid to a stop. There was a rippling and clashing as seat belts clattered open. The passengers, talking loudly in at least five languages, pressed hastily towards the door. Since H.M. and Maureen occupied the two foremost seats on the starboard side, they lingered and were more leisurely. Nobody had sat opposite them.

Up rose H.M. in all massiveness, goodly and great behind his corporation. On his head he firmly placed a Panama hat, with a vivid band and a down-turned brim. His light Palm Beach suit was set off by one of those revolting hand-painted ties which would have caused a shudder in Regent Street.

"Sir Henry," suggested Maureen hesitantly, "wouldn't it be better if you went first? I mean, you'll have to move sort of sideways down the aisle towards the door, and it would be much less awkward."

Even H.M.'s suspicious eye could detect no insulting reference to his corporation.

"Clever good!" he agreed, turning himself sideways and hopping down the aisle with his arms in the air like a ballet dancer. "Burn me, how good it is to sneak into a place where nobody knows you!"

"But, Sir Henry . . ."

"Sh-h! Call me Mr. Herbert Morrison, or else Pop."

"But I couldn't call you that!" Maureen was genuinely shocked. "Anyway, what is all that commotion down there outside the door?"

Though it was much warmer now that they had landed, the still-misted windows showed little outside. But it was evident that the fog had gone. Across the Tangier airport, built in mountain country far above and behind the city, a spiteful little wind still blew.

But shouts, imprecations now rose and boiled up round the portable steps which they had rolled against the open door. Each passenger, as he or she hurried down the steps, was whisked adroitly to one side; and all were lined up against the plane like those about to be shot.

"It's nothin', my wench," H.M. scoffed airily. "When Spaniards or Portuguese or Arabs begin yelling at each other, and you don't know more'n a dozen words, it sounds like there's goin' to be a murder; but it only means they're arguing about one peseta on the bill. Sh-h! Y'see . . ."

By this time *he* was at the door, where the steward bowed so low he nearly fell flat. H.M., handing him money, had hurried three steps down the stairs before he looked up. Directly ahead of him, about forty feet away, ran the long, rather low line of the airport station, with a row of glass doors along the front.

Then H.M. did look up, and surveyed what was before him. His neck swelled, and his eyes slowly bulged out behind the big spectacles. If he had not established a firm grip on the handrail, he would have reeled.

"Oh, lord love a duck!" he whispered.

CHAPTER TWO

And, for once, H.M.'s call for compassion was not without reason.

He scarcely heard the thunder of cheers, from what seemed thousands of lusty North African throats, which nearly blew off his hat. His blurred eye first saw the two lines of red silken ropes, each line looped through an upright metal support at ten feet or so, which ran from the foot of the portable steps to the central door of the building, forming a broad path to divide the multitude.

Still blurred, his eye moved upwards. Above the central door loomed three immense messages woven in tropical flowers, their entwined hues flaming against the old green-brown hills. Each was in a different language, set one above the other thus:

Salud y Pesetas y Cosas Nuevas a SIR HENRY MERRIVALE!
Vive le Vieux Bonhomme, SIR HENRY MERRIVALE!
Salamun Aleykum, SIR HENRY MERRIVALE!

The last greeting was in Arabic characters which we need not torture the printers to reproduce. But there was more. Beyond the right-hand red rope, motionless and without an eyewink, stood a twenty-piece band whose instruments were mostly of brass. Even a newcomer could deduce that the band was composed of Tangier policemen. They wore white-painted helmets, rather like American helmets, over dark-complexioned faces. Their uniform shirts and shorts were of light khaki; a white cross belt passed a whistle hung round the neck on a chain, descended across the chest to a white belt with a white truncheon. Rigidly disciplined, they waited for a hidden signal.

Then the whole band burst like artillery into the face of Sir Henry Merrivale, and the tune was "God Save the King." The civilian population, on the other side of the red rope, cheered so wildly as almost to equal the band.

Maureen Holmes, on the step behind H.M., bent forward and spoke timorously at his ear.

"You know, Sir Henry," she said, "I'm afraid *somebody* knows you're here."

"Well . . . now," growled the great man, obviously of two minds about how to treat this. Then he was galvanized. "Oi! My wench! Look there!"

It was the crowning triumph, *le moment suprême.* At the central door of the airport stooped two Arab boys, perhaps nine or ten years old, in jacket and breeches suspiciously white. Both wore the red tarboosh, with tassel, which nowadays means only that the wearer is a Mohammedan. And they stooped on either side of what looked like an immense and broad roll of red carpet.

With a concerted word to each other the boys darted forward like monkeys. The red carpet unrolled swiftly towards the portable steps.

"Hem!" observed Sir Henry Merrivale, with a strange new note in his voice.

"A red carpet for you!" said Maureen. "Isn't it wonderful?"

"Oh, nothin' much," sneered H.M., with a gesture of indifference. "I don't care about it, if that's what you mean." Again he broke off, shivering, and cupped his hands round his mouth.

"Hoy!" he bellowed.

When we remember that the band was at its most deafening during the second playing of "God Save the King," and the spectators were making noises so loud as can be heard only in Tangier, it is remarkable that even H.M. could have made himself heard. But he did.

"Hoy!" he bellowed again.

Briefly the red carpet stopped. Two small faces, brown and alert, were raised towards him under two red tarbooshes.

"You're swingin' that bloomin' carpet too much to your right," thundered the visitor, with gestures. "In one more minute you'll have it under the tail of the plane. Swing it to your left, here, so's I can walk on it!"

In a country where one sentence may contain words in five languages, with explanatory gestures, it is easy to make yourself understood. There were two grins and two white eyeflashes as the Arab boys nodded. The red carpet flashed forward and ended dead at the foot of the stairs; the boys, again at some secret signal, disappeared.

"Hem!" repeated Sir Henry Merrivale.

With a casual gesture, like a magician handing a used prop to his female assistant, H.M. offered his hat to Maureen. The remaining steps he descended at a lordly and pigeon-toed walk. Then, putting his hand on his heart, he bowed left and right as low as his corporation would permit.

"Muchas gracias," he bellowed. *"Je vous remercie. Naharak sai'd.* Members of the Conservative Party, I thank you."

The noise was now louder than the heaviest ack-ack barrage in a London blitz ten years ago. Maureen, feeling guilty because she held H.M.'s hat, stole down the stairs to stand behind him.

"I dunno what we're goin' to do now," admitted the distinguished visitor. "It's been a fine show, but where's the M.C.?"

Relief, however, was in sight.

Governed by that same mysterious but hidden signal, the band stopped abruptly in the middle of their fourth playing of "God Save the King"; so abruptly that one whump of a trombone sailed out and could not be recaptured. The civilian crowd, streaked through with colourful costumes, ceased to shout. Maureen could feel her head buzzing from the silence.

Out and under the right-hand rope there ducked and stood up a lean young man who was a little above middle height. Though he was faintly swarthy and had black hair, there was about him not the slightest suggestion of the quality called oiliness. His tweed sports coat, with grey flannel trousers and a sombre dark-blue tie, might have come from Bond Street. Though his best friend could not have called him handsome, his thin face showed traces of an intelligence and humour which were masked, as a result of his official duties, by a formal courtesy close to stateliness.

In his left hand he held a small sheaf of papers. He bowed formally to H.M., and then raised the red-brown eyes which were his best feature.

"Sir Henry," he said, in English without a trace of foreign accent, "may I be the first to welcome you? I am Alvarez, the Commandant."

(Commandant of what? And in sport clothes? It might have meant anything. But H.M. did not pursue the matter.)

"Y'know, son," he said, dubiously tugging at his ear lobe, "this is uncommon handsome of you. It really is. But are you sure you're settin' off illuminations for the right man? I'm good old Herbie . . ."

Alvarez stopped him with a small, hardly noticeable gesture. The Commandant's eyes, coldly formal, took a glance at the great flower messages towering behind him.

"If I might suggest it, sir," he said with deepest respect, "would it not be wise to drop your incognito now?"

"H'mf. Well. If everybody seems to . . ."

"Sir Henry!" interrupted a new and feminine voice. A girl ducked under the rope and ran towards them. Maureen Holmes's eye was instantly fixed on her; though, under lowered lashes, Maureen scarcely seemed to notice her.

The newcomer was clearly British, clearly in her middle-twenties, and clearly friendly. Her thick fine-spun hair, of a truly golden colour, was worn long in a page-boy bob. Under thin and arched but unplucked eyebrows, she had dark blue eyes with heavy lids. The slightest exertion flushed her fair skin. Though she wore very little powder and no lipstick, there flowed from her an aura of sheer femininity like a physical touch. She was hardly conscious of this, though an outsider would have sworn differently. Over her shoulders she had thrown a light coat. But her Paris dressmaker, in the Place de France, had designed for her an unorthodox silk summer frock with a deep V between the breasts, and clinging tightly to her admirable figure. She was without stockings, and wore openwork sandals.

"You must forgive me," stated the coldly formal Juan Alvarez. "May I present . . . ?"

"I'm Paula Bentley," cried the newcomer, and attached herself to H.M.'s arm. "Bill (my husband, you know) was supposed to meet you. But old J.—that's the consul—wouldn't let him go. Will I do instead?"

"Oh, my dolly!" said H.M., powerfully dazzled. This was his type, breathless but not much inhibited.

"You see," Paula explained, "they're always sending poor Bill"—unreserved love made rich her voice whenever she spoke of Bill—"to some dreadful place all over the world to write a report about mud or bananas or machinery or something. The report is always miles long; and old J. wants to study every word. And of course Bill returned only three days ago, and we . . . I mean . . ." Paula's face went scarlet, and she stopped.

"Sure, my dolly," H.M. soothed her. "You've got a lot of intimate talking to do; that's it."

"Well . . . something like that. Yes. Thanks." Happy again, the dropped brick forgotten, Paula Bentley suddenly became conscious of Maureen on the other side of H.M. "Er—" she began.

Maureen, throwing back her fur coat still farther, lowered the lashes over her green eyes. Casually she strolled forward, and took affectionate possession of H.M.'s left arm.

"I am Sir Henry's secretary," she announced, in her receptionist's beautiful voice.

Dead silence.

Maureen did not explain her reasons for this sudden about-turn. Perhaps it was just as well. All four faces in that group were worthy of study afterwards.

H.M., whose poker-face is still famed at the Diogenes Club, remained as imperturbable as an oyster. Yet Commandant Alvarez, though not a muscle moved in his face, somehow conveyed—suggestion, telepathy!—the gesture of one in England who puts his hand before his mouth, coughs delicately, and raises his eyebrows. There was anger in his look, too.

H.M., about to shout, "I am absolutely innercent," choked back the words just in time. Alvarez inclined his head in stately fashion towards Maureen, and for the first time showed fine teeth in a smile.

"I fear it is my fault, Miss . . . ?"

"Holmes," grunted H.M. "Maureen Holmes."

"It is my fault, Miss Holmes, that we were unaware of your arrival. May I bid you, in the name of my—my authority, the most cordial welcome? We shall try to make you as comfortable as we can."

"Of course we will!" cried Paula. Dropping H.M.'s arm, she hurried round to Maureen and extended her hand.

"It was awfully decent of you to come here!" Paula went on. "I've heard a great deal about Sir Henry's secretary in London—I think he calls her Lollypop—but you're from the States, of course."

Now, in fiction, even to this day, the English girl is always depicted as cold, haughty, and aristocratic, which is almost comically the reverse of true. The American girl, on the other hand, is always shown as bright, "cute," asking questions twenty to the dozen; which would hardly be an accurate description of the reserved Maureen or so many like her.

And yet, at the beginning, it must be confessed that Maureen had the darkest suspicions of Paula Bentley. She thought the English blonde had shown too much sex appeal, too much—well, you know. But that had changed. At the deep sincerity in Paula's dark-blue eyes, at the warmth and friendliness of her handshake, Maureen's heart melted.

"Do you know, I spent six months in New York before I was married," Paula said eagerly. "As a matter of fact, my younger sister is at Columbia now. Iris Lade. I don't suppose you've met her?"

"No. I was at Wellesley. That was some time ago, of course."

Hoy!" roared Sir Henry Merrivale. For a moment there was complete silence.

"Sir?" murmured Alvarez, again the complete stuffed shirt.

"Now that all the goo-goo is over, son, do I walk across that red carpet, or don't I?"

"Certainly, sir."

"What I mean," said H.M., instantly aloof and disdainful, "is we've got to get our passports stamped in there, and have the customs people look at our luggage. Those passengers you lined up against the plane are goin' stark gibberin' mad, I tell you! They can't leave until we do. Hadn't you better start the march?"

Unobtrusively Alvarez snapped his fingers. Maureen, who saw this, observed that an inconspicuous man in plain clothes melted away from the civilian crowd.

"As for your passports, sir," continued Alvarez, slightly lifting one shoulder, "I can have them stamped for you and Miss Holmes in one minute. Our friends the French, who control all customhouses both here and at the port, have given you diplomatic immunity; your luggage will not be touched. Over there," he nodded to the right, beyond the band, "waits the motor car in which I shall be happy to drive you to your destination. Another car, of course, will follow us with you luggage and that of Miss Holmes."

H.M. seemed dazed.

"Looky here, son. Are you *sure* you've got the right man?"

"Quite sure, sir." Again Alvarez bowed. "In fact, we need not go into the building at all, save that . . ."

"Let's have it, son. What?"

"Well! If you will be so kind as to walk across to the airport amid your admirers, you will confer on them a great favour. A bow, a smile, perhaps even an encouraging word? Since they know you so well . . ."

What d'ye mean, they know me so well?"

For the first time Commandant Alvarez seemed at loss. His dark eyebrows gathered together over the red-brown eyes. Then, as though happily, it seemed that the truth reached him.

"Come, I have it!" he declared. His shoulders went back in military fashion. "You imagine that here in Tangier we live away from the world? Pardon me; not so. In addition to the English *Tangier Gazette,* we have newspapers in Spanish, in French, in Arabic. These good people have followed your career. Not merely your thrilling detective adventures; more, in particular, your capacity to absorb incredible quantities of strong drink and your relentless pursuit of—er—fair ladies. Believe me, sir, it is deeply admired here."

"But it ain't true!" yelled H.M. "It's all newspaper lies!"

Fully drawn up, with impregnable courtesy, Alvarez quelled the outburst by ignoring it.

"Miss Holmes, will you be good enough to give me Sir Henry's hat? Thank you." Alvarez placed it at a definitely rakish angle on the great man's head. "Now! If you will take his right arm, Mrs. Bentley, and you his left arm, Miss Holmes. . . . Please be ready to proceed at the first note of the band. I shall follow you three. Is all understood?"

Paula Bentley, though rather subdued, was enjoying herself. Maureen was not so sure. But they both did as they were told.

"Excellent!" said Alvarez, and brushed imaginary fluff from the lapel of this tweed coat. He snapped his fingers to the right; he snapped his fingers to the left.

"Forward!" he cried.

With full flourish the band boomed and brayed; the audience went mad with delight. And the blood of the Merrivales could no longer resist. All his life H.M. had dreamed of somebody putting down a red carpet for him, and here it was. Majestically, his corporation outthrust, he moved forward at a pigeon-toed walk, with a pretty girl clinging to each arm. The boom of the band poured out its lofty strains.

Come, come, come and make eyes at me
Down at the old "Bull and Bush," (da, da!)
Come, come, come and drink booze with me
Down at the old "Bull and Bush!" (da, da). . . .

"Regard there the old goodman," shouted an ecstatic voice in French. "To Tangier he brings *two* poules, eh? It is magnificent, that!"

"Y bellas muchachas con tetas grandes!" yelled a delighted Spaniard, pointing to what should have been the rest of the flower message.

"Allah! Allah! Bless the wine-drinking unbeliever with

many sons!"

"Do you realize," Maureen called across to Paula, "that we're supposed to be concubines?"

"I never was anybody's concubine, except Bill's," cried Paula. "But I should dearly love to look like one."

H.M. had now completely lost his head. Dragging off his hat, with Paula still clinging determinedly to his arm, he waved the hat and was bellowing back amenities in return. His French was fluent, if you do not mind the speech of a Parisian taxi driver. But he knew few words of Spanish. And, though it may be remembered he had picked up a fine vocabulary of Arabic in Egypt, these were mostly words not to be spoken in public.

But inspiration darted into his brain. If he pointed to himself as he spoke, giving a dignified, tolerant smile at the same time . . .

"Khanif!" roared a revitalized H.M., pointing to himself. His attempt at a smile can only be called hellish. While Paula had to stand on tiptoe and try to hold his hat near his head while he pointed at himself, H.M. cut loose.

"Ya illa illa Allah!" screamed a voice in pure ecstasy.

If H.M. had deliberately wanted to be popular, he could have taken no better course. The Arab has that very primitive sense of humour which rejoices in the mere use of improper words. As there poured over them such a string of indecencies and vile obscenities that even Commandant Alvarez blenched, a king of explosion shook the crowd. Strong men, either in *jalebah* or modern clothes, were doubled up with tears of mirth. Even the women, including those slim ones in the beautiful grey *jalebahs* with flat hoods and laced *yashmaks,* had turned away and were rocking helplessly.

And then, as the dauntless three neared the glass doors, ghostly figures flitted or crouched across their path. Newspaper flash bulbs glared and rippled, then faded away. In another moment H.M., now turned the other way round and still cursing mightily in Arabic, was borne backwards through the central door by his two "concubines" and Commandant Alvarez, as the band crashed into "Knocked 'Em in the Old Kent Road."

"Oh, God," whispered Paula Bentley. Puffing out her

cheeks, shaking back the heavy golden hair, Paula gave H.M. a curious look before she gave him his hat. Then, light and graceful, she raced off towards a public telephone to reach her Bill at the British Consulate.

Alvarez took from Maureen a green passport, and from H.M. a blue one. Hurrying toward a large cubicle, in frosted glass above the middle, Alvarez put his head through a window. Maureen and H.M. stood in a core of silence amid huge noise outside.

'Wot—cher?' all the people say,
"Oo yer goin' to meet, Bill?
Do yer own the street, Bill?'
Laugh? Gord! Thought I'd nearly die—
Knocked 'em in the Old Kent Road!

Well, H.M. had knocked 'em. As usual, with the populace if not the authorities, he had scored a hit—with what effect at the moment, he could not guess. He merely stood there, hat on, with an insufferable look of complacency on his face, and waited to be praised. He was not praised.

"Sir Henry," said Maureen, with that same look of doubt she had kept for some time, "I'm scared."

H.M. was taken aback. "Scared, my wench? Scared of what?"

"Wait! Why do you call Mrs. Bentley 'my dolly,' and call me 'my wench'?"

"Come to think of it, I dunno. Would you rather I changed it the other way round?"

"No, no! If you must call me something like that, I'd prefer—the second. But never mind that. Under all this ceremony, it's *wrong*. It's like something in *Through the Looking Glass*. The whole Government can't be crazy, even in Tangier. Wait, now! I know what they say isn't true. But they wouldn't give you an official welcome just for getting tight and chasing blondes, would they?"

Maureen had removed her fur coat and hung it over her arm. Her sleek black hair, parted in the middle and drawn across the ears in bands at the back of the head, gave a quiet intensity to every expression on her face. Surreptitiously she had removed most of her lipstick, because Paula Bentley wore none.

"Oh, probably I'm wrong," admitted Maureen. "But I still think that under the surface it's all deceptive and maybe dangerous. You and I and Mrs. Bentley can trust each other. But what about this Commandant Alvarez?"

She glanced quickly towards her left. Alvarez, standing at the window of the glass enclosure, had drawn a telephone to the window ledge; Maureen heard the whirr and click of the dial.

"Who or what is he? We don't know a thing about him. Though I admit he is . . . rather nice."

H.M. gave her a sharp sideways look.

"Uh-huh. For a Spaniard, he's not bad. No pomade on his hair. No loud clothes, just like me. No loud speech or wavin' his hands, like me again. Good family; probably been in the army. Best of all, not a ruddy ring on any finger. By the way, you noticed he was awful smitten with you?"

"How utterly ridiculous!"

"So? You're not very observing, my wench. When he thought my 'secretary' meant my Scotch warming pan, he was as mad as hops. When I used some fine old terms in Arabic, he went white and looked at you because he thought you might understand 'em."

"But—but you couldn't have seen that! You only glanced back once! You couldn't have seen!"

"Couldn't I?" said H.M. "I'm the old man."

Then his tone changed. He pointed a finger at Maureen.

"Now I'm goin' to ask *you* a question, and I want the truth. Why did you suddenly change and decide you'd pretend to be my secretary after all?"

Maureen lowered her green eyes, which always animated her face and (in a sense) betrayed her. Several lies flashed through her mind, but the "old man" had too disturbingly penetrating a look.

"If I tell you, Sir Henry, will you promise not to get mad?"

"Me? 'Course I won't get mad!"

"Well," and Maureen moistened her lips, "at first I

thought I couldn't. Absolutely couldn't! And then . . . Listen, Sir Henry! I know you've got all the brains in the world, and everything like that. But sometimes you're so—so *childish*. I was afraid if I didn't look after you, that the first crook you met would fool you or swindle you."

There was terrible silence.

Maureen did not know she had said the unsayable thing. But H.M., though he shivered, did not explode. He merely folded his arms.

" 'Childish,' eh?" he murmured, with his eye on a corner of the ceiling.

"Please! You promised you wouldn't get mad!"

"Who's mad?" inquired the other, with vast surprise. "I'm cogitatin', that's all." He cogitated. " 'The first crook' I meet will—" Then he sighed. "Y'know, I wonder if you can guess how many crooks I've flumdiddled and turned wall-eyed at their own game? But I'm not going to tell you. I'm going to *show* you. I'm goin' to take you . . ."

"Take her where?" interrupted the soft, quick voice of Paula Bentley, who had raced back from the phone.

"Take Miss Holmes, and all of us, out by the side door," said the formal voice of Alvarez, hurrying back from his own phone. "Much haste is necessary, I point out. We do not wish for there to be trouble."

"What d'ye mean, trouble? Why, son . . ."

Though the muted roar could be heard from outside, even above the band, Alvarez nodded towards the glass doors. Policemen, their white hard-rubber truncheons drawn, stood motionless along the whole line of the doors.

"I fear, sir, you have made yourself too much admired," explained Alvarez with some dryness, and handed H.M. two stamped passports. "There are many who would rend all the clothes from you and take them home in pieces as precious souvenirs."

"Have you seen to that luggage?" asked H.M., turning slightly green. "Then why don't we cut along? Now!"

Twenty seconds later they stood outside, in a large if somewhat rocky open space beside the largest and most modern of Packard cars. A little distance away stood a very modern Buick, in whose back seat sat a bronzed old gentleman who wore the green tarboosh which indicates a holy pilgrimage to Mecca. H.M. eyed that green fez with a longing bordering on greed; Maureen could almost see the clicking thoughts which transferred it to his own head. Behind them was a new Ford station wagon, into which short muscular Arabs were piling luggage.

Maureen, who had expected to see old rattletrap cars, swallowed her surprise. Opening the back door of the Packard, Alvarez handed in Paula Bentley, who was an old acquaintance; he even managed to shove in H.M. But, when he opened the front door, Alvarez lost his suavity and even became awkward.

"Miss Holmes, I trust—that is to say, for example: will you do me the honour of sitting beside me when I drive?"

"I'd love to," Maureen answered conventionally; but even this had its effect on the Commandant.

Slamming the door, he hurried round to the other side and slipped into the front seat. Then things began to happen. Moving into top gear almost at once, Alvarez sent the powerful car whizzing up a low embankment, wrenched the wheel violently to the left, and bucketed down a not-too-even road at such blazing speed that even the tumult at the airport faded away.

H.M., flung backwards on his spine and thrashing to get up, could be heard distinctly speaking in Arabic. Paula Bentley, saving her modesty only by pulling over her knees a short silk skirt under which she wore little, rolled in the other direction.

For sometime, under a damp overcast sky, they shot down a long and winding road without a word spoken. H.M., one of whose few fears is fast driving when he is not himself at the wheel, struggled to regain breath and dignity. Paula, crossing her knees and drawing the light coat round her shoulders, sat up and found nothing strange in eighty miles an hour among bends and boulders.

These hills, Paula had always thought, looked disappointingly unforeign. The left of the road might have been Dartmoor; the right might have been Hampshire. Then she heard Maureen gasp. Some distance away, a very old man in a dirty robe and a wide-brimmed conical straw hat was ploughing a field with oxen behind a plough that might have been used in Biblical times.

"By the way, son. . . ." An impassive H.M. addressed Alvarez, who inclined his head but did not turn round. "I think I told you that was a slap-up welcome. Who arranged it? The Sultan of Morocco?"

"I fear, sir, you are not quite up to date," said Alvarez. Sideways, in the rear-view mirror, you could see Alvarez's long straight nose, his broad but tightly compressed mouth. "The Sultan of Morocco has merely nominal authority. Tangier is what is called an international zone: it is ruled by the representatives of many nations. For instance, the head of the Government is a Dutchman."

"Lord love a duck, think of that! What d'ye want with a gin-swillin' squarehead?"

His right hand resting carelessly on the wheel while he still pressed down on the accelerator, Alvarez turned round almost fully to face H.M. Alvarez, driving by instinct or casual glances, regarded H.M. with what was almost a smile.

"Mynheer Hoofdstuck," he said, "is a gentleman of great ability and uprightness. True, he has what you would call somewhat Puritan principles . . ."

"Is Tangier a Puritan city?"

"No, sir. Definitely not."

"Uh-huh. Well?"

"I was speaking of the various government heads. The French, as I had the pleasure of telling you, control the customhouses. The Belgians control the police. The Spanish . . ."

"For the love of Esau, look where you're goin'!"

Turning back carelessly, Alvarez avoided a thick low palm tree with a slight flick of his wrist, and whirled round another curve. Though the padded upholstery gave the passengers no shock, it threw them all together again.

"Without wishin'," said H.M, "to cast any aspersions on your sanity, do they issue drivers' licenses to every loony like you?"

"But, sir—"

"No, no, keep your eyes on the road!"

"But I am considered the most careful and moderate of drivers," protested Alvarez, with surprise and obvious truth. "Come, Sir Henry! Wait until you see the cars pour down into the Place de France by day; or, better still, through narrow streets down into the Grand Socco! And each driver with his hand on the button of the horn!"

"I'm savourin' the pleasure," said H.M., and glanced out of the rear window. "Well, that little luggage van is after us right enough. Did you tell 'em we were goin' to the Minzeh Hotel?"

"The Minzeh!" exclaimed Paula. "But that's where Bill and I live! We . . ."

"I said nothing," Alvarez observed slowly, "about driving to the Minzeh."

A chilly silence fell in the car, though a bright streak of sunlight streamed down outside.

"I said, if you remember," continued Alvarez, "that I would drive you to your destination."

CHAPTER THREE

Again they could hear only the low, heavy tiger hum of the car. Maureen, who had been staring straight ahead with the determination to show no sign of anything unusual even if they crashed into one of the low walls built of loose stones, felt all her forebodings congeal again.

She stole a quick look sideways at Alvarez, whose teeth were set and his hands locked on the wheel, as though he hated what he had said. The old road dipped and swung amid higher, darker trees; the speedometer needle flickered round ninety.

Then H.M. spoke drowsily, always a bad sign.

"I say, my dolly." He touched Paula on the arm. "Would you mind changing places with me?"

"Lord, no. But why?"

A low-flying bee whacked against the windscreen with an audible report. Paula Bentley maneuvered her knees over H.M. as the latter slid across the cushion to the left hand side behind the driver. The speedometer needle flickered over ninety.

"I dunno whether you've heard of the trick, son," H.M. remarked drowsily, "but from this position I can break your neck quicker'n a hangman."

"Perhaps, though, you might find it difficult." Alvarez still spoke in a steady, formal tone. "And yet, sir, if you attack the driver this car will run wild. Miss . . . that is, all of us would be injured and possibly killed. Because of this, and this alone, I yield."

The speedometer needle dropped steadily back to seventy, then sixty and fifty to forty. In the windscreen Paula could see by the reflection that Maureen's face was very white.

Although Paula was far more emotional than Maureen, she was less sensible of physical danger. She had seen too much of it in a London girlhood. Paula smoothed her yellow hair; her pink lips parted in an expression between amusement and annoyance.

"Juan!" she said quietly.

"Yes?" said Alvarez.

"You *are* silly," Paula told him in her soft voice. "Is this bit of nonsense what I think it is?"

Alvarez may, or may not, have shrugged his shoulders.

"Well, I shall tell them what I think it is, if you won't. You're 'under orders,' I suppose. Oh, Juan! Sir Henry and Maureen have done everything you asked." Colour flamed through the fair complexion of Paula's face. "Can't you at least tell them? Wouldn't that be the decent thing? The sporting thing?"

For some reason only that word "sporting" made Alvarez wince. He looked at Maureen, who stared steadily ahead. Slowing down the car to a stop, Alvarez yanked on the hand brake. He turned to the back, the nostrils of his thin nose dilated.

"Sir Henry, I assure you—and Miss Holmes—that you are not being kidnapped. You will not be harmed or molested in any way. If you and Miss Holmes wish to walk the six or seven miles to the Hotel Minzeh in the rue du Statut, you are at liberty to leave this car. Or you could ride in the station wagon with the luggage."

All dangerous signs had faded in H.M.

"Oh, son! I'd rather be kidnapped than walk *one* mile. And bouncin' in that luggage van wouldn't be good for my behind. To tell you the truth, I don't particularly care where we go, as long as I can rest. What d'ye think, my wench?"

"I don't mind either," Maureen answered instantly and cheerfully.

"Wait a minute!" said H.M., with sudden alarm. "This hokey-pokey isn't goin' to snare me into police work, is it?"

Alvarez cleared his throat.

"Sir, aside from petty larcenies and minor assaults, there has been no crime here within the past two months."

"Haah!" said H.M, letting out vast relief. "That's all I wanted to know."

"We have come some distance," Alvarez told him instantly. "We are now on the Old Mountain. A little distance ahead, and at my first turn, we shall be on the Old Mountain Road. Up here live many of the retired, the affluent, the gentry." His voice grew intense. "I ask only to drive you to one of these, which I can do in three minutes. There you will have perhaps ten, perhaps twenty minutes' talk with a certain gentleman. Afterwards you may, of course, do as you like."

"I still don't understand the reason for all this mysterious hocus-pocus . . ."

"There are reasons, sir! Believe me!"

"Oh, son, it's all right!" said H.M. "I enjoy a little *causerie* with anybody. Maybe it's that ruddy Dutchman with his bottle of schnapps. Drive on."

Alvarez, so relieved that faint sweat appeared on his swarthy forehead, whipped round to the wheel. Starting the car, he slid it into top gear and shot forward like a thunderbolt. Then he seemed to remember something, and glanced at Maureen.

"Miss Holmes," he said awkwardly, "I—that is, I have been accused of too-fast driving, which seems extraordinary. Do *you* think it too fast?"

Maureen turned and smiled at him. She still could not decide whether she liked or disliked him.

"Well," she answered, "If you *could* manage to drive a little more slowly . . . ?"

Almost instantly the Packard's pace dropped to that of a rather rheumatic snail. Paula Bentley, again sitting back in one corner with her knees crossed and light coat draped on her shoulders, winked at H.M. in sheer delight. But the great man did not notice.

Alvarez's tactics had been bad. The bright-painted station wagon, plunging after him, evidently did not trust its brakes to avoid a collision from behind. It shot straight out across an open field, fortunately unfenced, with a realistic imitation of a bucking bronco at a rodeo. Then, making a sweeping turn on two wheels, the station wagon bucked its way back, rejoining the road and avoiding another near collision by at least two feet.

H.M. closed his eyes. He did not say anything.

But, after a moment, he leaned forward and tapped Alvarez on the shoulder.

"Son," he suggested, "did anybody ever tell you about the stork? Or that there's a difference between a jet plane and bus goin' to Croydon? What I mean—sort of a compromise?"

"I fear I cannot do that, sir. I am sorry. I must go violently one way or the other."

"Well," observed Paula, all innocent-eyed, "your wife will always know where you stand."

"Wife?" cried Alvarez. "What wife? I have no wife!"

Yet the car moved forward at a steady thirty-five. They were now on the Old Mountain Road, with the sun at noonday warm and even hot. On their left, where the hill sloped up steeply, a house or villa was all but invisible amid thick trees. On their right, they still could not see down to Tangier in the valley because of thin but monstrously high hedges. But a tropical luxuriance seemed to have crept into the vegetation that was very sweet to Maureen.

Then, on their right, some distance ahead, appeared a smallish mosque painted pink. Nobody except Alvarez and Paula saw a broad opening in the tall thin hedge to the left, beyond which the hill sloped steeply.

Alvarez, jamming his foot on the accelerator, yanked the wheel to the left. They plunged through the opening in the hedge, then slightly to the right up a steep earthen tunnel walled on each side with dark-green moss or grey stone once whitewashed, and bunched trees overhanging. They seemed to have climbed a good distance when Alvarez, driving on more power in top gear, whirled the car to the right.

Now they raced on gravel past a high brick wall, parallel with the wall because the path was so narrow. Up ahead sprang a pair of gateposts, also parallel with them in the narrow path. The eye of Sir Henry Merrivale saw doom ahead of him.

"Looky here, son! You're not goin' to turn left through those gateposts? You can't do it! Nobody can make . . ."

But Alvarez did. Even the Packard skidded as its rear end swung round under the wrench of Alvarez's left hand. Gravel spurted wide, or clattered up under the wings. They were still ascending when they had passed through the gateposts, but on a gentler gravel drive which curved up at the side of a garden planted with great wild-olive trees. And they caught their first rational glimpse of the house.

The House of the Wild Olives, very high and very broad, was of white dressed stone as smooth as concrete; against it many lines of windows, with wooden shutters painted green, stood out vividly. The actual ground floor, you could see, was a kind of cellar: it contained only kitchens and kitchen offices. The true ground floor, with the front door, was above it. Across this had been built a broad terrace with a marble balustrade, along which stood at intervals smallish marble nymphs and vases. A stone staircase against the front wall went up to the balcony; and beneath the balcony had been built a broad garage.

Seen now, under the sunlight and amid a bickering of birds, it seemed stately yet kindly. Though the house could not have been very old, forty years perhaps, it carried well the grace and colour of its country.

Alvarez, moving slowly, sent the car idling into the dim garage and stopped.

"You see?" said Paula Bentley. "Since Juan insisted on being so horribly mysterious, I kept my mouth shut. But there wasn't the least danger, Maureen, or I should have stopped it. And there *wasn't* any danger; was there, Sir Henry?"

H.M., deeply in one corner with his hands folded over his corporation and his squashed Panama hat drawn down, opened one eye.

"No-n-o," he said, with a rumble from deep in his chest. "No danger. Absolutely. In this country all you got to worry about is the morgue. Will somebody help me out of this treacherous capsule?"

Alvarez sprang down and opened the door for him. Out poured what seemed a shapeless mass, which reassembled itself like an evil-minded goblin. H.M., reaching into his pocket, brought out a cigar case, took one of his vile black cigars, sniffed at it with ghoulish voluptuousness, bit off the end, spat it out, and lighted the cigar. As he inhaled, his face grew almost human.

"Sir, you will have the kindness to remember?" Alvarez was eager, on wires. "Your instructions?"

"Why not?" asked H.M. "I ain't dead yet. Burn me if I can tell you why I'm still alive, but I am."

"Out there," Alvarez pointed towards the mouth of the

garage, "you saw the stone staircase going up to the terrace above us now. There you will find . . ."

"Sure, sure, the Dutchman gettin' whiffled on Bols gin."

"No, sir. No! This gentleman is not Dutch. He is a Belgian."

"So?" inquired H.M., and his eyes flashed open. "That's better. That's much, much better!"

"Thank you. I shall take the ladies for a short stroll, explain the situation to them, and return."

"Take your time, son. I can find my way."

H.M. nodded, setting his hat at a more seemly angle. He lumbered out of the garage, and a good distance along the high stone wall of the staircase. Then, turning back on his tracks, he went up the stairs, soothing his lungs with poisonous smoke.

He found the floor of the balcony—and stopped short. From this high place, the view should have been seen by the romantic Maureen. But even H.M. paused.

One marble nymph on the balustrade wore a long garment of yellow flowers. A marble vase foamed thick, light-purple blossoms, which spilled over to the floor. Beyond the balustrade, Tangier fell away in ridges of dense dark green far down to the long, blue shimmering bay and the dark hills rising beyond the bay. The slope was thickened with red-roofed white houses, looking from there like toys of white or yellow-brown or pink. One sole jarring note was a water tower, seeming high only because it was on a ridge, but dwarfing the slender brick towers of mosques. Far to the left the higher battlements of the Kasbah, the ancient Arab Quarter, rose above an invisible yellow beach.

But it was not alone the view; there were as good views elsewhere. It was the air, the very feel and texture of the air, entwining the languour of the Mediterranean with the harshness of North Africa. It was a leopard's skin, all claws removed. It was bright, timeless, proud, yielding. You drank that air, and were at one with the pagan.

H.M., suddenly waking up, removed the cigar from his mouth and looked round.

"Hem!" he said.

The balcony was floored with red unglazed tiles. It extended only part way across the house, since the far side ended in the projection of the house wall with a French window, and it lay half in shadow and half in dazzling sunlight from the overhang of the floor above. On the red tiles stood a number of cushioned wicker chairs.

In the middle of the terrace stood a wicker table whose red top was loaded with bottles, glasses, an ice bucket and a soda siphon, as well as a very neat pile of reports and dossiers. Beside the table, having stood up from his chair, was a short, stoutish man, capless but otherwise in full khaki uniform including Sam Browne belt, with the red tabs of a staff officer and insignia of a Colonel in the Belgian Army.

His large head was covered with short white hair cut *en brosse,* showing the pink scalp underneath. His face was red and jovial; even as he stood at attention, so that the stoutness round the waist made his uniform tunic stick forward like a strut, he fired off a string of chuckles. His bushy eyebrows were black streaked with white. What you first noticed was the twinkle and intelligence in his blue eyes.

"Sir Henry Merrivale?" he asked, in a gruff but genial voice.

"Ça va, mon gars?" returned H.M., with his deplorable taxi-driver familiarity. *"Votre femme n'a pas couché sur le pin de votre chemise? C'est vrai: je suis le vieux bonhomme."*

"Oh, I speak a little English," said the other, putting his head on one side with the concealed glee of one who knows he speaks it very well. "Come, let us talk in English! It will be good practice for me."

"Fine!" said H.M.'s "They tell me I got an Addisonian purity in my style. You remember what I say, and bob's-your-uncle."

The other, looking slightly puzzled, covered this with a string of chuckles.

"Then I present myself," he beamed. "I am Colonel Duroc."

Colonel Duroc shot out his hand at the same time as H.M. The handgrip was strong and sincere, because each man instinctively realized in the other a kindred spirit.

Sir Henry was not aware that Duroc's daredevil (or idiotic, if you prefer) escapades had carried him scatheless through two world wars. There was a time when no machine gun could nip him, no prison hold him. He always appeared when they didn't expect him, amid a shower of grenades, and was never there when they did. He had acquired so many decorations that he did not trouble to wear any of them. Though H.M. did not know this, he sensed it. Duroc, on the other hand, was familiar with H.M.'s more regrettable exploits, and they delighted him.

"Ah, but I mislay my hospitality!" he cried, and fussed at the table. He brought up a rich box of excellent Havanas, and offered them. "Will you try one of these, my friend? Ah, no! I see that already you smoke."

H.M., inhaling a deep lungful, let the poisonous smoke drift out into his companion's face. Duroc did not shudder or wince, but merely reflected.

"Got anything like that in Tangier?" inquired H.M.

The little white-haired Colonel shook his head darkly.

"Worse!" he said.

"Honest?" demanded H.M., instantly alert.

"My friend, have you never tried the truly black cigar of Marseilles? No? I will order them for you."

Down sat the Colonel, and with meticulous handwriting in French he wrote in a notebook: "Sir H.M. Cigars of the most dreadful. Obtainable at Tangier, Attention, Sergeant Chocano." Then he bounced up with his red face shining.

"Allons prendre un verre!" he cried, with a phrase as truly Belgian as the Boulevard Gaston Max. A Frenchman would have said *"quelque chose a boire,"* and with far less gusto.

"That suits me, Colonel. I mean, *est-ce qu'il y a du visky-soda?"*

"Mais naturellement. Vous êtes anglais, voyons. Ici vous voyez le Johnny Walker, Le John Haig, Le White Horse . . ."

Two minutes later they were seated opposite each other, close to the balustrade in full sun, with tall glasses and ash trays on side tables, while Colonel Duroc smoked a Havana. But for the first time Duroc's chuckles died away. Under the bushy eyebrows his blue eyes seemed disturbed.

"My friend!" he began abruptly, taking the cigar out of his mouth. "Before I say what I wish to say, I must explain to you a small deception which was played on you."

"I've been waitin' for that explanation," replied H.M. in

a sinister voice. "Maybe you thought it was funny, but I didn't. Lord love a duck, I nearly got murdered!"

Colonel Duroc bounced from his chair.

"Quoi? Assassiné?"

"Well, now . . . Maybe not exactly that. But I'm telling you"—H.M.'s voice blared back—"when anybody here tries to drive a car, all of a sudden he's as scatty as a blind owl. His dearest wish is to smack into somebody else or wrap himself round a tree. I've got blood pressure, Colonel! I'm practically an invalid!"

Relieved, Duroc sank back. This time his series of chuckles made the gold buttons of his tunic behave alarmingly.

"Ah, that? That is nothing! In a day or two it will pass out."

"I'm not goin' to make the obvious answer," retorted H.M. "But I'd like to ask an obvious question. I know your name and your rank. What's your official position?"

There was a slight pause before Duroc replied.

"I am what you would call in London the Commissioner of the Metropolitan Police."

"Yes. I sort of guessed that, when I heard the Belgians controlled the police and you were a Belgian. Well, you've got the floor. Go on."

Old Duroc's red face brightened.

"Observe," he cried, "this fine house. It is not mine, though I too live on the Old Mountain. My house is in repairs; my wife has departed for a holiday in Belgium. I lease this house from a good friend of mine, also English, who is also absent from Tangier. Is it not large, full of valuable things, with all the comfort modern? *Hein?"*

"Sure. It's first-rate. What about it?"

Colonel Duroc, with deep solemnity, pressed his glass of visky-soda against his heart.

"When I hear you are coming to Tangier, and to a hotel at that, I say no. No, no, no! Hotels!" added Duroc, holding his nose in disgust. "While you are in Tangier, my friend, you must be my guest here."

H.M. grunted and looked at the floor. The old sinner was rather touched.

"I have here," Duroc pursued, "a large staff of Arab servants, with a *fatima*"—he pronounced the word *fat'ma,* as did everyone else—"who speaks French and English. If you wish to rest, is not this terrace much suitable? Snap your fingers (so!) and there will be a swing or a deck chair."

"Y'know, Colonel, that's very decent of you. I appreciate it."

"Only half an hour ago do I learn, when Alvarez has telephoned from the airport, that you had brought with you your—ah—secretary. Yes. 'Well, well, well?' said I; 'the lady must by my guest too. We will put them,' said I, 'in adjoining rooms upstairs, purely,' " Duroc added in haste, with a delicacy which could give no offence, "as a matter of convenience, should he wish to dictate letters.' Yes. *Voilà!* You see?"

"I bet that pleased Alvarez no end, didn't it?"

"Pardon?"

"Never mind." H.M. threw the end of his cigar over the balustrade. "I can't speak for the gal, Colonel, but I'd be howlingly pleased to accept your invitation."

"Ah! Now I am delight!"

"But who *is* this bloke Alvarez, anyway?"

The bushy eyebrows went up in surprise.

"But he is the Commandant of Police! In criminal matters, my right hand." Colonel Duroc frowned. "And yet often I do not understand him. It seems to me he is a rowboat."

"A . . . what d'ye mean, a rowboat?"

"Ah, bah! A man of machinery. You press a button; he walks. You press another button—"

"Oh, son! You mean a robot."

"But that is what I say: a rowboat." Duroc spoke somewhat irritably, and his short white hair bristled up. "I sounded the *ot,* yes? I too am well spikking the English *et Robert est votre oncle.* However," he brooded, "Alvarez is very, very intelligent. Like that." Duroc snapped his fingers three times. "Also all dubious characters are terrified of him. He is a famous boxer and swordsman; worst of all, he is bad in a street fight with a truncheon, because he has no mercy. Yes. This is puzzling. In my younger days, alas, I have often run mad with a bayonet and think nothing. Yet to punish with the blood cool . . . Yes, this is puzzling.

H.M. made fussed gestures.

"But stop a bit, son! Alvarez is a Spaniard, ain't he? Then, with the rest of you Belgians—"

Chuckling again, the Commissioner of Police took a deep pull at his visky-soda and set it down.

"Listen, *mon fils,*" he said. "I tell you what all know. The commanding executive officers are Belgians, yes. Unfortunately, there are too few of us. All my detective officers are Spaniards: all intelligent and well trained. My policemen—*les agents, vous comprenez*—are Spanish and even with some Arabs. They are trained and drilled like an army. Yes, by God! And as good as an army!" Despite the chuckles, pride rang in Duroc's voice. "Each man must fluently speak French, Spanish, and Arabic. Should he commit any discourtesy, let him beware!"

"But wait a minute, son! What I wanted to know . . ."

Sitting upright, chest puffed out, Colonel Duroc ignored this.

"And our policy, you ask?" His blue eyes twinkled tolerantly. "Well! We regard human beings as human beings; and why not? Provided they do not make too much a public nuisance, and too much we interpret broadly, let them do as they please. But a serious crime . . . Ah, that is different! When Alvarez suggested the small deception we played—"

"So it was Alvarez, hey? That smooth-talkin' snake! Stop; I'm askin' the questions now. How'd you know I was coming to Tangier, let alone the time of the plane? The newspapers, I s'pose?"

Colonel Duroc was very tactful and did not chuckle.

"No. Your newspaper friends at New York are in truth your friends. They sent out not one word of your—I have it—sneak departure."

But all H.M.'s suspicions were again roused. Malignant as the evil one, he stuck out his horrible face.

"Then how'd you know about it?" he demanded.

Colonel Duroc, the Havana stuck at an angle of his mouth, went over to the chair by the wicker table, sat down, and riffled his thumb up neatly piled documents. He sighed.

"Wherever you go in the world, my friend, I fear a police cable will precede you by twenty-four hours." From a folder he took out a cablegram fully two pages long. "This one from New York, for example. 'Leaves La Guardia TWA . . . 9:30, 3/31/50. Arrive Lisbon about dawn. Lisbon-Tangier 9:30-11:30. Must warn you . . .' *Rien du tout!*"

H.M. slapped the top of the balustrade.

"If that cable was signed by a weasel named Finnegan," he roared, "then there's not a word of truth in it. It's all lies anyway!"

"I believe you," said Duroc, putting back the cablegram. "Still! Even if you were inordinately addicted to wine and women," he winked broadly, "where is the harm in that? Pah! The police could supply you with—" He stopped, coughed heavily, and went on. "However! I credit you. I think your actions have been made from pure cussedness, of which you are full. Yes?"

"Then what was the idea of that show this morning?"

"Ah!"

"I'm a modest man, Colonel," H.M. assured him earnestly. "Practically a shrinkin' violet. But, burn me, to judge by the welcome I had, you might have thought I was Bacchus and Priapus rolled into one. What was the game?"

The shrewd blue eyes regarded him sideways.

"Let us suppose," Duroc mused, "that there is to arrive here a famous detective for a purpose, and you wish to conceal that purpose."

"What purpose?" demanded H.M.

"Let us further suppose that this man is an amateur detective, more recently of fame in the press for his athletic prowess at—hem—*criquet* and football. We-el! Yesterday, when we have gained news from the New York Police, we speak to our own journals. Who, in our arrangements, will think anything of the detective, if we stress only *criquet* and football? You see?"

"Oh, I see," glowered H.M. "I've been seeing for a long time. But, just in the interest of holy lyin', is it true there's been no serious crime here for two months?"

"Quite true." The other nodded. "But that is what we must discuss now."

Bouncing up, he began to pace back and forth in a kind of nervous dignity, his hands clasped behind this back and the cigar, gripped between this teeth, sending out short furious puffs. A little wind stirred the blossoms on the marble nymph; it seemed warm, yet it had a cold centre of the wind from the Sahara.

Wheeling round, Duroc strode over to H.M. and stood in front of him.

"Tonight." he said formally, "there is in Tangier perhaps the most clever criminal who ever lived. I do not speak lightly, no."

"Uh-huh?" said H.M. "When did this bloke get to Tangier?"

"This morning. On the same plane as yourself."

"What's that, son?"

"If this man were an ordinary criminal, we could deal with him. But he is not. His feats, I swear it, defy belief. Veritably he is a ghost; he disappears, and makes things disappear with him! He is a grotesque, inhuman. Frankly, my friend, I ask for your help."

Flipping his cigar over the balustrade, Colonel Duroc spread out his hands.

"You are the Maestro," he said. "You are the Old Man. These magics and strange doings are for you the food and drink. If you do not help, I fear we shall have on our hands, perhaps even tonight, a situation which I can only call . . . impossible."

CHAPTER FOUR

There was a long silence.

"Impossible, hey?" murmured H.M., in a strange and croaky voice.

His eyes moved lovingly to the soda siphon on the table, then back to the top of Colonel Duroc's head. He shuddered. Then, gaining control by gripping the arms of the chair, he impelled himself up and stood looking out over the balustrade.

"It's fate," he declared, gathering voice power, "it's Mansoul, it's economic law, it's a ruddy reincarnation!" He turned round. "Colonel, I can't do it; and that's flat. Maybe you were right about my cussedness, but I can't. I explained all about it to Maureen Holmes today. I can't say another word."

But he did. For twenty minutes, in fact, he gave a powerful oration covering the same things and more, while Duroc listened respectfully. The Ford station wagon, scarcely heard by either but carrying H.M.'s and Maureen's luggage, clattered into the garage below, after which invisible Arab servants bore the luggage up through a door in the garage to the house. When he wound up his peroration, H.M. was in a mighty state of martyrdom.

"And that's that," he concluded. "About that invitation of yours: thank'ee, but I'd better push off. The old man's never much wanted when he can't sing for his supper. I . . ."

H.M. stopped abruptly, his mouth open.

For the first time the burly little Colonel was really in a rage. He stood with shoulders back, uniform tunic sticking forward as though he had outthrust his small corporation. There was a blaze in Colonel Duroc's blue eyes.

"Sir," he began, his pronunciation often slipping. "If you imagined my offer was any form of breebeery, I am far from being too old to use a sword or a pistol."

"Oi! Stop the bus!"

"At the beginning, I merely think it would be more comfortable for you. Then I meet you. I find in you a good old puffer like myself, and I like you. If you don' credit this, you shall 'ave the satisfaction. If you do credit it, I tell you I can quite understand how you wish to have no trouble with what is not your affair, and only an impertinence of mine. If by some chance you still wish to be my guest, I should be the proudest man in all Tangier."

"Oh, for the love of Esau!" groaned H.M., his colour coming up. He understood these formal Continental courtesies and secretly approved them, though they only embarrassed him and made him hot under the collar.

"Colonel," he said, "I'm not much good at this kind o' thing. But what I mean: I would like to stay."

Duroc was rather embarrassed too. But he found inspiration.

"Let's take another glass!" he exclaimed.

"Good!" thundered H.M., who was very English and to whom this seemed the obvious, indeed the only, solution to the problem. "Let's drink every bottle on the table!"

Hastily snatching up the two empty glasses, Duroc put them on the table. He filled each exactly half full of whiskey. He was just flicking a spectral dash of soda into them when light, hurrying footfalls, the tread of youth, ascended the stone steps outside.

Paula Bentley stood on the red tiles of the balcony, her fair complexion heightened by the wind. Colonel Duroc looked with outward sternness but inward applause at Paula's tight-fitting white silk frock, at her bare legs and sandals. He shook an admonitory finger at her. But Paula, smiling, merely ran over and kissed him on the cheek.

"Ha ha!" exclaimed Colonel Duroc.

Behind Paula—as she had arranged—appeared Maureen and Alvarez. Maureen's black hair and green eyes made her seem less like stained glass in a Spanish cathedral; she was too alive, too excited. As Alvarez bent over her, only someone very close could have caught his cryptic word: "Caravel?"

"Well—yes!" whispered Maureen. "Unless I have work to do."

"But you are not his . . . I mean, not his sec— Never mind. You have told me!"

Maureen hurried forward, looking at Paula. The view from the balustrade dazzled her, even with that water tower, down over red and white and green to the bay.

"Commandant Alvarez," she said, "has taken us for a lovely walk along the Old Mountain Road. Even places from which we could see the town. . . . Oh!"

Maureen saw the chuckling Colonel Duroc, and stopped short. Alvarez, wooden-faced, strode forward to the table, came sharply to attention, and saluted.

"Miss Holmes," he said, "may I present Colonel Georges Duroc, our Commissioner of Police?"

"Enchanté, mademoiselle!" said Duroc, taking her extended hand and lifting it to his lips.

"Très heureuse, monsieur!" replied Maureen. She made a wild attempt at a curtsy, and got away with it. Her school-and-college French seemed to slip as smoothly as a dream speech. Never in her life had she tried anything like this. But Maureen was intoxicated, without anything to drink.

Whereupon Colonel Duroc, seeing his subordinate, became stern. Discipline, he thought, was very dear to him. He sat down in the chair behind the wicker table, and rapped his knuckles on it.

"Commandant Alvarez!"

"Yes, sir?"

Colonel Duroc decided to use English, though he would be at a disadvantage against the flawless speech and pronunciation of his subordinate. If he had been less preoccupied, he would have noted that strange twitching and ripplings were going over Alvarez's face, like that of a man about to burst.

"I find, Commandant, that your small idea of a small deception played at the airport has misshot. The conduct of Sir Henry Merrivale . . ."

"I am sorry, sir. The c-conduct of S-s-ir Henry M-m-m-m . . ."

Whereupon Alvarez did what nobody could ever have expected of him. He began to laugh, and laugh like a lunatic. First it was the full-throated guffaw with which we greet the antics of the Marx Brothers or Mr. Chaplin. He stamped and whooped and howled, flinging out his arms. Then, as it took him like a stomach cramp, he bent over and laughed in helpless gasps, at the same time piteously trying to gibber words of explanation. All were surprised, but Duroc was astounded.

"Commandant!" said the scandalized Colonel, and whacked his fist on the table.

Alvarez made a Homeric effort, and managed to straighten up.

"I r-r-regret!" he stumbled. "No d-doubt I have as ch-childish a sense of humour as the Arabs. B-but to see Sir Henry M-merrivale, forced backwards through the airport door by these ladies and myself, yet st-still heroically sh-shouting obscenities in A-arabic . . ."

The Commandant's distended cheeks burst again. Leaning across the table, he laughed straight into the face of this outraged Colonel.

"What was so goddam funny about it?" yelled H.M.

"Oh, let him laugh," Maureen pleaded to Duroc, and then looked at Alvarez. "All these years you've been behaving like a stuffed shirt, to impress people or scare them; and it's not you at all. Go on; laugh. It'll do you good."

"There's much w-w-wisdom in that," advised Paula, who was quietly having hysterics.

Alvarez had now gained complete control over himself, though tears still ran down his cheeks. Colonel Duroc hesitated. Though discipline was discipline, the culprit was defended by two pretty girls. Furthermore, he had never before heard Alvarez laugh, and the Commandant might not be altogether a rowboat. All these things disposed Colonel Duroc to be lenient.

"You understand, Commandant," he said darkly, "that your offence might have had serious consequences?"

"I do, sir."

"Well!" said Duroc. "Then I forget it." Yet his wrath boiled over. "But here is an end, Commandant. We will have no more of this, burn me, or Robert is your uncle!"

"What?" said Paula Bentley. Then she turned away and went off the deep end again.

Though Alvarez remained grave, lines of perplexity deepened in his swarthy forehead.

"It shall not occur again, sir. But, if I may respectfully ask with regard to this uncle—Robert who?"

Colonel Duroc, gleefully waiting in ambush, slapped his thigh with a heavy hand.

"He is the idiom English!" cried Duroc, again all gold buttons and chuckles. "You do not know it? You, who have spent most of your life in England? Almonds to you, Commandant! That is the slang American, which I have learned in the Parade Bar."

"If you will pardon me, sir, I believe the term is 'nuts.' "

"What nuts?" demanded the Colonel.

" 'Nuts to you,' sir."

"Then nuts to you!" shouted the Colonel, and paused with his fist in the air. His hand dropped, and his red face grew more red. Under his cropped white hair, his brain floundered amid confused and distorted words which would not drop into a straight line. This was very bad. He must not be jovial before subordinates. He must sink his teeth in dignity and discipline.

Therefore he looked round under his bushy eyebrows until there was dead silence.

"Understand me, Commandant. I am not angry because you laugh, which is perhaps a good sign. No! But your bungling today," elaborated Colonel Duroc, with great unfairness, "has quite rightly made Sir Henry refuse to help us with our case. Sir Henry Merrivale . . ."

He made a gesture in that direction.

For some time, excluding his one outburst, nobody had noticed H.M. But he had not moved. He stood with his back to the balustrade, left elbow cradled in his right hand, fingers of the left hand massaging his big jaw. He was chewing some blue flowers. Over these his eyes never wavered in a look, both thoughtful and malignant, at Maureen Holmes.

Maureen, previously too much absorbed in other matters, saw it now and jumped back with a start. She glanced down over herself to see what was wrong. She peered for laddered stockings, and pressed at her hair.

H.M. spoke through the chewed flowers, one eye fixed on a corner of the balcony roof.

" 'Childish,' " he observed, with the air of one who quotes. " 'Childish,' hey?"

Enlightenment came to Maureen.

"Oh, please don't bring that up again! I didn't mean it! Or . . . Well, if I did mean it, it was only in a partial way. I was only trying to help."

" 'The first crook you met,' " continued H.M. without remorse, " 'would fool you or swindle you.' All right. I said I'd *show* you, didn't I? Even when I hadn't the ghostiest idea how I could? All right again!"

"Oh, you *are* childish!"

"Are you still my secretary?" leered H.M. "Stayin' on at this house to take notes?"

"Yes, I am!" retorted Maureen, instantly and defiantly. "You say you can show me. I don't believe it. Well, go ahead and try."

During these exchanges Alvarez, in some consternation, had been looking from one to the other.

H.M. turned round, and spat the chewed flowers over the balustrade. He addressed Colonel Duroc in an offhand, apologetic manner.

"If it's all the same to you, Colonel," he said, "I'd like to change my mind. I'd like to give you all the help I can with this ghost-feller case. And we'll nab the blighter good and proper."

Colonel Duroc jumped up from his chair.

"You are serious?"

"Dead serious, Colonel."

Duroc spoke with the intensity of a man who prays.

"Grand God!" he said. "If my small organization, with your help, can capture Iron Chest and make stupid the great police forces of Rome and Paris, then I shall die happy in a dog kennel!" He paused, swallowing. "When do you wish to begin?"

"Now."

"But lunch," protested Duroc. He glanced at his wrist watch. "*Tiens,* it is now long past the hour. My servants have forgotton it. If you tell an Arab exactly what to do, with writing and diagrams, he will do it and do it well. But, if you forget this, he will think you do not want it and he will forget too. At the same time . . ."

"Lunch be sugared," H.M. said crudely. "Just gimme some sandwiches and the good old visky-soda. Trot out every report, every bit of evidence, anything at all you've got on the ghost bloke. Clear away the rest of these people except . . ."

Some distance away, by the chair over which she had thrown her fur coat, Maureen stood haughty and aloof, except for a superior kind of smile which she hoped would annoy him. But H.M.'s look had grown uneasy. When his lips silently framed the words, "Can you take shorthand?" she immediately nodded.

"Clear 'em away," said H.M., "except for my secretary."

"Well, *I* must fly anyway," cried Paula. "I promised to pick up Bill. Colonel Duroc, may I run upstairs and phone for a taxi?"

"Nonsense, nonsense!" said the harassed Colonel. "Commandant Alvarez shall drive you down in my Packard."

Paula Bentley slipped across to Maureen.

"My dear," she said with her usual sincere forthrightness, "on any other night, of course, we should have taken you out somewhere. Will tomorrow night do?"

"I'd love to!"

"Good. But, you see, tonight's a special one for Bill and me. We're going to the Ali Baba for dinner, then for a swim, then . . ."

"A swim in this weather? Won't it be too cold?"

"Oh, I don't mean that beach down there!" Paula smiled a secret smile. "But the Mediterranean is always warm, along the miles and miles of beach beyond Cape Spartel. You must try it."

"I intend to," Maureen assured her. "But, to tell you a dark secret, I didn't know what would be fashionable. I thought I'd wait and buy a swim suit here."

Paula regarded her in amazement.

"A bathing suit?" said Paula, and laughed. "But what on earth do you want with a bathing suit? You're miles and miles from anybody."

"Oh!" said Maureen. She considered the possibilities and hastily turned away her thoughts. Besides, an insufferable voice had boomed above the clatter of talk.

"That's straight, Colonel," said Sir Henry Merrivale. "I'll make a little bet, say a thousand quid to ten, we nail this blighter in forty-eight hours."

"My friend, you do not know his record!"

"I don't give two hoots and a whistle what his record is. Who's taking my bet?"

Alvarez extended his hand, which H.M. shook. Alvarez, with his long straight nose, his red-brown eyes gleaming, and a smile on his broad mouth, had become a thoroughly human being.

"I won't take your bet, sir," he said, "because I want you to win it. It was jolly decent of you, offering to help us."

"Not a bit, son." Deliberately H.M. raised his voice. "I'm goin' to teach a lesson to a little bean pole who mistakes a fine natural dignity, sort of, for sheer cloth-headedness."

"Excuse me, sir." Alvarex first hesitated, then poured out words frankly. "Between ourselves, I know Miss Holmes isn't . . . related to you in any way, so to speak. But will you keep her here all evening taking notes?"

"Goin' on the razzle-dazzle, son?" inquired H.M., with interest and approval. "No. She'll be here only a couple of hours."

"Razzle-dazzle?" Alvarez was horrified. "No, no. Only to dinner."

"Ooh!" said Maureen to Paula. "Have you ever," she whispered, clenching her fists, "met a man who makes you so mad you lose your head and want to scratch?"

"Juan Alvarez?" Paula was puzzled. "But he hasn't . . ."

"No! I mean that *awful—!*"

"Oh, Sir Henry!" murmured Paula, with a grin. "Darling, you'll never understand that type of man until you learn to laugh at him. If you don't laugh, you'll stay angry all the time."

Colonel Duroc, all discipline again, was smacking his hands together.

"Commandant Alvarez! You will drive Mrs. Bentley to the British Consulate. Then you will go to the 7th Arrondissement Station, and send the car back here. No one has telephoned to me about the passengers' luggage," he added cryptically, "but it may take a long time. Perhaps you will have news first. In any case, telephone me in one hour. *C'est entendu?* Good. I go now to have the fat'ma prepare the sondveech, and to bring our best evidence. Go!"

In another two minutes, the terrace was quiet. Colonel Duroc's Packard roared backwards out of the garage. Paula, in the front seat, was crying back to Maureen that she really didn't need a bathing suit; and Alvarez, shocked, was trying to shush her. Colonel Duroc walked through a front door, two green-painted high doors set open, into a lofty hall floored with marble. He called snappishly in Arabic, and was answered by a hurrying of slippered feet.

H.M. sat down in his chair by the balustrade, adjusted his hat, and lit another vile cigar. Maureen drew a wicker chair near the table. For a moment H.M. smoked in silence.

"So you decided to stay here, eh?" he asked her.

Maureen already had her answer prepared.

"It's much better than paying an enormous hotel bill, isn't it?"

"Was that the first thing you thought of? Don't lie to me, my wench; it was too pat. Oh, and another thing!" H.M. made a face, remembering. "So far as I can judge this feller Alvarez is A-I. But don't you go too far until *I* give you the wire. Got that?"

Maureen breathed hard.

"Well, really!" she said inadequately. "I ought to have my head examined. I'm as spineless as I-don't-know-what. Any other woman would have told you exactly what she thought of you, and walked out on you. I must be hopeless."

H.M. shook his head.

"Oh, contrariwise," he grunted. "You've got too much Irish-American stubbornness, even though you know you're battlin' a crafty old professional ten times your mental weight." H.M surveyed her, with outward dismalness. "You've got looks, y'know. You've got a good heart. You're as loyal as blazes to anything or anybody you think needs help. You're not bad, my wench."

Maureen, who had experienced an exciting day, was near tears.

"You can say nice things," she retorted, "in the most outrageous way I ever heard!"

"I can't help it. I'm like that. Futhermore," added H.M., unintentionally cutting away the compliments, "you're as crawlin' with curiosity as I am about this ghost-man case. Didn't Alvarez tell you something about it when you went for a walk?"

Maureen nodded.

"Then, lord love a duck," H.M. said uncomfortably, and

glared at her. "Are we friends, or aren't we?"

"Well . . . All right," admitted Maureen.

Strutting footsteps approached through the marble hall. Since the sun had sunk far behind the house, putting most of the terrace in shade, the interior of the hall was gloomy. Colonel Duroc carried under one arm a chest of iron or steel, perhaps two feet long by one foot high, with curious carvings which the watchers could not make out. The Colonel deposited it with a bump—its dull polish made it seem iron rather than steel—near the front door.

Then he strutted out on the terrace, sat down by his documents, and took out a pencil.

"Now we come to business!" he said. "Where, my friend, do you wish to commence?"

Maureen had taken from her handbag one of those notebooks, together with a sharpened pencil, with which we all determine to keep a copious diary but never do.

"Don't make a note," H.M. levelled his arm at Maureen, "unless I say. 'That's important, put it down.' You're challenging me, hey? Then you'll see how the old man works."

He turned to Colonel Duroc.

"First, son, a bit of background. Has this feller got a name, by the way?"

"Unfortunately, none that we know. The police of many cities merely call him 'Iron Chest.' His record in not much more than a year, between the 27th February, 1949, and the 1st April, now 1950, has been amazing, *épatant!*"

"Sure, sure." H.M. puffed at the cigar drowsily, not much impressed. "You've said he can do this, or do that; but what does he actually do? What's his racket?

"He is the most dangerous and modern burglar now at large."

H.M. groaned.

"Oh, my son! I've said before that the professional criminal is the dullest dog on earth!"

Colonel Duroc smiled a catlike smile.

"Believe me, my friend, not this one."

"H'mf. Well. No photographs or fingerprints, I s'pose?"

"Alas, none."

"Any good descriptions by an eyewitness?"

"Alas, not any good one at all. He has been seen many times on occasion at fairly close distance. Only once has he been seen face to face, and that . . . Well, you will hear."

H.M.'s eyes narrowed, and his lack of interest ceased. Sitting up straight, he half-turned towards Maureen; but he decided against it, and said nothing for a note.

"Now, Colonel. Has he got any peculiarities—you know what I mean—by which you can pick him as the particular man who did the particular job?"

"Ah!" pounced Colonel Duroc, lifting up his hands with palms outwards. "Indeed, yes! In effect, yes! So many, my friend, that I do not even need my notes!"

Here Duroc carefully stressed the points on each finger.

"First, he has never been known to—what do you say in England?—crack a private house. Always he cracks a modern small bank or a modern small jeweller. Second, always he uses an electric drill on the safe, in itself an unusual thing. Even this drill is unusual, called a Spandau after the German Spandau machine gun. Three times he has broken a drill, having to replace it with another and leaving the first behind. The drill mechanism can be made to march on any current; you plug it in any socket. By damn, this is good!

"Third," pursued the Colonel, "at jewellers he takes only diamonds, cut or uncut. Nothing else. At small banks he touches no gold or silver. Only banknotes whose numbers are not registered. For example, my friend, in England, is it true that the one-pound notes are not registered and cannot be traced?"

H.M. nodded, chewing the cigar.

"That's right, Colonel. They take the serial numbers only of fivers or above."

"So! Good! With our man, it is the same principle of currency. Though he make a good haul of diamonds, and he crack two jewellers to one bank, yet with money in any country he leave behind a big profit for a safe one. Now, please, your attention. Fourth and last!"

Colonel Duroc's expression grew intent.

"On every one of his raids, *every* one, he has carried under his left arm the iron chest such as you see now in the hall."

"Hold on, now!" muttered H.M., and slowly rose to his feet. "Write that down," he told Maureen; "it's important, though maybe not in the way you think." He turned back to Duroc. "But, if that's the chest he carried, how do you happen to have it?"

Duroc chuckled. The Colonel was very proud of his criminal *per se;* though, as he had said, he would have died happy in a dog kennel to see that criminal behind bars.

"Because, my friend, in two cities—once in Amsterdam, once in Paris—he has had to drop and leave a chest when almost the police get him. And we know, from a report with which I will not trouble you now, he has four such chests. All more or less alike, all carved in much the same way. So he carry another one, when he raid again."

"But, burn me, why?"

"Aha!" exclaimed the Colonel, who had been lurking in ambush for that question. "That is the first problem we have. Consider this problem!"

"No, son. You consider it. You're burstin' to."

"Well, well! It may be. But consider. This chest is not a mighty and overbearing weight. It is made of sheet iron rolled thin. It can be carried under the arm, though with some difficulty and awkwardness. Now diamonds he could carry in his pockets. Banknotes could be fitted into a small attaché case. Yet he carries this chest! In every way it hampers him; it endangers him in a quick away-get . . ."

"Don't you mean getaway?" Maureen asked with real innocence.

Colonel Duroc was incensed.

"Pah! This English! I make myself clear, God love a goose? Yes! Well. I repeat: this chest halts his getaway, it obstructs his gun hand—for I tell he is a killer—and, when two discarded chests are found, they are empty. It is not at all necessary. Yet he always carries it. Why?"

There was a silence.

"Is the feller by any chance a loony?" asked H.M.

"No, no! That will not do. It is too easy. Besides, every move he makes is planned by careful strategy as at chess. There is some reason for his carrying it. But what?"

H.M. scratched his chin, a man clearly bothered. Maureen, making aimless marks with her pencil, did not know whether she was pleased or disappointed. Her imagination was caught by this faceless figure, deliberately laden with an iron chest, in the dark streets of the Continent. H.M. went back to his chair and sat down.

"I want more information!" he said querulously, and took the cigar out of his mouth. "Though it's just possible that . . . No, never mind. More information!"

Inclining his head, Duroc took out and opened a brown folder, which contained thick sheets of typewritten flimsy.

"Excellent!" he said. "I should like to recount a typical Iron Chest adventure, the more maddening because it was the only time his face was ever seen at close range. It occurred in Brussels, my own city. I was there at the time, with my wife, on holiday, and so was Mark Hammond."

"Stop! Who's Mark Hammond?"

"He is a good fellow," Duroc returned promptly. "He writes modern science books, and lives here at Tangier. He is American, with excellent manners and without any comic-paper talk. Perhaps he drink a little, but seldom too much. He . . ."

"Uh-huh. Never mind Hammond. Get back to the crime."

"Sir Henry, are you familiar with Brussels? Do you know the Bourse?"

H.M. reflected, still smoking.

"The Bourse, hey? I've never been inside it. But I remember, years ago, a tiny little street full of cafés with pavement tables; it was in front of the Bourse, and just on the right hand of it as you faced the building. You couldn't buy anything but wine or beer or apéritifs there. They even iced the soda siphons, curse 'em; and you got the shock of your life when you pressed the siphon handle and out squirted lemonade."

"You have it, you have it! The rue du Midi!"

" 'Course," said H.M., "you could always buy whisky at a shop and drink it at home."

"But attend! Just beyond the rue du Midi, and along the right hand side of the Bourse itself, there is a quiet, narrow little street with trees and street lamps. There are only dignified homes, with a few shops of the first class. But one is the great Parisian jewel firm of Bernstein et Cie., which has a branch at Brussels and another here at Tangier.

"Now picture what happens, on a warm spring night. Many people rustle their newspapers or rattle their glasses outside the cafés, separated only by the bustling crossway of the rue Neuve from that silent street of trees made green by lamps. It is ten o'clock on the night of May 5, last year."

Nobody else spoke. Duroc's bushy grey-black eyebrows drew together. He rippled his thumb across the typewritten flimsies as though he had memorized them; which, in fact, he had.

"All the Brussels police are alert for Iron Chest, since he has cracked two nights before. Yet at ten o'clock not a hundred feet from the nearest café, he is already at work on the great steel front doors of Bernstein et Cie. To open such doors, with picklock or form of key, is very difficult. The slightest touch will set off the burglar alarm. But it is not uncommon in these days.

"Well, Iron Chest does it. He slips inside, leaving the doors very slightly open because he wish no more trouble with that lock. The premises, the doors, are too thick for anyone to hear his electric drill. He takes fifty uncut diamonds; nothing else. And why? That is easy. Well-known jewels in a shop are too obvious. A good diamond cutter and polisher, who keeps his mouth shut, can make those little grey lumps unrecognizable. Iron Chest moves for the doors.

"And then . . . A policeman, an *agent* named Emil Laurant, was pacing along the same side of the street. Just beyond the doors of Bernstein et Cie. there is a street lamp, partly shadowed by thick green leaves. Ordinarily, it might have gone unnoticed. But the policeman was alert. He saw the line of shadow where the outer steel doors were not quite shut. He knew there was no other entrance or exit. He stood and waited.

"One of the steel doors very softly opens. Someone, carrying the iron chest under his left arm, steps out on his left foot so that he can maneuver the chest outwards in a straight line. And the policeman comes face to face with the unknown.

"The policeman dives straight for the chest, which is longways in front of him. He remembers getting a good grip over and under the chest, feeling even the carved monkeys, and desiring to drag it away because he thinks it contains loot. He remembers raising his head and getting a good look at the unknown's face, by the light of the street lamp. Then the other man's right hand whips up and over, holding a Browning .32 automatic. And he shoots the policeman pointblank into the forehead."

Duroc paused, and slapped his hand on the table with such dramatic effect that Maureen jumped and dropped her pencil. She could almost hear the shot.

"There's something very rummy about that, son," objected a scowling H.M. "If this copper was polished off like that, he's dead. How can he 'remember' to tell you anything?"

Duroc's mouth made an ironic grimace.

"Because he did not die."

"Oh, ah. You mean there was a . . . ?"

"Exactly. Your knowledge of medical jurisprudence—are you not a physician as well as a barrister?—will remind you of many victims who have received a worse injury to the head than a light .32 bullet, yet have survived?"

"Sure."

"Yet in most cases," frowned Duroc, "they are not quite mentally the same. They are not mad, no. In most things they are clear enough. But their minds do not run always on a plain track. Thus the policeman, Emil Laurant, is fairly clear about everything up to the time he saw the iron chest; and at once the man fired. Then—no! His eyes blazed before fire; his hearing deadened to darkness. This shot brought on a kind of paralysis. He cannot recall any detail of Iron Chest's face. If the man stood before him now, that policeman could not identify him.

"But hear what happen, a demi-second after the shot is fired. . . . *Quelle sensation!*

"A half-second after the shot, those in the cafés leap up or dash out to see. Those in the rue Neuve, which is a transverse street even closer, turn round to look. Many persons see the policeman stagger back from the pavement into the road, slip, and fall on his face. But nobody, nobody at all, sees Iron Chest. He has vanished."

"Now, stop the bus again!" exploded H.M., quickly getting rid of his cigar. "What kind of eyewash are you tellin' me?"

Colonel Duroc raised his hand as though taking an oath.

"It is the truth I tell you," he replied firmly. "All people rush into that little street *en masse,* like a blockade. Iron Chest does not run or even walk towards them. Other people, at the other end of a short street, have heard the shot and hurry from the other direction. Iron Chest does not go towards *them*. He does not step backwards through the open door of the jeweller's, because they think of this and search. All, of course, have read about him in the newspapers . . ."

"Put that down," H.M. interposed suddenly, and snapped his fingers towards Maureen. "That last sentence. It might be important."

Colonel Duroc did not even hear him.

"Iron Chest," he continued, "did not try to shrink into a doorway, open a door, or get at any window. There was no manhole in the street for him to go down. He did not even climb up into a tree, or the lamps would have shown him among the leaves. And, in any case, the zealous tried them all. No. *C'est tout*. He simply disappeared."

There was a long silence, while Duroc gently closed the folder.

"A pretty problem, eh?" His chuckle was not mirthful, but tinged with satire. "Our first ghost glimpse." He tapped the folder. "Here is the testimony of honest and respectable witnesses. Is there any question, my friend, you would wish to ask?"

"Cor!" grunted H.M, in a voice which secretly delighted Maureen. He was sitting with his elbow on the arm of this chair, chin in hand, a mass of concentration.

Maureen, forcing away the thoughts uppermost in her mind, looked down at the long light dying over the city. She tried to visualize how others would picture that grotesque scene in the grey Brussels street of trees and lamps: the policeman looking over a carved chest at the face of—what? Some would picture a horror, like the Phantom of the Opera; some (she almost laughed) would see a gentleman-burglar in evening clothes; others, more sensible, might choose a drab unobtrusive person combining viciousness with prudence.

Irresistibly her thoughts drifted again. Tonight she was having dinner with Juan Alvarez at—abruptly her thoughts stopped, and her memory began to grope wildly. Ca . . . Co . . . Ci . . . Ciro's? That would be more like it.

"Colonel Duroc," she said in a low voice, "I'm sorry to intrude like this, but is there a restaurant in town called Ciro's?"

"Yes, yes, an excellent one! You must tell Henry I sent you." The Colonel, always gallant, beamed at her; but he immediately turned back to H.M. "Come, my friend! Have you no questions?" he added slyly.

"Well, yes," said H.M., and scowled. "Tell me this. Was there any rain on the night it happened?"

"I—I beg your pardon?"

"Just that. Was there any rain on the night Iron Chest cracked Bernstein and Company's safe?"

"I cannot understand why you ask. And I do not remember. But I know you never ask a question which is not relevant. Therefore I will find it in the report."

Opening the folder, Colonel Duroc began slowly and carefully to go through the typewritten pages, missing nothing. H.M. turned a lordly look towards Maureen.

"Better write down both question and answer, my wench," he said offhandedly. "It's very important."

Maureen's first impulse was to break the pencil in two pieces, and fling both of them into the face of Sir Henry Merrivale. The old so-and-so was doing this deliberately to annoy her; and already her annoyance and perplexity had reached their limit. She couldn't stand this! She wouldn't stand it!

Fortunately, at this moment, the Arab fat'ma appeared in the doorway, pushing a white-painted iron tea wagon whose wheels rattled like the plates of sandwiches on its top. On the shelf underneath lay a carelessly opened copy of today's *Tangier Gazette.*

The fat'ma, who was actually very fat, wore a blouse and skirt of faded blue and white, and a white cloth over her head without a *yashmak* to conceal her round, brown, smiling face. She rattled the tea wagon to the right of Maureen's chair, and padded away. But it gave Maureen an opportunity to conceal her own furious face. Bending over to adjust the newspaper, Maureen was about to close it when her eye caught a small advertisement. She read it again. There!

Colonel Duroc uttered an exclamation.

"It is incredible!" he said, looking up from the typewritten flimsies. "Sir Henry! On that day in Brussels there were several small showers. The last shower, so light that it did not even trouble the café-loungers under their awnings, began at about nine-fifty P.M. and ended at about ten-five P.M., some twenty minutes before the firing of the shot. Our burglar worked for some time on that safe, of course. But how a fiend's name did you know this?"

"Hem," said H.M., with a modest cough. He did not even look at Maureen, which was even worse and made her frantic. "If you don't mind, Colonel, I won't answer just now. After all, you did bowl me a hard one."

Now it was the Colonel's turn to triumph.

"A hard one? A difficult one?" he asked, in elaborately simulated surprise. "Oh, my friend! This disappearance in Brussels, I told you, was a pretty problem. But it is nothing!"

"It ain't?" demanded H.M., sitting up straight.

In the silence they could hear faintly what sounded like the noise of an ancient rattletrap car toiling up the tunnel towards the house. Maureen, still furious, carefully noted down an address from the advertisement.

"A bagatelle," smiled the Colonel. "Why, in Paris, he made a whole table load of diamonds disappear from plain sight."

CHAPTER FIVE

The sky over Tangier, at half-past ten that night, was a soft arch of bluish-black with small stars so brilliant that they seemed pierced through it.

Here, many miles away and below the House of the Wild Olives, and near the meeting of the Mediterranean with the long landlocked bay, the gentle waters of the Mediterranean whispered and slapped against the base of a tower built of ancient stones. It was a large square tower, appearing very high only by reason of its position. Then, too, it stood on the quietest edge of the Kasbah, beside its orange garden below.

If you looked over the parapet straight ahead, with the Mediterranean on your left, you could see the harbour of Tangier with its great concrete mole. One medium-sized cargo and passenger ship displayed a few yellow-shining portholes or deck lights, with broken reflections trembling in the water. Other and lesser craft showed riding lights. If you looked ahead and somewhat to the left, on a clear day of glassy space you could just discern the grey peak of Gibraltar, troubled by white cloud. But tonight sky and stars seemed a hollow of darkness, whispering, empty, except for a breeze from the Straits.

From this parapet, in a jewelled dead age, arrows had whistled from the short Moorish bows. Now the top of the tower was scattered round with a dozen or more tables, with chairs and benches, and they brought you glasses of hot mint tea, heavily sweetened.

The only light came from a lantern of Moorish work hung under the stairs some distance away. Beside it, on a bench, drowsed an elderly Arab in a white *jalebah* with a peaked hood. And, on either side of a round table at the front, Paula Bentley and Bill Bentley sat and looked at each other over forgotten glasses.

"Bill," Paula began tentatively.

"Yes, my baggage?"

Paula wore a white pullover and blue slacks. Her elbows were on the table, her arms up and hands buried under each side of the heavy silken hair. The dark-blue eyes, wide open now, searched his face with that strength of intensity and love which only Bill knew.

"Darling," she said, "you're worried about something. What is it?"

She studied him, as he sat across from her in his open-necked shirt and his old grey flannels. Bill's brown hair was cut short in military fashion. His eyes were brown. Though he was not particularly good looking, which for some reason delighted Paula, he had a humourous mouth and cleft chin. Unlike Alvarez, say, he had broad shoulders and a tapering waist; but he was probably not much taller or heavier than the Commandant.

Paula reflected that not once had he criticized her for anything since their marriage five years ago. (But, seeing the matter through Bill's eyes, it was simple: he worshipped her and could see nothing to criticize.) Bill never complained of or even noticed what he ate. He never even inquired what she spent, though she was not extravagant; they had a joint banking account, and she did as she liked.

An outsider would have thought him the average sort of fellow with good background, good public school, good university: dependable, but not very ambitious. And this, in a sense, was true. What Paula knew, together with only old J. and a few members of the British Consulate, was the lightning-swift quality of his brain. He could arrange facts as a conjuror handles cards; he could draw the gist from a report with one glance down each page; he could supply, out of a remarkable memory, any fact required on any subject.

One hidden wish of his, which he knew to be hopeless, was to read every book ever written on the subjects which interested him. Again unlike Alvarez, he did not much enjoy knockabout farce. Like Colonel Duroc, his secret relish was for satirical wit: the poison stings of Swift or

Wilkes or Whistler. These barbed darts he could fire himself. But, since they were always directed at himself or at things (never persons; he was too good-natured) which everybody disliked, people considered him merely a young man of good common sense.

Which he wasn't.

But now, Paula said, "You're worried about something. What is it?"

At the end of such a noble evening, Bill considered such a question unfair. Borrowing a car from Mark Hammond, he and Paula had dined at the Ali Baba. Then they had driven over twisted roads and ways, down to the stretch of a deserted beach. The long flat water ran and foamed swiftly up a flat sand beach, all black and white. They swam far out into the warm sea. They made love on the beach until both were tired, relaxed, and a little drowsy. Then, determining to return home to the Minzeh Hotel, they had fallen into a romantic mood and decided to drink mint tea on top of the old tower.

"Look here, baggage," said Bill, "why should you think I'm worried about anything?"

"Because I know," Paula answered simply. "I can always tell, can't I?"

"H'm," said Bill. She nearly always could, at that.

From the floor between them Paula picked up a bag which contained her bathing cap and two towels, and deposited it on the other side of her.

"Darling, pull your chair round beside mine. There; that's it. Kiss me."

This was a long process, confusing both minds and emotions. A cooler breeze surged at them from the great hollow of darkness and water. Far away in the Kasbah dim and angry voices were raised. A dog barked. But they did not hear it.

"Oh, Bill, we've been so lucky!"

"You mean *I've* been lucky."

"No! I was running wild in London—"

"S-sh! And I wasn't doing much in G.S.I.* Sitting in an army lorry while we moved up through Italy. Look here—er—let's go back to the hotel, shall we?"

* General Staff Intelligence

But Paula, even at her most emotional, was always practical. She pressed her cheek against his, and whispered.

"Darling. What's *really* worrying you? It's something about money, isn't it?"

Bill gave a start, and almost drew back his arm from her shoulders. He did not want to tell her the truth as yet, though there was no reason why he should not have done so. Pay in the Consular (which, like the Diplomatic, is controlled by the Foreign Office) is seldom large, but Bill had a few hundred a year of his own. He searched his mind to find some excuse which, while convincing, must also sound true. And he found it.

"Didn't you notice, Paula, that I had to borrow a car from Mark Hammond?"

"I didn't notice anything," murmured Paula. "I hardly know what we had to eat at the restaurant."

"Then I regret to tell you that Lothario went to his well-earned rest this afternoon. He conked out and expired just at the entrance to Colonel Duroc's garage."

"Bill!"

Lothario was their car. A louder, noisier, more sputtering little four-seater than Lothario would have been difficult to find. He had been ready for the scrap heap years before Bill bought him.

"I didn't want to tell you about this," continued Bill, who was genuinely sorry for the old junk pile, "and spoil the most noble of evenings."

"Mm," agreed Paula, pressing closer to him. Then her eyes opened wide. "But when were you at Colonel Duroc's house?"

"They told me," said Bill, "that I got there about twenty minutes after you'd left in Duroc's Packard. We must have passed each other on the road."

"But why on earth did you go up there?"

"You phoned me from the airport, remember? About the stupendous welcome of Sir Henry Merrivale?" Bill smiled. "Also, that you thought they were luring him to Colonel Duroc's house, and inveigling him into helping with the Iron Chest case?"

Paula nodded. Excitement had come into Bill's voice.

"Aside from wanting to carry you away like young Lochinvar," he said, "I was a bit curious to meet the Old Maestro himself. He was there on the terrace, right enough. And Colonel Duroc. And a Miss Holmes, who's rather attractive."

"She's nice," said Paula. "I mean, she really *is* nice." (Here Bill felt her body grow tense in his arms.) "But if you go and fall for . . ."

"S-ss-t! My pet! She's attractive, but not the sort for me. I prefer a buxom wench like you."

"I am not buxom!" exclaimed Paula, with such intensity that she did not see her husband's grin. "How I loathe the word! It means buxom all over, and I'm not. You know I'm not."

"Sorry, Paula. But seriously, now. You're not jealous of every woman I meet, are you?"

"Of course I am," said Paula, raising her head and looking at him with astonishment. "Some of them, when I've seen them with you . . ." She paused, remembering the horrible surgical tortures which (or so she believed) she would like to have performed. Scratching out the eyes was a mere preliminary. But she asked quickly: "Aren't you jealous of other men?"

"Well . . ."

"Aren't you?"

"Yes, damn it," snapped Bill, and felt every muscle in his arms and shoulders grow tense. In his way, he was worse than she was. "I don't trust anybody in this town. It's in the air, all this what-does-it-matter? I don't mean Juan Alvarez; he's the best friend I've got. But Hammond—!"

"No, Bill, please!"

He had erred in asking the original question; it brought on a nerve storm which he had to soothe.

"Paula, wait," Bill said, with her hair against his cheek while she held him more tightly. "We've gone over this a hundred times before. Let's go back to my visit to the Colonel, shall we?"

"I'm sorry," said Paula in a muffled voice. "Go on."

"All I did was phone for a taxi. Then I had to keep it waiting for nearly two hours; the driver just went to sleep. They insisted on my staying."

"Who insisted?" Paula asked rather quickly.

"Old H.M. himself. Nobody else." Bill's brown eyes became ironic. "I have a funny reputation in Tangier. They think I've got common sense, which isn't true; and they think I can keep my mouth shut, which is true. The Colonel wanted suggestions." Now Bill spoke very slowly. "I didn't say much, but I think I have them."

"Bill, your heart's beating like a fire engine! What is it?"

"You'll see. When I first got to the house—they heard Lothario chugging up the tunnel—the Colonel was telling them the stories of Iron Chest. Paula, how well do you know the history of Iron Chest?"

"Well—what's been in the press here. A little of what I heard today."

Bill's eyes were shining, though they seemed to see nothing; Paula felt faint disquiet.

"As it happens," he went on, "I know it inside-out. First, somebody here keeps a complete scrapbook from press-cutting agencies everywhere. You know her: Countess Scherbatsky."

" 'Countess,' " repeated Paula in a certain tone, but did not comment further.

"Well," he reminded her tolerantly, "everybody in Tangier has a title. Some of them are quite genuine. Anyway, you're not jealous of Ilone Scherbatsky; you know her too well."

"Ilone's all right," giggled Paula. "Usually she's too funny to take seriously. Also she . . ."

"Never mind that! The point is, second, that her latest boy friend is in the detective bureau. Inspector Mendoza, to be exact. He tells Ilone everything they know here, straight from the stable; and Ilone tells me."

"Tells you what?"

"Let's take a look at Iron Chest. His last coup was in . . ."

"Lisbon!" said Paula, fascinated and sitting up a little.

"Got it, my pet. Whang in the gold. In Lisbon, ten days ago: March 23. His previous one had been in Paris, a fortnight before that. Of course, the Lisbon police had been put on the alert. But Lisbon is an air centre, to say nothing of railways. Dozens of planes go in and out all the time. Ever since that coup in Paris, the Lisbon police had to keep an eye on the customhouse.

"Their trouble was that nobody had the remotest idea what Iron Chest looked like. Their one high card was that he had to get his burglar's kit, including that electric drill, through the customs inspection. As for the actual iron chest, that was still worse.

"Remember, the Lisbon police had no particular reason to expect him, by air or train, except for that direct air route between Lisbon and Paris. He might be anywhere. Furthermore, how many people—including customs inspectors—could recognize a burglar's kit if they saw one? Could you?"

Paula shook her head.

"I'm afraid not," she confessed.

"Well, neither could I. In stories they always use something called a jimmy, but if you showed me one I couldn't tell it from a crowbar or a spanner. In any case, everything seems to have been quiet, until the night of March 23. Then Iron Chest burgled a small private bank in the Avenida de Libertad. Same drill, same kind of haul in dollars—and pesetas. Lisbon exploded.

"Now they were in their worst difficulty. Iron Chest couldn't hole up in Lisbon for long; he never does. And customs authorities can't search the luggage of *outgoing* passengers, unless they have reason to suspect a particular person or persons, which they hadn't.

"The police brought in all the customs inspectors, and hammered them with questions about arrivals in the past two or three days. But you can't expect much of men who see so many suitcases and trunks that they dream about 'em. Meantime, all the various airlines had been co-operating by checking the list of arrivals who hadn't yet left.

"And this morning, my pet, it all happened at once."

Bill paused. He reached out for the glass of mint tea, which was very cold. He drank some of it, and set down the glass. Paula, clinging to him, wondered what he really meant behind this talk. She felt a little more apprehension in case he would get into some kind of danger.

"Yes, darling?" she prompted him.

"In Lisbon, at half-past nine, an off-duty customs inspector rushed into the police. He said he'd cudgelled his wits and thought he remembered something about the evening plane from Paris on March 21, two days before the burglary. The customs inspector seemed to remember a man—couldn't remember face or any detail, of course—

who carried a kit of tools, mostly smallish. The man explained this by saying he was a locksmith; a very convincing explanation, too. The customs inspector had a notion, unsure, that the luggage tags had a name beginning, 'C-o-l' something. There was another suggestion, but I won't bother you with it.

"By the time this customs inspector had finished, the police were so excited that they fired a phone call to the airport. They got quite a reply. It had just been discovered that a G. W. Collier had arrived in the Paris plane on the twenty-first. G. W. Collier, making a hasty last-minute booking because the plane wasn't full, had just done a bunk in the nine-thirty plane for Tangier, which left ten-fifteen minutes before.

"That's about all. But the Portuguese police, sighing with relief, phoned Colonel Duroc and were glad to hand somebody else the baby. Duroc had been waiting, ever since that burglary in Lisbon. Tangier was the possible, even the probable, next jump. Iron Chest arrived on the very same plane this morning with H.M. and Miss Holmes."

"But the Colonel didn't say anything about that when I was there!"

"He said a good deal about it when I was there," retorted Bill, making a grimace by wriggling his short-cut hair back and forth on his scalp. "And more. Baggage, I wonder if you've ever realized what a canny old bird the Colonel really is?"

"Nonsense!" protested Paula, who remembered only gallantry and chuckles. "That's silly!"

"Is it? Think about old H.M.'s stupendous reception at the airport, which you thought was funny."

"But it was!" gurgled Paula, relaxed now. "You'd have thought so too, if you'd been there. Not only that, but those poor gibbering passengers held up in a line against the plane, not even allowed to move until long after . . ."

Abruptly Paula sat up with a look of wonder and half-enlightenment in her face. Her pink lips opened, but closed without a sound. She glanced inquiringly at Bill.

"Got it again, my pet," he smiled. "They stayed there while all their luggage was instantly whisked into the airport station, and the French customs had a real beano. Furthermore, they were kept in a queue for a passport examination which lasted over an hour.

"Meanwhile, the customs inspectors were doing a royal job. They didn't concentrate on G. W. Collier's luggage alone. Luggage tags can be transferred; suitcases interchanged. So they pitched into everybody. They measured for false bottoms and compartments; they flung out everything; they followed a dozen measures Duroc had written down for them. Ilone's boy friend, Inspector Mendoza, who was in charge for the police, says the whole shed looked as though a hurricane had struck the clothes departments of Selfridge's."

Paula tugged at the collar of his shirt.

"Bill, wait!" she urged. "What about this G. W. Collier himself?"

"Well, what could Inspector Mendoza do?" asked Bill. "He could look at the passport, ask where Collier was staying—at the Riff Hotel, down near the bay—and search Collier himself. The man had nothing on him except a lot of money in many currencies. But nearly everybody has that, because the city's a changing centre and any currency is good. Were you at the house there when Colonel Duroc said he was expecting an important phone call from the airport or from the 7th Arrondissement Station?"

"Yes, I do remember that!"

"It was to learn the result of the search at the airport. The call got through when I was there." Bill drew a deep breath. "Paula, in all that luggage there was no kit of burglar's tools and no iron chest. Nothing that could be disguised as them; nothing remotely resembling them. Absolutely nothing!"

There was a long silence.

"But, Bill! If Collier is Iron Chest, hasn't he given himself away horribly? They know what he looks like."

"Oh, no, they don't!"

"Why not?"

"Old H.M. and Colonel Duroc think, and I agree, that Collier isn't Iron Chest. Otherwise, would he have been fool enough to do what you just said? Or enter and leave Lisbon under the name? No, my pet. Iron Chest must have only one accomplice: his diamond-cutter and polisher, who travels with him. And that's the 'Collier,' "

"Yes. I can see . . ."

"But the real Iron Chest, who planned and managed everything," Bill told her, "was tucked safely away in that same plane. Nobody saw him, in the sense of observing. They let 'Collier' go, of course; if he weren't the man they wanted, he would be bait for the man they wanted. But Iron Chest slipped invisibly through the barrier and into Tangier."

Paula shivered. Turning her head to the right, she looked past the silhouette of a leaning palm tree to the long light-spangled ridges piling up from the bay against a sky of lighter blue.

"Bill," she said, "I'm frightened. Oh, not physically, or for myself, but . . . according to what I've heard or read, this man simply vanished out of a narrow street in Brussels. In Paris he made a whole table-load of diamonds vanish before the eyes of the police. Now he's gone again, and made burglar's kit and iron chest vanish with him! It's creepy. It's . . . It's unnatural!"

"It's unnatural, right enough," he agreed. Then his usually low voice rang out. "But what an opportunity!"

"Opportunity?"

Bill sprang to his feet, making table and glasses on the table rattle. His wide shoulders were squared; and a colder breeze down the Straits of Gibraltar belled out the back of his shirt. His gaze was fixed without sight on rippled little reflections of light on the waters of the harbour. Paula sensed, as she always did, that his quick brain was sorting and arranging facts as swiftly as the man behind the private boxes at the British Post Office flicks each letter into its proper box.

"Iron Chest is tricky, he's spectacular; he's got a satirical sense of humour," Bill said to the harbour. "Have you seen those photographs of the iron chest? Or the chest Duroc had sent specially from Amsterdam as soon as he suspected Iron Chest would strike in Tangier?" He was not listening for a reply. "The carving round the edges is of monkeys putting out their tongues at you. Besides, Iron Chest is matched against H.M., who's even trickier and more spectacular. All the same . . ." Suddenly his tone alters. "Paula!"

"I'm here, Bill," she answered quickly, in the same soft tone she used when sometimes he called out or mumbled, twisting, in troubled sleep.

"Paula," he went on, "can you guess the total amount of the rewards, from various cities, for the capture of Iron Chest?"

"No, dear. But . . ."

"It's well over seven thousand pounds." He spoke blankly. "Paula, suppose *I* caught him?"

Now Paula was really frightened. These thefts and ghost vanishings might be all very fascinating and disturbing, in their remote way. But she was interested only in him. If *he* became involved in such dangers, if they threatened her and Bill's happy life, then he must be rescued from them as from a horrible disease.

"Bill," she said in her most yearning voice, "sit down and put your arms round me. Don't you want to?"

"Of course."

He sat down and held her tightly. Gently he lifted her hand and kissed it. Yet she knew his mind was still far away, sorting and arranging facts. Then Paula had an inspiration, based on her knowledge of him, which she felt with a sting in her heart must be true.

"I know now!" she whispered. "Darling, I know why you're troubled about money; and it's all my fault." Paula loved to take the blame on herself. "We've been too extravagant, that's all. We've been living and having our meals at the most expensive hotel in Tangier, which you can't afford. But I remember . . . Yes! An advertisement in the *Tangier Gazette* today . . ."

She did not tell him fully of her inspiration, hugging the secret.

"If we could get a little flat, and I did the housekeeping and cooking, it would change everything. We all grouse, darling, but let's face it: living in Tangier is the cheapest in the world. As I say, if we could get a little flat . . ."

Bill, waking up from his daze, blinked at her.

"What flat?" he asked. "Who's talking about a flat?"

"Never mind, dear." Then she chided him. "Anyway, why do you want to win all that money?"

"It's not the money, so much." He shook his head and brooded. "Though that would get us free from this consular grind, and we could retire somewhere. Perhaps—England."

"Bill! Aren't you satisfied to live with me? Here?"

"You? Oh, God, yes, you know that! I couldn't be anywhere without you!"

This was all Paula wanted to know. She sighed.

"Then what's this dreadful nonsense about the money?"

"I told you; it's not so much that. It would be . . . the prestige."

"Prestige?"

"Yes, don't you see?"

They looked at each other. For an instant it became achingly clear that she did not understand his motives, and he did not understand hers. A gulf opened between them, terrifying because they had been so intimate. It might have grown worse if Bill had not kissed her for some time, so that healing warmth destroyed mere words.

"Paula, I'm a blasted fool!" he said at length. "Forget what I said, won't you? I didn't mean it!"

"If you ever want to be involved in a thing like this," whispered Paula, and almost believed she meant it, "I won't stop you. Truly I won't."

"I'm not going to get involved."

"Anyway," Paula attempted that man-to-man tone which she, of all people, could never manage, "you'll at least think it over, won't you?"

"There's nothing to think over. There it is."

"Bill, I'm getting terribly cold, with only a jumper and slacks on. Couldn't we . . . go back to the hotel?"

"Of course, immediately. I'm sorry."

In the Flying Standard car, Bill could have driven them home by a more direct way. Instead, for reasons of his own, he took a slightly more circuitous route. Paula, glowing inwardly and hugging her inspiration from the *Tangier Gazette,* lounged beside him with her eyes half-closed.

Over Tangier, even in what seems the blackest night, there hangs always a faint greyness as of hidden lamps. When the car swung into the Grand Socco, it was only a quarter to midnight. Electric lights, as well as curling yellow tallow flares, faintly brushed pink or white colour on the grime of huddled houses. The odours of the Grand Socco are more mixed than savoury.

It was quiet tonight, though for blary raucousness you had only to descend a curving slope into the Little Socco, which never sleeps. In the earthen market place amid the cobblestones of the Grand Socco, few donkeys or horses or carts now remained. The crooked trees shadowed squashed fruit and dead flowers, which were to have been sold. A group of hooded Arabs crouched, their heads together, as though in sinister conspiracy, round a wise man who was telling fortunes with bones. Down the narrow hill of the rue San Francisco roared two modern cars, their horn buttons punched and screaming.

But what is noise, as such? Who shall hear it?

Certainly Paula did not notice that her husband, as he turned the car left towards the entrance to the rue du Statut, was driving so slowly that the Standard's engine almost stalled.

Later, she wished she had.

Now the rue du Statut is a very long street with intersections. Beginning in the Grand Socco, it first ascends a slight slope, with shops on either side. It grows steeper when it is bisected by the rue du Sud on the right; and, on the left, by a downward slope and a broad flight of stone stairs descending into the semi-darkness of the rue Waller. Afterwards, it continues up a steep hill and finally into the Place de France.

But we are concerned only with the lower part, just before you reach that intersection. Paula, at the left of the driver in an English car, was peering out and up through one open window on the left.

"Bill!" She was delighted. "Look here!"

"Eh?" her husband said absently. He was letting the car creep along close to the right-hand curbstone, and peering out.

"Well, you can listen," Paula pointed out.

On the roof ledge over a draper's shop, at the left-hand side of the rue du Statut and squatted cross-legged, sat a very fat Italian with a guitar. His head was flung back, so that you could see the huge cavern of this mouth and even his bald head. Thus on the rooftop, above the twang of the guitar, he poured out his longing in a frenzy of Neapolitan self-expression.

"Che be-la co-sa," warbled the rich tenor, *" 'na iur-na-ta'e sooo-le?"*

"Isn't it rather lovely?" asked Paula, leaning back cosily.

"His behaviour is perfectly natural to everyone; not even the police would ask what he was doing there. It isn't quiet here, but it's so peaceful. So restful. So . . ."

Then it happened.

Across her words ripped the violent, continuous *clatter-clang* of a burglar alarm.

It drove into the ears like a drill into a safe. It even seemed to grow louder and more deafening, as though a mechanical voice cried guilt into the night. Across the street, the guitar fell and smashed unheard on the pavement. A mutter of voices swept up from the Grand Socco.

There were now only a comparatively few doors between them and the intersection of the rue du Sud. The instant that burglar alarm had clattered out, Bill Bentley jammed on the handbrake and stopped the car. Now he jerked open the handle of the right-hand door.

Paula, peering past him, could see the front of a familiar shop. It was a jeweller's. It had a broad display window on either side of the front door; but windows and door were now protected by a folding steel grille which not even a ghost would dare to touch in an open street. Over the shop, in large separated gilt letters, ran the sign, "Bernstein et Cie."

Then Paula, who had seen it so often, remembered and looked straight ahead. On the left-hand side of the building ran a narrow alley, and there was a side door to the premises of the jeweller.

Bill Bentley flung open the car door and jumped out on the pavement.

"Bill! No! Bill!"

"I knew it!" he shouted. "A stuffed dummy could have guessed it!"

And, taking only one glance at the locked steel grille across the front, he raced down the dark alley towards the side door. The burglar alarm still clanged and clattered to the night.

CHAPTER SIX

Frantically Paula pushed herself across the seat, under the driving wheel, and leaped out to the pavement. She was facing straight down the dark alley, and heard Bill's footsteps on stone. Paula remembered only afterwards that she had choked back a scream of, "Bill!" for too many things happened at once.

Over the side door of Bernstein et Cie. there flashed on a large but dull-burning electric bulb under a round and flat tin shade. Bill, in the darkness, had run past the door by eight or ten feet; Paula saw him whip round as the light appeared.

Then came the nightmare.

The side door, an ordinary-sized door, was flung open. Out stumbled a man with a felt hat pulled down on his head. Clutched heavily under his left arm but partly across his body was a familiar object from which the light struck a dull gleam—especially on the frieze of monkeys' heads. The burglar alarm stopped, and silence smote like a blow in the face.

The man, adjusting his burden, ran for the mouth of the alley. Out of the side door plunged Colonel Duroc and H.M., one stoutish and one very stout man getting in each other's way.

But Bill, the instant that door opened, had taken off like a sprinter. His head was crouched low. Paula could see the expression on his face, lips drawn back of the teeth; he would get Iron Chest or get a bullet. Miraculously Bill dodged past H.M. and the Colonel, overtook his quarry—and dived at him with a Rugby tackle from behind.

Only Iron Chest's sneering luck, again as Paula remembered afterwards, saved him then. Bill's right hand hooked round the runner's right knee, and strove to send his arm round to the elbow. But he made exactly the same mistake as had the policeman in Brussels. Bill's left hand darted up to seize that accursed, maddening chest, and his fingers slipped on a too-smooth surface.

Off-balance and dragged face-forward, Bill would still have kept his grip on the right knee if the burglar's trousers had held. Six inches of some thin material ripped off under Bill's hand. The solid phantom kicked viciously backwards into his adversary's left shoulder; Bill, still groping, fell heavily on his side and rolled over on his back.

Even then they might have nabbed him, if H.M. and Duroc had been quick enough. Iron Chest was staggering and almost down. Yet he half turned behind. Paula caught the gleam on a snub-nosed but heavy revolver, and he fired almost point-blank at Bill's body.

And now the hobgoblin, little more than a black silhouette, raced for the mouth of the alley and came face to face with Paula.

They were about four feet apart. There was just enough light, perhaps, for her to have seen his face. But her vision was concentrated all on those shiny monkeys; her mind flew past to Bill. Blank face's gun hand, encased in a rubber glove, snaked up over the chest and he fired two shots at Paula's head.

Whereupon, again heaving his burden, he ran hard a few feet up the rue du Statut. But he did not turn right, into the rue du Midi. Instead he whipped to the left, taking the steep street instead of the broad stone steps which led down into the rue Waller.

Suddenly police whistles seemed to be shrilling from everywhere.

Paula stood rigid. In this nightmare she had not time even to be frightened when the hobgoblin fired at her. Two flashes, two reports, had been no more than grotesque incidents, seeming quite natural at the time. But she saw that Bill was immediately on his feet. Bill raced to the mouth of the alley, glanced left and right without seeing any quarry, and then hurried to Paula.

At the same time Colonel Duroc, in full uniform and cap, plunged out with a red and frantic face and stared round. Momentarily he glanced back to shout to someone invisible in the alley. Now he spoke only French.

"Inspector Mendoza, where is the Commandant?"

"My Colonel, I don't know! He has not been here at all."

"Our men were to have been placed so that not even a snake could have left! Where are they?"

"My Colonel, the Commandant was to have given the orders. You know the Commandant. He does not show himself at all. Myself, I am lying on top of the wall at the back of the alley. I dare not give the orders until . . ."

"My God!" whispered the Colonel, and lifted both arms to the sky. He paused. His gruff voice thundered out like a fog horn, yet with every word clear.

"Listen, all agents of police. Listen, police. Our man is departed into the rue Waller! After him, all of you! All!"

Now the street was alive and drumming to the sound of running feet. There were ghostly glimpses of white helmets, white belts, white truncheons in hand. Among them flashed a number of sprinters who could easily overtake the fugitive.

The Colonel still shouted.

"Throw a line across the end of the rue Waller! He must not get out, into the market up one side, or down. Keep him in the rue Waller, and he is trapped. We have him!"

A thunder of running footsteps whacked so fast that its turmoil was dying away. Up from the Grand Socco poured Arabs in *jalebahs,* Arabs in robes, Arabs in ordinary clothes but wearing the red tarboosh. Few people on earth can grow more excited about a street row.

"Ten thousand pesetas," yelled Duroc, first in French and then in Arabic, "to the man who has him!"

The turmoil went mad.

"I am an executive, an administrator!" fumed the Colonel, flinging out his arms to empty air. "And yet . . . Forward!" he cried, and himself raced in the crowd towards the rue Waller.

During all this, Bill Bentley had run across the street and seized Paula. Two questions were thrown at once and by each of them, sounding together.

"Are you all right?"

"Are you all right?"

"Yes!"

"Yes!"

Frantically Bill ran his hands over her face, her hair, her arms and shoulders, her breast and stomach, while she tried to laugh.

"Darling," she said, "are you *sure?* I mean, about you?"

"Yes, not a scratch."

This, strictly speaking, was not quite true. There was a blackish smear on the left shoulder of his shirt, covering a long purpling bruise underneath. His right sleeve was torn, with blackish stone scratchings oozing blood. A trouser knee was torn, and both wrists scratched on their underside. But it was all so little as to be nothing, even if Paula did not think so.

"Bill, you *are* hurt! We must wash those and put iodine—" She paused, remembering Bill's loathing of what he called being fussed over, and said no more.

It was unnecessary to say more. Out of the alley lumbered Sir Henry Merrivale, his hat gone and his bald head gleaming. His look was evilly dispirited, half-abased, and altogether bad. He approached Paula with the same old question.

"You all right, my dolly?"

"Of course I am!" smiled Paula. In the reaction she wasn't, but she would have died rather than admit it. She spoke in the same calm voice she had used after a thousand-pound H.E. bomb had fallen two doors away.

In fact, both she and Bill had instantly sprung apart before they heard H.M's footsteps near them. An outsider, seeing this British couple in street or restaurant, would have said that they might feel a dull domestic comfort, but they could never possibly be emotional.

"And you, son," said H.M. Adjusting his spectacles, he peered at Bill. The latter, though his look could not conceal bitter disappointment, showed himself unhurt.

"Now that's very interestin'," growled H.M. "Come with me, both of you!"

The tumult now boiled at its highest down in the rue Waller. Policemen, heaven knows why, persisted in blowing their whistles. There was a high neighing and heavy stamping of frightened horses in a nearby stable. But H.M. led Paul and Bill into the alley.

Now they could see that the wall opposite the door of Bernstein et Cie. was composed of very small shops. Each consisted only of a lower cross door and an upper cross door. Fold back the upper door and your lower door became a counter with all the stock in a small space behind the seller. Now all doors were shut and locked into a long row of dirty grey-or-brown-painted upright boards.

Taking an electric torch from his pocket, H.M. directed its strong beam along the lower boards and the ground.

"Son," he said to Bill, "do you mind getting your clothes messed up again?"

"Not a bit. Why?"

"Well, fall down and show me exactly where you were when Iron Chest took a shot at you."

Bill studied the ground, but much study was not necessary under H.M.'s moving light. The stone-paved alley was thick with dirt as well as grit, and they could see the marks where Bill had been thrown and dragged. There lay a flimsy piece of light-brown material torn from the unknown's trouserleg.

Nodding approval, Bill first lay down on his right side, where Paula had seen him fall, and then rolled over on his back with his left shoulder touching grimy grey boards; just as before.

"Now!" grunted H.M.

Sending the beam of the torch along Bill's length, he next lifted it and played it along the boards above. All could see the bullet hole, clean-drilled in grey wood except for a slight furring on the right side because the goblin had fired backwards and partly sideways.

"No, don't get up. Look!" admonished H.M. "Now, I saw that gun. It's the American revolver they call a Colt's Banker's Special, .38, very short barrel, but heavy fire power and deadly at short range. This humourous feller shot at you . . . well, not exactly at point-blank range, but very close. And yet look at the bullet hole! . . . he missed you by two feet."

Bill scrambled up from the ground.

"And you, my dolly," said H.M., turning to Paula, "are you certain you don't feel any powder specklings on your forehead? No, not powder burns. But this was only four feet away from you. Usually there are stings from unburnt powder grains after a near miss."

"There aren't any," she answered positively.

"D'ye see, then? The bullets must have gone wild over your head."

For the first time, in the wearing away of shock, Paula imagined the crash of a bullet into her forehead or face.

"There aren't . . ." she whispered. Her knees were trembling.

Bill immediately put his arm round her. Partly to divert attention, Bill began cursing himself with round, vile, expressive oaths particular to Tangier. Then he stopped short.

"It's my own fault," he added more soberly. "If I'd hit him with a clean tackle for both knees, he'd have gone over flat. But, no. Oh, no. I had to make a grab for that chest. Even then I might have done it. But the damned iron was polished; kind of film on it, like polished steel; my fingers slipped on it, and down I went. But if I'd had any sense! The rewa—" again Bill stopped.

H.M. grunted, pulling at his underlip. Momentarily he turned away, to inspect a chalk drawing on the wall of Bernstein et Cie. This drawing was not exactly of the most proper variety.

"No, son," said H.M., "it wasn't your fault. It was pure cussedness. Just as it's happened every other time." He turned back, and his diffidence was explained by this look of secret guilt. "Burn it, what about me? I was standin' here as paralyzed as a straw ghoul—and so was the Colonel—with my eyes bulging out because I thought you'd got him."

"*If* I'd got him! Lord *if* I'd got him!"

H.M. sent the beam of the torch round the alley, including the chalk drawing on a yellow wall. He switched off the torch and dropped it into his pocket. Now the only light burned dully over the side door.

"Son," said H.M. in a heavy, serious voice, "I want you to think. And think hard, just the same as you did at Colonel Duroc's place this afternoon."

"Well, sir?"

Bill's eyes were shining again, and Paula's heart sank as she saw the detective fever burn once more.

"For about ten hours," said H.M., with the beginning of a martyred look, "the Colonel kept pourin' reports down my throat. I know more about Iron Chest than his own mother, except I don't know who he is. Now consider! In twelve spectacular burglaries, thirteen if we include tonight, Iron Chest has been seen making his getaway no less than nine times. In every instance he's fired shots, sometimes several shots, at people who weren't quite close enough to nab him."

"Yes?" prompted Bill.

"And yet, with all that gunplay, what's the result? With the exception of a poor-devil policeman in Brussels, who recovered, and a powerful woman in Madrid who wanted the reward, and got a hip wound, Iron Chest hasn't hit a single person for all his shootin'. How do you explain that? Hey?"

Bill, pondering, shifted from one foot to the other. He rubbed the side of his jaw with a grimy hand.

"Do you think it's important, sir?"

"Important? Cor! Remember, he's performed only three miracles. he vanished smack out of a street in Brussels. He made a table-full of diamonds vanish in Paris. Here in Tangier he seems to have vanished with all his kit and possessions. Yet, other times, he's seen and he's kept firing without much result."

"Putting aside the idea that he's simply a rotten bad shot," observed Bill, "you could have it another way. As, for instance, when he shot at me. He took a snap shot at me: off-balance, half-turning, and weighted with that heavy chest. More or less the same with Paula; he was still half-staggering. It all comes down to this: *why* does he insist on carrying that damned chest? Is it a kind of mascot he thinks will bring luck?"

H.M. sniffed.

" 'Tisn't as easy as that, son. Or Iron Chest bein' a loony, which he's not. I formed sort of a different opinion from my first one." H.M. glanced back at the lighted side door, inside which someone seemed to lurk. "Anyway, regarding the jiggery-pokery the police played here tonight . . ."

Satiric lines appeared round Bill's mouth.

"If you'll pardon me saying it, sir," he said, "it was fairly obvious what you and the police would do. Also, what Iron Chest would do."

H.M.'s face turned slightly purple.

"What d'ye mean, obvious?" he demanded.

"It was tolerably certain Iron Chest would have a go at Bernstein and Company," said Bill. "First, he'd burgled their branch at Brussels, and he can't have a very high opinion of their locks. Second, for weeks it's been in the newspapers that a West African potentate, the Sultan of Somewhere, I forget, was bringing one hundred uncut diamonds to Tangier, and handing over the little grey shapeless masses to Bernstein and Company to be cut and polished as a necklace for his third and final wife."

"Uh-huh," agreed H.M. in a strangled voice. "Anything else?"

Bill tried to look deprecating, but failed.

"Iron Chest, I decided, would reason thus: 'They'll think I mean to be low and reconnoitre for a night or two, as I usually do; therefore I'll hit 'em tonight.' You, on the other hand, would reason: 'He may not strike tonight; but, in case it's a double bluff, we'd better have that jeweller's heavily covered just the same.' Proof, sir? I was here when the fireworks began."

H.M. put his head on one side.

"Y'know, son," he observed thoughtfully, "I told the Colonel this evening you had a lot of grey matter floatin' about unperceived. I say, son." He coughed. "I'm not interested in rewards. Y'know, when they talked about fees or rewards in America, I got so frothing mad they had to pull me down from the ceiling, and they couldn't understand it. Still, if you'd like to take a hand in this . . . hey?"

Paula glanced quickly at Bill. Bill, in a somewhat overheroic attitude, did not even look at her.

"I'm afraid I can't sir. You see," he said, telling lies with the fluency made necessary by his job, "there's a lot of extra work at the consulate I've got to handle. Decisions, you know. And, since—er—I've got a lot of influence over the consul . . ."

"Sure," said H.M., "you mean your wife has got a smackin' influence over you." Then H.M. became equally dramatic, attempting a far-off look of melancholy in a narrow alley. "Some wives are tyrants. Awful tyrants. Instead of bootin' 'em in the stern . . ."

"I'm not a tyrant!" said Paula, indignant and rather shocked. "You ask Bill if I am. He's p-perfectly free to do anything he likes, and he knows it."

Now *she* was becoming noble. And yet, though she was now very calm, horror seemed to crawl inside her skin.

Never, never again must she meet that hobgoblin with no face and a pistol with a two-inch barrel, or she would go mad or do something silly. Nor must Bill ever meet him again. Put all this together and mix it—still, her curiosity was stronger than her fear.

"Sir Henry," she asked hesitantly, "what *happened* here tonight? Why were you and the Colonel inside the jeweller's with Iron Chest? Where was Juan Alvarez? And those hundred diamonds—how many did Iron Chest steal?"

An expression almost of serenity crossed H.M.'s unmentionable face.

"Not one ruddy diamond," he said. "Not one jewel. Not one peseta or anything else."

"Wow!" said Bill, and gleefully slapped a torn knee and winced.

"Y'see," H.M. explained, "early in the evening Duroc phoned 'young' M. Bernstein, who's about fifty and the last of an old family who've had a jeweller's in Paris since the eighteenth century. But he's a fine feller, and he helped us to the limit. He drove down here with us, gave the Colonel all his keys, and sent away the night watchman. Bernstein wanted to stay, but the Colonel chucked him off his own premises. Bernstein was sort of . . . Cor! I forgot! He'll be sittin' by a telephone now."

H.M. wheeled majestically round towards the side door behind them. His bass voice was pitched in that strange, highfalutin' way with which he spoke any foreign language.

"Monsieur L'Inspecteur Mendoza!" he called.

Out under the overhead lamp stepped briskly a tall, bony, rather handsome man with a narrow line of black moustache. His felt hat showed heavy dark hair with grey at the temples; he was well dressed in civilian clothes, and smoked a cigarette rather nervously.

Oui, Seer Henri?"

Since Inspector Mendoza was reputed to be the latest conquest of Ilone Scherbatsky—plump, kindly Ilone, who gave *keef* parties and was generous in every sense—Paula regarded him with interest. Paula had never been jealous of Ilone because Bill secretly but savagely hated all Russians, even (which was very unfair) White Russians like Ilone.

H.M. attempted to put polish on his taxi-driver French.

"Be good enough," he entoned like a soothsayer, "to telephone to M. Bernstein and tell him that he need no longer be in the apples."

"Pardon me, Sir Henry?"

"Ah, bah! It is an expression of slang. So-and-so it! Have the kindness to inform M. Bernstein that the robbery has failed and not a jewel is missing."

"Very good, Sir Henry," said Mendoza, and disappeared back into the doorway.

"But what *happened?*" Paula insisted again.

"Can't you guess, my dolly? For nearly three mortal hours, ever since it got good and dark at nine o'clock, Duroc and I hid in Bernstein's private office. Look!" H.M. pointed. "That side door leads to it. It's partitioned off from the front of the shop. The safe is against the wall opposite the side door; and, on the left, there's a pretty big cupboard. That's where Duroc and I hid.

"Y'see, the place was all dark. The cupboard door," H.M continued, "was open only about half an inch. I got all the view there was, because Duroc couldn't move me. His language was shockin'. Oh, my dolly! If your pure ears were ever stained by that stupefyin', godless . . ."

Paula giggled. H.M., glaring at her over his spectacles, climbed down from his virtuous pedestal.

"All right!" he growled. "Iron Chest got there about a quarter to midnight. He found that opening the side door was as easy as shellin' peas. What he didn't know, and we did, was the little trick Bernstein had kept there for years."

"Trick?" interposed Bill. "What trick?"

"Y'see, the main burglar alarm ain't attached to the door or windows." The old reprobate was faintly amused. "It works from hidden button, set flush with the floor, in front of the safe and just under the lock. Even in daylight it's hard to spot. Iron Chest prowled in with a torch. He put down the chest, which had the burglin' tools—you'd be surprised how small and light the kit was—packed inside in velvet. He didn't open 'em; just looked at 'em and put 'em back. He prowled over to the safe with his torch, and then . . . whang!

"Burn me, I never knew a burglar alarm could possibly be so loud!

"For a couple of seconds I was as petrified as the Colonel. Then this little bounder, who was wrestling and cursin' at me because he wanted to get out of the cupboard first—that was my right, wasn't it?—got both of us stuck in the door. Iron Chest got his burden together, put the torch in his pocket and pulled out a short-nosed Colt's Banker's Special, and hared out. You know the rest. Except that something seems to have gone wonky with the police net outside."

H.M. made a noise deep in his throat.

Then, shaking his head in a dissatisfied kind of way, he walked to the mouth of the alley and then out into the middle of the rue du Statut. Paula and Bill followed. Far down in the rue Waller, it was almost quiet except for the noise of footsteps and the occasional thud of a horse hoof. H.M., the corners of his mouth turned down, was surveying the folding steel framework across the front of Bernstein et Cie. His gaze moved to the shop next door, down towards the Grand Socco: a very grimy shop window across which ran the enamelled letters, "Luisa Bonomi," and under them, in Spanish and French, "Masks and Costumes." Then H.M. turned round.

"Sir Henry," said Paula, "that rue Waller really is a trap if they put a cordon across the far end. Do you think they'll catch him?"

"No, my dolly," replied H.M., pulling at his underlip. "Y'see, they don't know what they're looking for."

"You mean, for whom they're looking?"

"No, no, no!" H.M. made fussed gestures. "I mean just exactly that—they don't know what they're looking for."

As Paula and Bill exchanged puzzled glances, H.M. held up a big hand.

"And as a specific instance of what I mean, I'll show you," he declared. "We've never once had even a tolerable description of Iron Chest, have we? Right! Now both of you saw him tonight, and at close range. Describe him!"

There was a silence.

"Do you know," Bill suddenly remarked, and scratched what was left of thick brown hair after an army-style haircut, "that for the life of me I can't remember. I grabbed his knee; nothing to describe about that. When he took a shot at me I was lying on my back, eyes in the wrong direction, and all I saw was a flash. No; I can't describe him."

"Well, I can't," Paula said defensively. "He was a—a dark silhouette. Anyway, I was looking at that dreadful iron chest with the monkeys. I rather think he had a hat on."

"I'm not askin' for any Bertillon measurements." H.M. spoke patiently. "Only the general details. Was he tall or short? Fat or thin? Anything at all about the face?"

"I don't know," both Bentleys answered together, after a long silence.

"Then there you are," said H.M. wearily. "It's the same with other people. But *why* don't they know? Solve that, and you've got half the answer. Even providin'," he added, "it *was* Iron Chest we saw tonight." At this cryptic announcement, as though he still concealed much, H.M. made a violent gesture.

"Lord love a duck, no!" Again he forestalled their thoughts. "I'm not being one of these feather-witted goops who've got the right answer but let corpses go on fallin' all over the place because they won't tell the police anything until everybody's been polished off. I think I've got half the answer, that's all. And I'll tell the Colonel fast enough tomorrow. Or even tonight, if he's not so mad that flames are spurtin' up from under his collar. Y'see . . ."

He broke off, because the subject of his talk was strutting down the short distance towards them. Only in the figurative sense did flames spurt up from under Colonel Duroc's collar. His short, stoutish figure in the khaki uniform carried real dignity. Formally he kissed Paula's hand, and shook hands with Bill.

"Well!" he said in English, and with an effort. "We have lost our man again. Yet every door, every shutter in the rue Waller was locked on the inside. Four of our fastest runners, Arab policemen, passed Iron Chest, saw him, and stood in a line under a lamp street at the end of the rue Waller. But no, no, no! Again he performs a vanish trick." Colonel Duroc paused for breath. "And who is responsible for this?"

"Now don't you look at me!" blared H.M. He appealed to the others with power of sympathy. "I get myself almost murdered again, bein' cloth-witted enough to drive down in the Colonel's car. Haa, that reminds me. You promised I could have what I wanted. I know just how to travel in this town. Do I get what I want?"

The Colonel waved his hand grandly.

"It shall arrive," he announced, "by special plane from Lisbon tomorrow morning. But, my friend . . . No, no, I did not mean you." He raised his voice. "Mendoza!"

Out of the side door hurried tall Inspector Mendoza, with his bony handsome face and narrow line of moustache, and hurried along the alley to the street. Flinging away what was presumably still another cigarette, he stood uneasily at attention.

Colonel Duroc, as though his throat changed gears, shifted into French.

"Inspector Mendoza," he purred in a soft voice. "You were second in command to Commandant Alvarez of the men outside the jeweller's. Myself, I was inside that office accursed since nine o'clock. Our men were huddled into doorways, crouched everywhere in the wrong places, without orders. Since the Commandant did not see fit to appear, and indeed has not yet favoured us with his presence, why did you not give orders yourself?"

"I have told you, my Colonel, I did not dare! Pardon me; the Commandant is a martinet . . ."

Duroc's purring voice seemed to creep nearer.

"Yet a dozen telephones were near you, Mendoza. Did it not occur to you to telephone to the Central Office, and send men out in search of him?"

"My Colonel, I did! At least ten times!"

"Ah, you did? Very well . . . And then? Come, I can well understand your wish not to speak badly of a colleague." The Colonel's tone altered. "But it is I who command you!" he cried, sticking out his stomach. "Speak!"

Now Mendoza rattled out syllables so fast that Paula and Bill had to strain their ears.

"I believe, my Colonel, that the Commandant had arranged to meet a young lady, a Miss Maureen 'Olmes, at the restaurant Caravel to dine at seven-thirty."

"The restaurant Caravel? But . . . no matter! A man may dine at seven-thirty, and yet report for duty at nine hours!"

"True, my Colonel. However, according to the waiters and the boss, the Commandant arrives too early. At half-past seven he is still inscrutable. When the lady does not arrive at eight hours, his fingers drum the table and his boots strike the floor. At eight-thirty, when still she is not arrived, the Commandant calls for glasses of brandy. And, according to the waiters . . . By blue, how this man can drink! Now, if I may digress . . ."

"Continue, continue!"

"It seems that the young lady, in some fashion, thought the Commandant told her to meet him at the restaurant Ciro, in the rue Raphael."

"The restaurant Ciro!" muttered the Colonel, striking his hands together. "Yes, this is true. I have heard her say it myself."

"Then the rest is not much. When the Commandant does not appear at eight-thirty, this young lady throws plates on the floor and bursts into tears. Henri and all his staff try to console her. Yet she leaps into a taxi and returns to your own home, my Colonel, on the Old Mountain."

"And the Commandant?"

"Well, then, they have found him in his own flat. He is unconscious and black-drunk."

In the heavy, vibrant silence which followed, bill Bentley whispered in his wife's ear.

"Has Juan Alvarez really fallen for the American girl you told me about?"

"Bill, I'm sure of it!"

"Fine. Do him good to go out and get blind for once. Good old Juan!"

Unfortunately the meditating Duroc overheard this. He turned round.

"Then that is good, Mr. Bentley?" he inquired, in a soft and sarcastic tone. "Through the negligence of Commandant Alvarez, and the weakness of this Mendoza, it is good that we have lost a certain capture of Iron Chest? It is good that we have lost our best—stop; our only—opportunity to catch him? Regard—" he swept his arm round, his gruff voice rising—"here is a city of money. Stuffed and bursting with money . . . Fortunes made overnight . . . Already becoming well known as a jewel centre, and banks everywhere! Yet now we have no notion of where Iron Chest will strike, even where he is. That is good, eh?"

"Who-ah, there!" interposed the voice of Sir Henry Merrivale, who was sitting on the curb with his head in his hands. "The more I think over this, the less I see you have to grouse about."

"Indeed, my friend?"

"Yes. You haven't lost your great or only opportunity. You haven't even *had* your big opportunity. Did the feller get any of the Sultan's hundred diamonds, a fortune in themselves? No. You prevented the burglary, didn't you?"

Colonel Duroc puffed out his chest and expelled a sigh of relief.

"There is much in what you say, yes. But this talk of our biggest opportunity . . ."

"That's because you don't understand Iron Chest, son. He's half to three parts full of vanity. You've scratched his vanity, and scratched it hard. You talk a lot of gibberish about not knowing 'where Iron Chest will strike.' Oh, my eye! I dunno when, of course, except that it'll be soon. But I can tell you just exactly where."

"This is so, then? Very well; where will he attack?"

"Why, curse it all, *there,*" retorted H.M., turning round to stab one finger towards the locked steel framework of Bernstein et Cie. "He'll have another go at those diamonds, just to show you. He'll do it, Colonel, if you put fifty coppers round the safe. What's more, I'm bettin' he'll get away with it."

Then H.M. spoke in a hollow voice. "But, burn me," he said, "how in blazes is Iron Chest going to do it?"

"Probably you are right," mused the Colonel. "But, at the moment," he added ominously, "I think of what I will say to Commandant Alvarez next morning!"

CHAPTER SEVEN

On the next morning, at half-past seven in the large, comfortable bedroom at the Minzeh Hotel, Paula Bentley slipped from the side of her snoring husband, and edged softly and silently out of bed.

At that hour it was bitter cold. Paula shivered. Hastily she donned a pair of pajamas, which felt colder still, as well as dressing gown and slippers. She tiptoed to the bathroom, closed the door, and switched on the light. After a quick but warm bath, she "did" her hair and face, the latter requiring only a little powder because of her glowing health. At hand were the clothes she meant to wear, surreptitiously put there before she had gone to sleep the night before.

As Paula quickly dressed, she glanced more than once at the copy of yesterday's *Tangier Gazette* on the edge of the bathtub, and at the advertisement she had marked.

She was completely happy. The idea which had come to her last night, on top of the tower, seemed even better by morning. She had determined to solve all difficulties—worries about money, or so she imagined—by getting a small but modern flat, and doing the housekeeping and cooking herself.

Her only deadly fear was that someone had got there before her. Small flats, especially modern ones and in a respectable district, are almost as difficult to find in Tangier as anywhere else. Paula had romantically resolved to get there first, and camp on the doorstep.

"I'll get it," she told herself. "I *must* get it."

Completely dressed, in dark blue which almost matched the colour of her eyes, Paula switched off the light before opening the bathroom door. The alarm clock would not ring until eight; and nothing could wake Bill until then.

Pausing only to pick up a handbag and a light coat, Paula slipped out of the room and let the door close without any click of the latch. She moved down across the thick carpets of the hotel, pushed through the revolving doors into the upper hill of the rue du Statut, and found almost at once the most modern of taxis.

The sky was still whitish grey, with a broad pink band towards the east. Paula, the newspaper clenched under her arm like a talisman, sat back and dreamed.

Twenty seconds after her own cab had gone, another taxi swerved away from the curb and followed her at the fast, even pace of the first.

Though Paula did not read the newspaper, many phrases of the advertisement were printed in her mind. True, it contained only one large bed-sitting room, but by day the bed could neatly be disguised as a couch. It had a kitchenette—Paula's American friends and the films had made her familiar with the term—and this kitchenette could instantly be hidden behind sliding doors. The bathroom contained every modern comfort. "Excellent for transients," no! . . . "Inspection invited," good! Though it added no telephone number, it gave a price absurdly low.

Best of all was the address: number 40-bis Marshan.

"Next door to Dr. MacPhail," whispered Paula to herself. It couldn't be better.

Twenty-odd years ago, when Tangier had been only a handful of mud or stucco houses clustered round the squat towers of the big Kasbah, nobody expected that its position in North Africa would make it mushroom out into a city of a hundred and thirty thousand inhabitants, with so much money made by ways both legal and dubious that some people made a living by playing the rise and fall of currencies against each other.

Hence the city had spread ever upwards and outwards towards the mountains, with buildings and sedate villas and Spanish blocks of flats, in yellow stucco and green blinds after the post-Franco style. Marshan was a vast flat open space, very respectable. At one corner stood Dr. MacPhail's nursing home, as up-to-date as any in London.

Paula, as the heavy taxi whipped up the rue du Statut, past the broad silent Place de France, and again uphill by way of the rue du Fez.* was still far away in thought. She grinned as her mind drifted back to very late last night, to the final violent argument between Sir Henry Merrivale and Colonel Duroc before all left for home.

"Come, we must not stand here in the open street," Duroc had spluttered. Carefully he gathered up the torn piece of trouser material, to derisive remarks from H.M. "Now, I tell you. We must all have a last drink, a cup of the stirrup. You agree?"

And so he had led H.M., Bill, and Paula to the Parade Bar.

Though Paula had often visited the Parade Bar, she was always uneasy in case she and Bill should find Mark Hammond there. Mark Hammond, long and lean, almost completely bald though only in his middle thirties, wrote popular science books which gave him a steady if not an overly great income. He lived in Tangier, but he was forever travelling on the Continent.

Hammond, though never offensive even when he was drunk, was sometimes disturbingly frank. Paula, as well as Bill himself, had been embarrassed by such remarks as, "I suppose, Mr. Bentley, you know I am in love with your wife?" Or: "But please don't think I shall make any advances. I loathe exercise; by nature, thank God, I am thin. But I hear you are a pretty fair middleweight, not perhaps as good as Alvarez *le terrible;* and I won't have my head knocked off for unrequited love." Here Hammond had laughed and was friendly.

But Paula, entering the Parade Bar last night with Bill and H.M. and Colonel Duroc, had been relieved to find Hammond absent. The Parade is comparatively small, discreetly lighted, with a touch of red and black in the furnishings. Over the bar counter hangs a canopy, under which

*It should be explained that, with the exception of certain quarters, street signs in Tangier are usually printed in three languages: Spanish, French, and Arabic. To avoid confusion and irritation when the characters in this book go anywhere, the French names alone have been used. Though by far the greatest part of the population is Spanish and Arabic, the French have a strong influence; and other nations have colonies relatively or very small.

last night had gathered a chosen few who were tipsy but not noisy. Since the proprietor is a large, slow-moving, amiable Texan, the customers are for the most part Americans or British.

Round the walls runs a red-padded bench, with tables, at which you may have excellent food as well as drink. H.M. and the Colonel had taken a far corner table, where they sat down side by side. Bill was beside the Colonel, Paula beside H.M., like acolytes.

"Alors," said the Colonel, tapping his fingers on the table, "you believe that our criminal will again try to crack the safe of M. Bernstein?"

"Uh-huh. And I'll bet you," leered H.M., "we'll catch him this time if *I* give the orders."

Surprisingly, both of them spoke in soft voices. They emphasized a point only by facial contortions, though for the most part the Colonel had regained all his old suavity.

"Come!" he said. "Then I am stumbling in my strategy?"

"No, no! You're all right. But this is a very rummy case, Colonel. You oughtn't to use the whole blinkin' police force. What you want are fewer men at better points."

"There has occurred to you," the Colonel asked suavely, "no difficulties in this?"

"What difficulties?"

"Well. 'Young' M. Isaac Bernstein cannot have been very happy regarding tonight. What if he should merely remove the Sultan's diamonds to a safer place?"

But H.M. shook his head.

"He won't, Colonel, if I talk to him again. First off, he's an A-1 sport. Second, it seems he's got a sort of admiration for the old man, because a lot of cloth-heads in Paris got together and—burn me if I know why—they gave me somethin' called the Grand Cross of the Legion of Honour."

"Sweet Saviour!" breathed Colonel Duroc, in awe.

"Y'see, Bernstein is French. He liked that fine. Though," said the mystified H.M., "all I did was keep one of their big pots from bein' poisoned. Finally, and as a practical point for a practical man, can you think of a better place for those diamonds than in Bernstein's own safe? I mean, when he knows you're always guarding 'em, and you spiked the robbery tonight?"

Colonel Duroc meditated. His short white hair stood up

like the foam on a glass of lager beer.

"Perhaps yes," he assented, not without pride. "But again! If there should reach Iron Chest some whisper that the jewels are not at Bernstein's . . ."

"You mean he wouldn't attack again?"

"Exactly. Be assured; he will have watchers there, perhaps many paid Arabs."

"Then the more the merrier. That's easy. Bernstein simply closes his shop for a day or two. Nobody goes near it. Above all—are you followin' me?—every one of your newspapers shouts glee that for the first time Iron Chest has been beaten; he can't fool the police here; those diamonds are still in the safe, and he can't get 'em."

Here H.M. paused, with a facial distortion which would have interested a professional actor.

"That may not be strictly true, y'know," he added. "Because it seems, I say it *seems*"—here he put faint stress on the word—"that he's been almost nabbed twice, once in Amsterdam and once in Paris. But never mind! If your newspaper stories don't slice open his vanity and pour sulphuric acid in it . . . Oh, my eye! He may be wild enough to have a go tomorrow night."

Colonel Duroc purred and smoothed his hand across the table.

"And," continued H.M., "speakin' of watchers and accomplices. Let's think of this feller called 'G. W. Collier.' We're pretty sure he's Iron Chest's one accomplice and diamond cutter. We haven't seen him personally; but lots of others have, including Mendoza. You ordered him turned loose, as bait. What's become of him? Are you keeping an eye on him?"

"Ha ha ha," said the Colonel. "That type!" Despite the Colonel's chuckles, he much disliked what he had heard of G. W. Collier; and his mouth tightened. "You need not worry, my friend. We do not fail here. He sits at the Riff Hotel; his telephone is doped . . ."

"Easy, Colonel! Do you by any chance mean 'tapped'?"

"That is what I say, tapped. No move this man makes is unwatched. When he go out of the hotel, he has always on him a behind."

"A tail, son. Just tail will do."

"Une petite histoire? Pah!" said the Colonel, looking

suspiciously at H.M. "My English . . . never before am I called impure! But no matter." Suavely he folded his arms over gold buttons. "Tell me, please: what is your great plan for the capture of Iron Chest?"

H.M., though seemingly dubious about something Duroc had recently said, merely frowned.

"I've got to have a pretty big map," he announced. "Then there's somebody for you to supply. This man you've got to supply can't be swarthy complexioned, like your police and detectives. Don't ask me why! . . . He's got to have a good deal of courage. And he must be an A-1 first-class shot with a revolver or an automatic."

It was now the Colonel's turn to behave like a magician.

"Behold," he beamed, moving his wrist to the right, "your candidate himself. Mr. William Bentley. He is the best pistol shot in Tangier."

Paula sat up straight. Even she had never known this, because Bill simply had never troubled to mention it.

Bill, now somewhat pink, moved his shoulders and attempted to see Paula without looking up. He failed.

"I'm not too bad with a revolver," he muttered. "But no automatics, thanks. Sometimes they jam and they do a funny jump."

"No!" Paula had blurted out instinctively. "No, no, no!"

Suddenly her remembrances of the dim-lit Parade Bar, with its voices and its clink of glasses amid dull red and black, were whisked away and dissolved like a dream.

"No, no, no!" Paula said aloud, and roused herself out of reverie.

She was sitting, cold and huddled, in the back of a swift-humming taxi which carried her up through the streets towards her destination at number 40-bis Marshan. The taxi windows were steamed over. The monumental moustache of the taxi driver turned slowly round.

"Is all well with you, my lady?" he asked gruffly in Spanish.

"Yes, thank you. I was thinking. Drive on, please."

Wiping the windows, Paula discovered that she was in a familiar neighbourhood and close to the address she wanted. The light was a clear, deceptive white, with tinges of purple in the sky.

Bill was in danger. She *must* get that flat!

Paula's first instinct, as usual, was correct. Her second, more confused, was a cloudy feeling that both of them would be safer if she and Bill moved from downtown Tangier to an upper district like this, to say nothing of the saving in money. Bill wouldn't like it, of course. But Paula knew she could persuade him. Though she never nagged, never argued except quietly or even timidly, Paula had a different way of persuasion which made her smile dreamily. If even this failed, she must be downright dishonest and use tears. Bill swore and stamped and raved; but he couldn't hold out against tears.

The heavy cab swung into the open space, and turned to the right across it. Paula could see the square solidness of Dr. MacPhail's nursing home. The driver had automatically turned towards the doctor's, assuming it was where she wanted to go, and pulled up in front of the stone gates.

"The doctor?" he asked with a shade of triumph.

"Not exactly," replied Paula, glancing at the dashboard clock of the taxi. "But this will do. It is enough. You may go now."

Absently she thanked him and overpaid him. A flood of Spanish thanks, like the burst of a concealed radio, poured from the car as it shot backwards and missed a tall tree by inches, then slurred round wildly to be off again.

For a moment Paula looked at the nursing home. Lights were burning behind lace curtains. It gave her more a sense of loneliness that of comfort. All else except herself seemed asleep, hushed. She could hear the noise of her own sandals as she walked on hard-packed sand, scattered with tiny pebbles.

The house next door was separated from the nursing home only by a flower-bordered path which led straight back to Dr. MacPhail's house at the rear. As for the house next door, it was so well concealed by an immensely high tropical hedge over a low stone wall that Paula could see only the roof until she came to the wrought-iron gates.

Yes, this was unquestionably the block of flats.

The gates squealed as she pushed them open. The building was very long, though only two storeys high, and set back a short way from the road. Some modern builder had tried his hand at old-style Spanish instead of new. It was of yellow stucco with a roof of green curved tiles. Across the front, between the upper and lower floor, ran a narrow balcony with a railing of lacy wrought iron, with arches of laced iron both above and below. Lines of windows had each a pair of wooden shutters painted green and fast shut.

Except . . .

As Paula went up the stone-paved walk, some flash of movement crossed the corner of her vision. She glanced up at the line of windows upstairs. On the left side, though with a good space between it and the left-hand wall, was a window considerably smaller than most. There was a corresponding window on the ground floor, and several others along the facade. Paula supposed them to be bathroom windows.

Yet only that small window in the upper left-hand had its closed shutters painted a bright crimson, solitary crimson against other shutters green. As Paula glanced up, a man on the balcony had been crouched close to that window. Suddenly he darted back, bent low, and disappeared round the left-hand side of the balcony.

At the same moment, though she did not know it, the cab which had been following her slid quietly to a stop well opposite number 40-bis.

Paula was far from being alarmed. That figure on the balcony, seen through faint mist and behind the scrolls or twinnings of iron work, might have been illusion. But the crimson-painted shutters stood out on her mind, and her heart beat faster. There were two main entrances.

Unhesitatingly Paula chose the entrance on the left. She could hear somebody whistling inside.

But here she was greeted with too much sticky cordiality. A stocky little Greek, with a spit curl in the middle of his forehead, was sweeping the entry with a Biblical broom. In fluent French he oozed a welcome as though to royalty. He told her his name, his wife's name, the number of his children, and was beginning his life story before Paula, flourishing the newspaper and pointing, could ask for Flat 3-B. Sadly he gave her directions.

"Que vous étes belle!" her informant whispered insinuatingly, and ran his hand up her arm. *"Que vous . . ."* Paula, long used to such attentions, merely smiled and got away.

Hurrying up a broad stone staircase against the left wall, she took the first corridor again on the left. The block of flats, though modern, had already run to seediness in this climate. The walls, done in some plaster composition and faintly painted to resemble stone blocks of cream colour, were already dingy. So was the once-good carpeting.

In the first corridor on the left, Paula passed the green-painted door of 1-B, the duplicate of it in 2-B, and paused before its third duplicate in 3-B, the last door down on the left, which was her quarry.

For a few moments Paula stood motionless in front of that green door with its rusting nickelled numbers and its nickelled electric bell push at one side. In the roof of the corridor two shallow domes of frosted glass, inverted, illuminated brave shabbiness. For the first time Paula realized the ridiculousness of her position.

When she looked at the dashboard clock of the taxi, the time had been ten minutes past eight. Hardly five minutes, ten at the most, could have passed since then. To rouse up the tenant at this ungodly hour . . .

If the tenant were a woman, Paula could easily explain. If a man, there might be anything from surliness to another amorous approach. Best of all would be a couple, but there was no indication.

Yet she *must* do this! There was nowhere to sit down, unless the wanted to sit down on the floor, her back to the wall, for an hour or so. Drawing a deep breath, clutching the newspaper under her arm, Paula pressed hard at the electric doorbell.

Nothing happened; at least, Paula could detect no sound of ringing or buzzing inside that small flat. Dead silence in the dingy corridor, under the depressing lights. Undoubtedly the bell was out of order. Paula, daunted, knocked at the door, but with so light a knock that perhaps it went unheard. Automatically her hand fell on the nickelled iron knob, and a soft twist showed that the door was open. Either by instinct or fever-pitch curiosity. Paula swung open the noiselessly moving door until she could see most of the room.

Then again came the nightmare.

It held her body rigid, her mind frozen in a soundless scream.

She was looking into the one large, square room described in the advertisement. Its walls, of cream-coloured plaster, were even more dingy than the corridors outside. In the wall well towards her left, folding doors were closed on what must be the kitchenette. In the same wall, towards the front, an open door showed a narrow bathroom with closed shutters painted crimson even on the inside.

Facing her from some distance, in the wall opposite, was a small fireplace with a small grate in which a bright coal fire burned against the cold. In the right-hand wall, as Paula saw when she turned her head, were two large windows with crimson shutters held locked by a wooden bar.

There were several other things, but Paula was conscious only of one.

At a heavy mahogany table in the middle of the room, his back turned to the door, sat a man with a jeweller's lens in his eye. Because of a rather high easy chair, Paula could see only that he had a very short thick neck, and a head of abundant hair—at once darkish and yet fiery red—parted and plastered down with hair cream.

At his left, on the crimson table cover, stood the iron chest itself, the famous chest gleaming under the half-domed, inverted roof lamp. In front of the man, set out in rows, were more uncut diamonds that Paula's numbed brain could count.

Still silence . . .

A draught of wind, beginning some distance away in the rather unsavoury corridors, crept along and stirred at the door. Paula could feel it on her neck, on the backs of her calves. The draught strengthened. On the table, to the right of the red-haired man, lay a few light sheets of writing paper. One of these sheets gently fluttered into the air, hovered, and sailed away.

The man in the chair knew now. Quietly he put down the lens. Then, fast and sudden, he jumped up and whirled round to face Paula.

Of that man, beyond the dark yet fiery red hair, Paula noticed only that it seemed to her—she could not analyze it, save that it was a whitish ordinary-looking face—one of the most unpleasant she had ever seen.

"Who in hell—" he snarled in English, with a thin raspy tenor from a heavy body.

And, both arms extended with fingers crooked, he plunged forward towards her.

CHAPTER EIGHT

With the very shock of those words, all Paula's weakness was gone and her mind moved again. Springing back out of the doorway, she slammed the door and even gripped her hands round the knob with some wild, impossible notion of holding it against him.

Iron Chest! Probably she had seen Iron Chest himself, with his own chest and jewels. Now Paula prayed. If only somebody were here to help her! If only *somebody* . . .

Then she realized that the red-headed man was not trying to attack her. On the contrary, she could hear a bolt shot into its socket, and a click of a key that further locked the door.

At the same moment, very quietly and swiftly, Commandant Juan Alvarez moved towards her from the other end of the corridor.

"Juan!" whispered Paula. Her knees trembled with relief, but she was outwardly calm.

Today Alvarez wore full military uniform, with Sam Browne belt and gold leaf on his cap. On his hands were brown gloves of light leather. Though his red-brown eyes were still faintly bloodshot, like those of a man who had passed a bad night, yet they were clearing to brightness. His high, intellectual forehead contrasted with the tight line of his mouth.

"You were in no danger, Mrs. Bentley," he said gently, and smiled. "The man inside that flat has been followed since . . ."

"But he's probably Iron Chest! He has red hair. He . . ."

"I'm afraid not, Mrs. Bentley. The man's name is G. W. Collier, and he has been putting up at the Riff Hotel. Whether you have heard it or not, we believe him to be the accomplice of Iron Chest. As I say, he has been followed since he left the hotel at seven this morning. I led the chase myself, without troubling to communicate with Colonel Duroc. . . . You also were followed, but for a different reason. We too saw that curious advertisement. You might be in danger. And your bravery is great, Mrs. Bentley."

Awkwardly, diffidently, he patted her shoulder in praise. Yet there was something of courtliness in the gesture.

"But don't you see?" Paula persisted in a fierce whisper. "Whoever he is, he's got the iron chest and—oh, I don't know how many—but at least thirty diamonds. If you don't hurry, he'll get away!" And quickly she related all that had happened.

Alvarez's eyes flashed open. He snapped his fingers. Down into the corridor hurried three policemen, their white helmets and belts bold against khaki shirts and shorts. In front of them moved Inspector Mendoza, his jaw showing a grim determination not to make last night's mistake.

Inside the big room of the flat Paula imagined, or thought she imagined, very faint sounds she could not identify. Her thoughts pounded with hurry, hurry, hurry!

"He cannot get away, Mrs. Bentley," Alvarez said very softly. "A man of ours has stood on the balcony outside ever since he arrived. But diamonds! As real evidence . . ."

The underside of Alvarez's gloved fist struck three hard blows at the door. His voice, ordinarily low-pitched that it might have been anyone's voice, was a heavy baritone when he spoke out.

"I am a police officer," he said, "holding a warrant for the search of this flat. Open the door!"

Only silence, while Paula tried to remember those very faint sounds. Anyway, they had something now. Unless . . .

Footsteps slowly approached the door, in no hurry about anything. The bolt was shot carelessly back; and, after a deliberate pause, the key was turned. The man with the red hair opened the door wide.

Only Alvarez and Paula went inside the room. Neither of them looked first at Collier. Paula's glance flew to the mahogany table in the middle of the floor. Its crimson-velvet cloth, where only a brief time ago had stood the iron chest and rows of diamonds, was now empty except for an ink bottle, a few pens, scattered sheets of writing paper.

Gone. Vanished. Paula felt almost physically sick. But they couldn't have vanished; they must be here. Alvarez, despite his own glance, remained impassive; his voice, again low-pitched, spoke with icy politeness.

"Mr. Collier?" he asked.

"Yeah; that's me."

The red-haired man, Paula thought after a quick look at him again, seemed somehow different. No; she knew what it was. He showed no anger, much less rage. Under the heavily plastered-down hair, the large face with the flattish nose was quite expressionless. Collier's eyes were so pale that you could see little under the drooping white lids. No, his whitish face displayed nothing—except perhaps a faint air of weariness, or the hint of a sneer at his left upper lip.

He was older than he first appeared; at least forty, probably more. He was an inch or so below the height of Alvarez, though he must have weighed six or seven pounds more than Alvarez's middleweight eleven-stone-five. Paula, who knew her athletes from Bill and also from a strong interest in men, estimated that Mr. G. W. Collier was in almost perfect physical training despite his deceptive complexion. Mr. Collier also wore a whitish lounge suit, without waistcoat, but with unnecessary shoulder-padding which made him look bulkier. He had a bow tie, blue with pink spots, and his thumbs were hooked in his belt as he watched without interest.

All this swept through Paula's mind, together with the distinct impression she had seen him somewhere before today, in the second before Alvarez could speak again.

"Very well, Mr. Collier," said the Commandant, "I am here to . . ."

"Look, buddy," interrupted Collier, with a sharpened weariness, "I don't want any trouble with you boys. You wanted in? Okay, so I let you in."

"Well?"

"But be smart, that's all; just don't make me sore. it's not healthy. Catch on?"

Alvarez looked him up and down.

"Your sensitive feelings, Mr. Collier, are no concern of mine."

Collier, eyelids drooping still further, partly turned as though to address an invisible companion beside him.

"Wise guy," he murmured, and turned back. "Know what I am, wise guy?"

"Perfectly."

"I'm an American citizen, wise guy." He flipped open the

right side of his coat to show the breast pocket. "I got a passport here to prove it."

"Yes?" said the unimpressed Alvarez.

"We're smart, see? America didn't sign any screwy international-zone treaty. But we've got a place called a legation here, to see nobody pulls a fast one. So what? So we're the big boys around here. Don't you forget it, junior." The corner of Collier's lip turned up. "Why, if I ever pulled a job in this lousy whistle stop, which I haven't and wouldn't, you spicks couldn't do a thing about it. Not a thing. I'd have to be tried by the American Legation."

"Quite true," Alvarez agreed. "You forget, however, that you must first be detained and questioned by the Tangier police." The Commandant's tone was a low growl, purely animal. "Believe me, sir, you will be."

Then, ignoring him, Alvarez turned his head over his shoulder and spoke in Spanish.

"Inspector Mendoza, remain just outside the door. No object, nothing of any kind, is to leave this room. You others, in here."

The three policemen, impassive, came into the room and stood in a row along the wall beside him, whereupon Alvarez turned back to Collier.

"Now to business. A while ago, on that table, was an iron box two feet long by one foot broad by one foot high, as well as a great number of diamonds. . . . How many diamonds, Mrs. Bentley?"

"I didn't have time to count." Paula spoke sweetly, with a calm gaze of appraisal and repulsion on Collier. "More than thirty, I'm certain. He's hidden them, of course."

For the first time Collier's face muscles moved, as though in sheer amazement.

"What?" he said, and his rasping tenor went high.

Curtly Alvarez explained, and the result was curious. Collier did not laugh; nobody ever heard him laugh. But the bulky figure writhed. His unpleasant face grew almost pleasant, in the sense that it had qualities of faint amiability and enjoyment under the plastering of dark-fiery red hair. At the end he was almost as brisk as a salesman. Unhooking one thumb from his belt, he slapped his side and again addressed an invisible companion.

"Well, whadda ya know?" he inquired in wonder. He turned back to Alvarez. "I still don't get it. But you've handed me the best laugh of the year. Go ahead and search."

"Where have you hidden the diamonds?"

"I ain't got any. The dame's a screwball, though she's a swell dish to look at. Didn't you hear me, wise guy? Go ahead and search. I don't even wanna see your warrant, though"—here his eyelids dropped in threat—"I could make plenty trouble for you if I asked to see it."

Instantly Alvarez whipped out the warrant from inside his tunic, and held it spread out in front of Collier.

The latter, lowering his bulky shoulders, studied the document; his lips moved a little. Though it was written in French, Paula saw that he could understand it. Yet, when Collier straightened up, he was as unruffled as ever. His fishy eye suggested that Alvarez had made a bluff, not he.

"Okay, so you've got a warrant," he said wearily. "How dumb can you get? Go ahead."

"Do you object to a personal search?"

"What have I got to lose?" inquired Collier, and automatically lifted his arms.

Alvarez's hard, competent hands did a thorough job, but he found nothing.

"Satisfied, pal?"

"For the moment, yes. Now go and sit down."

Alvarez, very straight-backed but as alert as a terrier, made a swift, comprehensive survey of the room. Then he hurried to the right-hand wall, in which the two large windows were covered with crimson wooden shutters and locked with wooden bars. Alvarez unlocked and threw open both windows. Outside each one stood a detective in plain clothes.

Alvarez spoke in French. It was clear he did so with an eye on Collier, to make sure the latter understood.

"Has anyone entered or left by these windows," he snapped, "since this—this gentleman arrived?"

Both were emphatic in saying "No."

"Has any object or objects, anything whatsoever, been handed or thrown out of these windows since then?"

The clear morning light, against the pallor of desk lamp and pale firelight, showed up the walls of the room as even more dirty and dingy under their cream-coloured paint.

"Nothing, my Commandant! Nothing at all!" Both plainclothes men were emphatic.

"Remain at your posts, then. See that nothing is."

Closing and locking the shutters again, Alvarez hurried across to the bathroom at the other side of the room. From where she stood, Paula could see the crimson and locked shutters of the small window facing front. Alvarez opened it, to find a third plain-clothes man, whose denials were emphatically the same as the others.

"Nothing, my Commandant! Except"—and here his eyes encountered Paula's—"when that young lady has arrived here, I have moved back to the angle of the wall. But never have I taken my eyes from the window! Nothing has come out, ever!"

"Good. Rest there," said Alvarez. He pulled down the frosted-glass window, then closed and locked the shutters.

Paula ran lightly and gracefully over to Alvarez as he stood at the bathroom door. Bending down his shoulder, she whispered in his ear.

"Juan, you've *got* to find those diamonds and the chest! You must! Or else that *poisonous,* sneering . . ."

"Gently," murmured Alvarez through his teeth. "We will find them. The windows are sealed. You and I stood outside the only door, which is watched now. He is in a trap at last."

"Having a good time, wise guy?" asked Collier, almost pityingly.

Alvarez strode to the large mahogany table. For a moment he looked down at the crimson-velvet tablecloth, smooth and unmarked save for the ink bottle, the pens, and writing paper. He looked up and across at the three motionless policemen.

"It is very well," he barked out, again in French, "that we came here prepared for a search, though we did not know a search was necessary until Madame there informed us. Now go downstairs, fetch your tools, and return. You know what we want. Find it! Find it, if you rip down this flat like a doll's house. That is all."

The policemen, breathing hard, almost ran for the closed door to the corridor, outside which waited Inspector Mendoza. They almost ran into Colonel Duroc, marching in.

Alvarez and Paula had gone towards the door, but they moved back as Colonel Duroc entered. Duroc's khaki tunic stuck forward; his cap was a trifle awry; his tufted eyebrows hovered with thunder. Since he had not yet seen Alvarez this morning, he boiled with words for a man who had been blind-drunk when on duty.

He opened his mouth, then shut it. He should not humiliate a subordinate before an outsider, even Paula Bentley. Alvarez, clearly, was in such a state of mind that he had forgotten his misdemeanor.

"I thank you, Commandant," said the Colonel, in gruff and formal French, "for having telephoned to me from here. This flat; yes, well? We knew of it. We spoke of it last night, before you . . . that is to say, before this morning. What now?"

Alvarez, in a quick mutter, related the story up to the present.

Colonel Duroc's face grew far less ruddy as he listened. Once he glanced towards Collier, who had sat down in a chair at an angle between the wall of crimson windows and the wall towards the corridor. A lighted cigarette was fastened to the corner of his lower lip, and smoke dribbled down the flattish nostrils to show boredom or derision.

"But here we have the same story—" began Colonel Duroc, and hesitated. "Then the little Paula, you say, came here to seek an apartment furnished?"

"The little Paula" nodded. She was too frightened, or perhaps too puzzled, to employ the cajoleries with which she usually made the Colonel chuckle. Paula stood with her back to the closed folding doors of the kitchenette, bent a little forward from the waist, the heavy golden hair slanting down long below her chin, her dark-blue eyes fixed with wondering look on none other than G. W. Collier. But her own nod woke her up.

"It is true," she assured Duroc in fluent French, and handed him the newspaper with the marked advertisement. "I wished this apartment furnished, certainly. But—dear Colonel—the story is too long to be told now. Except that—you comprehend?—I arrived too early. That grimy type over there did not expect me."

"Good," muttered Alvarez.

"Pah!" snorted the Colonel, slapping at the folded newspaper. "We have agreed, the Commandant and I, that this is purely a trap, a bait for someone. But not for you, little one!"

"I—I thought not. But why?"

"Regard the words," said Duroc, and again slapped the newspaper. "The price is too low for residents not to be suspicious; clever residents, that is. Ah, pardon! The term 'kitchenette' is American, never used here by the English; seldom by the Americans." He glanced towards Collier. "Above all, regard what is of the most importance: 'Excellent for transients.' Eh?"

"Yes, I saw that," Paula admitted. "All the same . . ."

"For transients! Well! This man Collier, this camel, has prepared a trap for someone. But for whom? I ask you, for whom?"

Outside the closed door to the corridor, there was a dispute of voices. Yanking open the door, Colonel Duroc peered outside, and his mouth opened wide.

"Inspector Mendoza," he snapped, "permit mademoiselle to enter."

And in walked Maureen Holmes, much surprised and confused, with a copy of the same newspaper and the same marked advertisement.

The Colonel removed his cap for a moment in order to smite his forehead. He almost danced.

"The obvious," he groaned. "Always the obvious. And one never sees it." He extended his hands towards Maureen in supplication. "My dear, will you tell me how *you* have in some fashion become involved with Iron Chest? Or why the camel Collier should set a trap for you?"

At the same moment the corridor door banged wide open. Past the watchful Mendoza, in strode the three eager policemen, now followed by a fourth, all laden with a weight of tools ranging from small chisels to long-handled instruments ending in a broad knife-sharp steel blade.

The floor was of concrete, partly covered by a shabby brown carpet. Down went the tools with a long clatter and crash. Colonel Duroc wheeled round to cry encouragement.

"To work, my braves ones!" he shouted, both in French and in Spanish. "Go to it!"

And they did, while the door was again firmly closed. Duroc turned to Maureen, and repeated his question.

Maureen groped after her French, but it would not slip glibly. Her green eyes, with the long lashes, she tried to keep fixed on the newspaper, so as to avoid meeting those of Alvarez. Today she wore her own white silk dress, altered and shortened overnight so as to resemble Paula's of yesterday. It was clear that under it she wore as little as Paula herself, though Maureen had donned stockings and fashionable shoes.

"But I don't understand any of it!" she protested, in her own language. "I don't even understand why there's such a rumpus, or why the police are here, or anything at all!"

"You are sure?" persisted Colonel Duroc, also in English. "You have not earned—for instance, it may be—the enmity of this Iron Chest? Or of Collier? You know something?"

"No!" said Maureen. "Colonel Duroc, do you remember late yesterday afternoon on the terrace?"

The Colonel made a strange noise.

"Your fat'ma," Maureen went on, "wheeled in a tea wagon with sandwiches on top and the *Gazette* on the shelf underneath. You see, I happened to notice that ad . . ."

"With my eyes," groaned Duroc, pointing to them, "I saw you do it!"

"I'd just decided that Sir Henry was simply *intolerable.*" But Maureen was not angry; her green eyes showed a rueful smile. "He's not really maddening, because he never really means it and also he's funny, as Paula said . . ."

"Oh, you *are* nice!" Paula burst out, her heart warmed by Maureen's copy of her own frock.

"Thanks, Paula. . . . But I did mean it at the time, and I thought it would be wonderful to have a little apartment of my own, and eat out. And much less expensive than the hotel. But . . ."

Maureen paused, wrinkling up her smooth forehead.

"But this morning, when I looked into Sir Henry's room," she added, "he was still asleep."

"Ah, that Morpheus!" said Colonel Duroc, in agony. "I too have seen him. Pah! I think him dead, dead and buriable, except that his snores make bump the ceiling like a lid on a kettle. So I depart on my own."

"I called to you," said Maureen, "but you couldn't hear me. I followed in a taxi. But I knew . . ."

"Go on, go on."

"Well, I knew I couldn't do it," said Maureen. "You and Sir Henry and—and Mr. Alvarez have all been too nice. If you want me to stay, I'm sorry I ever thought of leaving. But, since I was near the place, I decided I might as well see the place and go away. That's all."

But it wasn't all. Maureen's New England conscience still writhed. The dull light ripped on her glossy hair as she raised her head, and looked straight into the eyes of Commandant Alvarez.

"Juan—" she began tentatively.

It was remarkable, Paula thought, to see this fellow of ferocious self-control (why did he need it?) turn into a wild, stumbling human being.

"Maureen!" said Commandant Alvarez, swallowing hard as he tried out the name. "If I could make only one apology out of ten thousand . . ."

"But it doesn't matter . . . I know, Sir Henry told me! We went to different restaurants."

"I should have thought of that! I should have searched! Instead of this, I must go home and get—"

He stopped. Maureen extended both hands, and he gripped them in gloved fingers of such murderous pressure that it must have hurt badly. But Maureen, either because she did not notice or did not want to complain, made no protest.

"It must not happen again!" said the anguished Alvarez. "It is enough . . ."

Through these amenities chopped the voice of Colonel Duroc.

"It is indeed enough," said the Colonel, who was furious. "Shut that! I will have no more spoonerisms while there is work to be done. Commandant Alvarez! . . ."

It was Paula who had the inspiration and silenced Duroc. Pushing among them, she rolled open the folding doors of the kitchenette, which was no deeper than the narrow bathroom in front, and had no window at all.

"Maureen, this is where we can help!" Paula spoke excitedly. "This is where we can do the job better than they. No, no; don't ask questions! I'll explain as we search. Look here: there hasn't been a bit of food here for weeks!"

"Good!" almost beamed Duroc, speaking again in French. "Commandant Alvarez! A word!"

And he drew Alvarez aside.

"I will speak to you presently," he added grimly, "of other matters. For the moment, don't you understand? Here we have, with one happy difference, the affair in Paris all over again!" Colonel Duroc paused. "I will tell you a secret. Yesterday I prayed to the good God—yes, I!—that we might beat Paris and Rome. At Paris, in exactly this position, they found no iron box and no diamonds. We must find them!"

"I agree with you, my Colonel." Over Alvarez went a shiver, perhaps of superstitious dread. "But—but if we should not . . ."

"We must! It is impossible that we can fail. We *must!*"

There was a *cr-r-ack* of wood as one workman, who had removed the smooth crimson cloth, worked with a small chisel to pry up the mahogany tabletop. Another policeman had hurried into the bathroom, whence issued rattling sounds of a porcelain cistern lid set high. The third policeman, who had raked out the fire with no result whatever, was now putting on a dirty canvas coat to explore the chimney.

Just to the right of the mantelpiece as you faced it stood some long bookshelves shaky and hastily knocked together by a careless carpenter. Yet they were filled with handsome-looking books of all sizes; and the fourth policeman was whipping them out for a quick examination of each before flinging it on the floor.

"Now what interest," muttered Alvarez between his teeth, "would Collier have in books? Any book?"

G. W. Collier got up from his chair, adjusting his bow tie. From his lower lip he detached the burnt-down cigarette, dropping it on the concrete floor and stepping on it. He lighted another cigarette, flicked the burnt match towards the helmet of the policeman at the table, and moved towards Colonel Duroc. Mr. Collier, the padding in his shoulders making him seem bulkier than he really was, sauntered with the arm-swinging gait of a prize fighter.

"Look, you with the spinach," he said to Duroc. "You think I don't savvy your frog lingo. That's where you're not smart. Languages!" he was disgusted. "Jeez, why can't everybody talk English!"

Across Alvarez's face went a broad, fixed smile.

"An excellent idea, Mr. Collier," said the Commandant. "I strongly recommend it to you."

There was a pause, almost like an explosion. But Collier remained unruffled, and addressed his invisible companion.

"Here's wise guy again," he said. Warily he lifted his knuckles and inspected both hands, the cigarette rolling in his mouth. "I can't be bothered with you, wise guy. Or you'd wish you'd never been born."

"Now why don't you try?"

"Look, you with the spinach." Collier turned to Colonel Duroc. "Just don't let your punk here, that talks like a de-ah old Limey, get me too sore."

"You spoke to me, my man?" asked the Colonel, as though smelling something faintly offensive.

"Yeah; sure, 'my man,' " mimicked Collier. Triumphantly he shot out the next: "Ain't I as good as you?"

"No," said the Colonel.

Collier, who clearly had been expecting "Yes,"—an answer far too readily given—did not stop.

"Funny," he said. "I was feeling friendly, too. I just wanted to warn you." The eyelids drooped almost shut. "If your punks keep on busting up my apartment, I could make big trouble for you. Big trouble; catch on? I say I *could.*"

Maureen and Paula, behind them, had been swiftly sorting through the little kitchenette. But Paula had turned to look at them. Collier, taking the cigarette out of his mouth, pointed the lighted end towards Colonel Duroc. Alvarez, strung up, did not fail to catch the look on Paula's face before she whipped back again.

"But get this," said Collier, "maybe if you give with a coupla hundred bucks, maybe I'll forget it. I don't say yes; only maybe. You're in big trouble, pal."

Colonel Duroc's eyebrows gathered and lowered.

"Indeed? Do you own this flat? Or lease it?"

"Pal, I just wouldn't know."

"Oh, *I* know," said the Colonel, "having talked by telephone with the owner of the block of flats, M. Jacques Bullier. You rented this place by cable and money order from Lisbon, much less than a fortnight ago. You signed and returned a lease by post. Any damage will be fully paid to the owner. Not to you."

"Okay; so I got a lease." Collier almost smiled, returning the cigarette to his mouth. "Just business, that's all. I try to outsmart you; you try to outsmart me. No harm in trying."

"Some of us believe," said Colonel Duroc, "that there is great harm in trying."

"Well, I ain't one of 'em."

"No," said the Colonel slowly, "you are not one of them." His tone altered. "Now return to your chair and remain there."

"I think you're cute, too," said Collier. "So is wise guy."

And, letting smoke drift into the Colonel's face, he sauntered away with his prize-fighter's swing.

Every time Alvarez had looked at him, a close observer

would have seen the small, blue, blood-gorged veins stand out on his upper forehead. Nobody ever guessed by what inhuman effort he remained "correct." Now, maddened, he began to supervise the search himself.

From the bathroom issued a crash as the metal plug was forced from the bath drain. On his left, against the wall between the kitchenette and the bathroom, Alvarez saw an overstuffed sofa with three seat cushions, on which lay a handful of small and large nails together with a hammer which the police had not brought.

The policeman at the table had removed the top, explored the hollow legs with a very long and thin steel probe, and was now putting down a police microscope of the kind which can detect any tampering with the smallest of solid wood.

"There is nothing in the table, sir," he reported. "Nothing!"

"Very well," said Alvarez. "Push it back against the corridor wall, and investigate this easy chair facing it. As for the roof light over it . . ."

But, glancing upwards, Alvarez could see that the shallow, inverted glass dome had already been unscrewed, showing only a naked bulb.

"Find anything?" called Collier from his corner, and almost laughed.

Ignoring this, Alvarez strode towards the mantelpiece. The policeman who had put on the dirty canvas jacket, together with a canvas hood, now had his head almost stuck in the flue, but seemed to be peering upwards by the light of an electric torch.

Alvarez glanced at the wall above the mantel shelf, stopped, and then looked more closely. In the dirty cream-coloured plaster were a number of tiny whitish digs, where a nail had been very lightly tamped to show the position in which the nail would later be driven.

There was . . . Yes, there was a pattern! Alvarez, plainly desperate, studied the wall with his red-brown eyes burning like the whites of them. Suddenly he snapped his fingers and nodded.

At the same moment, the grimy canvas hood and jacket of the policeman ducked out from under the chimney, amid a rattle and shower of soot.

"No good," he growled, spitting soot. "Up there, not far,

very close, is a crossed-iron grating. Fixed there. Not to be moved." The policeman, an Arab, rattled out rapid Spanish as he flung off hood and jacket, replacing the first with his white helmet. "Nothing could go through the grating."

"And the bricks?"

"Secure, Commandant. I tried them. Nothing hidden anywhere here. See for yourself."

And, as may be admitted, he spoke the truth. Taking the electric torch, Alvarez thrust his head up the chimney, played the beam of the torch upwards, and knew it. With a face of furious disappointment, he ducked out again without soot and gave the Arab policeman the torch.

"Very well, Abou Owad! Fetch a stepladder, and our biggest magnifying lens. Search every inch of these walls for a hidden cavity."

"But, Commandant!" The Arab, much excited, gabbled with eager wistfulness. "May we not tear down the walls, as promised?"

"Trust Allah, my friend!" soothed Alvarez. "Listen! If anything be hidden, the smallest crack or line will show it. Be off, now. Hurry!"

"Find anything?" drawled Collier, and almost laughed again.

Alvarez whipped round to the shaky unpainted lines of bookshelves. At one side, now fallen over, was a small garden sickle, with dead grass on its blade. As for books, the man who searched them had finished, and was now knocking apart a straight chair. Many of the books he left on the shelves, but most he merely threw to the floor. Alvarez glanced over every title, with mounting surprise. Though large or small, plain or decorated, in every language, each book was a copy of the Bible.

"Find anything?" asked Collier. "Yeah, wise guy; that's my job. If you'd seen the card I filled out, you'd have got smart. I'm a Bible salesman.

Alvarez closed his eyes.

"You'd be surprised," said Collier. "Educated Mohammedans know our Bible as well as we do. Don't kid yourself: best-selling book on earth."

"And that, of course, is the reason for reading it?"

"Why not? I got ideals. Friendship, everybody happy, no wars—that kind of stuff. Them's ideals. I got 'em."

Still Collier's large candle-coloured face remained expressionless between the red hair and the spotted bow tie. But he had half-finished his second cigarette; he took it out of his mouth, and looked wearily for a place to flick it.

In the middle of the room, the first policeman was now gutting the easy chair with a long knife, and working the legs loose. Mr. G. W. Collier, seeking amusement, held the burning cigarette tightly between thumb and second finger. He flicked it forward, straight and hard, and the lighted end struck the policeman on the cheek. Then it bounced down and burned acridly against the carpet.

"Pretty good," Collier said complacently, and let his eyelids droop.

For an instant the policeman stood motionless, head and helmet down, gripping the sides of the chair. You could see his heavy biceps and corded wrists strain out against the arms of the khaki shirt. Suddenly he whirled round towards Collier.

"Ce fils de putain!" he shouted. *"Tapette! Gul de macquereau! Espéce de . . ."*

Instantly Alvarez was beside him. The Commandant's left arm shot across the man's chest, holding back even that fighting weight.

"Doucement, mon vieux," he muttered, and whispered a few words at the side of his companion's helmet. The policeman's eyes glistened, and he subsided.

"Jeez, another toughie," sneered Collier. "If they only was good, how good they'd bc!"

The shaken voice of Paula Bentley, raised as though it might quell the dangerous atmosphere, called from the other side of the room.

"I'm sorry, Juan," she said, "but there isn't a single thing hidden in this kitchenette."

As Alvarez strode across towards them, Maureen Holmes saw in his face the beginning of a doubt freezing towards despair. Yet something else sustained and upheld him; she could see that too.

"One moment, please," said Alvarez, frowning. "This what-do-you-call-it—kitchenette—looks as though it has not been touched."

"That's because we put everything back tidily." Paula pushed back one wing of her hair with the outside of a begrimed hand. "You men simply threw everything on the floor."

"It's true!" Maureen assured him. She would have touched his arm except that her hands were grubby too, and as a result she felt grubby all over. "Years ago, I used to have one just like this. Look! There's a small electric stove, a little electric refrigerator under the drainboard, and on each side closed cupboards for china or cans for flour and sugar and the rest. No food here; nothing concealed. We tried the walls; no cracks or secret cupboards. There isn't even a vent for steam or smoke, though you're supposed to have one."

"Find anything?" asked Collier.

Colonel Duroc, who had been standing near the group at the kitchenette, wore a white mottled face of nervousness and near-collapse.

"We must find them," he kept muttering. "We *must*."

Now the search ran fast to its close, though to Paula's nerves every second seemed a minute and every minute an hour. Every piece of furniture was taken to pieces, the sofa disembowelled and examined. Agent of Police Abou Owad darted round with his stepladder, scrutinizing every inch of the walls and then the ceiling. The Spanish policeman from the bathroom hurled away the carpet and went over a floor of solid concrete.

Alvarez, scarcely knowing what he did, kicked savagely at burned coals and heavy bits of ash; he kicked the andirons; he almost kicked a fallen Bible. Colonel Duroc stood with head turned aside. Maureen, discovering with joy that the hot-water tap worked in the kitchenette, washed her hands along with Paula; they had no soap, but here was a roller towel. Again both felt clean all over—but, by the mere fact of this, more miserable.

Slowly a silence, of hearts and minds as well as hammerings, gathered in the room.

It was the Spanish policeman, the one first at searching the bathroom, who spoke out a sentiment in most minds.

"Commandant," he said in French, "in the bathroom that *lavabo* does not match; the chain to the plunger in the cistern has not been used for weeks or months; it is broken and even corroded. Nothing is hidden down the drain of the tub or the wash basin. Nothing hidden anywhere!"

Voices in many languages volleyed out.

"Or hidden in the walls, or floor, or ceiling, by Allah!"

"Or in the chimney, the fireplace, or on the hearth."

"Or in any piece of furniture, or the smallest trinket."

"Or in the kitchenette; please believe that!"

"Or sent out of this room. All windows, the one door, are guarded and watched!"

"These things, in effect—have vanished."

Paula, for the second time that day, felt that in a moment she would be physically sick. Maureen, the taller and more slender of the two, put her arm round Paula's waist.

"One little moment!" cried a white-faced Colonel Duroc. "You have searched everywhere, I do not deny it. But one place alone you have not searched. That is the chair in which the man Collier has been sitting all this time."

Collier, who had been lighting still another cigarette, raised filmed eyes. He seemed to ponder, behind a slight lifting of the lip, whether he ought to rib this old stumblebum any further. Instead he sighed, got up, and moved to one side.

"It's all yours, spinach," he said, moving up his thick shoulders. "Search it. If you find I've been sitting on a hatful of diamonds or an iron box two feet long, be a pal and tell me. Eh?"

Three policemen, with knife, upholstery tools, and microscope, flung themselves at the chair. Time seemed to have no end. A tension of nerves grew so taut that Maureen pressed one hand over Paula's mouth. At last the chair, fully gutted and closely examined, lay on its back; and there was nothing.

At last Collier condescended to laugh out loud when he looked at Alvarez.

"You're licked, wise guy," he sneered. "You haven't got a thing on me, and you know it."

CHAPTER NINE

And then, in black despair when all but one were ready to concede defeat, the atmosphere subtly altered and the luck began to flow the other way.

Afterwards all argued about the change in atmosphere. But Maureen knew. The closed room, with its dismembered furniture all pushed back against the walls, was half-stifling from locked windows and locked crimson blinds. The room was an open space of dirty concrete flooring.

But Maureen, all of whose thoughts were concentrated on Alvarez, saw that the atmosphere came from him. Juan Alvarez, seeming leaner in his trim, tight-fitting uniform which brought out the breadth of shoulder, stood in the middle of the open space.

And Maureen, who had her arm round Paula's waist, felt her imperceptible start. For the first time since Paula and Alvarez had been at the door of this flat, Paula heard the Commandant let out the full power of his voice.

"I am not at all convinced of that, Mr. Collier," said the Commandant. "You fool! We have not even begun to show our evidence!"

Dead silence.

The Arab policeman whistled. Collier, lounging against the wall near one crimson shutter, the cigarette paper stuck to his lower lip, merely breathed out smoke.

"You still don't get it, wise guy. I can't be bothered with you saps much longer. I've got business. I've gotta go out . . ."

Colonel Duroc's voice, now cold and calm, struck in.

"You will not be permitted to leave here," he said.

"So I won't?" asked Collier softly, lifting red eyebrows and mouthing smoke. "So there'll be plenty big trouble at the legation, when I spill it. Suit yourself."

Alvarez made a gesture which made even his Colonel

pause.

"Are you a betting man, Mr. Collier?" he asked in English and with a voice which seemed inspired of the devil. "If so, I will accept any wager you care to offer that within fifteen minutes we shall have enough evidence to take you away in handcuffs."

There was a buzz among the policemen, who were required to speak French, Spanish, and Arabic, but not English. One who evidently knew a little of the last-named language was hissing an explanation. Collier merely looked weary. And Colonel Duroc unobtrusively plucked at the Commandant's sleeve.

"Alvarez!"

"Yes, sir?"

"A word aside with you. Come over to this dismembered couch near the bathroom door. Good."

Their whispered talk, in French, did not carry to another person in the room.

"Alvarez, is this a bluff?"

"No, sir. I never bluff, and I despise those who do."

"You would be a bad strategist in war, Alvarez."

"Of that I am aware," said Alvarez, who could feel humility as only those of high soul can feel it. "It is my one imbecile's principle, sir. I would prove that for the rest I am not stupid. May I explain?"

Clearly Alvarez could not see that Duroc was inwardly raging, all against the Commandant. More bitter in the Colonel's mind was Alvarez's dereliction of duty last night; his greeting of Maureen this morning; bitterest of all, the vanishing of the diamonds now, which he also blamed on Alvarez. Colonel Duroc was not himself. Though retaining something of his outer suavity, his mind had darkened.

"Continue, Alvarez," he said huskily.

"I was not present at the conference between you and Sir Henry Merrivale on the terrace at your home . . ."

"Ah! If I could but lay my hands on that sleeping beauty!"

"This conference lasted from early afternoon until seven o'clock in the evening. Then you, Sir Henry, and Miss Holmes drove down from the Old Mountain, and you stopped briefly to see me at the Central Station to tell me what had been decided."

"Yes, yes? And what is this to our sheep?"

"Pardon, sir. You had decided that this man Collier, a diamond cutter, was the accomplice of Iron Chest; and that Iron Chest himself slipped invisibly from the scene. Sir, sir," pleaded Alvarez, "your deductions were admirable and had sound reason . . ."

"You flatter both of us," murmured the Colonel. "Also practical, perhaps, since Sir Henry foresaw the attempt to rob Bernstein et Cie. last night?"

Alvarez swallowed hard.

"True, sir. But your main deductions, I respectfully submit, must remain suppositions and not facts. Both you and Sir Henry are fond of playing the game of the clever against the super-clever, the super-clever against the supreme-clever, as you think Iron Chest will do against you. But it becomes too involved."

"Indeed," the Colonel said flatly.

"In my humble opinion," begged Alvarez, "and as you said yourself a while ago, it is the obvious we do not see. I believe this man Collier *is* Iron Chest himself; that there was no second person. Using sheer daring—always his weapon—he walked straight through our immigration and customs as he did through Lisbon. Sir, may I be allowed to pin him down?"

Though Duroc spoke no more curtly, the inside of his mind grew blacker.

"You may," he said. "But my position, as well as administrative, is also diplomatic. If you make one mistake—"

"Thank you, sir," said Alvarez, and turned on his heel and swung round.

The policemen, whispering and gesticulating, were now drawn up in a long line across the front of the fireplace. Paula and Maureen, by some commonly shared impulse, stood with their backs to the kitchenette sink. Alvarez's footsteps struck hard on the concrete as he strode to the middle of it.

"If I speak in English," he said clearly, "is because I wish," he nodded towards Collier without referring to him, "clearly to understand every word I say." Now he did look at the thick figure in the whitish suit. "Mr. Collier," he added pleasantly, "much depends on certain questions I should like to ask you. Will you answer the questions?"

Still lounging against the wall, Collier turned his head and in a dreary way let smoke fall out of his mouth.

"How silly can you get?" he asked, referring to himself. "I should say something without a lawyer here? Shove it, wise guy."

"I might remind you," Alvarez said pleasantly, "that you are not even charged with any offence, much less imprisoned. You do not need a lawyer."

Collier did not condescend to reply.

"Well, that is your right," Alvarez conceded, still pleasantly. He took a step away, and then swung back. "But it is interesting," he added, "to confirm my original opinion of you. You are merely a fat coward, without courage to answer questions when you are unprotected."

And that tore it.

A yell of pure ecstasy went up from the one policeman who understood English.

Collier swung round, tearing the cigarette from his lip and flinging it away. Slowly, at his languid but truculent prize-fighter's walk, he moved over and faced Alvarez in the open space.

Maureen, more sensitive than the English girl, felt that she could not stand the tension much longer. But not Paula. Paula stood upright, face rather flushed; cool, almost eager, calm eyes of appraisal on Alvarez and Collier.

"Now look!" snarled Collier. "Make another crack like that—"

"Yes?" prompted Alvarez, raising his eyebrows politely and looking still more pleasant.

"I'd hate to hafta hurt you, sonny," said Collier languidly. "I'd just smear you all over this floor."

"But I thought you could not be bothered. It would be unpleasant for me," Alvarez smiled silkily, "if you hurt me."

"Yeah; sure; now you're catching on." The sneer on Collier's large face seemed less pronounced. "Just don't get me sore; I warned you. Now look! You think I never been around? You think I was never on the witness stand?"

"Quite often, I should imagine."

"And you're not kidding, either. They send their smart lawyers against me, and I tie 'em up in knots. It'd kill you! You got some questions for me? Okay, smart guy. Give. I'll answer 'em."

"Thank you," said Alvarez. He pointed to Maureen's copy of the *Gazette,* still clutched in the Colonel's hand.

"Can you deny," asked Alvarez, in a slightly different

voice, "it was you who put that advertisement, about leasing this flat, in yesterday's *Tangier Gazette?*"

"Pal, I just wouldn't know. And you couldn't prove a thing."

"No?" said Alvarez, instantly producing more documents. "You sent it to the newspaper three days ago, by cable and money order when you first ordered the flat, from Messrs. Cook's main office in Lisbon. You asked for the advertisement to appear yesterday. When you were interrogated at the airport, you of course were secretly photographed. A radio-photo was sent to Lisbon last night. This morning a cable," he held up the cable, "identifies you as the man who sent the advertisement to the *Gazette*. Do you deny this?"

Again Collier regarded him with a fishy half-smile.

"So I get me a room at the Riff Hotel. So I get me an apartment, too, and then think maybe that's not so good. Having both, see? So I wanna sublet the apartment." Collier's pale eyes opened wide, in a simulation of real interest. "Say, Counseller, is any of them things a crime?"

"This flat was a trap. Which of these young ladies did you try to trap—Mrs. Bentley or Miss Holmes?"

Collier put his head on one side.

" 'Have you stopped cheating at poker?' " he jeered. "Now what kind of a question is that? A judge would jump all over it. You better let me help you, wise guy."

"I asked you—!"

"Look. You wanna know about the dames? I never seen either of 'em before. Did I try to 'trap' either one? Shove it. They tried to bust in; one of 'em did bust in; and I tried to keep 'em out."

Collier lifted his hand, and also his padded shoulders, to forestall objection.

"So you wanna talk about diamonds and iron chests?" Now his flat nostrils grew wider. "So what? Did you get 'em? Did you find what a screwy broad told you? Don't make me laugh. You haven't got a thing on me, and you know it."

Maureen Holmes' heart sank. The questioning seemed to have been going badly for Alvarez. In the background, motionless and without a word, stood Colonel Duroc.

"Jeez, what a rotten lawyer *you'd* make," sneered Collier. "I twisted you up in knots, didn't I? Like I said. Why, even this cable—" Casually he stretched out his hand.

"Don't touch those papers, swine?"

Then Collier's tenor voice went high.

"So you *want* trouble, wise guy?"

"Yes!" roared Alvarez. Instantly his heavy voice sank to a polite, suave growl. "But not until you have answered another question, Mr. Collier."

In two seconds something would explode, and everybody knew it.

Despite his languid face, Collier was shaking with rage. Alvarez was controlled, except that occasionally he would loosen his shoulders in the trim, tight-fitting uniform. Paula Bentley, noiseless in her sandals even on a gritty floor, crept out to a position against the corridor wall, so that she saw the two men in profile. Beyond them stood the line of policemen.

"So the poor sap wants a question," said Collier to his invisible companion. "Ain't I done enough to help him? But okay, wise guy, give."

"What is your nationality, Mr. Collier?"

Collier seemed—almost, at least—amazed.

"Didn' I tell you?" He pushed out his chest. "I'm an Amurrican citizen!"

"Er . . . naturalized, of course?"

Collier took a step backwards, while Alvarez put away the documents.

"Now palsy-walsy is being funny. What are you trying to slip me, palsy-walsy? What's this stuff about being naturalized? Why?"

"Because you are not like any real American I have ever met," said Alvarez. "And I have met many. You are the jabberwock fake American, whom we find as a rule only in films and cheap fiction. . . . May I see your passport, please?"

"Now suppose," said Collier, putting his head on one side, "I just couldn't be bothered to show you my passport?"

"Then, unfortunately," smiled Alvarez, "I will take it from you."

No doubt Alvarez imagined he was keeping a straight, pleasant face. But one thing perhaps he was not aware of and could not control: his expression of sheer contempt.

"Maybe I'm funny, in a way," drawled Collier, his head still on one side. "Yeah, that's it; maybe I'm funny. But I just kind of don't like the look on your pan, see? I just don't like being looked at as if I was dirt."

Alvarez was puzzled.

"But what else are you?" he asked, in obviously genuine surprise.

Dead silence.

Then the blood rushed into Collier's face, and all his languid airs flew apart. Fists clenched, lightly balanced, he fired a straight, hard left jab at Alvarez's face.

All the joy of heaven shone in the Commandant's eyes. Contemptuously slipping the punch, Alvarez countered with a murderous right cross to the side of Collier's jaw. Instantly, his footwork too fast to see, Alvarez drove an even harder left hook—his deadliest weapon—to the other side of Collier's jaw. The two blows seemed to whack almost together, like chops on meat.

"Oh, well done!" Paula blurted out uncontrollably. "Beautifully done!"

From the policemen came a roar and stamping of delight.

Alvarez did not put his opponent completely on the floor, of course. With an experienced fighter, such as Collier at least seemed to be, that is not easy.

But the Commandant almost did it. As the left hook whacked home, a film as of vacancy slid over Collier's eyes. He reeled back four steps to the right, wildly tried to steady himself from falling left; then instinctively he fell on his right knee, right hand supporting himself against the concrete, head down.

Nobody moved or spoke. Alvarez, who might badly have damaged his gloved hands, had not done so; he merely waited, arms loose at his side. Colonel Duroc opened his mouth to speak, but, thinking differently, he remained silent.

Collier knelt, head down, until a referee might have counted to eight and just on the word of nine.

Then his heavy body bounced up, the film cleared from his eyes. Though his jaws had reddish marks which were beginning to swell and must have hurt like poisoned teeth, Collier showed no slur in his speech. The casual sneer was still on his face. Carelessly thrusting his hands in his pockets, as though he could not be troubled with more fighting, he sauntered forward. His pale eyes, under the drooping lids, conveyed the impression that it was he who had put down Alvarez for a count of nine.

"I get it," he said to Alvarez. "You box. Fancy Dan stuff. I don't; I fight. If we ever tangle for keeps," and his left upper lip curled up in disdain, "remember I just keep coming on, just keep coming on, till I land one punch. And what'll you be? Hamburger; that's what."

The policeman who understood English laughed with much derision. A fire iron went over with a crash on the hearth tiles.

Alvarez snapped his fingers, looking at Collier.

"May I see your passport, please?"

Momentarily Collier hesitated.

"Why not?" And he shrugged his shoulders. "They already took the number at the airport. It's no skin off mine if you wanna take the number again."

Drawing the green passport from his inside pocket, Collier threw it at Alvarez, who caught it neatly.

"What's so wrong about being naturalized?" Collier demanded.

"Nothing whatever, if you are a credit to your adopted country. . . . Ah, here we have it," said Alvarez. " 'Place of birth: Moscow, Russia. Date of birth—' " Alvarez paused, thoughtfully tapping a gloved finger on the passport. "He was naturalized, I see, at the earliest date permitted by American Law. Even within that time, he could not have learned such fluent gutter language in the United States. His gutter manners also he could have found elsewhere." Alvarez's face showed faint disgust. "Moscow, Russia," he added, in deeper disgust.

"So what?" leered Collier. "So now I gotta prove I ain't a communist?"

"No. Your politics are none of my business or of anyone else."

"Good thing, sweetheart. I couldn't help you, see? You're too dumb to get the right answers for yourself."

"You think so?" murmured Alvarez, almost with sympathy and pity. "Poor simpleton."

Then Alvarez whipped round towards the Colonel, who was still standing silent in the background. The Commandant pointed to the wall above the fireplace.

"Colonel Duroc!" he continued in English. "No doubt you observed the small marks of nail holes, set in a pattern, of something to be hung here over the fireplace?"

The Colonel, grim-faced, merely nodded curtly.

"Good!" said Alvarez.

He strode over to the gutted sofa which was between the kitchenette and the bathroom door. From there he picked up the hammer which had not been brought by the police. It was not a claw hammer, but a machinist's hammer. While the policemen scattered to each side of the fireplace, Alvarez strode back and snatched up the garden sickle from beside the bookshelves.

With one instrument in each hand, he reared up and slammed both against the wall with such savagery that plaster chips flew. Yet, when he moved them a little, they fitted exactly into the tiny pattern of nail marks. The crossed hammer and sickle sprang out against the grimy wall.

Holding them there only long enough for everyone to see, Alvarez flung hammer and sickle into the fireplace.

"Sir," again he addressed Colonel Duroc, "there are several more plain indications of this 'Collier's' strange beliefs. For instance, if you will look at . . ."

"Commandant Alvarez!" interrupted the Colonel sharply.

"Sir?"

Colonel Duroc also spoke in English. But his voice had an odd sound—cold, hard, yet with a strangled quality. Though he fashioned each syllable with care, he seemed to have difficulty in speaking.

"All this," he said, "has no concern with our affair." He nodded towards Collier. "This . . . gentleman is the naturalized citizen of a friendly power—"

"Sir, the Americans will only laugh at him! Let them speak to him for one minute, and they will know him for the fake and undoubted crook he is."

"I did not refer to the Americans, Commandant."

"Surely, Colonel," asked the astonished Alvarez, "you cannot refer to our Soviet insects?"

"The Soviet Union," said Duroc in a fierce voice, "is a . . . friendly power, a signer of our international treaty, part of the government we serve. Never again, Commandant, will you use that insulting term, or any insulting term! Do you understand?"

Alvarez bowed slightly.

"I understand the ways of diplomatic usage, sir."

"Enough of your childish sarcasm, Commandant."

"I also understand," said Alvarez, "that in your heart you

know, as I do, that this man Collier has attached himself to the high ideals and open-hearted methods of the . . . of the Soviet Union."

Paula Bentley glanced towards Maureen beside the kitchenette sink. The dark-blue eyes were as bewildered as the green eyes. Hitherto Collier in the Colonel's eyes had been "this camel," or similar French insults; now he was "this gentleman." Though both Paula and Maureen could understand the diplomatic beehive of a police commissioner in Tangier, they were bewildered by his suppressed rage, like rusty clockwork at the back of his throat.

"Furthermore," snapped Colonel Duroc, glancing at his wrist watch, "you promised to produce evidence, within fifteen minutes, of Mr. Collier's guilt in theft or attempted murder. You have not done so, and your time runs out. Well?"

"Ah, the evidence!" said Alvarez, snapping his fingers as though at some half-forgotten trifle. Whereupon he became very straight and formal. "With your permission, Colonel, I will now produce that evidence. . . . Mrs. Bentley!"

"Yes, Juan?" answered Paula, in her softest and sweetest voice.

Paula lounged there, rounded chin held up, in a careless position. Her close-fitting blue-silk frock brought to the eyes of the policemen a glisten of sympathy, if not some other and stronger feeling. But Paula saw very clearly the truth in her mind, and knew what she must do.

"Mrs. Bently," Alvarez began gently, facing her from in front of the fireplace, "I do not wish in any way to distress or upset you . . ."

"Oh, you won't," laughed Paula. "Really you won't!"

"Thank you." Alvarez nodded towards Collier, who had swung round to face her. "Will you look at this man, please?"

This time Paula did gasp, but it was no stab of fear; it was merely repulsion as she saw the indomitable Collier, with his sneering face and his thumbs hooked in his belt.

"When you and I came into this flat, Mrs. Bentley, it seemed to me that you several times looked at him as though wondering where you had seen him before. Is that correct?"

"It is, Jua—Commandant," said Paula. Sensing the deadliness under this formality, Paula made her voice almost prim.

"Observe, in the presence of witnesses, that I do not attempt to suggest anything to you, or put words into your mouth. Did anything else happen later?"

"Oh, yes."

"What was it?"

"I definitely and clearly remembered where I had seen him before."

Alvarez, like a crafty prosecuting counsel before a formidable judge, carefully refrained from leading his witness.

"Will you explain that, Mrs. Bentley?"

"For the most part, it was a gesture."

"Go on, please."

The room, in earthly silence except for their voices, had grown hot and stifling as the sun neared midday. Paula felt no dampness on her body; she was quite cool, except for a pulse throbbing somewhere.

"Miss Holmes and I," she went on, "were standing facing the kitchenette. You and Colonel Duroc had your backs to us, facing out into room, when that man"—she nodded towards Collier—"with a cigarette in his mouth. . . ."

"Yes, Mrs. Bently?"

"I turned round," said Paula, "while you were talking. I looked at that man. He took the end of the cigarette out of his mouth, and pointed the lighted end at Colonel Duroc with an awfully odd kind of gesture, like this." She extended her arm and wrist, turning them partly upwards in a snake-like motion. "That was when I remembered everything, even his face."

"Explain that, please!"

"It was the movement of his gun hand," said Paula, "when it came up over the iron chest and fired two shots at me last night. He was only four feet away. There was a street light not far from his face, and I can now remember his face distinctly. He had a hat on, concealing that red hair. And those filthy padded shoulders are deceptive; he was wearing a thin suit. But I know his face. Whether or not he's Iron Chest, he's the man who tried to rob Bernstein and Company last night."

Colonel Duroc opened his mouth, and shut it. Alvarez turned to the Colonel. The rest stood concealed, while one of the policemen softly rattled out a translation.

"Do we need more evidence that this identification, sir?" inquired Alvarez.

Then Collier's rasping tenor again soared high.

"Why, the lying little floosie!" he screamed. "I'll cut the tramp's throat out for this!"

Alvarez, turning back to him, whipped the glove off his left fingers with his right hand. With all the power of his arm he slashed the glove across Collier's left cheek; then, backhand, across Collier's right cheek. He was so fast that the glove was back on his left hand before anyone could follow it.

"Though you are only a fat coward," Alvarez said loudly, "will *that* make you fight?"

Collier, who was certainly not fat and possible not a coward, squared again to throw his left. Only in Alvarez's delighted eyes could you see he meant to go for the body, left and right, with a flurry of piston-rod belly punches.

But both men were stopped, rigid, by what was in sober fact a terrible voice.

"Commandant! Assez! Assez, je dis! Venez ici!"

Few now remembered how Colonel Duroc, less than a decade ago, could use that voice or his power of eye to subdue his savage Belgian guerillas.

Alvarez turned round and walked over to him. The little Colonel stood with feet planted wide, uniform tunic stuck out, hands gripped behind his back. Paula and Maureen, remembering the chuckling and amiable Duroc, who winked at them and chided them, were more bewildered than ever. Their instinct was correct. For Colonel Duroc, upon whom misfortune piled on misfortune (all somehow seeming to centre in Alvarez), was not quite in his right senses.

"Commandant," he said, "once more I speak English so that our men will not understand." He forgot one of the policemen. "Let me now give judgment on you. Your 'identification' evidence might, or in my opinion would not, be valuable in a court of justice . . ."

"Colonel, that's absurd!" cried Paula Bentley.

The little Colonel gave her a glance, but spoke to Alvarez. "Let us consider your record, Alvarez. Last night you have commit the most serious offence known to the Department of Police. When supposedly on duty, when you might yourself have caught a dangerous criminal, *étant noir* . . . that is, you are black-drunk and incapable. Even last night I meditate on whether you shall be only demoted, or dismissed from a duty of which you are not capable."

"Sir, you must know I bitterly apologize for that! I offer no excuse. I only . . ."

"I do not want your apologies," said Colonel Duroc curtly. "What good are they? Keep them! But I come to today, offences quite as serious. Do not speak. *I* will speak.

"Well, I pass over small matters, as when you and—and Mr. Collier exchange blows. He is the aggressor; you are correct to strike back. But then what do you do? In the presence of witnesses, as I have tell you, you insult a friendly power of our Government. And lastly—"

The breath whistled through Duroc's nostrils. His fingernails, on hands gripped behind his back, dug blood from the flesh. Not a soul dared speak.

"Lastly, Commandant! Because you are annoyed, you have take off your glove and splash on this man's face, daring him to fight. Why? Because you think you can beat him to a jelly. *Merde, alors!* You do not see, no? Now you give him the chance to say to all that the police of Tangier used the methods of what they call third degree. This is not true—leave such things to the Arab Mendoubia!—and well you know it. Very well! If you wish to remain in my service in any capacity, I now give you your order!"

Whereupon the Colonel completely lost his head. He pointed at Collier.

"You will publicly apologize to that man, now! And in full!"

Collier was almost triumphant. Up went his high, sneering laugh.

"Better listen to the Colonel, wise guy," he said. "He's the McCoy. And crawl, wise guy. That's what I wanna see. Crawl!"

Alvarez, shoulders back, looked straight down into the inflamed eyes of Colonel Duroc.

"Are you serious, sir?"

"You will find, Commandant, how serious I am."

Alvarez, in the daze of a man who cannot believe his ears, slowly turned and, still vaguely insistent, pointed towards Collier.

"Apologize to *that*?" he asked, still wonderingly.

"You will obey my order, Commandant!"

Alvarez whirled back. "Excuse me one moment, sir," he said quickly.

Turning his back on the Colonel, Alvarez walked with ringing steps towards the corridor wall, near the point where Paula stood. Pushed back against the wall was the big mahogany table, now with only three legs put back and its cover placed on shakily like a lid.

But round it on the floor were still a few sheets of writing paper. Snatching up one, he tried to balance it on the unsteady tabletop. He drew out a fountain pen and wrote several lines quickly but unsteadily before Colonel Duroc's voice cut across the room.

"Alvarez! What the devil are you doing?"

Alvarez signed his name. He blew on the paper and shook it in the air to dry the ink. He marched back and handed the paper to Colonel Duroc.

"It is my resignation from the Department of Police, sir," he said, "to take effect at once. You find it in order, I hope?"

"Quite in order," answered the Colonel, taking the paper and running his eye down it. He folded it up and put it into his trouser pocket. "There might be formalities, but I waive them."

"Thank you, sir. And now . . ."

And now burst out the loudest clamour yet heard in that red-shuttered room. Already there had been a heavy buzzing, as of wasps streaming out, as one policeman explained the matter to the others. Paula, with a cry of protest, ran across and seized the Colonel's left arm. Maureen ran from the kitchenette and seized his right arm.

"Colonel," said Paula, "you're behaving like a foolish little boy." Her soft voice grew softer and more cajoling. "What's the matter, *mon cher?* If I kissed you now, you'd probably hit me. But what's happened to the nice, pleasant person I used to know?"

"Please, Colonel!" begged Maureen. She could not help it; tears came into her eyes. "I know it's none of my business. But I'll just bet you I can tell what it is. Because Sir Henry's still asleep, and you couldn't find the diamonds"—here Colonel Duroc winced, but kept a face like Napoleon going to St. Helena—"you were furious and took it out on poor Juan. What better detective do you want? He found a criminal, didn't he?"

Paula, inspired, turned to Maureen without letting go the Colonel's arm.

"Darling, that's exactly it! I *can* identify that man. It's true! Colonel Duroc must know any court will accept it. Instead of admitting it . . ."

Whereupon, the angry policemen crowded up and pinned a protesting Alvarez between themselves and Colonel Duroc.

They held the Commandant far more in awe than the Colonel. Though they knew Alvarez for a strict one, they admired his iron fairness; they liked the fact that he never bullied and he never bluffed. Now, as a real crown, they simple-heartedly but sensibly like him because he was a human being and had got drunk.

"It's a good thing, eh?" jeered the heavily muscled one, in French. "You lose your best man because he catches your criminal. *Vive la logique.*"

"Allah will not bless you for this, lord of policemen! Look to it!"

"And because of the Russian filth who sells Bibles and yet is foul?"

"Mother of heaven! I spit!"

"Silence!" shouted Colonel Duroc, in such a voice that the tumult subsided.

The little Colonel stood among them, hands still locked behind his back, showing a very real dignity.

"It is possible," his English began to slur, "that perhaps quite already in this affair I 'ave been too hasty." He shifted into French. "Pah, but that Alvarez! That villain! He deserves the bastinado, the water torture, the . . . Alvarez! Where the devil are you?"

"Standing immediately in front of you," retorted the villain in question, looking down at him.

"Well, Your orders—"

Alvarez smiled broadly.

"You forget, sir, that I am no longer under your damned orders. I am a civilian. Therefore I propose to that 'Mr. Collier' . . ."

Swinging round, shoving past the policeman, Alvarez took two steps and stopped short. He looked wildly round the room. So did everybody else, after a moment.

Collier was not there.

Only a ghost of Collier's unruffled sneer seemed to hang in the room, mocking them all.

Whether or not he was a civilian, Alvarez raced for the only door, and threw it open.

Outside—a fine, lean, handsome figure of a man, though hesitant and not over-bright—stood Inspector Mendoza, patiently waiting.

"Inspector Mendoza!" Alvarez's throat was thick, but he tried to clear it. "You have not permitted anyone to leave here? A man, pretending to be an American, with a white-grey suit and an unspeakable bow tie?"

"Pr-pretending?" Mendoza answered his Spanish. "But, Commandant! The gentleman *was* American. And very pleasant. He showed me his passport, with photograph. He told me you would or could not detain him, since all Americans are answerable only to their own legation. And this is true, is it not?"

Alvarez stood motionless.

"No matter," he said at last. "I have been the stupid one, my friend."

CHAPTER TEN

Late that afternoon, amid the noise of the Little Socco, Maureen Holmes and Juan Alvarez sat at a round iron table amid many before the dirty fly-specked windows of a café. They drank the vilest coffee ever brewed.

Since the Little Socco is a street narrow and not too long, it is difficult to believe that so much brawling can occur here. You descend to it through an arch in the wall of the Grand Socco. But you must be careful to go down by the little winding street on the right, past the church. Never, never branch off in any street to the left, or you will find yourself lost and cursing amid the strange-smelling labyrinth of the lower Kasbah.

This afternoon the Little Socco, under dust and sun glare, almost drowsed. At the end of it, painted a nightmare yellow, loomed the low-roofed Vox Cinema. On many an ancient wall, too, you could see the red tin placard whose white letters bore the mystic lettering, "Coca-Cola,"

On the right, as you went down, were the booths of money changers, who would give you a sporting flutter on today's exchange in any currency. There was a tobacconist's, as well as many of those narrow courtesy "hotels," with upper shutters tightly closed, which abound here and in nearby streets. Of course, the proprietor does not actually protest against a guest who merely wants a room there.

On the right were several long café fronts. The red tarboosh bloomed everywhere. Past Maureen and Alvarez staked Arabs in *jalebahs,* powerful dark-burnt Arabs in collarless robes vertically striped yellow and black like a wasp, and young Arabs in modern clothes whose pinched-in waists and white ties made them resemble wideboys from Soho. Even the donkeys, some with bells, trod with statelier air and even statelier odour over cobblestones so packed down with ancient animal dung that they now resembled a smoothly paved street.

Despite the babble of voices, an anxious Maureen made herself heard.

"Juan," she said, "you're not really depressed about all this, are you? After that good lunch, and the wine?"

"No. Of course not," said Alvarez.

He lied. Alvarez now wore a sombre grey suit of London cut instead of his uniform, but still no hat. His elbows were on the table, head lowered, hands clasped over his ears. He was in that blackest of depressions which can be felt only when the Latin temperament is armoured by a British training which will not allow him to show it.

"It was my temper," he said, still with his hands over his ears. "That is why they call me a stuffed shirt; because I must always control my temper. Once or twice it has broken loose, and—"

He shivered, and tried to climb out of the pit.

"Well, I have failed," he added. "I attempted to show that by my own hard work I could attain a good position. Now it becomes merely comic. I have lost my job."

Though Maureen's impulse towards crying had long gone, she felt her heart contract. Silently she opened the catch of her handbag.

"I—I have a little money," she said, powerfully embarrassed. "If you need . . ."

For a short space she thought he had not heard her. Still with head in hands, he was staring across the street at the tobacconist's small shop. The tobacconist, an alert Arab, eagerly held up a tin of fifty Players cigarettes in one hand and fifty Gold Flake in the other.

Alvarez did not see him. He turned his head and regarded Maureen with a strange expression, as though she were something holy.

"You would do that?" he asked wonderingly. Then he smiled, a genuine smile, and snapped shut the clasp of her purse. "Put it away, little one. Of that, at least, there is no need. I have more money than any man can possibly spend in his lifetime. Yet deeply I thank you for—for . . ." He paused. "We know so little of each other, you and I."

"I—I didn't want to ask," said Maureen, who in fact was burning with curiosity but restrained herself. "After all, we haven't had much time, have we?"

"No," mused Alvarez. "No." He smiled again. "But I have

little to tell. You see, I am a Spanish Royalist. When our last King was driven from the country—was it in '30, or '31?—I was a mere boy. They sent me to England, where we had powerful relatives."

Here Alvarez's gaze wandered away into a dream.

"I remember a large house in Eaton Square, and a stately butler who corrected my pronunciation with unobtrusive courtesy. For a time I had a private tutor. Then I was sent to . . ."

Maureen, aching to prompt this reluctant man, spoke the first words that came into her mind.

"Eton and Oxford?"

"No, no, no," said Alvarez, taking the question very seriously. "Rugby and Sandhurst. I wished to be trained for the Army. Before I had finished Sandhurst I became a naturalized British subject, though, I hope, with more credit to my adopted country than Collier is to yours." He made a wry face. "Moreover, when I had left Sandhurst the Spanish Civil War was over. But we had not long to wait for the Second World War. I served with the British Army for six years. That is almost all; and little enough, I think.

"Oh, but for one thing," he added, turning back and again looking into her eyes. "I would always be open with you, little one. My Christian name really is Juan. But my surname is not Alvarez." Inside his eyes was a fierce pride so deep that it did not show on the surface. "I am not at all ashamed of my true name, Maureen. It has been known to Spain—yes, and to all the world!—for over eight hundred years."

Shrugging his shoulders, Alvarez attempted a smile but failed.

"In these days," he concluded, "I suppose I should apologize for such old-fashioned sentiments. But I cannot apologize, little one. In fact, when I hear the true hypocrites and idlers jeer at the sons of old families that they are spivs and drones, that they will not work or cannot work . . ." Suddenly he clenched his fists, kept the blood from his face, and remained aloofly pleasant. "You notice? The strongest feeling can be overcome."

Whereupon, as always, the unexpected happened.

Maureen had not the slightest intention of blurting out the words she spoke. They were not even in her mind, she believed, an instant before. Yet her lips formed them unbidden, as she looked down at the dingy dark-green tabletop.

"I suppose you've known a lot of women?" she asked.

Alvarez looked startled.

"Yes, of course," he answered. Then his expression changed altogether. "But you—that is different. . . . That is another thing. . . . That is—"

Now he was in worse plight. Turning back, he lifted a cup of cold coffee and slowly drank it to the dregs.

"Pope-corn!" sang a youthful voice, above the clatter of metal and wheels with hard-rubber tires. *"Pope-corn!"*

Amid the crush of red tarbooshes and sinister-looking felt hats, a young man in red fez and green jacket was pushing a green machine broadly inscribed "Popcorn" along the side. This was not easy, since everybody walked in the middle of the road. Against a pink wall Maureen saw another advertisement for Coca-Cola. Dust blew along the yellow Little Socco. A smartly dressed French girl, clearly a tourist, was buying cigarettes. The babble rose higher.

But the flowering of romance in Maureen's heart withered away; she felt cold all over. Why didn't he speak? Well, but she hadn't wanted him to speak, had she? Maureen did not know. She knew only that she felt miserable, and hoped he would change the subject. Alvarez did.

"Thus you understand," he was saying, in a matter-of-fact tone, "that the pleasure of being Commandant of Police was only for its work and its prestige. Now I am free! Now I can become a private detective, and track down Collier for myself."

"You don't mean to keep on with this?" demanded Maureen, now bitterly sorry he had changed the subject, and determined to bring it up again. But the possible danger to Alvarez drove it momentarily from her mind. "You don't mean . . . ?" her voice died away.

"Yes, of course. I have a little grudge to settle."

"But won't that be horribly dangerous?"

"Maureen, my dear," and both of them started slightly when he said that, "what else have I been doing for the past four years? Believe me, there are characters a dozen times tougher here in Tangier than this sneering Collier even believes he is. Er—didn't you hear the news of this afternoon?"

"No!" said Maureen, and fear deepened again. "After lunch I went back to the house to get a bath. I dozed a little. But you made me promise to meet you here—"

Alvarez drummed his fingers on the top of the table.
"Well!" he grunted, half to himself. "I was permitted twenty-four hours' grace to gather up the effects from my private office, and leave behind those belonging to my department. Many phone calls went through my office. You realize who is in the deadliest danger of all?"
"Who?"
"Mrs. Bentley, of course!" He rapped his knuckles on the table. "She alone can identify Collier as would-be thief and attempted murderer. I myself think he is Iron Chest, and the only Iron Chest, but others think differently. In any case, he is closely allied with Iron Chest. He will not hesitate to kill Mrs. Bentley, as he promised."
"Paula," murmured Maureen. "I love Paula!" she said, thinking that Paula would easily have known how to deal with an emotional situation like her own.
"Collier," said Alvarez, his eyes nearly closed and his mind concentrated on other matters, "is now a fugitive on the run. Every net has gone out. His photograph will be known to every hotel, every bank, every money changer, every drinking house. But there are so many crooked small hotels, crooked money changers, criminal dives, that he may have gone to earth already."
"Then whatever can they do?"
"Mrs. Bentley must be protected every moment of the day and night. Outside her hotel, of course, she will be preceded at some distance by a plain-clothes detective who must not look like one and followed at the same distance by another. But this is not good enough."
"What *is* good enough?"
"Bill Bentley, her husband," Alvarez's look was grimly appreciative, "has got leave from his consulate to be at her side, in the literal sense, every minute. And this prospect, I gather," he smiled slightly, "does not in the least displease Mrs. Bentley."
"She's very much in love with him," Maureen observed thoughtfully.
"And I—no matter!" said Alvarez, and seemed to wince. Again he became grim. "Collier, when I searched him this morning, was not armed. He will be armed now. But so will Bill. And God help Collier if he tries gunplay. Bill, whether you have heard it or not, is the best pistol shot in Tangier."
"Do you know," said Maureen, "that's the first time—

well, perhaps except for myself—I've ever heard you call anybody by his or her first name?"

"I like Bill," Alvarez said simply. "Up to now," he glanced at Maureen quickly, and looked away again, "he is the one person with whom I could be natural. To whom I could talk, pour out my doubtless mad ideas, with the certain knowledge I should not be mocked or laughed at. I understand the English. The Americans"—again that fierce gaze rested on Maureen—"I am not so sure I understand."

"But why am I hard to understand?" cried Maureen. "There are thousands of girls just like me. I . . . I only . . ."

Alvarez leaned across the table, and with both hands seized hers in that paralyzing grip. Then he turned back, and once more changed the subject.

"As for Bill—" Alvarez stopped, puzzled. "You have met him?"

"Who? Oh! Oh, yes. He was up on the terrace late yesterday afternoon. Easygoing, rather slow-moving boy in a long raincoat and an absurd conical straw hat, to keep the evil-minded engine of his car from spitting oil at him even after it died." Here Maureen laughed loudly, from sheer strained nerves. "He talked about wanting to join the detectives, or something."

"Well, he has had his wish," agreed Alvarez, and brooded. His tone grew light, almost joking. "I myself, of course, shall stalk them everywhere in my role of private detective. Should it come to fighting with fists . . ."

"Can't Bill handle that?"

"In my opinion, he could slaughter Collier in one round. Yes; say three minutes. Bill is as fast inside the ring as he is slow outside it. He is careless with his guard. But he has a death in his left hand and pure high explosive in his right."

Maureen wanted to give him a lecture, a real old-fashioned lecture from her home town of Bradshaw, near Boston. *He not understand her?* When she could not in the least follow his own bewildering changes of mood? Yet, in Maureen's mind, there rose the large, candle-coloured, murderous face of red-haired Collier; and again apprehension drove out anger.

"Then why—why?—must *you* get into more trouble?"

"Because, as I told you, I have a score to settle. I would give a hundred thousand pounds—and I mean that, little one—to face Collier for one minute. Three, I think, would not be necessary."

Alvarez meditated.

"Confound it, little one! It should be fairly simple matter to protect Mrs. Bentley, if they are careful. The New Quarter, with such a guard, should be safe by day; and perhaps safe even by night. But never must she go into the Old Quarter, day or night. In the Kasbah there are too many nooks and holes and corners where a knife may strike. He promised to cut her throat, you remember. No, they would never let her go there! Unless—"

"Unless what?"

Maureen was alert. Though she had never seen the Kasbah, her imagination pictured it by night with tolerable accuracy: high-built, a maze, muddy underfoot, half-brawling and half-asleep, narrowness, high white walls blue under a blue-black sky.

"Unless," answered Alvarez, "Colonel Duroc received precise information as to where Collier had gone to earth. Then they might send Mrs. Bentley as bait."

"But they wouldn't dream of doing that, surely?"

"What other course would they have? I do not know."

"Oh, it's impossible! Colonel Duroc wouldn't! Anyway, Bill Bentley wouldn't allow it, that's all! And Paula simply wouldn't go; she's brave, but she isn't an idiot. It's ridiculous!"

Maureen, in the midst of pictured horrors which were to come all too true, now saw Alvarez in the most unusual mood of all.

Mirth, beginning in his lean stomach and shaking from his ribs up to his shoulders and then into tears of joy, threatened to whoop out.

"Oh, Juan, please behave yourself! What's wrong now?"

"Little one," quavered Alvarez, shaking worse, "I have not told you all. This crafty villain, Sir Henry Merrivale . . ."

"Sir Henry! I didn't think to look in his room when I went back to the house. Good heavens, he isn't *still* asleep?"

"No. N-no-no. The wily Ulysses, I say, was not even asleep when you and the Colonel saw him. When you both departed, he arose fully dressed. He followed you in a—" He broke off, overcome with laughter.

"Juan! Stop it! It's not funny!"

"I beg your p-pardon." blurted Alvarez, who yesterday had admitted he possessed a very primitive sense of humour.

He steadied himself. "He departed in a conveyance which he had persuaded Colonel Duroc to be flown by specially chartered plane from Lisbon this morning. All this morning, and part of this afternoon, he has been on what I can only describe as the razzle-dazzle all over Tangier."

"But how do you know all this? Have you seen him?"

"No, But he phoned my office when I was there, inquiring as to whether I was having a good time. I fear, little one, my reply blistered the wires. He requested me to tell him all about what had happened in the room with the crimson blinds."

"You—you didn't tell him to go jump in the lake?"

"On the contrary," replied Alvarez, whose shoulders had begun to shake again, "I told him the story in detail. Saying he was at a carpet dealer's in the Kasbah and must hurry, he asked me to repeat it all over again. Well, I did."

"But what else happened?"

"I don't know. I gathered he later visited the Colonel's office in state, with somewhat chaotic results. Being no longer Commandant," Alvarez lifted his shoulders, "I did not attend. But I hear that Sir Henry issued a long explanation, followed by the sounds of Colonel Duroc smashing furniture."

"We've got to find him!" persisted Maureen, as though H.M. were the wanted Collier. "Where is he now?"

"I have not the slightest . . ." Casually Alvarez turned his head to the right, and looked a little way up the very narrow thoroughfare winding down into the Little Socco. Then he sat as though paralyzed. His eyes, after growing wider and wider, were filled with tears of ecstasy as he turned away.

"Oh, *brulez-moi!*" he whispered.

Maureen looked wildly to the right, and at first saw nothing. True, the Little Socco was strangely quiet except for low, deep murmurs of respect and humility. Each head in a red tarboosh, each head in hooded *jalebah,* each bare head or head in the modern hat of a pious Moslem, bent a little in awe. Decent-minded visitors always follow the custom of the country; Maureen could see the smartly dressed French girl, a Danish sailor, and a young American with a camera slung round his neck on leather straps, all move with the sons of Islam as the latter pressed back against walls on either side, offering open passage to something which slowly approached down the little street.

It was a sedan chair.

Alvarez could have told her it was a Spanish sedan chair, late eighteenth century, broad and strong with heavy shafts, notable for its outside tapestry work and gold nail heads; and that it came from the collection in the Museum at Lisbon.

Now it was borne by four brawny Arabs, two in the shafts in front and two in the shafts at the back, their faces rapt with holiness and their bare feet slapping the dust at a snail's walk. Maureen caught a glimpse of the holy man in the sedan chair; and, for a brief instant, there still seemed nothing wrong.

The passenger was an ancient, venerable, barrel-shaped patriarch. On his head, somewhat rakishly, he wore the green tarboosh, which is the symbol of the pilgrimage to Mecca. His large brown face was lordly, yet deeply sad as with long meditation on the world. Under his nose was a spreading white moustache, though insignificant compared with the broad white beard which rippled down over his thick robe of subdued yet rich colour.

"Juan!" said Maureen. "But that . . ."

Her second glance had shown that the patriarch wore large shellrimmed spectacles. From one corner of his mouth projected upwards, at a forty-five-degree angle, a long black cigar which he was smoking with relish.

"Excuse me sir!" called out a voice at a distance.

As the patriarch's equipage neared the entrance to the Little Socco, the young American could no longer restrain himself. Slipping the camera out of its case, he moved a little out and sighted for a picture.

To this move the patriarch did not seem to have any objection. On the contrary. Into his venerable white beard, and in a deep guttural voice, he muttered some word which made the bearers of the sedan chair instantly stop.

Putting his left fist on his hip like Victor Hugo, the patriarch glared out into nothingness with a stern, stuffed look. The camera shutter clicked. The young American quickly moved back.

"Thanks a lot, sir," he called over his shoulder.

The patriarch waved one hand in a majestic gesture.

"Not a bit, son," he intoned.

The American leaped at least two feet into the air, whirling round to see who could have performed this feat of ventriloquism. All the brown faces were grave and stern.

"Juan," pleaded Maureen, "he'll get into trouble. You know he will!"

"My dear, from the beginning of his life he has never been out of trouble."

"But suppose they find out he isn't what he seems? I mean . . . a holy man from Mecca?"

"If you will look across the street, Maureen, you will see a peddler with a tray trying to sell red tarbooshes to a tourist at a hundred pesetas each. The sons of Islam are proud that any man should wear their emblem. Still, the green one . . ." Alvarez's eyes narrowed, and he stood up. "You may be right. Follow me."

Feeling like one who clutches at the coattail of a comet, Maureen hurried after him as he strode forward, shoulders back. Uniform or not, all in the Little Socco recognized the terrible Commandant, who, they believed, had no human feeling at all. A deep growl ran among the packed lines.

Alvarez, who had never carried a gun and refused to carry one, paid no attention. He approached the sedan chair of Sir Henry Merrivale—whose identity can no longer by concealed. Making a bow of deference, Alvarez spoke for a few seconds in Arabic. His clear, respectful voice changed the growls to deep hums and cluckings of approval.

"What did you say?" whispered Maureen, clutching at his shoulder.

"I said," muttered Alvarez, without opening his mouth, "that the holy man for his own safety must not travel in a place so crowded, lest he receive injury."

Yet Alvarez could not help admiring the old reprobate's ingenuity. H.M. had found the one way to move about in Tangier without being shoved or jostled or murdered by a car. He bent forward.

"Do I not speak truth, O venerable student?" Juan asked in Arabic.

The venerable student, head down, looked up at him—from under large white adhesive eyebrows—with a glare of pure evil.

"Ik moogle ik," the holy man intoned into his beard. *"Hi-ho-kafoozalum.* Lemme alone, can't you?"

Alvarez raised his head and his voice.

"The venerable one has spoken," he said. "The venerable one has a little torn place in his robe, which he wishes to be mended by a tailor, even a infidel tailor." Alvarez improvised. "Let this conveyance," he commanded, "be turned round the other way."

The very solemn-faced bearers (Arabs are natural actors) instantly whipped the sedan chair completely round, so that the rear bearers now faced the front. In their haste it was done somewhat clumsily, the sedan chair swaying so dangerously that its occupant would have been shot out in front if his great bulk had not kept him pressed in. From the sedan chair issued vile obscenities, and puffs of smoke suggesting it was on fire.

"Forward!" said Alvarez.

While the crowd pressed back or flowed away, the procession marched back up the same narrow street. Alvarez knew every shop in Tangier, including what went on behind it or above it, legal or illegal. His eye watched the right-hand side of the shop fronts, and he called a halt about thirty paces up.

"Here," he said to the bearers in Arabic. Moving round to the front, he made a gesture indicating that H.M. should get out.

"Be pleased to descend, O patriarch. We are here. . . . Let the conveyance await us outside."

The patriarch, who understood the gesture if not the words, yanked himself loose from the seat, and moved out in stern dignity between the shafts. His robe, a really fine one of some thick material lined with silk, was a wine-dark red with trimmings of white and silver at breast and sleeves, the gentleness of its slope concealing much of his corporation and covered by the beard stretching below his waist.

Emerging from the shafts, he glanced evilly at the rather large shop front. As always in this quarter, it was also dingy and bore the enamel letters, "René Taupin: English Tailor." Below it explained in French, "Formerly of High-Life Tailors, Paris."

H.M., still quivering with wrath, raised his hand in blessing to anyone in sight, and pushed open the door.

"After you, little one," Alvarez said to Maureen, and followed her.

The premises of M. René Taupin were gloomy but fairly spacious. Out at the visitors blew every thick fragrance of the old clothes man. A very long row of suits hung on the right, jackets and topcoats on the left, and down the centre ran tables of shirts and socks of such insufferably loud colours that H.M.'s eyes began to gleam. Nevertheless he carried himself forward some paces, and then swung round in all his pride. Now he glared at Alvarez from under the adhesive eyebrows, and clutched at a handful of beard, as he dropped his cigar on the floor and trod it out.

"What's the game, hey?" he thundered. "Why do I get scooped off the Little Socco like a Jermyn Street tart? Lord love a duck, I ought to get a medal for the work I've done today!"

Alvarez was at his most formal.

"I deeply regret it, Sir Henry. But it is best that you do not wear that green tarboosh in public, or even the disguise in general."

H.M. reached up one finger behind his skull and tilted the green tarboosh forward on his head, leaving exposed a bald patch unstained by the walnut juice on his face.

"What's the matter with this tile?" he asked hotly. "I got it through co-operatin' with that fine gal Luisa Bonomi."

"Sir Henry!" said Maureen. "You haven't – I mean, you aren't making passes at some dreadful woman *already?"*

The Ancient One's martyrdom returned.

"Y'see?" he demanded, pointing to Maureen. "What low minds people can have? And me a holy man at that? No! I am absolutely . . ."

" 'Luisa . . .' " Alvarcz whistled. "Come, I remember now. 'Luisa Bonomi: Masks and Costumes.' That is the costumier's next door to the jeweller's firm of Bernstein et Cie., in the rue du Statut."

"Got it!" agreed the patriarch, almost complacent again as he stroked his white moustache and mighty beard. "See thesc whiskers? It's real human hair. No flimmery-flummery of hookin' it round the ears, either. You gum each single hair to the chin first, and build it up until you attach it to the real thing. Son, there hasn't been a beard like this since Moses."

"But why?" insisted Maureen. "I mean, why must you put on these awful clothes?"

"'Cause I'm disguised!" gritted H.M., as though it were the simplest explanation in the world. "And is it a good disguise? Looky here! . . . I told you," he went on with a leer, "I've been all over this place. I've visited shops and – hem – other places in the Kasbah. I went through the fish market.

I've visited the British Consulate . . ."

"You haven't!" cried Maureen. "Not as a holy man, surely?"

"Well . . . now," admitted H.M., with another darkly sinister look. "Maybe not. But I used to play golf with old Hack Jefferson, who's consul here now, and I wanted to have a good crack with him."

"Crack?" repeated Maureen.

"Oh, my wench! Talk! Conversation! Swingin' the lead!"

"All right! I only . . ."

"I also had 'em row me out in the harbour . . ."

"What on earth for?"

"Never you mind what for," said H.M., again tilting forward his green tarboosh like a noble Arab mobster, and leaning one hand on the table of shirts beside him. "But they didn't twig me once. S'posin' I don't speak Arabic except swear words? I'm holy man, ain't I? I'm practicing French and English so I can preach to the unbelievin' monsters at Brighton or Dieppe."

Here H.M. stood up straight. His eyes narrowed. The whole atmosphere of the gloomy tailor's shop seemed to alter.

"At least," he growled, "I don't think they spotted me at that carpet dealer's in the Kasbah. That's where I bought this robe. Lots of other things to buy, too. Snaky little feller—" H.M. absent-mindedly extended his hand to the improbable height of four feet—"with his front teeth stickin' straight out ahead. Rummy voice, too. Between what you might call a bat's squeak and then lower down to a purr. Bat's squeak: 'In Tangier one may buy all things,' down to purr: 'at a price.' Uh-huh. I sort of tested him."

Maureen and Alvarez exchanged glances.

Whether or not Alvarez felt it, Maureen became still more conscious of the dingy premises amid a thick air of old clothes, the row of suits topped by a high and ghostly conference of hats. She could have sworn she heard somewhere noises all but inaudible—whispers, murmurs, movement—whose source she could not identify.

"Finally," thundered H.M., with such a change of mood that she dragged back her thoughts, "I did just exactly what I promised to do."

"And what was that, Sir Henry?" asked Alvarez with formal politeness.

"I went to Colonel Duroc's office, son," said H.M., "and I told him everything. I explained how Iron Chest vanished out of a street in Brussels. I explained how the blighter brought his burglar's kit and his iron box invisibly through the customs shed here. I explained how twice, once in Paris and once here, a table-full of diamonds and the same iron chest vanished. When the Colonel saw how simple it all was, he sat and looked at me for about thirty seconds. Then he began to smash the furniture."

Slowly and dismally H.M. shook his head, the great beard wagging below his waist. "And, oh, my eye!" he groaned. "How simple it all is!"

CHAPTER ELEVEN

"Simple, you say?" inquired Alvarez in his most polite, repressed voice.

"Uh-huh."

"For three hours this morning," said Alvarez, "Miss Holmes, Mrs. Bentley, and I—to say nothing of Colonel Duroc or his men—went through pure hell, because we could not find the objects you mention. Sir, if I use the tortures of the Inquisition, I will discover the truth now."

Behind him, someone coughed discreetly but with significance.

Alvarez, swinging round, found that M. René Taupin, the proprietor, had been patiently waiting. M. Taupin, a lean and cadaverous Frenchman whose black hair extended in cropped side whiskers to the jaw, wore a tape measure round his neck. He had given a start when he heard H.M. speak; no more.

"Monsieur the tailor," continued Alvarez in French, so courteously that M. Taupin bowed, "we are in need of assistance. That gentleman there," he nodded towards H.M., "is in fact a milor' English, who has assumed disguise for a joke."

"Ah, that!" breathed the tailor, enlightened and brightening visibly.

"Exactly. Now his robe . . ."

There was a heavy sound as H.M. put down his foot, both literally and metaphorically.

"Any howlin' baboon who tries to take this robe, or the whiskers either," he glared, "is goin' to get a fight that'll wreck the whole ruddy street. Got that, son?"

Alvarez made a gesture of despair.

"But the green tarboosh must go, Sir Henry. Also the brown paint off your face."

"We-el . . ." half-conceded the great man, to whom the

tarboosh was awkward because he could not fashion it firmly to his big skull. Turning a little way, he caught a glimpse of himself in the embrasure of a full-length mirror, and was pleased. Then inspiration caught him, and turned him round.

"A top hat!" breathed H.M. in French. "Is it that you have a top hat?"

M. Taupin, picturing the hideousness of this, shuddered.

"The milor' English," he promised, "shall have a hat. And a hat," he added like French grammar, "which fits him. Excuse me a little moment."

Hurrying away round the left-hand side of the line of tables, he pushed forward a rolling stepladder to climb up past the line of suits to the long shelf of hats above. Across a table of shirts Alvarez faced Sir Henry Merrivale, who had backed into the mirror embrasure.

"Now, if you please," Alvarez continued, "let us have an explanation at least of how the diamonds and iron chest vanished from the sealed flat this morning."

A mulish expression overspread H.M.'s face.

"I'm not goin' to do it," he said.

Maureen, on the same side of the tables as H.M., peered round at him surrounded by many lofty images of himself.

"Oh, Juan, he's impossible!" she said. "Just when you think he's going to be nice again . . ."

But she was cut short by Alvarez's very slight gesture.

"Sir, can you give one good reason why you cannot speak? This mysteriousness of yours—yes, I have read of it before!—may seriously hamper us . . . that is, the police."

"Oh, no, you don't!" retorted H.M. "I've gone straight to Colonel Duroc, and told him everything I know. Bang! I've cut the ruddy ground from under the people who say I'm always leerin' over a crystal ball. What more do you want?"

Alvarez gave a slight, rueful smile.

"But you do not wish me to have the information. Well! I cannot blame you; it is fair enough."

Abruptly H.M.'s attitude changed. He was glaring down at the floor. But Maureen saw that under the wine-red robe the old man was writhing with embarrassment.

Now looky here—" he began in far too loud a voice, and stopped. Then, much as he hated it, the embarrassment showed. "Y'know, son," the big voice almost pleaded, "Colonel Duroc really is a very fine feller."

"I have never doubted it, Sir Henry."

"What I mean," persisted H.M., seizing his beard. "he sometimes goes off the deep end, over a matter of discipline or maybe diplomatic duty. Now he's no more fond of red Russians than you or I or any sane person. But you go off the deep end too."

"I am also aware of that, sir."

"Now looky here!" sputtered the patriarch, with an air of one offering a fair business proposition. "Duroc's as depressed about that resignation business as I bet you are. Why don't you go and see him, son? Tell him you were a trifle hasty, that's all. He'll slap you on the back, and pour a magnum of champagne down your gullet, and tell you to tear up that ruddy resignation for good. It'll be doing a favour for both of you, honest."

"Sir Henry," answered Alvarez, and swallowed hard, "it was all my fault. How many times must I acknowledge it?"

"I dunno, son. You did a very shrewd bit of detective work in that flat."

"Thank the lord *somebody's* admitted it!" cried Maureen.

Slim and straight in her white silk frock, Maureen faced Alvarez with her green eyes shining and her chin up. Yet Alvarez hardly appeared to notice her, and Maureen suppressed a groan at the expression on his face. She could almost read his mind.

"Sir, I will not apologize," said Alvarez. He lifted one hand to shade his badly puzzled eyes. "Don't ask me why, because I do not know. I—I don't understand. But I cannot and I will not apologize."

H.M. eyed him steadily. "Conquistador," he said.

"I beg your pardon?" Alvarez straightened up.

"Nothing, son," H.M's big voice was soothing. "Nothing at all. I was only cogitatin'."

"And even if it were not for that," persisted Alvarez, "there is another matter which—" for the twentieth of a second his eye flickered towards Maureen, then back to H.M.—"which—well, I have no hope at all and I should not have mentioned it. Forget it, please."

Maureen knew intuitively what he had started to say. She knew Alvarez was in love with her. Then she sensed, sickeningly, that she was not even in his thoughts as he faced Sir Henry Merrivale across the table.

"Sir," said Alvarez, "I will make you a sporting proposition."

"You will, hey?" demanded the patriarch, and stuck out his neck.

"Yes. I am still maddened about the disappearance of the diamonds and the chest from that flat. Possibilities I might have overlooked. You won't tell me about it . . ."

"Easy, son!" growled H.M., again embarrassed. "I couldn't tell you, burn me, because the Colonel made me promise not to. He said you ought to have worked it out for yourself."

"The Colonel again? Indeed. Could *he* work it out for himself?"

"Well . . . no."

"Then hear my proposition. I will admit to the Colonel's face that my whole behaviour was wrong—though no apology, under any circumstances whatever—if you will answer questions about the vanishing of the diamonds and the iron chest. Furthermore, sir, you will answer without any misdirection or—or jiggery-pokery?"

"Jiggery-pokery? *Me?*"

"I have heard much," Alvarez said courteously. "of Chief Inspector Masters."

"That crawlin' snake? Oh, son! He couldn't tell the truth if . . ."

"On your word of honour, sir, will you answer with fair play?"

H.M. still studied him, his eyes glaring yet somehow not unsympathetic under the adhesive eyebrows, while he stroked his beard in meditation.

"All right, fair enough!" he said.

"Good!" retorted Alvarez.

The former Commandant was leaning against the long side of the table, resting his weight with both hands on a pile of shirts. Alvarez's mind seemed far away; he had no idea of what he was doing. Vaguely conscious that some discomfort was under his hands, he thrust the obstacle out of his way. The shirts toppled and slid, one by one, to the floor.

"First question!" breathed Alvarez.

"Drive on!" said H.M., giving a sinister twist to each side of his moustache.

"I have been haunted by this. Was there some hiding place we overlooked? Perhaps a cavity in the walls or floor or ceiling, undetectably concealed?"

"No," said H.M.

"Do you make that statement without reserve? They were not hidden in any place we *did* search? Furniture, or the like. They were not hidden in any place we searched?"

"No, son, they weren't." Here the fervent patriarch crossed his heart and lifted his right hand. "No hokey-pokey, either! I'll tell you if you're getting warm."

"Not hidden in any secret place we did not discover," muttered Alvarez, "yet not hidden in any place we did search."

"That's right, son," agreed H.M., though he seemed disturbed about something. "But you're warm. You're gettin' warm!"

Alvarez, in spirit, was again pacing and peering up and down that flat with the crimson blinds. It may be accounted as doubtful whether he even heard H.M.'s last speech.

"Then there is only one thing left!" cried Alvarez, slapping the table in triumph.

"You think so, hey?" leered H.M., leaning forward on the remaining pile of shirts.

Atop the stepladder, M. René Taupin turned deadly pale.

But either the politeness of his nation, or the more practical politeness to a customer, held him silent. With shaking hands he explored a high edifice of hats which must be handled with care lest they fall.

Maureen, who could see nothing amusing in this (who can, when it happens?), did her desperate best.

"All goes well, Monsieur the tailor," she called in French. "They are children. They only talk."

"Then I repeat," snapped Alvarez, his unblinking gaze on H.M., "there is only one other possibility. The windows were locked and watched. The door was watched. Yet . . . yet there was much confusion."

"Uh-huh. Well?"

"This man Collier, this red-headed swine, in some fashion spirited these objects out of the flat."

"No," said H.M. "Colder, colder, much colder!" He made mesmeric passes with his brown hands. "Come back, now, come back!"

"But any other course is in the realm of madness!"

"Oh, my son! Lemme lead you. All the stuff you're talkin' about was in the flat when you searched it, and was still there when you'd finished."

"What?" cried Alvarez.

"Honest Injun, son," the Old Man pleaded, "I'm trying to tell you the strict, literal truth. But there's . . . burn it, there's shades of different meanings in words. For instance, you keep talking about these things being 'hidden.' "

"Yes, yes, yes?"

"Well! In a sense, yes, they were hidden. But not in the way you mean; not a bit in the way you mean. In another sense, they weren't hidden at all. They were smack in front of your eyes the whole time. But you couldn't see 'em."

"Do you tell me," said Alvarez in a strangled voice, "that these things were invisible?"

"As good as invisible, yes."

Extending a long forefinger, Alvarez pointed it across the table at H.M.'s nose.

"This is hokey-pokey," he declared.

"It ain't, son! I swear it ain't!"

"This is hokey-pokey," Alvarez repeated slowly, and pushed his forefinger within an inch of H.M.'s nose.

"No!" cried Maureen.

The crafty patriarch, instinctively lumbering backward, almost stumbled over two well-filled fire buckets which M. Taupin kept more or less out of sight beside the mirror embrasure.

"Another question," gasped Alvarez, "if this be not hokey-pokey! Are the diamonds and the chest still in that room?"

"No, I don't think so. Y'see . . ."

Through their words clove an agonized voice in French.

"Milor' English! Monsieur the Commandant! Is this seemly, I ask you? Is it of the grand politeness?"

Alvarez, only hazily conscious that the tailor had said something, was anxious to brush it away.

"Monsieur the tailor," he murmured, blandly but firmly, "I am sure you are a man of understanding. We speak of serious matters. Be good enough to remain silent!"

The high stepladder was behind Alvarez. Without taking his eyes from H.M.'s malevolent ones, he reached behind him and gave the stepladder what he sincerely believed to be a gentle admonitory shake.

Unfortunately, it was not so. M. René Taupin, choking back a scream, rocked wildly on his perch. Maureen Holmes ran round the other side of the tables to steady him. M.

Taupin steadied himself by clutching the wooden ledge above the rack of suits. But, in doing so, he disturbed the towering edifice above. And down on his head poured the avalanche of hats.

There were soft felt hats, hard felt hats, many bowler hats, straw hats, conical straw hats, top hats, caps in profusion, tarbooshes, all hats of east or west. Indeed, it may be said that one side of the shop momentarily disappeared under a deluge of hats.

They made little sound in landing on the floor, save for skittish bowlers bouncing on thin brims. But light straw hats took flight like birds.

"By George, I've got it!" said Alvarez, and again smote the table with his fist. "I think I've got it!"

"Drive on, son!"

Alvarez's red-brown eyes, now luminous with inspiration, were so locked against the awful gaze of H.M. that neither man was conscious of the descended hats.

"You say that these articles were in the flat," said the hypnotized Alvarez, "yet are not now in the flat. Now a question! Are they still in the same block of flats—the same building?"

"Yes!" thundered H.M. "Son, you're getting hotter than blazes! Now a little step more, in logical reasoning . . ."

"Good God!" said Alvarez. "When I myself observed . . . never mind."

H.M. seemed malignant yet whistling, like an old-time photographer holding up the dicky bird beside a camera.

"If they're not in Flat 3-B," prodded H.M., "where else are they practically bound to be? Hey?"

Alvarez whipped out a notebook, uncapped a fountain pen, and scribbled something on the pad. Returning pen and notebook to his pocket, he handed the slip to H.M. The latter took one glance at it, and tore the slip into many pieces.

"Got it!" roared H.M. triumphantly. "Bull's-eye!"

"Then it's what I've been saying all along. This swine Collier *is* Iron Chest!"

"No!" said H.M. "Get that notion out of your onion, son. I haven't got time to explain now; but since this afternoon the Colonel's had a lot more information about Collier, and there were some things you didn't know before. Mind! Collier's dangerous . . . here! Why that rummy look on your dial?"

" 'Collier's dangerous,' " quoted Alvarez. "I will keep my thoughts to myself, Sir Henry."

"Anyway," retorted H.M., after peering at him over the big spectacles, "Collier's a smart aleck. He's got no brains. He could no more have devised that vanishing trick than he could have written *Hamlet*. The real Iron Chest showed him how, d'ye see? And let him try it twice."

"But what will happen now?"

H.M., tilting the green tarboosh to the other side, scratched the side of his brown head.

"I prophesied last night, though you weren't there . . ."

"To my deep regret, Sir Henry," said Alvarez with a face of agony, "I was as tight as a tick."

"We-el! Who isn't, generally speaking? But what I mean—I said Iron Chest, the real Iron Chest and not your bunglin' Collier, would make a raid tonight on those same premises of Bernstein and Company."

"And will he?"

"No, son." H.M. sighed gustily. "That's washed out. 'Cause why? 'Cause Iron Chest has got a fortune in diamonds—well, you know where—at that block of flats. He's *got* to snaffle 'em tonight, in case we tumble to the trick. He thinks we haven't; but we have. Colonel Duroc will be there, with enough men. But if Iron Chest squirms through the net—" He paused.

"And Collier, sir?" asked Alvarez, with another wide and murderous smile.

"Collier!" grunted H.M. He was uneasy. "Yes, Collier's loose. But I think I can guess . . ."

Abruptly, perhaps because Maureen was speaking, H.M. woke up from his mental trance and really looked round him. So, to a certain extent, did Alvarez. H.M. blinked with astonishment at the opposite floor covered with hats, hats decorating the tables, hats rolled under the tables almost to his feet.

"Well, lord love a duck!" he said.

Across the shop Maureen stood halfway up the stepladder, her arms extended over her head in pleading like a white angel in a Victorian painting. On the top step of the ladder M. René Taupin—his face corpse-white, his eyes set in horrible glassy fixity—sat and gibbered without speech.

"What's that feller trying to do?" demanded H.M., and

sternly pointed a finger at him. "Chucking hats about! Cor! If you want to display hats, why don't you bring 'em out one at a time? And not chuck 'em about like a popcorn machine?" He looked at Alvarez. "Is he loopy, do you think?"

M. Taupin understood some little English. A spasm went through him.

"I have never found him so," replied Alvarez, taking a few steps backwards and sideways to look up. Unconsciously he trod on three or four hats, with a loud crunching noise of brims which sent a last spasm through the tailor.

"Ah, now, enough, then!" screamed M. Taupin in French. He leaped to stand up on the ladder, nearly banging his head against the ceiling. "This goes too far! It is finished!"

In one hand M. Taupin held a Napoleonic cavalry helmet, heavy metal with plumes. In the other hand M. Taupin held an old-fashioned bowler hat with a heavy, curly brim.

"Regard!" he hissed, making a sibilant of the *r.* And down went the heavy cavalry helmet towards the head of Former Commandant Alvarez.

Only Alvarez's cat-footed quickness saved him. He darted back, amid a further crunching of hat brims, as the helmet crashed on the floor. M. Taupin's good right hand tightened on the brim of the bowler hat.

"And now!" he said with drama.

The mad tailor (or hatter, if you prefer) was no whit madder than Sir Henry Merrivale. You would have sworn that his face was not brown but purple, and that it distended. His eyes bulged behind the big spectacles as he looked upwards.

"And it is I, eh," cried M. Taupin, "who am a candidate for the mental hospital? Villain, assassin, I give you the lie!"

Any public-spirited person, who has secretly longed to snatch the bowler hat from the head of a friend and send it skimming, will discover that the brim fits finely to the hand; and, with sharp twist of wrist and arm, remarkable accuracy is possible.

This knowledge must have been born in M. Taupin. The bowler hat whizzed and curved down across the room. Its hard, heavy brim smote full and true into the lower nose of Sir Henry Merrivale.

"Vive la France!" shouted M. Taupin. *"A bas les rosbifs!"*

But it was his own gesture, flinging up one arm like Marshal Ney, which cost him his balance. Twice he reeled round on top of the ladder, flapping his arms, while Maureen vainly tried to hold the ladder steady. Then M. Taupin fell.

It is not known by what miracle he landed upwards and on his feet. But M. Taupin did, crashing down with both feet on the heavy table in front of H.M. Meanwhile, he had not seen the patriarch, with the quintessence of all evil in his eyes, slip softly to one side and with loving hands take up one of the well-filled water buckets. He did not see H.M. before him as M. Taupin landed with a crash of both feet and stood up straight. But, just as he stood up, H.M. gave him the full contents of the water bucket squarely in the face.

Once more, momentarily, M. Taupin's head and shoulders may be said to have disappeared like the diamonds.

For a brief instant, nobody said anything.

After all, this was the smallest of incidents here. *C'est Tanger, vous savez.*

M. René Taupin stood still upright and motionless, a man now bereft of his reason. Nobody would have believed that one bucket of water could have made anybody so wet. M. Taupin looked like a man who has stood for ten minutes under Niagara Falls. With water smoothing his lank black hair across a streaming and cadaverous face, he would have made admirable statue of a Barbary pirate in some public fountain.

"Not bad, eh?" remarked H.M, with satisfaction. Gravely he handed the empty bucket across the table to Alvarez, who absent-mindedly took it and put it down beside the stepladder. "Of course," mused H.M. "I could have done better with a fire hose. But you can't expect everything, now can you?"

And then, from the back of the gloomy shop, a woman screamed.

It must hastily be stated that this was not a scream of fright, of fear, or of any emotion usual in a sensational chronicle. It was the parakeet scream of a woman, perhaps hyper-thyroid, who underlines the faintest emotion with noise as she underlines words in a letter.

But it shocked Juan Alvarez completely into his wits; he was once more alert, dominating them all.

"M. Taupin!" he said in a low, sharp voice, yanking so hard at the Frenchman's trouserleg that the tailor blinked round.

From his pocket he slipped out two English banknotes, of very large denomination. M. Taupin's eye focussed quickly. Alvarez, folding up the notes, slid them under the contents of the table by his right hand. Though the socks, underwear, and shirts of this table had been well soused by H.M.'s attempt with the fire bucket, the underside of them remained dry.

"It is necessary to be discreet," Alvarez whispered rapidly in French. "Not a word; it is understood?"

Down scrambled M. Taupin, amid his wet-flying locks. Casually abstracting the banknotes, he attempted to move with dignity towards the back of the shop. Then, overcome, he uttered a wild yell and ran. He passed two persons who were mere shadows, a woman and a man, who turned to look at him as he shot past.

"I *thought* I heard voices or something back there," said Maureen in a low voice, remembering her earlier impression as she climbed down the stepladder now.

She followed Alvarez, who was striding towards the front so as to circle round the tables on H.M.'s side. Both of them crushed and stumbled amid hats.

"But what's back there, Juan?" Maureen asked.

"Nothing but a low-to-middle-class French gambling club," smiles Alvarez. "The—er—alleged sophisticates are sometimes here for a good run at chemmy or twenty-one."

They had now rounded the tables, and hurried down an open aisle towards H.M.

"But gambling isn't illegal here, is it?"

"No, little one. But there must be some show of discretion by playing indoors. Otherwise we should have certain people playing at the curb stone, and whacking down piles of notes on the pavement."

Briefly Alvarez paused, looked at Maureen with intense tenderness, and reverently touched her cheek.

"Now as for you, Sir Henry—" he began, swinging back.

"I ain't me," said H.M.

Carefully adjusting his green tarboosh to the proper position, he folded his arms across his beard, set his features to the holy man's look, and backed slowly into the mirror embrasure. Motionless, his eyes closed, H.M. stood there like some special exhibit at Madame Tussaud's.

"But who *are* these people?" whispered Maureen. "I mean, the man and the woman coming towards us."

Alvarez smiled slightly.

"One is the Countess Scherbatsky," he whispered back, "and the other is Mr. Mark Hammond. Mr. Hammond is a very good sort. But the—er—Countess, though she is good-hearted, is the most blatant gossip from here to Algiers. Don't be surprised at anything you hear or see; but take care what you say!"

CHAPTER TWELVE

Ilone, White Russian Countess Scherbatsky, again screamed piercingly. This was because she recognized someone, Alvarez, whom she had not seen in perhaps three days.

Her Hungarian first name of Ilone contrasted with the Russian title. There were other contrasts, too, as Maureen observed when the Countess Scherbatsky hurried forward out of gloom.

Ilone's dresses were always of the eternal Parisian black like the satiny affair she wore now; she ordered them from Paris. Her hat was a black band across rather coarse black hair, the hat continuing in long white feathers horizontally to the rear, rather in the flattened war-bonnet style of a red Indian. Ilone's earrings, unfortunately, were very large and they were also real diamonds. Once she must have been very pretty; and now, despite the suggestion of dew laps, she would have retained attractiveness if it were not for heavy mascara on the lashes of black eyes, and lipstick which came off too easily.

Most persons, offhand, would have called Ilone fat. But she was not. She was merely heavy and thick-bodied. Given the proper training, she should have rowed stroke oar or put the weight against any man. This idea, no doubt, would have horrified her. But, though she would have given her soul to attract all men with a battery of languishing glances and lip movements, Ilone in fact did not have much sex appeal.

Still, she tried. Her money and above all her good nature won her some lovers, whose names she proudly paraded whenever possible.

Now she came rushing down the aisle, and stopped within six paces of Alvarez. Carefully Ilone placed her handbag on the nearest table. Then she threw wide her arms.

"Von, *mon três, três cher!"* she cried, almost always using English with an admixture of French. "It is vun, two veeks since I zee you! Now I zee you! You are here!"

"Your eyesight, madame," bowed Alvarez, "is seldom at fault."

"Ah, Von!"

It was Ilone's custom, when thus affected, to hurl herself against somebody (male or female), to fling her arms round the person's neck, and to plant a lipsticky kiss on both cheeks.

Alvarez was no longer Commandant, with an enforced courtesy. And yet, though he remained punctiliously polite, it is possible that with many things he was fed up. As Ilone rushed forward, he braced his weight as well as tightening his chest and stomach muscles. Ilone cannoned into him, and, to her astonishment, merely bounced back.

"Von!" pouted Ilone like a small girl. She sought support against a table, and straightened her long-feathered hat. "Zat was not nice! Zat was naugh-*ty!* Never, never, vill I again forgive you!"

"I ask your pardon, Countess Scherbatsky. I was a trifle off-balance."

"Never, nevaire vill I forgive!" Ilone stopped. Slowly her dark eyes rolled upwards under mascaraed lashes. Her throaty voice became one of tragedy. "Yes! I forgive you, poor Von. I am R-r-r-ussion! I veep; I laugh! Nobody know vich! *Hélas!* forgive everybody. Zat is my veakness."

Ilone bowed her head, the big diamond earrings trembling. Suddenly she caught sight of Maureen, who was sidling closer and closer to Alvarez. Ilone's head came up. She emitted another tough smaller scream.

"But zis," cried Ilone, whose smile could be attractive when she chose, "zis must be ze sharming American girl vich arrived yesterday in ze arrowplane! Ah, *mon enfant! Que vous êtes chic! Que vous êtes belle!*"

And again Ilone flung wide her arms, ready to pounce.

Maureen, who had taken an intense dislike to her on sight, was also afraid of her for some reason she could not explain. But she need not have worried. Casually Alvarez moved to the side of Ilone Scherbatsky. When he dropped his hand on the back of her neck, no observer could possibly have seen in the gesture anything except one of mild affection.

But Alvarez's long, powerful fingers tightened on the sides of Ilone's neck, and they tightened hard.

"Miss Holmes," he said easily, "may I present you to the

Countess Scherbatsky?"

Now we can well understand why Paula Bentley was not jealous of Ilone as regards Bill. But anyone who took Ilone for a fool would have been badly mistaken. Ilone understood the reason for that deadly pressure on her neck, though she gave no sign of it except a wicked little look on her broad good-natured face. Again she smiled.

"'Ow you do, Miss Holmes?" she inquired, and graciously extended her hand. "Permit me to say again zat I find you sharming."

"Thank you so much," said Maureen, taking the large hand and almost immediately dropping it.

Alvarez's fingers relaxed. Ilone straightened her heavy shoulders and gave another little scream.

"Ah, but I too forget! I have someone vich I must present. Oh, *pauvre moi,* and my handbag!" She turned her head. "Mark, *chéri,* you will bring me my handbag."

The handbag lay all of six inches behind her on the table.

But the man, who had been standing well back, moved forward, gravely caught up the handbag, and just as gravely gave it to Ilone.

"Zis," cried Ilone attempting a dance step, "is Mr. Mark Hammond, my dear. *Grand écrivain américain! Grand"* — here she let her dark eyes roll and languish — *"grand savant de l'amour! Vous avez compris?"*

That woman, Maureen was thinking furiously, wouldn't pick up a coffee cup from one end of a table, and put it down at the other end of the table. She's simply bone-lazy.

This was true, though perhaps not quite fair to Ilone. Having had money for most of her life, Ilone expected service and received it. In Tangier there really is no income tax, no tax of any kind whatever except a twelve-and-a-half per cent duty on anything you import. Thus the most modern American conveniences and cars can be imported wholesale, and, even with that duty, sold at a profit. Ilone, having money, was in paradise.

But this time it was Maureen who impulsively extended her hand to Mark Hammond. She was delighted to meet an American writer of popular science books. He grasped her hand in a way she understood.

"How do you do, Miss Holmes?" said Hammond in homely tones. "I'm afraid I must warn you, though, against both charges Ilone Scherbatsky has made against me. I'm not even a very good writer, and certainly I'm not — the other thing. I wish I were."

"I'm sure you underrate yourself, Mr. Hammond," smiled Maureen.

Hammond smiled back wryly. As Ilone always moved amid a cloud of perfume which had an oddly exciting effect, Mark Hammond moved amid a deep aura of gin. But he was not in the least drunk. Thin, rather fragile looking and stoop-shouldered though of decent height, Hammond was almost bald in his middle thirties. He had a long nose, pale eyes, and the air of one who has known many cities. His clothes were as sombre as those of Alvarez.

"How are you, Commandant?" he asked, shaking hands with pleasure. A satirical look rippled up wrinkles in his forehead. "We've known each other — how long? Two or three years, isn't it? I wonder when you'll break down and call me by my first name?"

Alvarez also laughed.

"It has become some kind of necessity," he admitted in a shamefaced way. "No doubt it would interest the late Dr. Freud. But I cannot do it, Mr. Hammond."

"And yet," remarked Hammond, with the thought of Paula always nagging inside him, "you call Bill Bentley by his first name."

"Bill, yes. He is my closest friend. Perhaps my only friend."

"But he's English, old man; and you're Spanish."

"I am English by naturalization," replied Alvarez, his eyes hardening. He lifted his shoulders. "Perhaps because my instincts are English. I call myself Spanish — well! As you in your country call yourselves Irish or Scottish or Dutch or German, though your grandfathers and greatgrandfathers may have been born on American soil."

Ilone, tugging at the triple tier of pearls round her neck, was furious. She could not bear to be left out of a conversation for one instant. Now she screamed at her loudest, and was noticed.

"Bah!" she said. "Zat Bill Bentley! I hate heem!" She hesitated. "And yet," Ilone let her eyes languish round, conveying an untrue suggestion, "in some vays he is nice. Yes. But he is Anglich, as you zay! He is not *galant!* He is not *amoureux!* He cannot conwey ze you-know-vat even ven he teach you ze peestol shoot!"

"The what?" exclaimed Maureen.

Dramatically, Ilone thrust out a heavy arm.

"Bang, bang, bang, bang bang bang," she said.

For Ilone made two gestures in the matter of sport, which even then were not precisely what the word implies. She would go bathing in the reasonably respectable surf on Tangier beach, dressed in an almost non-existent bathing suit. Though she had not the figure for this, at least she attracted attention. Also, for ulterior motives, long ago she had persuaded Bill Bentley to give her lessons at target practice with a pistol.

Ilone now explained the matter clearly.

"And this Anglichman!" she screamed. *"Bon Dieu!* He say, 'Damn it, vooman, aim at ze bull-eye?' Or, 'It is not necessary, cone-found it, to shoot the man vich change ze target.' Bah! But if it had been a Frenchman . . ." Here Ilone's tone changed, and she sighed dreamily.

"Un français!" she repeated, in a kind of hoarse, shrill murmur. "Always he vould visper ze pretty compliments in your ear; and you g-know you are a vooman, yes? If he must touch your arm to steady ze gun, it is not alone he touch there! No, no! He touch here. And here. And here! And you g-know he vish to . . . do this-and-that, *comprenez?"*

Maureen cast a quick sideways glance at Alvarez.

Whenever he heard a pungent word used in her presence, he had gone pale under his faint swarthiness and looked murder. Maureen's mind seethed with a confusion of a little admiration and much anger. Didn't Juan think she heard ten times worse every day, at the offices of Jones, Howard & Ramsbottham? Or used the same words herself, among her friends?

Furthermore, only a few minutes ago, he had gently touched her cheek with a kind of reverence. This was even worse. It might be all very well, in theory, to be treated like something made of stained glass. But Maureen didn't like it.

"And zis Anglichman's vife!" she heard Ilone crying in disgust.

In any of the better-class bars they would tell you that even the good-natured Ilone hated Paula Bentley because of the latter's good figure, but mainly because the tolerant Paula refused to take her seriously.

The mild-mannered Hammond spoke sharply.

"Take it easy, Ilone!"

"But I say nossing against her," cried Ilone, hurt. She took a few dramatic steps backwards, hand on heart. "No, no, no. . . . *Pauvre* Mark!" Ilone went on, in her small girl's manner. "How he like her! But do I not love everybody? Do I not give parties for everybody?" Again the small girl pouted, her pulpy mouth pressed out. There would have been real tears in her eyes if she could have risked damage to the mascara. "It is true. It is my poor veakness. Of this Paula, poor girl, I say only that she is wulgar. *Wulgar!*" screamed the Countess Scherbatsky.

Taking another step backwards, she swung to her left, came face to face with H.M. in the mirror embrasure, and stood paralyzed.

Over all the patriarch's barrel-shaped figure, not a fold of the wine-dark robe moved to show that he even breathed. His eyes were closed, face smoothed out with meditation or prayer. Nor was there a single twitch of arms folded across beard and corporation.

"And vat is zat?" cried Ilone, pointing with scarlet-nailed forefinger. She backed her broad behind against the table.

Alvarez stepped deftly in front of the embrasure, as though discreetly veiling the Tussaud exhibit.

"This gentleman, madame," he said, "is the Moslem prophet named Hassan-el-Mulik, or Hassan the Leader. He has meditated many years in the desert, and has now come to study the most secret writings of Islam." Alvarez hesitated. "I suggested that he might wish to try modern clothes. Er—I fear he did not like them."

Mark, trying to stifle curiosity for some time, could not be repressed. His long nose and bald head seemed to gleam into the group.

"It's fairly obvious he didn't," agreed Hammond, nodding towards the damp shirts, the wilderness of crushed hats. "In fact, he seems to have wrecked the joint completely. But why all the water?"

Alvarez was not at a loss.

"The fire bucket, as you see, stood near the stepladder. In some fashion M. Taupin fell from the ladder and became entangled with the bucket."

"Entangled! Great Scott, he must have dived head-first into the bucket! However," and Hammond suppressed a chuckle, "it's none of my affair."

But Ilone was not interested in this. Being accustomed to

wreck the joint at every party she attended, she saw nothing interesting in mere confusion.

"Oh, I love zis prophet!" she cried out, clapping her hands. "I tell you! For heem I give a special *keef* party. Vith booze too, of course." Then Ilone beamed at Maureen. "Have you tried ze *keef,* my dear?"

For the first time, the prophet Hassan-el-Mulik stirred in the slightest degree. One eye partly opened, the eye bulging with ghoulish hope and fascination. It closed so quickly that nobody saw it.

"No, Countess Scherbatsky," Alvarez interrupted in a cold voice. "Miss Holmes has not."

Now Ilone smiled playfully at Alvarez. A close observer might have thought she had not—not quite—forgotten the marks on either side of her neck.

"Chéri!" she yearned at him, picking up a string of pearls and nuzzling them between fine white teeth. "About you, I have also forgot! Ve is old friends, yes? Zen I ask you a k-vestion and you shall answer it!"

"What question, madame?"

"Ve-el," mused Ilone. She dropped the pearls from her teeth. The black eyes grew soulful. "I tell you! At vat time tonight, *chéri,* shall your police raid ze block of flats at number 40-bis Marshan?"

Dead silence.

They could hear the crowd slapping and raucously crying in the street. But the mustiness of the gloomy shop seemed to press down more heavily. Nobody moved except Hammond, who glanced angrily at Ilone.

"Where did you get that information, madame?" Alvarez asked quietly.

"Ah, zat? My 'eart . . ."

"I am not interested in your heart, madame, or in any other organ you may or may not possess. *Where did you learn that?"*

Ilone laughed delightedly and unaffectedly. She was proud to parade her own affairs, as well as to administer a small sting at dear Juan.

"You 'ave been in London? Yes, yes, of gourse! I mock myself. The London policemen, vich is called bobbysoxers, are very nice. Zese foreigners say, 'Your policemen, how sveet!' "

"Well, well, well?"

"Why, zen," coquetted Ilone, all archness and coyness, "might zere not be anosser—better, a policeman vich is also an officer, an inspector of police—also sweet? A littul stupeed, perhaps, but handsome! Ah, how he adore me! How he made love! Poor José! Shall I give you a teeny-veeny hint of his last name? *Il est ici à Tanger.* His last name begin with *M.*"

Up to this time Alvarez had no knowledge of what Paula and Bill Bentley already knew.

"Mendoza," whispered Alvarez, and clenched his fists. "Inspector Mendoza!"

"Ah, *quel amant!*"

"Did he tell you what happened today?"

"Ah, bah!" said Ilone, momentarily dropping her dreaminess. "Have I not follow zis affair of Iron Chest from the start? Have I not much, many scrap books all about it?"

"What did he say today?"

Ilone pursed out her lips, and lifted her thick shoulders.

"He told me most of vat has happened inside ze flat at 40-bis Marshan. Ze man G. W. Collier, and you do not find ze beeg chest or ze diamonds. Poor José could not tell all, because he is outside ze door and he cannot catch every word.

Clearly Mendoza had not heard of Alvarez's resignation, or Ilone would have used it as her first taunt.

"Did Inspector Mendoza tell you anything else? About the afternoon—or later?"

"Ah, poor me! Am I arrest? No! Jose told me only, in ze afternoon, he has passed ze door of ze office of Colonel Duroc. Wulgar man; he tell me . . . no matter. In thees office is an enormous fat man, vich is no good because he never draw a sober breat' all ze year. Ze fat rummy, vich is an Anglichman as you might g-know because zey all go zeir club and get drunk and never visper pretty compliment to zeir voomans . . ."

"Never mind that! What did Inspector Mendoza tell you about the afternoon—or later?"

"But I am spikking!" screamed Ilone, and danced heavily on the floor. "Zis dronkard has said zat zere vill be a raid tonight on ze block of flats, because ze things are still zere. Zat is all he heard; zat is all José told me. And he told me"—Ilone used all her body when she swung to point towards the rear of the shop—"not half an hour ago ven he came in to see Mark and me, and left by ze back vay. Zat is all I know. All,

all, all, *all!*"

The piercing voice stopped. Ilone, breathing hard and re-arranging her long-feathered hat, retired into icy dignity.

"Do you mind if I interrupt, Commandant?" asked Mark Hammond, in a stronger, sharper voice.

"Not at all, Mr. Hammond," smiled Alvarez, rather startled. "Can you help us?"

"That depends. Do you want to know anything about G. W. Collier as a boxer?"

I do. Much!"

"Well, I can tell you everything. The point is, I've followed boxing for more years than I like to count."

The change in Hammond was surprising. His pale eyes had emerged as a sharp, penetrating grey. He had straightened up from his stoop-shouldered lounging. Though there was no flush on his face, something of healthy colour tinged it. Maureen Holmes, studying him; felt the reason as palpably as she might have felt the heat of a fire. Very few things in this life had the slightest interest for Mark Hammond. This was one of them.

"Yes, of course!" said Alvarez, snapping his fingers as though in remembrance. "I have seen you often at the gymnasium in the Boulevard Pasteur. But I never saw you with the gloves on."

The intense bitterness in Hammond's eyes faded to his usual amused tolerance."

"Is it likely?" he asked, and spread out his hands. "Bad heart, bad eyesight, since I was a kid? No weight? Arms far too short? No; forget that. But I don't think there are many people who've watched the game as I have. Watched 'em train in gyms, sometimes six months at a stretch; heard every order from the trainer; watched 'em spar, watched 'em work out; watched the champ's training camp and the little back-room athletic clubs; watched . . . Well, I couldn't flatten a stuffed cat, myself. But I know every possible move they make, as I know the moves at chess."

Hammond's strong voice seemed to batter at them. He shook his bald head, and made a short gesture to forestall interruption.

"When I heard Inspector Mendoza mention G. W. Collier as a prize fighter," he went on, "I remembered him because of what the initials 'G.W.' stand for. I hopped over to the phone in that gambling room and called Bob Beacon at the

American Cultural Center. Bob had all the record books. He read out what I wanted to know."

From his inside pocket Hammond drew an envelope. Being too vain to wear glasses, he blinked as he consulted the back of it.

"Can you guess what 'G.W.' stands for?" he asked without amusement. "No, don't say George Washington. It stands for Gregor Weehawken. And you can imagine what a noisy, would-be witty crowd"—Hammond's contempt at the word "crowd" baffles description—"would do with a name like Weehawken? But they'd remember it; that's the point."

"What's his record?" asked Alvarez, flinging aside all the rest.

"Ten years ago," replied Hammond, "he fought for two and a half years as a professional middleweight. His record's not very impressive. He had forty bouts; won twenty, lost eighteen, two draws. *But—*"

Hammond paused in astonishment at Alvarez's broad smile.

"Then the swine," he inquired, "is not all brag and wind? Good! That pleases me. He does know his business, then."

"Yes, and more. I admit he could never box worth two cents. And he's far past his prime now, of course. But he was a slugger, what they like to call a killer. He keeps on wading in, wading in, to land just one punch that will end the fight."

Hammond paused again, and looked Alvarez straight in the eyes.

"Commandant," he said with deep earnestness, "you're good. You're damn good. Your footwork is lightning; you're never off-balance; you can hit from any angle, even going away; you can block or slip or roll with any punch; you' ve got a fair right and a good left. *But* . . ."

"I am an amateur?" suggested Alvarez, with a sudden rasp in his voice. "Whereas Collier is a professional?"

"It's God's truth, all the same. The best amateur couldn't possibly, under any circumstances, stand up to an experienced professional."

"Perhaps you have not considered—"

"Listen, man. The amateur fights short distances; he doesn't know the tiring, paralyzing long distances. His stamina hasn't been fully developed, either to meet that or to meet killer punches. In clinches he's taught to break instantly: he doesn't know in-fighting, or the short body jolts that soften him like a layer cake. I could give you a dozen reasons; but put it down that he can't meet ringcraft and he can't meet heavy punches."

"Thank you very much for your advice, Mr. Hammond." Alvarez also was sincere. "Now, I am afraid, we must turn back to . . ."

"Commandant," Hammond interrupted quietly, "I hate to tell you this. I mean it only as a friendly warning; and I hope you take it that way. Don't try to tangle with Collier. Stay away from him. He'll slaughter you."

There was another bursting kind of pause.

Hammond saw, as Maureen saw, the dark blood rush into Alvarez's face, and the gorged blue veins at this temples. Ilone, strangely fascinated, stood against the table with her mouth pulled square. Slowly the blood receded from Alvarez's face. He spoke curtly but pleasantly.

"Mr. Hammond," he said, "we have a criminal case on our hands. It was my fault; I let you divert me with our talk. First catch our Collier! Will you accept my apology?"

Mark Hammond, with his famous good manners, unconsciously bowed after the Continental style. But all the personality drained out of him. His grey eyes, which could be sharp and penetrating despite his bad sight, seemed lifeless. He sat down, stoop-shouldered, on the table beside Ilone; and he pictured, or so he explained, only a long line of glasses containing gin-and-It.

But Alvarez was in a desperate quandary.

Maureen knew he wanted to give some signal or communicate with H.M. But Alvarez dared not turn his head, even towards the side glass. A signal between himself and the Prophet Hassan-el-Mulik, who was supposed to be in a trance, would be too obvious.

But Maureen herself had a good view of H.M. Her heart beat heavily. Her very pulses seemed to beat in time with those of Alvarez as she saw the idea jump into his eyes.

"Maureen, my dear . . ." he began.

Ilone screeched out in ecstasy.

"You call her your dear?" she cried. *"Encore de l'amour!* Juan, *chéri!* I am surprise! Before zis you vill go vith nobody except voomans of ze street. I . . ."

Alvarez gave her one look. But it was enough momentarily to silence even Ilone Scherbatsky.

"Maureen," he said more loudly, "do you think we ought

to telephone Colonel Duroc at once, and have Inspector Mendoza put out of the way where he can do no more damage for the moment?"

The prophet's head, mainly hidden by Alvarez, gave a faint negative shake as though he stirred in sleep. The tassel of his green tarboosh, which hung straight down in front, twitched outwards left and right as though he would indicate Hammond and Ilone. Maureen was guessing at this; but she guessed correctly.

"No, Juan," she replied in her clear voice. "I don't think Uncle Henry would want us to. At least," and her green eyes moved innocently towards the others, "for a moment."

"Ah, good!" said Alvarez. He looked at Ilone. "As I told Mr. Hammond," he went on briskly, "this is a criminal case, and we have much work to do. Now if you will . . ."

But Ilone was advancing towards him, so emotionally torn that all her jewels rattled, and her hands were clenched.

"'Out of ze vay?' " she gasped, sending back at him his words about Inspector Mendoza. "My José? You do not mean my Jose? You vill not punish him?"

"In the devil's name, madame, what did you expect?"

Ilone uttered a horror-stricken scream.

"Grand Dieu!" she cried, clapping one hand on her heart as she staggered back against the table, and lifting the other hand in the air. "Jose! I have betray him! Zis is *terrib-le!*

Maureen Holmes felt herself go hot and cold with rage. Mark Hammond had already stood up, put the envelope into his pocket, and consulted his watch.

"Come along, Ilone," he said with weary patience. "We were supposed to be at a cocktail party at five o'clock. It's now a quarter to six."

"Vat is cocktails?" hissed Ilone, twitching her head round. At each of the next four words, she stamped her foot so heavily that the shop vibrated. *"I vill not go!"*

"You think not, madame?" inquired Alvarez.

Ordinarily, of course, Ilone would have had to be carried kicking and screaming to the door; she was not the woman to take a subtle hint. But Alvarez merely locked up her right arm and elbow behind her back. It hurt; he meant it to hurt. He marched her to the door without fuss. Ilone, one shivering mass of fury, dared not even speak lest he increase the pressure.

Alvarez opened the door, to the pinging of the overhead

bell.

"Think you can take over now?" he asked, indicating the grip he held on Ilone.

"Oh, yes." With a swift dexterity, surprising in one who deprecated the use of his hands, Hammond caught the grip from Alvarez. But clearly he still brooded on one subject.

"Commandant," said Hammond, "there's only one kind of amateur who could possibly beat Collier in a short fight. That's a pure slugger," Hammond looked thoughtful, but made a grimace without speaking any name, "who'd trade punches like Collier himself, and might land a haymaker. Come along, Ilone!"

Ilone was making cooing noises over the sedan chair, whose bearers still stood patiently to the right of the shop outside its window as you faced it. She was again in a fury as Hammond marched her up the street towards the Grand Socco.

"I am ze Countess Scherbatsky!" was her last audible scream.

Alvarez, in a black mood, went back into the tailor's and slammed the door to the accompaniment of a sharper ping from the bell. He strode down the right-hand side, in the direction of the mirror embrasure. He did not even seem to see Maureen, who was waiting for him with an expression of outraged dignity, and he walked past her.

The question of the phone was solved. Far down on the right, the venerable Hassan-el-Mulik—now transformed into Sir Henry Merrivale because his tarboosh was crushed over one ear—had found the most modern of dial telephones. He was speaking to Colonel Duroc in a low, bass rumble in which no word could be distinguished.

Alvarez swung round again. His face seemed haunted and haggard. He looked at the utter confusion of the shop. Monsieur René Taupin had always been a good fellow. Unobtrusively Alvarez slipped another English banknote out of his pocket and slid it on the cleared table. He paced forward again . . .

"Juan!" called Maureen sharply.

Alvarez stopped, jerking up his head. His eyes partly cleared, and his face brightened.

"Maureen!" he said, and looked puzzled. "Somehow, you know, I thought you'd gone."

Again Maureen had to fight that force which brought

tears to her eyes.

"Did you want me to go?"

"No! No!"

"Then you knew I'd be here, didn't you?" Maureen stopped; she must put away this for the main question. "Tell me! Was it true—what that awful woman said?"

"Er—which particular part of what she said?"

Maureen was taken aback. There could be, of course, only one thing.

"Why, that you never . . . that is, went out except with women of the street, of course!"

"Oh, that? Yes, it's true," he said absently.

Maureen stood speechless, because she did not understand herself. According to all rules she should have been at least a little shocked or annoyed. But she was not annoyed at all. Only if Juan Alvarez had been paying these attentions to so-called nice girls, Maureen suddenly realized, she would have been furious.

But there was no dealing with him in this new mood, in which he seemed concentrated on something else. It was as though his clothes were sewn with needles and razor blades. Maureen would not have dared to touch his arm. There was no sound in the gloomy, eerie shop except H.M.'s low growl at the phone.

Alvarez was standing with his back towards the rack of fusty-smelling suits. They were hung high and heavy on their metal rod. He put his hands on the fairly filled table in front of him, leaned his weight on them, and lowered his head.

"Now," said Maureen, "will you please, *please* listen to me?"

She sensed that within him an emotional storm had burst and was passing.

"Forgive me," grunted Alvarez, without raising his head. "I warned you about my moods. I try my best, but it is never good enough. I am impossible."

"No," said Maureen clearly, from the other side of the table. She was breathing quickly, but she tried to keep her mind from utter confusion. "You're only unhappy. Partly because the world isn't as it used to be. Partly because . . . Why do you go with these women?"

Though he did not raise his head, she saw his jaw muscles tighten. Even when he as most moved, Alvarez's speech remained slightly pedantic.

"Because I will not make love under false pretences," he said. "Better go with a decent harlot than mouth hypocrisies to someone who may be hurt."

He lifted his head, still leaning on the table, and spoke across it to Maureen. Then came the real storm.

"I have never really loved any woman but you," he burst out. "In you there is every trait, save one, which can drive a man to madness." Astonishingly, his expression was dark and bitter. "You are generous; you would have helped me when you thought me poor. You are loyal, as witness Sir Henry. You are intelligent, not stupid. You are romantic-minded, and easily moved to tenderness. *But—*"

Here Alvarez straightened up, with the same bitter look.

"I have seen you before," he said. "Oh, yes! I have seen you, with your pale face and your slender neck and your green eyes and your death-black hair, all aureoled and glowing in a window of the Cathedral at Seville. I have no religion, thank you; and I want none. But I remember that window, with the burning light beyond. You are just as unapproachable. Just as remote. Just as cold."

"Oh!" said Maureen inadequately. But it was only a gasp of amazement and anger.

Though she had seldom spoken of it, and in fact prided herself a little on her reserve, Maureen was very far from being cold. She regarded this accusation as the deadliest of all insults.

"You think I'm cold, do you?" she cried out heatedly. "Well, why don't you kiss me and find out!"

Alvarez looked at her blankly.

"What?"

"D-d-didn't you hear me?"

He put one hand on the table, to vault over it and reach her. His gaze left hers for only a third of a second. But, when he looked up again, Maureen's whole expression had changed. Her large eyes, with tears on the long black lashes, had widened to full extent and they were fixed in a look of horror. She was not even looking at him. She was staring past Alvarez at the rack of suits behind him.

Alvarez spun round to the sound of hangers sliding on metal. He came face to face with Gregor Weehawken Collier.

Collier stood framed in an opening between the two lines of suits, his back to the wall where he had room to move, his hands up somewhere in the hangers. His hair was dyed a heavy black, and he wore a red tarboosh. Otherwise he was dressed the same and looked the same, with his drooping eyelids and his eternal sneer.

It went so fast that nobody had time to think of the simple explanation of how or why he had come there. After that stunned instant, Alvarez plunged for the gap in the suits. Collier's hands, up on the coat hangers, swept together that close-packed mass in his opponent's face. Then Collier's hands shot higher, gripping the metal rod above. It was not one very long rod across the shop, of course. It consisted of a series of comparatively short metal lengths fastened at intervals to bear the weight. Collier showed his own strength of arm and shoulder.

There was from each side a separate *craa-ack,* together with long tearing noises, as Collier ripped the whole rod from its screw supports, and flung the mass of suits outwards and downwards over Alvarez's head.

A fool's trick.

Alvarez, bracing himself, knew he could cleave through that weight and pin Collier flat against the wall. And he would have done it, except for Collier's eternal and never-varying good luck. As Alvarez settled his balance, he trod flat on two slippery hats; and both shot forward under him. He reeled back, completely off balance. He fell heavily on his back, a sick humiliation rising in his stomach, and the whole avalanche of suits pitched out and over his head, smothering him. The tables rattled back with a wooden scraping of legs.

"Wise guy," said the sneering voice of Collier.

Alvarez, still in sick humiliation and fury, fought his way up through what seemed a weight that pressed him down by its mere rolling softness. The time must have been short; he could hear Collier running for the door. There was a faint crash. He could not tell what it was. But Maureen had thrown a light chair at Collier's legs to trip him up. It did not trip him, but it slowed him for a second or two.

Alvarez, springing to his feet, was just in time to hear the bell ping and see the shop door close. He vaulted over the nearest table, reached the door in two strides, flung it open, stepped out—and stopped.

He must not rush out into the crowd, and fall for the old trick by which a fugitive presses himself close against the wall on a side of the door. Alvarez's head twitched to the right, towards the sedan chair. He saw his warning in the eyes of the bearers, one of whom started to point. Alvarez spun to the left, not quite in time.

Down on his head, towards the back, crashed the weight of a weapon which Collier would have called a sap. It was not a clean smash, but that hardly mattered.

Alvarez did not go down. He would not go down. In that moment of too-great rage, you could not have dropped him with half a ton of stones.

His head seemed to him to expand rather than explode. He was conscious of little pain; only a ringing noise in his brain. For an instant he felt his legs weaken, no more. His only trouble was with his eyesight, where images slightly dimmed and blurred. So he whipped round—and again faced Collier, whose back was to the wall and without elbow room to swing the sap.

Alvarez prayed to the God in Whom he did not believe. His right fist drove so hard into Collier's belly that Collier half doubled up, the breath struck from his body with a sound grotesquely like a man retching, yet louder.

Staggering, trying to clear his swimming eyesight, Alvarez steadied himself to throw his left. In vague surprise he saw there was nobody there.

Collier, even disregarding the worst body punch he had ever received, still would not meet him in an honest fight. Collier had slipped behind Alvarez. Even now he managed a high, giggling laugh of mockery. Again the weight of the sap crashed down on Alvarez's head.

CHAPTER THIRTEEN

At half-past seven that evening, Paula Bentley lay back motionless and soaking in a very hot bath. A bathing cap kept her heavy hair from draggling in the water, and her eyes were closed.

The bathroom of their quarters at the Minszeh Hotel was not large. Bill Bentley, in grey flannels and a short-sleeved shirt tucked in at the collar, stood at the wash basin with his back to her, the stand of the wash basin being close at right angles to the foot of the tub.

Bill, his head on one side, was shaving with an electric razor. The razor hummed softly as he twisted his neck. The mirror over the porcelain bowl often clouded with steam from the bath, and Bill patiently wiped it clean. It might have been the cosiest of domestic scenes, a young couple preparing to dress for dinner, except for one thing. . . . Round Bill's left shoulder and side was strapped the yellowish-brown leather of a shoulder holster. In the holster he carried a Webley .45 revolver. That calibre, as the War Office discovered, was the only one which could stop a maddened Jerry grenadier at the charge, and blow him back in his tracks.

Yet neither she nor Bill referred to her danger in the slightest way. They spoke lightly and casually, on all other subjects. The electric razor continued to hum softly in the windowless, steamy bathroom. Then Bill, with a new idea, shut it off.

"Baggage," he said.

"M'm?" Paula spoke drowsily, without opening her eyes.

"Going from great conceptions to small things," said Bill, contemplating the razor, "did I ever tell you my old man first set me up in life . . ."

"Yes, darling." Paula, being a wise wife, did not add, "About a thousand times." She went on, "As an electrical engineer. But you hated that, and tried to study painting. You could do still life, but your figures were dreadful." Paula kept the same drowsy tone. "I'm rather glad of that. If you'd ever had a model, I should have scratched her eyes out."

"Painters don't think like that!" objected Bill, and cleaned the mirror with his arm so that he could see her face to face. He craned his neck up and sideways. "All the same, you give me ideas."

"Do you think *I* don't have them?" inquired Paula, half opening her eyes. "But, darling! This isn't the time or place. Especially considering that . . ."

Since the door of the bathroom was closed and locked, they could not see or hear Colonel Duroc pacing up and down the soft carpet of the bedroom outside. He was waiting for the telephone to ring. So, although they would not admit it, were they.

Paula, settling back, considered her husband's face in the mirror: the broad, easygoing countenance with brown eyes and the absurd army haircut. Sometimes she wondered that his slow-moving careful-studying personality could hide such a quick brain. His wide shoulders, heavy biceps, and narrow waist made him resemble . . . No! That brought her thoughts back to Collier and horror.

Bill was violently aggressive at love-making, which entirely suited Paula. But—without disloyalty, since she loved him to a point of doing—she sometimes wished he were more aggressive in life. She pictured him banging his fist on the table amid a group of bankers, for instance. He had not even been very cross when she had tried to get that flat. Yet . . . No, it brought him into danger, which brought her into a worse state of mind.

Unknown to her, Bill was in a worse state than that. He did not in the least mind danger to himself. Though his face or his voice never betrayed the fact, it may be stated without further comment that, if he ever lost Paula, he would kill himself.

". . . And, in time," she murmured, "you want to retire. But, darling! Not London, please. It has—associations."

Bill shut off the razor and put it away. Hot and cold water rushed into the bowl as he bent to wash.

"All right. As I said last night, anywhere you like."

They slipped gently into one of those familiar husband-

and-wife debates, which can be on any subject, but which usually go on for years.

"And you will write a Book of Great Wits," said Paula. "But it will not include Mr. George Bernard Shaw."

"No, baggage. Definitely not."

"He was a very great playwright, you know."

"Granted. Without a struggle. But his alleged wit consisted of blurting out, like a child, things that everybody knows and everybody decently agrees to conceal."

There was a stir of water as Paula raised her head. She opened her eyes.

Bill, wallowing like a water buffalo, lifted his head from the basin, partly dried his eyes, turned round, and looked at her.

"By the way," he said, "love me?"

"Mmm!"

"That's all right, then." He plunged once more into the basin.

"Bill," said Paula with remote but real interest. "You understand, darling, I don't *mind*. But why can you never even wash your face without hurling about *gallons* of water, and flooding the bathroom?"

"Bl-because I'm having a wash." This point should be made clear to all wives. Bill raised his face and groped blindly for a towel. "I'm not using a tooth glass. I'm not squirting some so-and-so perfume on my dial. I'm washing. This process . . ."

Outside, in the bedroom, they could hear the telephone ring.

For an instant, both of them remained motionless.

Faintly but clearly came Colonel Duroc's voice at the phone: "Allo?"

Bill, with his big hands shaking despite himself, dried his face and flung away the towel. Keeping his back carefully towards Paula, he slipped the Webley .45 out of the holster, opened it as quietly as he could, saw that it was fully loaded in every chamber, softly clicked the barrel back again, and returned it to the holster. He had done this about twenty times already.

There was a whirl and splash of water as Paula sat up straight, tearing off the bathing cap so that her golden hair fell down round her neck. She slipped out of the tub and, not troubling to dry herself, seized from the opposite wall a long-sleeved robe of heavy towel material, which she wrapped around her. She tied the belt, and fumbled along the floor for her slippers.

Bill had unlocked the door when she reached it. Both of them slid sideways, together, into the bedroom.

Though outside it was not yet dark, the shutters and curtains had been drawn on the windows. Lights shone in the soft-carpeted room with its blue hangings. The telephone was on its small table at the head of the double bed; Colonel Duroc, in uniform, sat on the far edge of the bed while he spoke to the phone in Spanish.

"Good, good!" said the Colonel. "Continue."

There was a rasping sound from the receiver. The back of Colonel Duroc's neck turned pink with joy. His short white hair seemed to wave with it.

"Better, better!" he said. "But why do you say you have 'probably' trapped him?"

Bill, who had been holding the towel-wrapped Paula in his arms, looked down at her.

"Well, well, well?" Duroc continued impatiently. There was further exchange over the phone.

For an instant the Colonel twitched round his red face and saw Bill and Paula standing there. His left hand held the phone, his right a handkerchief with which he had been mopping his head.

But he turned back to speak.

"Have your men stop every bolt hole. If he tries to make a run for it, then shoot. But do not shoot to kill unless you must. I want him as a witness."

Again the voice rasped. Paula and Bill, who could not hear a word from the other side, were growing frantic with curiosity. They could not see the sweat on Colonel Duroc's forehead, but they saw him wipe his forehead with a handkerchief.

"You are careless with lives, Acting Commandant." Colonel Duroc moistened his lips. Then, after a pause, he said, "Very well. But you cannot have more men, because *I* lead a party to surround the—you understand?—forty-bis Marshan when the real Iron Chest strikes for the diamonds. *This* party cannot leave the hotel until it is well and deeply dark. This party will be commanded by Sir—to you—the Lord Merrivale."

Hesitantly the Colonel put back the phone on its cradle.

Again he mopped his forehead.

Through his brain, in a shorter time than it took to mop the forehead, went every aspect of this case. When H.M. had explained the 'miracles' of Iron Chest, Colonel had then swiftly and logically deduced Iron Chest's identity. He was very proud of this. But then there had come H.M.'s telephone tip from the Kasbah, where the latter sinner was on the loose in the same sedan chair as that of his morning's carousal; and Duroc must set moving the organization.

Finally, there had been H.M.'s final message about the adventures in the tailor's shop. The Colonel, in person, had raced down in his jeep—never using the Packard when on real business—to convey Alvarez to Dr. MacPhail's nursing home. He had hovered while the calm doctor quieted Maureen's hysterics, finally with sedatives. He had interviewed the Countess Scherbatsky at her house in the Place du Kasbah. He had spoken with Mark Hammond, who was having dinner at the Parade. And the Colonel knew, if H.M. did not, that at one o'clock Collier had shouldered his chunky frame into an all-day-open ironmonger's in the Grand Socco. There he had bought a knife with a blade sharpened to razor-edge on either side.

"Monsieur wishes," had stammered the Arab proprietress, in an amiable attempt at French, "to kill animals?"

"No," had said Collier, in bad but understandable French. "I wish to cut the throat of a blonde."

For fully five minutes, after he had slammed the door, the proprietress had giggled over this as a good joke. Then, suddenly, she had fled screaming into the street to find a policeman.

Now Colonel Duroc, sitting on the edge of the bed, made up his mind. He could feel two pairs of eyes, those of Paula and Bill, boring into his back. To keep fear away for a time, Colonel Duroc performed one of his better feats of acting.

"Ha ha," he carolled with mirth.

Putting away the handkerchief, standing up from the edge of the bed, the stocky little Colonel strutted over to a deep padded blue chair. He sat down, his shoulders heaving with chuckles, and faced the Bentleys. His blue eyes twinkled under the tufted brows. He was again Papa Duroc.

"It's—it's not really very funny," said Paula, in the long trailing robe which actually belonged to Bill. "You told us that would be Acting Commandant Somebody. What did he say?"

"Well? What *did* he say?" demanded Bill.

Colonel Duroc puffed out his lips as though it were of no importance.

"A trifle," he replied airily, in his excellent English. "Come! It can wait for a moment or two."

Whereupon he frowned with mock sternness, and shook his finger at Paula.

"By burn!" he said. "I ask myself, again and again, why this young lady can never appear in public without wearing the least possible clothes."

For once startled, Paula opened her dark-blue eyes wide.

"But I—I never think of it!" she protested. "That is . . ."

"It is I who tell you. I, Papa Duroc. And it is not what *you* think. It is what all young men think; yes, and old ones too!" The Colonel drew a deep reminiscent breath. "Have you not heard the remark of great Clemenceau, the old Tiger of France, as he sat sighing by the boulevard in spring? 'Ah, to be seventy again. . . .' "

"Put that in your notebook, Bill," Paula advised wryly.

Yet Bill's eyes had narrowed. The Colonel knew what Bill guessed: that Duroc would not speak until Paula was out of the room.

"Half a tick!" said Bill. "You haven't even told us everything about that row at the tailor's. For some reason, Juan and H.M."—only the Bentleys had dropped the "Sir Henry," for which the reprobate was grateful—"tore the place up. Can't understand that. Juan's the most steady-going bloke I know. Then Ilone and Hammond appeared. But what was *Collier* doing there?"

"Aha!" beamed the Colonel, and rubbed his hands together. This slight diversion pleased him, as well as pride in his own deduction of other matters. "Now, my friend, you shall tell me why! You shall use your wits. What *was* Collier doing there?"

Paula felt Bill's arm tighten round her. She sensed his mind was sorting thoughts quickly.

"Right," said Bill, beginning in his slow way. "Collier must have been sitting openly in that gambling room at the back of the tailor's. Right! We know Ilone and Hammond were talking about Collier. Ilone screams everything; Collier must have heard it. We know Hammond phoned Bob Beacon at the American Cultural Center to get Collier's record as a boxer. Right?"

The Colonel, instead of being pleased, was annoyed at this accuracy.

"Yes?"

"In that case," said Bill, speaking more rapidly, "Collier could easily have slipped into the tailor's after Ilone and Hammond. We know the shop was gloomy. We know the occupants were all very much preoccupied, at one side of the shop alone. We know Collier was found on the other side. It would have been simple for him to have slipped across and hidden behind what seemed to be a very long suit rack on that side, where he could listen to what concerned him." Bill's eyes were shining. "Inference: Collier was a member of that gambling club, or at least well known to it. Otherwise he wouldn't have been admitted. Secondary inference: Collier has a good protecting friend, here in Tangier, who introduced him there. Right? Shall I go on?"

Colonel Duroc fumed.

"No, no, enough!" he said, not wishing to have anybody steal his own thunder.

Then the Colonel pointed his finger at Paula, like a mighty sorcerer commanding a miracle.

"Be dressed!" he said.

The miracle was not instantaneous, of course. Paula, guessing very well why they wanted her out of the way but not wishing to comment on it, compressed her lips and scurried about the room with the long robe flapping about her feet. She opened cupboard doors and shut them, gathering clothes; she opened dressing-table drawers and banged them shut.

Bill, absent-mindedly pulling up the collar of his shirt, took a tie from a rack without looking at it. He put it on, tying the knot halfway towards his ear under the collar then pulling it in place, and finally donned the light-grey flannel jacket of his suit to hide the shoulder holster.

Colonel Duroc had again begun to sweat. Outside closed shutters it must be growing dark. The clock ticked steadily.

Paula, having gathered up the clothes she required, hurried into the bathroom. But at the door she turned for a final word.

"Blast you," Paula observed mildly. The door slammed and was locked—or apparently so.

Taking a light chair, Bill brought it up facing close to the

Colonel's easy chair, glanced over his shoulder towards the bathroom door, and sat down.

"Now let's have it," he said in a low voice. "Everything you heard on that phone."

Duroc told him, still with a sense of the minutes ticking on. He omitted no word which Acting Commandant Perez had said. Bill, left elbow in palm and his other hand on his cleft chin, listened without a muscle moving in his face and without a single comment.

Collier, it seemed, had been traced to the house of carpet and antique dealer named Ali. In the cellar of this great Arab house was his shop. The whole, apparently, was a honeycomb of galleries, little rooms, and bolt holes, making it an enviable hiding place. There was even a dummy window, of which the Acting Commandant had hinted that he knew the secret. Duroc had instructed that the house be surrounded and men stationed at every bolt hole, but, as they had no means, such as tear gas, of smoking out Collier—here, Duroc's voice sank apologetically—Perez had suggested that they use Paula as a decoy, since Collier had bragged openly that he would kill her at the first opportunity. "And so," the Colonel ended hastily, "if your good wife will assist?"

Still Bill Bentley remained motionless.

"I won't let you do it," he said quietly. "Don't you think you've got a hell of a cheek to ask?"

Despair pressed hard on Colonel Duroc.

"Yes, I acknowledge it," he said stiffly, and lifted his shoulders. "Still, if you refuse, it is finished."

"Look here," muttered Bill. "I admit—well, I enjoy any tom-fool stunt myself. But, when it comes to involving Paula . . ."

"Yes, yes, I comprehend!"

Bill sprang to his feet. So did Colonel Duroc, with Bill towering over him.

"What's the matter with your men?" asked Bill, his usually mild voice with a cutting edge of scorn. "Why can't they go in and smoke him out? No tear gas? Good God! Use old-fashioned burning sulphur, with an electric fan that works on a battery; I can rig up one for you. Yes, and I'll lead 'em myself! Don't I deserve first shot at Collier?"

"Your sulphur," said the Colonel, "was tried in a war when you were not even yet a child. Ourselves we may choke, and Collier escape. Stop! It might do, yes, if we knew the place in a building of honeycomb passages and hidden spy holes. But no! Will you hear reasons more cogent?"

"Such as?"

"You know that this Collier has named your wife. You know his threats to her; he is filth; he will keep the promise if he can. Yet now we have him trapped in a single big house; we are certain. It may be our only chance. Do you care to go with her, perhaps for months, holding a pistol, forever-time looking round for a blow which may—or, by burn!—or may not come?"

Bill hesitated, looking away and licking dry lips.

Now Colonel Duroc, a kindly man, hated what he had to say. But discipline held him like a harness.

"You are big enough," he challenged. "With your arm round her, and a loaded gun in your other hand, dare you not face one man?"

Dead silence, except for the stir at the window of a breeze from the bay.

The Colonel had said a thing you must not say to any man, let alone Bill. The colour receded from Bill's face. His eyes narrowed, and his heavy left fist darted back. Again he hesitated, and moistened his lips. Slowly the fist moved forward, and wiped his mouth.

"All right," he said. "I'll do it."

And, once having made that promise, Bill would walk forward in dead straight line, not deviating one inch if he walked against enemy tanks. The War Office could have told you that. But Bill instantly made his conditions.

"Mind," he said without much voice, "I said *I'd* do it. It's Paula's choice, remember. I warn you. I'm going to advise her against it; I mean to use every argument against it; and if I have any influ . . ."

Suddenly the door of the bathroom, which all this time had stood open a splinter's width, was flung wide open.

Paula had not progressed far with her dressing. Round the corner of the door she thrust out her head; and, to the regret of Papa Duroc, her shoulders as well.

"Of course I'll do it!" she cried, with an odd shining in her eyes. "What on earth did you think I expected you to ask. D-don't be silly!"

The door slammed, and this time was genuinely locked.

Colonel Duroc, by this time much upset and wishing he

hadn't mentioned the matter, sat down slowly.

"I love that girl," he said simply.

Bill's own fierce love, and his fear for her too, twisted his heart and even momentarily shone in his eyes. Hastily he looked at the floor. There was a long silence.

"Not bad, is she?" muttered Bill. There was another long pause before Bill added bitterly: "Anyway, in what she'll do for—people. And never say a word." He sat down and put his head in his hands. "But he won't hurt her. By God, he won't."

Colonel Duroc, to avoid further discussion, got up and hurried over to a window. He fumbled among light coverings and blue curtains before he opened one shutter and peered out. Though he could see a huddle of dark roofs and the lights of Tangier, the sky was as yet only a dull grey; not black. If, in the meantime, Collier should escape . . .

"If Collier—" he began, and stopped.

Colonel Duroc swung round and Bill leaped to his feet as there was a knocking at the door to the hotel corridor.

CHAPTER FOURTEEN

Bill's movement, if his companion had seen it, almost baffled the eyesight. Bill's hand whipped up towards the inside of his coat; without interval, it seemed, the Webley .45 was levelled at the door, Bill's arm pressed against his side.

"Entrez!" called Duroc, clearing his throat.

It was, at first glance, only Sir Henry Merrivale. Bill's tension left him as he slipped the Webley back into the holster under his coat. But H.M.'s presence, when he is in a mood, can have all the healing balm of a hurricane, and can seem to upset chairs even when he is not near them. Though not precisely in a mood now, he was nearing one.

"More trouble," he grunted.

Colonel Duroc clutched at his white hair.

Gone were the robe, the moustache and mighty beard, the walnut-juice stains, the green tarboosh of the Prophet Hassan-el-Mulik. But H.M. remained crafty. Having nicked an old-fashioned square Churchillian bowler hat from the tailor's, he had jammed it on and refused to remove it. His black alpaca suit fitted the occasion, if not him. An unlighted cigar was stuck in the corner of his mouth.

Moving his bulk and his corporation sideways through the door, he greeted Bill with real pleasure, noted the shoulder holster, closed the door, and sat down in a huge easy chair.

"No," he growled, raising his hand palm outwards, "I'm not goin' to tell you what the trouble is. You'll learn in five minutes; and, anyway," he rolled the cigar reflectively, "I'm not sure it's so bad as you think." Now martyrdom appeared. "But cor! If any livin' son of Esau had as tiring day as I've had—"

Colonel Duroc straightened up.

"You have had a tiring day?" he inquired. "Ha ha. Behold, may I goose a duck! What about Papa Duroc?" A

terrible thought struck him. "You are not still in that sedan chair?"

"Son, I wouldn't stir a step in this loony city without it! She's downstairs."

"She must go. For tonight you cannot use her—it, I tell you."

H.M., without replying, merely looked mulish and stuck out his chin.

"For the morning," declared Colonel Duroc, "all this morning, you gave me hot-and-cold fits by your carousal about this place in a sedan chair. Later I hear of your disguise, which is worse yet and did not deceive me . . ."

"Ho, didn't it fool everybody?" shouted H.M., not without reason. "Why, the Holmes gal herself said she wouldn't 'a recognized me if I hadn't stuck a cigar in my potato trap. In the morning, y'see, I was almost snookered because all the shops and offices, the Continental ones anyway, close at noon and don't open until four. My eye, what a way of doin' business! You people here . . . you . . . Stop a bit. What do you call yourselves—Tangerians?"

"No, no," said Colonel Duroc. "Tangerines."

H.M. contemplated him over the big spectacles. Then H.M. closed one eye, and looked at him with an expression rather like that of Donald Duck listening to a story about Father Christmas.

"No, *pas de blague!"* This is true, as Bill will tell you. . . . We are Tangerines!"

"Cor," said H.M. in a hollow voice, "this is one I'm not going to tell 'em at home. Or the Ministry of Food will drop its usual brick and import you at threepence apiece."

"We are . . ."

"Uh-huh. I know now. But stop interrupting me, burn it!"

"Interrupting you?" asked Colonel Duroc in a strange, wild tone. The same note has been heard in the voice of Chief Inspector Masters.

"That's right. As I was saying, I got in my best innings, before noon and after, in the Kasbah. That's where . . ."

"Sir Henry!" The Colonel, who had sat down again, bowed from the waist and at least attempted to speak with formality and deference. "For the deductions you have given me, as regards Iron Chest and the vanishings of people and things, I myself, my Department of Police, the Government of Tangier itself, cannot praise you too highly."

"Well . . . now," said the great man, taking the unlighted cigar out of his mouth to utter a modest cough.

"But how," persisted the Colonel, clutching at his tie, "could you deceive the Arabs? By burn! You perhaps know a small greeting or so. But, when we hear your true vocabulary, a squeamish one would faint himself. You cannot even speak their language!"

"Oh, son," H.M. said dismally, "that was the easiest part of all."

The Colonel put his head in his hands.

"Y'see, I've really read the Koran. In English, yes. But I've even studied it. And for some rummy reason," he hammered his head, scowling, "whatever goes into this onion always sticks there."

"But the language . . ."

"I'm telling you. I'd got a noble disguise, d'ye see, from the costume shop beside Bernstein and Company. It included a simon-pure authentic robe, which I didn't change until I bought another from Ali, the carpet dealer."

Here his little eyes grew sharp, but Colonel Duroc said nothing for the moment.

"So, when I was moochin' about in my sedan chair, just whistling for information, I didn't need any Arabic. Oh, except 'Peace be upon your house.' Then I'd speak in not-too-perfect English or French, which they understood. I said I was goin' out to preach in the infidel world."

"Dut . . ."

"Every time I got to the subject of sin, which the same is the most popular in any place, I'd look 'em in the eye—like this, see?—and I'd reel off about a page of the Koran. Cor! Their eyes got as big as soup plates. Y'see, most Arabs . . . burn me, I ought to say 'Moors'; that's correct, you ignorant so-and-so's . . . But I keep forgetting. . ."

"So do all of us," sighed the Colonel.

"Well, they can't read. There's very little written Arabic. They've got to get a wise man to read out their own newspaper. But they've heard a lot of old Mohammed's teaching, over and over. When they heard me spoutin' the Koran, they knew it was solid gold stuff. If they had any doubts, I ripped off another page and a half. When I saw 'em rushing to bring me food or coffee or mint tea, I was pretty sure I had the audience tearin' up the stalls."

Bill Bentley, his back to the wall of a cupboard door, spoke seriously.

"You know," he said, "you really *are* a crafty old swine."

"Thank'ee, son," said the gratified H.M., with another modest cough.

"Pah!" sneered Colonel. "It was pure luck, then, that you spot what you call to me the 'snaky little type,' Ali, in the Kasbah?"

"Luck, hey?" demanded H.M., turning slightly purple. "It was no more'n routine police work. I mooched about, just like an ordinary copper . . ."

"I also am much about." Colonel was withering. "Pah! You cannot speak your own language."

"But when it came to Ali," persisted H.M., "it was something else. I sort of hinted that to Alvarez and Maureen Holmes this afternoon. I knew he was a soul mate of mine . . ."

"Un—quoi?"

"Sure. I said soul mate. I can sense 'em. I can smell 'em. 'Course, he thought I was at least outwardly what I pretended; I poured the Koran on him like a shower bath. But he knew, and I knew, we were both as twisty and crooked as each other. When he kept saying, in that bat's squeak, 'In Tangier one may buy all things,' down to a purr, 'at a price,' well, I tested him.

"I asked him, for instance, if he could get me a forged passport. That was so easy the little feller only giggled with his teeth. 'Then I said, what about a good revolver. He asked me whether I'd like a fine Colt's Banker's Special, three-eight, with much ammo, at a price.' "

"But here is the pistol," said Colonel Duroc, "which Collier has used when he impersonates the true Iron Chest at Bernstein et Cie.'s attempted robbery!"

"Uh-huh. Couldn't you sort of sense Collier lurkin' about?"

"Eh bien, alors?"

"Eh, bien," said the Old Maestro, making a fiendish face, "I bowled the little feller, Ali, a mean one. I asked whether he could get me a lot of some mildish high-explosive like dynamite or T.N.T. That nearly snookered him. But you couldn't beat him. He went away for a conference, 'cause he said there'd been a recent call for it—as though it'd been cough medicine. But up he squeaked: 'Two, t'ree day? Yes? At a price?' " H.M. broke off suddenly, and glared at Bill over his

spectacles. "What's so rummy about this, son?"

"To mention nothing else," said Bill, "didn't he think you were one hell of a holy man?"

"Oh, son! He knew I was crooked. Or we couldn't have got so pally, or drunk mint tea, or . . . Haah! Stop a bit!" H.M. interrupted himself, like one who jams on the hand brake of a car. "My blood pressure," he added tragically, "is flaming awful. I expect I'm goin' to die, after the exertions I've put in to help you two. But there's something I've *got* to know, now!"

Colonel Duroc looked his consternation.

"My dear friend, but of course! What puzzles you?"

"It's this stuff called *keef*. I heard about it at Ali's. I even heard that old witch Scherbatsky talking about *keef* parties. I think you smoke it. But what in the name of Esau is *keef?*"

Colonel Duroc sighed with resignation. Bill grinned broadly.

"Keef," the Colonel explained patiently, "is a species of tobacco somewhat like marihuana, but much more mild and never with dangerous results. The Arabs . . ."

"Moors!" said H.M., pointing a stern finger in his face.

"Tut, tut! Always I forget. Yes, yes, *Moors*. Well, these Arabs, who are pious Moslems and do not drink, smoke *keef* instead. I repeat: its earlier effects," he raised the tufted eyebrows significantly, "are pleasant. Afterwards the Arab or other simply goes to sleep, with more pleasant dreams. Never does it make him run amok or have any ill consequences."

H.M. thrust forward a ghoulish and eager face. He glanced left and right, to make sure they were not overheard.

"Looky here, Colonel. Could you get me some?"

Colonel Duroc seemed mildly shocked.

"But you do not wish to smoke *keef!"*

"Ho! Don't I!"

"Its sale is not illegal. Anyone may procure it." The Colonel fussed. "Ah, by burn! My objections are not of what you call the Madame Grundy. Many persons smoke, I know. But it—it lowers the prestige as a European."

"But who's a European?" thundered H.M. "I'm no blinking European; I'm smacking well English! So's this bloke here. So's his wife."

"Come, come. 'European' is not a term of nationality. It is a term of—of social prestige. It is what used to be called, in

India, a—a . . ."

"Pukka sahib," supplied Bill, as the other floundered. *"Keef's* not bad; Paula and I have tried it. We try anything once; and, if we like it, we try it again. No, it's not bad, except that it gives me at least a devil of a headache. I stick to Scotch."

"Are you goin' to do it, or not?" sternly demanded H.M.

"Well, if you must have it," sighed the Colonel, "I suppose you had better have the best quality. I will make a note of it. *Keef* for Sir Henry. Good. Now!" he snapped, rapidly smacking his fingers together under H.M.'s nose. "To our affairs, yes? What else have you to tell?"

But H.M.'s mood had altered. Folding his arms, the Churchillian hat firmly pulled down, he settled back with an air of malignancy.

"Oh, no," he said sharply, "I've told you everything, supplementing the whole lot I said on the phone. Something tells me," he sniffed like an ogre, "you've got another message, and my tip about the carpet dealer was right. If so, let's hear it!"

Again an evil atmosphere seemed to press down on this pleasant bedroom at the Minzeh. Bill Bentley hurried to one window.

"It's getting pretty dark, sir," he said. From Paula in the bathroom there was no sound.

For the second time Colonel Duroc carefully repeated every word which Acting Commandant Perez had said. Meanwhile H.M., rising with difficulty, lit the cigar by whisking a large match across the seat of his trousers. Settling back amid a poisonous cloud, he listened without comment and remained silent even at the end.

"I see," he grunted finally. "You think it may be less dangerous if the—" He paused, cryptically, and Colonel Duroc nodded. Again H.M. reflected, amid viler smoke.

"Then you're leading the raid against 40-bis Marshan." He looked doubtful. "Y'know, I rather doubt there'll be an attack, even if the Greek helps." Again he was cryptic. "And, with that witch of a Scherbatsky talking all over the place . . ."

"Then what else can I do?"

"Nothing, I suppose," admitted H.M. " 'Cause you can't afford to let it slip past." He brooded. "Who's leading our crowd into the Kasbah?"

"You are."

"Oh, stick-a-pig!" groaned H.M., and shut his eyes. He opened them again. "Looky here, son. That Kasbah, even by daylight, is worse than Hampton Court maze was in 1900. By night, maybe, I could take some people in. But I'd bring 'em up two miles on the other side of Fez. *I can't do it, Colonel.* What you need . . ."

There was another sharp knock at the door, and another lightning draw from Bill's holster. The man who entered from the corridor door was Juan Alvarez.

Alvarez was a little pale under his faint swarthiness, very straight in his well-cut double-breasted suit of dark grey. There was only a slight bandage at the back of his head, though Dr. MacPhail would have had fits at the soft hat he had pulled tightly over it.

Bill hurried over to greet him.

They did not even shake hands. But they showed real pleasure at the meeting by giving each other a hard punch at each other's shoulder.

"I thought you were in the nursing home," muttered Bill, out of the corner of his mouth. "What's the game?"

"Slipped out," muttered Alvarez, also out of the corner of his mouth. "Had to see the old man." A brief nod flickered towards Colonel Duroc. "Back me up, whatever I say."

"Right."

Now it was Colonel Duroc in the easy chair, loftily contemplating a corner of the ceiling with his notebook across his knee, whose behaviour seemed to have become purely childish.

Alvarez, again fighting-fit and brisk of step, approached the Commissioner of Police.

"Sir," he said. "According to my promise," his eye moved briefly towards H.M, who was smoking furiously, "and according to my own wish, I desire to apologize. My conduct in getting drunk was so indefensible that, if it had not been for your generous hesitation, I should have been discharged on the spot."

"Hurrum!" growled the Colonel, still with his bright blue eyes fixed on a corner of the ceiling.

"As for my conduct today, it was even more unpardonable." Now this was not strictly true. But to Duroc, who knew he had lost his head and was in the wrong, this was healing and soothing; it mollified. "I said and did impossible things, which—er—only your generosity permitted me to save face by my resignation. I think, sir, that is all."

"Well, nobody could apologize better than that," declared Bill, to the room in general.

"Ah, zut!" exploded Colonel Duroc.

He bounced to his feet, hurling his notebook on the floor. For an instant he stood red-faced and embarrassed, before the usual inspiration smote him.

"Let's go take a glass!" he shouted, heaving all over with chuckles. He wrung Alvarez's out-thrust hand, and with his other hand Colonel Duroc pointed dramatically at the telephone. "Come, it is necessary that we command the champagne!"

"Not at all, my old!" groaned Sir Henry Merrivale in the same language. "It is necessary that we command the repast. The Châteaubriand, with mushrooms . . ."

"By blue, this repast disgusts me!" interrupted the Colonel. "Down with it! We will have no food." Beaming, he turned to Alvarez. From his pocket he took a folded square of paper which could be only the Former Commandant's resignation. Tearing it into small pieces, he threw them wide. "And there!" he added.

It was Alvarez, bowing, who restored the conversation to English and to some degree of sanity.

"If you will forgive me, sir, I do not know whether we may yet tear it up."

Colonel Duroc stiffened.

"You see, sir, I have every hope that I can persuade Miss Maureen Holmes to become my wife. She may not wish to remain in Tangier. But if she remains, as I think she will, then let the resignation be torn up."

"Commandant!" beamed the Colonel. "Then you will marry the little Madame Bentley? Commandant, I congrat . . ."

"Here, stop a bit!" protested Bill.

"Ah, but I forget!" cried the Colonel, with a strange look as he clutched at his face. "The different lady, but also nice! I love her!" Quite suddenly, as though by a miracle, Colonel Duroc's wits seemed to flash back. "Commandant Alvarez! Why are you here tonight?"

"Well, sir, I telephoned the central station, and they were good enough to put me in touch with Perez . . ."

Duroc still regarded him with shrewd eyes.

"Why do you come here? What do you want?"
"I want," said Alvarez, "to command this particular party, if only for tonight. I would not interfere with Perez, who is a good man. But I want to guide your friends. I know every foot of the Kasbah. I know the great whitewashed room, underground at the carpet dealer's, and every entrance to it. In short, I want to bring you Collier on a plate."
Again Duroc's eyes narrowed under the tufted brows.
"You would capture Collier, true. But first you would wish to smash him in pieces with your fists. Is it not so?"
"Yes, sir!" replied Alvarez. "Knowing about him what you know now, do you blame me?"
"On consideration, no. Well! Perhaps this is better than having him slashed to pieces with bullets from automatic rifles, which are but modified machine guns. Do as you like, Commandant. Here is my hand and promise."
"Thank you, sir."
"And now," cried Duroc, going a little off his head again, "to the ladies!"
It was at this moment that the bathroom door opened, and Paula walked out.
And Paula, though not a vain girl, expected (or at least hoped) she would make some impression on the men.
Her golden hair was burnished, curled under at the ends in the page-boy bob, her pretty face more vivid with the very slightest touch of make-up. Against the pink-and-white skin she wore a low-cut, sleeveless gold evening gown, with slightly flaring skirts to the floor. By some careless ankle-or-thigh turn, sweeping out skirts, she displayed high-heeled gold shoes.
Then Paula saw their faces, while the four of them stood or sat motionless. Colonel Duroc and Alvarez, with impregnable politeness, bowed and smiled falsely. Sir Henry Merrivale, throwing his cigar in the general direction of the hearth, uttered a deep groan. Even Bill, after hesitating, looked at the floor. Paula's consternation turned slowly to dismay near tears.
"You—you don't like it," she faltered.
"Baggage," muttered Bill. He raised his head and burst out, "It's wonderful! It's magnificent! But—"
Putting his hands on her shoulders, he edged her gently towards the bathroom door and inside, where it was now dark. Trying to kick the door shut, Bill only partly suc-

ceeded. But Bill did not care. He put his arms round her, and her head dropped against his shoulder.

"Angel-harlot." Bill shouted tenderly, "I repeat: you're wonderful! I never saw you so lovely! You're like an impossible beauty out of a Ben Jonson masque! You're like the vision of Helen to Faustus, like Pope's description of . . ."

Paula's arm stole round him, though he could feel her shivering.

"But it—" her mind was still on the gown—"it makes you feel so much better! It improves your morale so much!" She did not even complain of a Webley .45 uncomfortably brushing against her. "Bill, I only . . ."

"Baggage, that's just it. You can't go into the Kasbah in high-heeled shoes and trailing skirts. You can't go there in a gold dress, even if you wore a coat over it; you'd be spotted at twenty yards." He saw an opportunity. "Baggage, why must you go with us anyway?"

"Love you," said Paula in a muffled voice.

"But that isn't the point!"—Wrong tactics; steady!—"I mean, it isn't the point that you should run into danger just for me. It's wrong! Angel-face, why don't you stay here?"

"Shan't!" said Paula. "Love you. . . . Like me?"

Bill lifted her head and kissed her with such thoroughness that they both almost fell into the bathtub. Whereupon Bill, losing his head completely, mingled strong caresses with roaring such a string of bejewelled quotations, epigrams, and tributes to her physical charms that already he felt Paula go limp and forget most of her disappointment about the gown.

In the next room, three men tried to pretend they were not listening. The Colonel, detached but thoughtful, eyed a corner of the ceiling. Alvarez, eyes gleaming, was obviously making mental note of every remark, so that he could use it to Maureen. Only H.M., malignant as the Evil One, growled out that it was more canoodlin'; that he met canoodlin' wherever he went; and that he hated canoodlin' worse than anything.

"This canoodling," whispered the Colonel; "what does it mean?" Alvarez himself, surprisingly enough, did not know the term.

Whereupon H.M., who was deeply fond of Paula but would never have admitted it, uttered a majestic lie. He translated "to canoodle" with a short, well-known word which perhaps might be a description of love-making in *ultima thule,* but which could never possibly be used as regards the mild very "canoodle." The eyes of Duroc and Alvarez grew large and round.

"Cré nom!" whispered the Colonel, not without respect.

Presently Paula strolled out of the half-open bathroom door, and rearranged her hair. It may be said, as the highest credit, that she did not give anyone a mean look. On the contrary, her smile was genuine. She even hummed happily as again she dashed round the room, resurrecting wretched slacks, jumper, sandals, and light coat. For the last time Paula darted into the bathroom.

Bill, looking as guilty as a print in the Newgate calendar, sauntered out casually.

"She'll—er—wear the proper outfit," he mumbled. "Out in half a tick."

Alvarez surreptitiously slapped him on the back.

But Colonel Duroc's mood had again changed to wrath.

"Half a tick, half a tick," he snapped, with a general suggestion beginning the verses about the Light Brigade. Dashing to one window, he groped and peered out. "Not only is it pitch-dark, but we lose time and lose time! We are late! If the type Collier has already escaped . . ."

Diabolically, then, the telephone rang.

Being near the bedside table at the head of the bed, Colonel Duroc dived for the phone and snatched it up.

"*Allo?* Perez? . . . What? No, no, be off the line! . . . What?" His angry gaze moved to Alvarez. "For you," he added, and held out the phone.

"Maureen!" exclaimed Alvarez. "I didn't think it was possible! She's in a private room at the doctor's, under sedatives, out of danger, anyway. . . . Thank you, sir. . . .Yes?"

"Is this you, Alvarez?" inquired a man's voice in English.

"Alvarez here," he said. "Who is speaking please?"

"This is Mark Hammond," replied the voice, and Alvarez knew it for the true Hammond. "I've been thinking over what I told you today about Collier as a fighter, and since then I've looked up his record for myself. The police station said you'd probably be at the Minzeh. Are you still interested?"

"Even more so!"

Hammond's voice, though not loud, was so clear and rounded of syllable that every person in the room could hear each word, and bent to listen.

"I told you he's far past his prime, and slow," continued Hammond. "But there was one thing I forgot. According to my information, he hasn't even had the gloves on for years. Understand?"

"Yes. Go on!"

"He'll be sluggish, slow of reaction in mind and body, and his timing will be all off."

Paula, not much less dazzling in yellow sweater, black slacks, and a woolly tan coat pulled over her shoulders, crept softly from the bathroom. She was ready but silent.

"Don't carry a handbag," Bill whispered in her ear. "Stick anything you want in your coat pockets. Sh-h! I want to hear this!"

"Any tips you can give me from the record?" asked Alvarez, in a dead eerie silence.

"Yes, one or two," replied the small, clear voice. "He holds his right hand—that's the killer hand—too low; and he's a sucker for a left hook." As Hammond spoke, all of them saw the Commandant's teeth gleam. "You can give him any body punch without troubling him, except one: a belly punch just above the waistline. He can't take too much punishment there; it cost him five fights. You may, I say *may,* have a forty-sixty chance against him. But remember: he keeps his left high, to guard against a right cross; he'll never forget his ringcraft; and he's a heavy puncher. Good night, good luck."

"Good night, thanks," replied Alvarez, and put down the phone.

Almost instantly the phone rang again. This time it was Duroc who lunged towards it.

"That is for me," he declared, and he was right. For thirty seconds the carbon rattled with indistinguishable Spanish. Duroc put down the phone, and stood up straight, rather pale.

"Collier is trapped," he said. "They have stopped up every bolt hole. Collier is inside the house. Commandant!"

"Sir?"

"Forget *la boxe.* Never mind *la boxe.* Can you give me Collier?"

"Yes, sir," said Alvarez, so hoarsely that he had to clear his throat.

"With trimmings on," muttered Bill.

"Good! And the little lady, she is ready. I follow you down into the foyer. Good luck."

"You mustn't be afraid, Mrs. Bentley," Alvarez muttered against Paula's ear.

"But I'm not!" protested Paula wonderingly. "Isn't Bill here?"

Bill turned his head away, biting hard at his underlip. Alvarez smiled and patted her on the back as he and Bill closed in on each side of her. H.M., in his Churchillian bowler, turned off the lights. Colonel Duroc opened the door.

Now it was Collier—or nothing.

CHAPTER FIFTEEN

Upwards they mounted, on the very high but shallow flight of stone stairs, enclosed at a fairly wide distance by dirty white walls. Under the arch far below, the lights and brattle of the Little Socco dwindled way. Down on them pressed the secrecy and dimness of the Kasbah. Some say the Kasbah holds little harm. Yet they admit it is unpredictable. What may seem very sinister is in fact innocent. And what looks innocent may be far worse than a king cobra.

Paula walked in the middle, with Alvarez on her left side and Bill close on her right. Though Alvarez seemed to carry no weapon, under the side of his waistcoat, hidden vertically with loop down, rested the murderous rubber truncheon. At the reception desk of the hotel, too, he had picked up a smallish grey canvas bag, which he now swung in his left hand.

Sir Henry Merrivale, his Churchillian bowler pressing down his ears while he complained bitterly of his feet, lumbered after them as rear guard.

Paula, though not speaking loudly, was wound up like a gramophone and could not stop. So, though they afterwards swore to the contrary, were the others.

"But why must we go in on this side?" she whispered. "Do you know, in nearly five years Bill has never allowed me to go into the Kasbah at night. And this carpet dealer's must be far away on the other side. Bill . . ."

"No good at night," muttered Bill. "Anyway, not in the old days when it was wide-open."

"You see, Mrs. Bentley," Alvarez explained in a low voice, "admittedly I take you by a very long way round. But we must not meet the police party bang in front of the shop."

Here he gave a low laugh.

"Please have no fear, however," he added smilingly. "Here is almost a tourist resort. There is absolutely no . . ."

With a slap of hard bare feet coming down stone steps, there loomed up a thin, immensely tall figure in white *jalebah* with white peaked hood. By some trick of the darkness it seemed about seven feet high. Suddenly the figure veered towards them, muttering ugly words.

The Webley was instantly in Bill's hand. H.M.'s right hand, with astonishing swiftness, darted towards his deep hip pocket.

But Alvarez merely spat back a half-sentence in Arabic, with such snarling viciousness that the tall figure muttered and slunk away down the steps.

"Anything wrong, old boy?" Bill asked Juan casually. Back went the Webley.

"Oh, he was only cursing us for being foreigners." Alvarez laughed. "Pay no attention to such incidents. They are nothing. But if any of the thief tribe think we have money—keep an eye out to the right, Bill. I shall do the same on the left."

"Y'know," Sir Henry Merrivale said reflectively, "this place may be a second restin' spot for Allah. Or again it may not. That walkin' bed sheet was like something out of M.R. James."

"Not at all," smiled Alvarez. "Observe, now!"

They emerged, a little breathless, into fairly open flat space where dim little alleys seemed to pierce through tall brownish or whitish house walls.

"You notice," whispered Alvarez, nudging Paula, "that the municipal authorities have tried to light the Kasbah. They have not had the greatest success. Still . . ."

Paula, glancing uneasily to the left, saw the source of a very dim illumination. She looked straight up a very narrow street, empty, with all its ghostly doors fast shut without a chink of light. The lane ended in what seemed a narrower dead-end wall, painted robin's egg blue. A single electric bulb, hanging down from a plank across the roof, burned under a metal shade on which a number had been stencilled.

"You see the stencil?" asked Alvarez. "They keep exact account . . ."

But, in a dense neighbourhood where unseen life moves always about you, it is unwise to challenge. Somebody brushed past H.M., who cursed as only he can. A small dark object—a stone or a bit of rock-whizzed high up the lane. The electric bulb, struck squarely, exploded and gushed white light, then vanished.

"Uh-huh," growled H.M.

But Paula, fascinated, was now looking to the right on so twisted a street that you could not tell whether it ran up or down hill. Its darkness was lightened at only one shiny blur on the pavement. One door, in a pair of double doors, stood open so that they saw it sideways. The upper part of the door had a frosted-glass panel which, feebly illuminated, showed red lettering—in English, strangely enough—with the legend: "Satan's Hotel."

Paula, deeply fascinated, studied the door.

"Oh, my dolly!" said H.M. dismally. "Don't bother with it. It looks very fetchin', but it's not."

Alvarez turned face and teeth.

"You old canoodler!" he muttered, looking a trifle startled as he uttered the vile new English word. "You were in there yourself, I suppose?"

"Well . . . now," H.M. said querulously. "A man's got a certain curiosity, ain't he? Anyway, it's a swindle. They don't keep 'em on the premises," he added cryptically. "You've got to go out and fetch 'em in." His voice was full of intense disgust. "What kind of a way of doin' business is that, hey?"

"No more talking, please," hissed Alvarez. "Be quiet as I lead you."

They went down a long, humped, narrow street, inside high dirty white walls, then turned into another and still another. Several times the mud squashed into Paula's sandals and made her shudder. Often Alvarez had to use an electric torch. Sometimes, at sharp corners there would be a light, hidden in the arch of an old red-brown-white Moorish tower, so dim that it seemed yellow.

"Y'know," suddenly observed H.M., who had been brooding over Satan's Hotel, "there are a lot of those hotels that can be used for proper ordinary hotels. I knew a feller once who went to one and left his luggage. But he stayed out too late with some friends. When he got back, burn me if the proprietor hadn't slung out his luggage and re-let the room to a gal for business purposes. Being a bloke of decency and feelin', he couldn't intrude. Now could he?"

"S-ss-t!"

"Uh-huh. Suit yourself."

With Bill's right hand on the grip of the Webley as he pressed against her on one side, and Alvarez's right hand near the loop of the truncheon as he moved close on the other side, anyone who flew at Paula from in front would shortly be sausage meat. She knew this, and loved it. Yet, at every step farther, she grew more frightened.

Partly it was the sense of oppressiveness, of furtive unseen life pressing close like the pressing of cracked blank walls; of being choked between mud below and hard-pointed stars in a black sky above. Partly, despite her years in Tangier, she was terrified by mere foreignness. The streets were not really foul-smelling—it was the odour of foreign cooking (and Arab cooking can be nauseous), even of foreign garbage. It was the outburst of unseen dogs all the way down a street. Paula would have given much to see a lighted room.

Then, from behind a sealed door in a low white wall whose crenellated top showed like battlements against the sky, Paula heard music—of a sort. It had strings, pipes, and some rattling sound, in which you could make out a rhythm. Though not too loud, it seemed to whirl faster and faster to what seemed a heavy stamping of many feet.

Paula stopped; the others stopped too.

"Isn't that," she asked, glad of the darkness for a moment, "one of those places where Arab girls dance naked on a table, with the weirdest possible contortions of . . . of anatomy?"

"Yes," Bill growled in her ear. Then he looked very hard in the starlit gloom. "*You* don't want to go in there, do you?"

"We-el," murmured Paula, in the tone of one who means, "I shouldn't really mind."

"You? A woman? Why?"

"I don't know why," retorted Paula, with spirit and frankness. "But all women do like to see these exhibitions, if they tell the truth about it. It's natural, somehow."

Alvarez glanced at the luminous dial of his wrist watch. The squalling music grew faster; there was a heavier sound to stamping feet.

"Not long ago," said Alvarez, "there were many such places, all wide-open. And there was always the *cinema vivant*. But the President of the Council wished to suppress them. They remain, of course; but they have gone underground. The President of the Council . . ."

"Is that," H.M. asked ferociously, "the drunken Dutchman again?"

"But I tell you," protested Alvarez in the same tone he had used yesterday, "Mynheer Hoofdstuck is a fine and admirable man. He is never drunk."

"Then he ought to be," said H.M. "Do the poor fathead a world of good. Think of it! Trying' to suppress . . ."

"I agree," said Bill. "Baggage, you never told me you wanted to . . ."

"Please, we must go on," Alvarez insisted tensely, and again glanced at his watch. "We are losing time. We must hurry!"

Again the march went on, more quickly. Paula, completely lost, at least knew they must be moving downhill. The tower of a mosque, which by daylight would be pink, rose partway on the sky and vanished. Presently Paula more than guessed, more than sensed, that they were amid a region of knives. Both Alvarez and Bill were more alert, more sharp of eyes as their heads turned; she held one arm of each, and the arm was rigid. On one occasion both glanced backwards, as though they wondered how H.M. would fare.

They need not have worried.

This old pirate, though he wheezed and grunted, marched behind his corporation as steadily as they. His wicked little eye, darting right and left, was even more alert than that of Alvarez. H.M. had not mentioned one of his purchases that day. But the broad Riff knife, whetted on both sides, and with a tightly woven haft, rested in a leather sheath in his deep hip pocket. Once or twice, with an innocent and even holy look, he tapped the pocket to make sure.

"Listen!" whispered Paula. Again they all stood still.

It was, in sober fact, a menacing sound. From behind another black door in these windowless walls, a man's very deep, slow-speaking voice seemed to plead or argue, with a growl of approval or dissent from other voices, as though urging a sacred cause. On went the deep voice, with its frequent pauses for guttural assent. . . .

Then Paula caught Alvarez's smile.

"What is it?" asked Paula.

"Come along, Mrs. Bentley. And the rest of you." Again Alvarez urged them all forward. "It is only a wise man, who can read and write, reading aloud the daily newspaper in Arabic. The other voices make comments on its news or editorial policy."

"Are you jok . . . ?"

"Not at all. Do you imagine, in England, some country squire reading the *Daily Mirror* to his tenants?"

On they went at a pace which made them stumble and took Paula's breath away.

"You see, Mrs. Bentley," muttered Alvarez, "most of this region—as a rule, I mean—is as innocent as that. There is always possible trouble, of course. I do not think we are in danger now."

But they were.

H.M.'s eye had spotted what Alvarez had missed. Those who have seen only H.M.'s corporation, and do not remember a certain adventure of his in America, will have forgotten his unerring eye and his deadly timing.

Just ahead on the left—the three-abreast group were nearing it now—was another ill-smelling alley not much wider than the breadth of man if he walked through. Against its far wall, facing out, was what appeared to be a white patch against darker white. The thief-cum-throat-cut, who was not an Arab but some little Middle European with greasy hair bound round and round his head, wore a white Arab *jalebah* without a hood. He seemed to melt against the wall. His right hand, well behind him, held the slender knife which was meant to rip out and up into the entrails.

Alvarez, Paula, and Bill were just passing the mouth of the alley. . . .

H.M. lumbered closer. The whetted Riff knife was in his right hand. It would be possible to lunge forward if the thief's own right hand moved. But already he had guessed Middle Europe's tactics, because he saw the slight flick of the man's dark head.

H.M., slowing his pace, sauntered on as the other three hurried ahead.

The little thief, now crouching, saw in this man only what his favourite newspapers told him was a fat symbol of money and despotism. As the barrel-shaped man passed the mouth of the alley, Middle Europe would attract his attention, make him turn full face, and then . . .

"Uh-huh," softly murmured Sir Henry Merrivale.

He was now at the mouth of the alley.

White robe had moved out from the wall, tensed for his leap. Sharply a pebble rattled and rolled. H.M. twitched his head round, made a feint to turn his body round too; and instantly swung backwards and to the right. Middle Europe, over-coiled like a spring, could not stop his own leap.

Dimly you saw the white robe flash out of the alley, and a

glint of the knife which shot outwards and upwards against nothing. H.M.'s powerful left hand whacked down on Middle Europe's head, seizing and rolling a good handful of hair to hold hard. As he forced the man downwards, H.M.'s right hand drove the Riff knife through the side of white robe's throat, just behind the Adam's apple.

Instantly whipping out the knife, he swung Middle Europe away from him by the hair, to avoid jetting blood. He cleansed the knife on the writhing robe. Then, still clutching the man by the hair, H.M. let him fall back softly into the alley. The white robe still writhed and twitched like a coil of snakes. You could see only the whites of Middle Europe's eyes. But his hands scrabbled at a throat spurting blood from both sides.

"Hem!" said H.M., as though concluding some small but necessary duty like washing his hands. Though he slid the knife back into its sheath, he looked innocently away as he did so. Then he did not make too obvious haste to close in behind the others.

But Alvarez knew, by the slight turn of his head. The little matter had not been quite as noiseless as H.M. had imagined. Bill guessed, too. As for Paula . . .

Though she still walked steadily, the enormous pounding of her heart seemed to choke back her breathing. She prayed that the weakness would go from her legs. Presently: "Please tell me," she managed to say in a small voice, "H.M. killed or hurt somebody back there, didn't he?"

"Me?" breathed a voice of outraged piety. "Oh, my dolly! That's a shockin' thing to say." The voice became tragic. "I'm only a pore old man, with maybe a little too much weight from eatin' Tangier food. If some brisk feller had a go at me in the dark, I'd flop down in two seconds."

"Somehow," said Bill, "I doubt that."

Alvarez cut off the question at the root.

"Forget the matter," he said incisely. "Whatever was done, it was well done. And we are very close to our destination."

Paula's breath crept back, especially as they now moved or stumbled slowly. She almost sobbed against Bill's shoulder. If they left this creepy, queer-smelling place of crooked walls, she felt that she could face anything. It would have surprised her to discover how spotlessly clean are the insides of most Arab houses.

"I say," remarked H.M. conversationally, "has everybody

heard of the Place de France?"

This was almost too much for Alvarez.

"Of course everybody has! In Tangier, at least, it is our most fashionable square."

"H'm," said H.M. darkly. "Mind, I got only a glimpse of it. I mightn't even know it again. But here's a deeper, darker mystery attached to the Place de France than Collier and Iron Chest rolled together. Maybe it's some law laid down from the time of Charlemagne; maybe it's some creepin' secret society. You can do anything in this town. You can . . . Well, never mind. *But never, under any circumstances whatever, must you walk across the Place de France.* Why?"

"But that is simple!" Alvarez fussed. "It is . . ."

"No!" retorted the other, in a kind of whispered boom. "I want to work it out for myself, because it's got me gibberin'. Will the pavement turn you to dust? Or a lightning bolt conk you on the onion? Here's a fine, harmless square. But if I had ten children, and all of 'em dyin' in front of the Cintra Bar, never, under any circumstances, must I cross the Place de France."

"Quiet, please." Alvarez was now on edge. "Bear right at the turning; we are there."

For a few seconds you heard only the tramp or stumble of footsteps. They turned, stood motionless, and looked ahead.

Paula, sighing, released her hold on Bill's left arm. Though she felt hot all over, she shook back her hair and pressed both hands to a chilly face. Now, she felt again, she could face anything.

Straight ahead, at a very slight downwards slope, was a real street. That is to say, it was two-dozen feet wide; it was paved evenly with square stone slabs, very faintly glistening. At its far end loomed the silhouette of a squat Moorish tower, pierced by a broad and pointed arch with a light somewhere vaguely beyond it.

A cool wind stroked their cheeks. On their left, towards the arch, ran what appeared to be one long building, of stone once white; but there were different roof levels. Lying partly in heavy shadow, it might have been several houses. On their left, past a grey-stone wall only four or five feet high, ran a garden of orange and pineapple trees set close yet in neat Arab rows. Murmurous in the breeze, the garden went on to a house near the Moorish tower.

"Well?" asked H.M. "If we're here, where are we and what do we do?"

Alvarez glanced towards the shadowed side of the building on the left. It was plain he knew of some secret door there.

"Walk in the same order," he directed in a low voice. "Near the wall of this building here, but a little out; not too close to it."

But, in their present mood, the order had begun to straggle. H.M., brooding over the Place de France, lumbered some distance behind. Alvarez seemed to be studying the wall. Paula, slow-breathing and firm even with muddy sandals, pressed at least three feet ahead in her eagerness to reach the dim-lighted arch. Only Bill remained alert, his right hand on the grip of the Webley, his eyes roving towards the rustling thick trees against starlight.

Then it happened with blinding speed.

Bill's long left arm shot out in a lunge, closing round Paula and yanking her back to safety behind his left side.

"Down!" he yelled. *"Down!"*

Paula flopped down, as did Alvarez. Bill, whipping out the Webley, went only down on one knee and looked up. H.M. was well to the rear, and standing up. Only Bill and H.M. saw the streak of the thrown knife whip out of the tree, whistle downwards across the spot where Paula would have been standing, smash its point low against the stone wall opposite, and rattle down.

Bill, the Webley in his hand, sprang to his feet, studied the trees for a fraction of a second, and then fired twice. Somebody screamed, and the two heavy explosions had not died away before a body whacked out of an orange tree into underbrush, rolling limply to the ground inside the garden wall.

"Got him," said Bill casually. "I thought I remembered that place, four oranges together like a half-circle, where he leaned out to throw. . . . Baggage, are you all right?"

"Darling, yes!"

"Get behind me," said Bill, facing the line of trees. "Completely behind me!"

"I'm not the least b-bit f-frightened," gasped Paula, obeying his orders and putting her arms round his waist. "Really I'm not."

"That's my harlot!" Bill said tenderly. It was a form of

address he often used in private; Paula liked it; but only absent-mindedly did he use it in public. "Put both your hands behind me, baggage; completely out of sight."

Alvarez's hand fell on his shoulder.

"That was well done, Bill," he muttered, with suppressed delight. "They know we're here; and Ali must have a bigger gang than we thought." Alvarez hesitated. "That knife was intended for Pau—" He stopped. "It would have gone—" Alvarez's gesture indicated a motion down past the collarbone and into the body.

"Right," said Bill.

"She's the only one who can identify Collier," said Alvarez. "But Collier can't throw knives. He's inside. Wait here; don't do anything foolish until I return."

To Paula's shaky imagination, which gave back images as in a blurred glass, he seemed to melt down into shadows. Probably through a concealed door, she thought, to meet Acting Commandant Perez. As a matter of fact, she was quite right.

But nobody saw the red wrath deepen and heighten in Bill's forehead as he continued to study the trees of the garden.

"Come on, you sneaking bastards!" he shouted, swinging the Webley loosely. "Who's got the nerve to throw another knife?"

"Y'know, son," casually observed H.M., whose Churchillian bowler was pulled down to his ears and who stood completely unprotected with feet apart, "that's not a bad idea." He drew the broad Riff knife, not quite cleansed, in a not quite cleansed hand. "I never learned how to throw one of these ruddy things, like the bloke who used to do it in the music hall. But I can have a shot at it." Then *he* thundered out. "Come on! Who wants a sportin' go?"

Inside the garden a wild parakeet shrieked, so horribly like the voice of Ilone Scherbatsky that for an instant they imagined they saw her face amid the trees.

"By the way, son," H.M. remarked, holding the knife by the tip and balancing it, "things went so fast a while ago I couldn't follow you. Were you shootin' from the hip, or what?"

"You *can* shoot from the hip." Bill's voice was quiet and contemptuous. "It's possible. But only some ass in a film would do it. You can't . . ."

Again Alvarez's hand fell softly on his shoulder while the Commandant beckoned H.M. closer. His whisper was so soft that they could scarcely hear him.

"From now on, Bill, you must obey orders to the letter. Got that? No matter what happens, I repeat: no matter what happens, you must not fire that revolver. This is vital. Do you understand?"

"Look here, Juan." Bill's own whisper was friendly but warning. "You brought Paula here as bait; or, anyway, Colonel Duroc did. You know what almost happened. If there's the slightest danger to her, in any way . . . you know what you can do with your orders, don't you?"

"I promise you there will not be. If my promise is fulfilled, will you obey to the letter?"

"All right." Bill slid the revolver back into the holster.

"Sir Henry," went on the insistent voice, "go with the others to the end of the street,"—a dark arm pointed towards the arch—"turn left, then inside the house, then downstairs to the big basement where the carpets are piled. Make no sound; stand just inside the door; but, for the last time, do not move or speak unless I give some signal. Now I must leave you."

This time Alvarez vanished like a ghost.

"Cor!" muttered H.M., himself a little daunted. A breeze made the garden sigh and scratch and whisper; a night bird squawked; once more the Webley slipped from its holster.

"C'mon," grunted the Old Maestro; and again they moved ahead with H.M. in place of Alvarez. Bill's left arm was again about Paula; she threw her arms round his neck; and there were such entangled endearments that H.M. blew false raspberries of disgust. "Listen," he whispered, "we got work to do. I can't endure any more canoodlin'! Son, keep an eye on that garden!"

This roused Bill, who whipped round to study it again. For a moment they moved in silence.

"Nice H.M.," whispered Paula, receiving in return only a baleful glare. "But I've been meaning to ask you. What *is* this horrible meaning attached to canoodling? Juan looked shocked even when he blurted it out accidentally."

"Well . . . now. Y'see, my dolly, I sort of told Alvarez and the Colonel that it meant far more than it really does. See what I mean?"

Paula's dark-blue eyes, on any matter like this, instantly

saw with delight.

"On every occasion," she said, "I shall use it to shock Juan and the Colonel, especially the Colonel. If . . ."

"S-ss-t!" snorted Bill, slipping back the Webley. "Here we are."

They had emerged from the arch into a sort of modern-built tunnel, common enough in the Kasbah, and open left and right at both ends. A stronger breeze swept through, with a smell of the clean Mediterranean, of dead fish, and the thickish pleasant odour of Tangier itself. Underfoot the ground was hard and sandy.

On their left, as they emerged, was a newly whitewashed wall with a large Moorish-arched door a little way to the left. Two electric bulbs, under yellow small boxes against the wall, gave the only light.

"I—I know where we are," gulped Paula against that strong wind. "If the worst part of it is over now . . ."

"Baggage," Bill told her very gently, "the worst part hasn't even begun yet."

The quiet words struck them dumb, together with the steady intent look in Bill's eyes. They guessed he knew what they would find, but that he would march against it just as steadily. It was as though they had been struck with deafness too.

With one accord they moved three abreast, as before, and into the Moorish arch of premises which belonged to Ali, the carpet dealer.

Inside they could see a hall, also of whitewashed stone walls, perhaps ten feet wide. At the left a painted, graceful Moorish staircase ascended into darkness. At the right were several arches, but only one large one inside which, on the thickness of the wall, had been painted a black arrow pointing downwards. Underneath ran the black painted legend, both in English and French, "Carpets and Antiques."

Though this hall was feebly illuminated, they could not see the source of the light. The floor was of small tiles, faintly coloured with some painting now half-obscured. Nothing moved. No noise stirred. The whole house might have been empty.

I have visited this shop before, Paula was thinking, with thoughts so thin and faint they hardly existed. Ali, whoever he is, has a quite legitimate business in addition to . . .

Though it is nearly impossible to walk on tiles without

sound, these three almost managed it. H.M., now leading, thrust his head round the side of the arch, peering to the left and downwards. A wooden staircase descended into gloom faintly lit with a dim yellow light some distance away. H.M. framed his villainous mouth for lip-reading.

"Keep to the wall," his mouth framed the words, "and follow me down."

They did. Paula's thoughts now tumbled through her mind with agony and remorse and an even greater love for Bill than she thought she already had. It was Bill who had thrust her back and flung her down under the streak of the knife; it was Bill who, jumping up instantly, had fired two blind shots that whisked a would-be assassin out of a tree like a fish on a line. Yet she, sometime earlier in the evening when she wallowed in a hot bath, had vaguely wished for him to be more aggressive. Aggressive!

It grew confused in Paula's brain with her vision of international bankers, whom she somehow mixed up with warmongers, and Bill outwitting them and banging the table. The intensity of her remorse can be felt only by those women whose husbands are still their lovers. Paula wanted to be tortured in public. She wanted to sob, but knew she mustn't. Of course, it was no longer necessary for Bill to be aggressive; that helped, but . . .

"S-ss-t!" H.M.'s very soft whisper shocked her back to reality.

They now moved, in single line, against a long wall that ran at right angles to the foot of the stairs. Some little distance ahead there was a smaller Moorish arched door, from which yellow light fell distinctly out across the stone floor.

H.M. thrust his bald head slowly round the edge of the door, and surveyed what was in front of him. His lip movements, at such close range, were terrifyingly easy to read as he turned back. First, according to what he said, Bill slipped into the room and slid across inside with his back to the wall. Then Paula. Finally H.M. Since the room was carpeted, there was not a breath of noise.

Inside, her back to a whitewashed wall with Bill on her right and H.M. on her left, Paula found her gaze swimming to take in details.

It was a vast room nearly forty feet square, though with a rather low ceiling for such proportions. Not quite in the middle, but pushed somewhat towards the watchers' left, was a squared pile of carpets about three feet high. The carpets, topside-up, glowed with sombre, deep, and sullen colours; each one was twenty feet square; and, being thin, their surface was as hard as turf.

In the whitewashed wall towards the watchers' left, there were two tall arched windows of crimson-glass panes, the windows set very wide apart. They were partly hung with robes such as H.M. had bought, with what looked like the gleaming white-gold of a scimitar scabbard, with a dagger in a heavy dark-blue sheath, with a Moorish war hammer in steel. Between the two windows stretched the immensity of what might have been authentic Oriental furniture. But it more resembled a heavy, stretched sideboard of carved blackish wood: above it a long mirror in a black wooden enclosure, its surface scattered with grotesque curios.

In the wall opposite the spectators stood another presumed sideboard, as long as the first and set close to it. Thus, directly across the room from the Moorish arched door by which they had entered, was another door just like it.

The third and last side (not counting the cleared wall against which they stood) should have had more room away from the pile of twenty-foot-square pile of carpets, but on that side were big white painted pigeonholes containing bolts or long yards of cloth or velvet or damask; and, in the middle of them, an immense velvet-covered board artfully laid out with flat weapons. A large lamp of Moorish brass work, hanging from the ceiling, lighted the silent room.

All this Paula saw, through blurred eyes, in a twentieth of the time it takes to tell. Then her eyes stopped, like the others', on a single dominating figure.

On top of the pile of carpets, near the right-hand end of it and with his back to them, stood Collier.

CHAPTER SIXTEEN

H.M. held up his hand for even more silence.

Collier could not see them, could not even animally sense them, because he was too much concentrated on the door directly opposite across the room. Beyond the arch of this door burned a faint light, but it led to a crooked tiled passage. Apparently an empty passage.

At first glance Paula might not have recognized Collier himself, since H.M.'s account to Duroc that afternoon and Duroc's account to her had made no mention of red hair dyed black. But a second glance told her. The thick shoulders and body, the whitish European lounge suit, the set and swagger of him, the highly polished tan shoes with lumpy toes. . . . It could be nobody else. She touched Bill's arm.

There was not even a rustle of leather as Bill drew the .45 from the holster, and his hand went up. For an instant he glanced across at H.M. Again it must be insisted that lip-reading, at very close range, becomes terrifyingly easy.

"Never thought I'd shoot a man in the back." Bill's lips framed the words. "But Coll . . ."

Both H.M.'s hands swept across Paula's and tightened powerfully round Bill's arm.

"No," his lips outlined, with a weird and almost cross-eyed expression on his face. "You promised. You gave your word."

Though Bill protested in furious mimicry, he lowered his arm. H.M. glanced at the black head.

"That's—?" his silent query went out. Paula nodded.

Still Collier tensely watched the open arch opposite, with its dim-burning lamp inside and its corridor beyond of white-plastered walls over stone. Collier's right hand, formerly concealed in front of him, now slipped down to the side.

He was carrying a .38 Colt's Banker's Special. Once more Bill turned.

"He's got a gun," Bill addressed H.M. in a kind of silent shout. "If I ask him to turn round, we can shoot it out. That's fair play, isn't it?"

"And," silently roared back H.M., touching Paula, "have him fire at *her?*"

Instantly Bill's hand went down, and H.M.'s called for even more silence as they listened.

Now they could hear footsteps.

The footsteps were on the tiles of that turning or twisting corridor beyond the door which Collier watched so tensely. Collier's gun hand came up. He stood near the right-hand side of that three-foot-high pile of rugs as hard as turf, and bought up the gun still further.

The footsteps, making no attempt at concealment, walked slowly and steadily without the least haste. Round a turning, and past a hidden light into full view in the narrow corridor, came Juan Alvarez.

All could see him, though Collier was much closer. In the left hand Alvarez still carried that odd little canvas bag. Otherwise he was not armed except for something he paused to discard at once. Plucking out the loop of the truncheon, Alvarez drew it down from under his waistcoat. He sent the truncheon thumping and clattering along the floor behind him.

Then Alvarez walked forward at the same pace to take Collier with his hands.

Out went Collier's harsh tenor voice, even into falsetto. But it was not fear. It was pure triumph.

"So it's wise guy again, eh?" jeered Collier. "I thought it must be, when they let you in so easy." His voice changed. "But I ain't playing marbles, wise guy. Stay where you are. Don't move. Or you'll get plenty heat."

Alvarez's utter contempt for firearms, which had so often worried Colonel Duroc, struck the three spectators now. Alvarez, a sauntering gentleman from his soft hat to his dark-grey suit, merely smiled without amusement. He moved forward at the same pace.

Collier fired—and missed.

The sharp *crack* of the short-nosed .38 was at once intensified yet immediately muffled by a boom of echoes which closed back on it in this thick-walled underground room. There was a whirring thud as the bullet, ricochetting off one wall, smacked to shapeless lead against the plaster-covered stone of another.

Alvarez, his contemptuous smile broadening, walked still forward.

Again Collier fired and missed. This time, somewhere, the bullet smashed a window.

Alvarez was now almost at the door. Collier, though always prudent, ran forward on the right-hand side of the carpet pile, hardly five feet from Alvarez just inside the door. As the shots and their echoes rolled and reverberated, it seemed to Paula that each object here—the two scarlet-paned windows, with their robes and weapons, the sideboard curios, even the hanging lamp of brass work—seemed to vibrate or tingle.

Then Collier, to make sure, fired three quick shots at what seemed very close range. Actually, it was not as close as that. And, though Collier aimed for the heart, he missed again. The first bullet struck Alvarez in the left chest below the collarbone, spinning his shoulder and side partway to the left; the second and third bullets missed.

At the first of those three shots, Bill Bentley ripped loose from H.M.'s hands. Bill, though a heavy middleweight at eleven-stone-six, was fast and light. One leap carried him to the top of the carpet pile, and noiselessly he raced across it. Afterwards Bill swore he had kept to the exact letter of his promise, since he had not fired from his first position.

Now he rammed the muzzle of the Webley so viciously into the back of Collier's neck that the man's head jerked and he almost toppled off the carpet pile.

"Drop the gun," Bill said, not loudly. "Drop it now, or I'll blow the front of your head off."

Collier hesitated, without turning round.

"Look, bud," he said, with a weary sneer. "I don't know who you are, but I don't bluff easy. So just—"

Then Collier stopped abruptly.

A .45 has a hard trigger pull. Bill meant quite simply what he said. With the muzzle jammed hard against the back of his neck Collier could feel the very faint vibration of the frame as Bill began to squeeze the trigger.

"Okay, bud." As though indulging a child, Collier threw out the Banker's Special, which landed on the carpeted floor. "But you'll get plenty for this."

Behind Collier's back, and concentrating on the pleasure of pulling the trigger, Bill could not get a good view of Alvarez.

"Juan," he shouted. "Are you all right?"

Alvarez's voice, hearty and firm as usual, showed a trace of amusement.

"Very fit, thanks," he answered. "No wound that could trouble a baby."

"Thank God! I was afraid . . . Never mind. Pick up his gun, will you, and join H.M. and Paula at the other side. There's more space to move about there."

Nobody saw Alvarez stagger slightly as he bent to pick up the Colt. Still carrying the grey canvas bag, he moved round the carpet pile with such damn-you determination that still no one observed anything until H.M. saw him.

"Now, up with your hands," Bill said to Collier. "Better behave."

There are tones in voices which do not have to speak loudly or with threat.

Collier hesitated, and raised his hands. Bill made a hard, quick search with his left hand, finding nothing dangerous except the long thin dagger done up in wrapping paper which Collier had bought at the ironmonger's. This Bill flung behind him over the pile of carpets.

Still Collier lounged, his eyelids drooping. The fingers of Bill's left hand dug down inside his adversary's collar, and gripped there. With the Webley now jammed into Collier's back, Bill maneuvered him to the exact centre of the carpet. Darting back, Bill told him to turn round.

Collier lumbered round, his hands still up. Bill, on the carpet about eight feet away and facing him now, kept the Webley trained on the middle of Collier's belly. Alvarez, Paula, and H.M. stared at them as if hypnotized.

"Put your hands down now," said Bill.

Collier's heavy shoulders quivered as he put down his hands. His dull eyes opened wide, then narrowed as his lip lifted at the corner.

"What's the big idea?" he drawled lazily. "Whadda ya think *you're* doing, fancy-pants?"

"You'll find out," said Bill, giving him back just as meaning a look. "H.M.," he called, with no movement of his head or the Webley.

"All present and correct, son," returned the reassuring rumble of H.M's voice.

"I read somewhere you were either a barrister or a

doctor . . ."

"It's all right, son. In my younger and more asinine days I was both. I'll take care of Alvarez. Just stand there and think where you'd like to shoot the blighter when you do plug him."

"But I assure you, Sir Henry, that I am quite all right," Alvarez said, with a slight laugh.

"I know, I know. Where's that torch you were carrying?"

"In my right-hand coat pocket. Here you are."

"Thank'ee, son." H.M. hustled round to Alvarez's left side.

"Believe me, sir, I appreciate your concern. But there is not the least . . ."

"Shut up," said H.M.

Despite protests H.M. quickly unbuttoned jacket, waistcoat, and shirt, slitting down the under shirt and pushing it aside like the shirt. Then, slipping the knife back, he held back linen and cloth with his left hand and studied the chest wound with the torch in his right.

It did not take long. His fingers were gentle. Alvarez's fingers, as he impatiently replaced and rebuttoned the clothes, were not at all gentle.

H.M. moved round to his right side, dropping the torch into Alvarez's pocket.

"Now listen, son!" He spoke in a fierce whisper. "I think that bullet more than grazed your left lung before it ploughed up into the shoulder."

"Well?"

"Lord love a duck, don't you twig it yet? I said *lung*. Unless we get you to a nursin' home for an operation within half an hour or so, you're finished. You'll die."

Alvarez's look became terrifying because it was not angry; it was merely perplexed.

"Die? But what does it matter?" he asked. "Provided"—his right hand, still holding the snub-nosed Colt, stabbed out with ferocity towards Collier—"I first smash and then arrest *that*."

Suddenly something flickered in his eyes.

"Maureen . . ." he began, and stopped.

Paula, who had been kneeling beside him, now stood up. Since she had wiped blood-stained hands on her slacks and also touched her hair as she threw it back, she was as wild-looking a figure as any.

"Maureen will understand," she said.

"Sir Henry," Alvarez said gently, "you force me to remind you that I am still in command here." His voice hardened, though he coughed. Out he spoke on the old note. "Bill!"

"Yes, old boy?"

"Now be good enough," Alvarez said formally to H.M., "to climb up on the carpets, take the Webley from Bill, and keep Collier covered while I speak to Bill privately. Should Collier attempt to run, shoot him through the head. I am sure, sir, you understand the necessity."

H.M. had to relieve his feelings in some way. His voice went out at full power.

"It's a pleasure!" he bellowed, and the thunder echoed back.

H.M., with some difficulty as regards his corporation, climbed up on the carpets. He muttered instructions and took the Webley from Bill, who leaped down nimbly from the carpets.

Alvarez stood very erect, holding the canvas bag still in his left hand.

"First, Bill," he said, "I want you to pay no attention to what Sir Henry says."

"Juan, I didn't like that business. What *does* he say?"

"He thinks I am a little hurt. That is absurd." Smiling, he seized Bill's arm with his right hand. "Look at that pile of carpets. It's a natural ring, or near enough; it must be twenty feet square. It is as firm as ground underfoot, isn't it?"

"Yes, but—"

"I am going to smash him," Alvarez said through his teeth, and nodded towards Collier. "I am going to smash him first."

His left hand opened, and the canvas bag dropped to the floor. Its drawstring was loose. Out rolled a single boxing glove, presumably one of two pair in the bag.

"Me hurt?" He smiled. "It is nonsense. Look at me. . . . Watch!"

Squaring himself, Alvarez began to throw out the sketch of a left hook. His left shoulder went up, the arm darted out in time with his forward-thrust left leg.

Abruptly Alvarez stopped. It was not the intensity of pain which burnt through his shoulder. This he would not have minded. But he could not use the arm. He would have toppled straight forward if Bill had not thrown a quick left arm round his other side, and caught him in front with his right. Gently Bill eased him back to standing position.

"Easy, old boy. Easy does it, now."

Alvarez looked strangely at his left arm, and slowly lowered it.

"I can't do it," he whispered, in blank amazement.

"Easy, Juan, easy."

"I can't do it," repeated Alvarez, in horror.

Though Bill held him hard, again he attempted the blow with his arm. Again he failed.

For a second his mouth trembled like that of a man with palsy. Then such outward expressions vanished. His face became as rigid and emotionless as that of a red Indian. But he could not control the look in his eyes. Out of them looked all the torture, all shamed humiliation, that any man can know.

"I can't do it," he faltered.

Bill's expression seemed wooden, except for the flush under his cheekbones and the expression in his eyes, which he instantly lowered. Only Paula, facing him from the other side of Alvarez, knew the boil of rage and pity and sympathy in Bill's heart.

Bill cleared his throat.

"Look here, old boy," he said quietly. "Would you like *me* to have a go at him?"

Alvarez hesitated. He turned round.

"*Would* you?" he asked eagerly, in a low voice.

"Yes," said Bill.

"Hard to tell you this." Alvarez spoke rapidly, clutching at Bill's arm. "Sounds too foolish. But a word like—well, sportsmanship. That's my god. That's all I ever worshipped. Would be as good as smashing him myself. To see him smashed. By a sportsman."

"Here," muttered Bill. "That's all right," he added.

"*Can* you smash him, Bill?"

"Dunno," said Bill, wiping his mouth with the back of a heavy left hand. "May not have a ghost of a chance. But I'll try, so help me."

He threw off his coat, flung it on the floor, and did the same with his necktie.

"Let's get it over with," he said.

But Alvarez, though he did not know it, had bodily fever mounting into his head from his wound. He almost babbled.

"Now listen!" he whispered. "This afternoon, at the tailor's, Mark Hammond said something. Can I remember? Something like: 'There's only one kind of amateur who might beat Collier in a short fight. That's a pure slugger, who'd trade punches like Collier himself, and might land a haymaker.' "

Bill looked down at his hands, spreading the fingers.

"Wait, wait," urged Alvarez, as though talking against time. "You know his strength, and above all his weaknesses. That gives you more help. Do you remember what you heard on the phone?"

"Oh, yes. Funny, that. But I remember."

"Now hear *my* advice. Don't stand and slog with him—not at first, anyway. Don't let him crowd you or stalk you. Get in fast; punch hard; get out fast. Keep him moving. He may be sluggish and slow, but for God's sake mind his punch."

"Haven't got much guard," said Bill. "Got to stand and take it. To hell with him."

"Anyway, I think you've got a harder punch, especially your straight right and right cross. Measure him. Remember, this must be a short fight or he may give you too much punishment. If I see an opportunity for you, I'll shout, 'Now!' Got that, Bill? *'Now!'* Then go for him all out." Now the fever had reached his eyes. "Can't think—anything else. Must be lots."

"I've got everything," said Bill.

"Stop! Forgot. . . . Must have something else for myself!"

"Juan!" exclaimed Paula. "Where you going?"

"Back in a moment," he assured them. "Must fetch . . ."

Straight shouldered, Alvarez walked stiffly away along the open space towards their right.

There was only eerie silence. All this time neither H.M. nor Collier had spoken a word, standing motionless some eight feet apart. Paula and Bill could not see H.M.'s face; perhaps this was just as well, since it struck drumb even G. W. Collier. But they heard the sharp *click* as H.M.'s thumb drew back the hammer of the Webley so that it was cocked; it now became a hair- trigger which could be fired at the smallest pressure. As H.M. gently lowered the muzzle so that a .45 bullet would catch Collier well below the belt, his forefinger tapped and tapped lightly at the trigger.

Also, during the time Paula had faced Bill across Alvarez,

she had felt her fierce feelings of pity and sympathy change to terror. As Alvarez moved quickly away, Paula ran to Bill, Threw her arms round him, and put her head against his chest.

"No!" She spoke in a smothered whisper, shaking her head. "Don't do it! You mustn't fight him, Bill. . . . I won't let you!"

He tried gently, at first without success, to tilt her chin up so that she looked at him.

"Now, baggage." He smiled. "What's the matter with your hair? You've got blood spots in it."

"Bill!" she went on in that muffled frantic voice, head down. "You've done a lot of boxing. But you've never paid much attention to it. This man's a—a pro. He'll hurt you. He'll hurt you awfully."

"Sorry, baggage. Got to do it."

"But why, why, why?"

He leaned forward and kissed her hair. She felt the fast, heavy beating of his heart. His low voice was one she knew he used only when he spoke of their future, their ambitions, their retirement, their love; issued from deep inside him, so faintly she scarcely heard it.

"Got to *win,"* said Bill.

"Bad as that, darling?"

"Yes. There are some decencies you've got to . . . got to . . ."

Paula was openly crying. She did not care. She lifted her face, though the tears blinded her and she could hardly see him.

"All right," she said in a choked voice, and pressed him harder. "Then go in and smash him! Smash him!"

Alvarez returned. He had located a high, square table, with thick curved ebony legs and a mosaic top, which he asked Bill to move over to the edge of the ring. It stood on about the same height.

"Will you help me to stand up on this?" he requested, his face now composed and like that of a hanging judge. From the top of the table he looked down at Bill.

"Have you any more cartridges for the Webley?" he asked in a cold and steady manner. Bill fished in his discarded coat and gave him a handful, which he dropped in his coat. "Now get the Webley from Sir Henry, and bring it to me. There is one more bullet left in the Colt, and I can keep Collier from running."

Bill leaped up on the carpets and murmured something to H.M., who handed over the Webley. But the enormous old ghoul doubtless guessed what was afoot. He moved to the extreme right-hand end of the carpet, where he stood sideways with his fists on his hips.

Jumping down again, Bill put the Webley in Alvarez's left hand. Scooping the boxing gloves back into the canvas bag, he took the bag with him when he returned and stood beside H.M. The flush under Bill's eyes had grown, and he breathed hard.

Alvarez's voice ripped across the room.

"And now, Mr. Collier, we will deal with *you.*"

Collier stood alone. In the middle of the dark yet rich colours of the carpet, he stood with his back to one so-called "sideboard," with its mirror and curios. Another such sideboard almost touched it at the far angle of the left-hand wall.

And Collier's face, with the red hair so obviously dyed black, seemed to stand out vividly in candle colour. He had forgotten to dye his eyebrows, which remained red. The eyebrows drooped over his pale eyes, and his lip lifted at one corner. His broad, thick body seemed planted there, legs apart.

"Why, if it ain't wise guy again," he said, in a sort of bored recognition. "Whadda ya know!"

Again he addressed an invisible companion.

"Wise guy," he said, "is the soldier boy who always wants to fight. I hadda sap him twice, and put him out like a light. I ain't bad with a heater, too. See them bullet wounds?" Collier almost laughed. "Wise guy couldn't fight a toy panda now."

Alvarez's expression and voice did not change.

"Ah, yes," he said, "speaking of fighting. You are now trapped and surrounded. You cannot leave this room. I imagine you don't believe that?"

Skepticism showed in Collier's face like a pale gas globe.

"I just don't scare easy," he said. "What do *you* think?"

"What I think, either of you or of your half-witted style of speech, is of no importance. I *tell* you what is so. When you leave this room, you will be taken to the police station. Either you will leave here with one bullet in you, exactly where you fired it into me, or else you will leave quietly and with no shooting. The choice depends on you. To leave quietly, my good scum, you must first stand and fight."

"Fight?" echoed Collier. For a moment he hesitated, and his dull sly eyes seemed pleased as he licked his lips. "Sure, wise guy, why not? I been feeling"—he moved his shoulders—"like I needed a nice little workout. Who's the guy I'm gonna fight?"

"I am," snarled Bill, taking a step forward and emptying the two pairs of gloves on the floor.

Collier's head twisted round. His eyes narrowed as he saw Bill's torso, the exact build of the fighting man, in the short-sleeved shirt. Also, Bill was a little taller and heavier, and he had a wicked look in his eye.

"The carpets will be your ring," said Alvarez. "You will fight only three rounds. However, you may have professional three-minute rounds and fight according to American rules instead of International since you are a naturalized American. . . ."

Out roared Sir Henry Merrivale, with such suddenness that all stood motionless.

"Stow that gab!" said H.M. "I'm glad to say that communist louse isn't even a naturalized American. His passport's a fake."

"What's that?" demanded Alvarez.

"Oh, son! Didn't I tell you we, meaning the Colonel and myself, mostly the Colonel doin' the cabling had a lot more evidence about him, a lot you didn't know? Duroc got down to business as soon as I told him this hyena's passport was a forgery."

"But you did not see the passport."

"I didn't need to. I heard all about it. Son, don't you remember readin' it aloud at the flat? Place of birth: Moscow, Russia. That's all right. But this feller here had to make it too clever. He stuck on a rubber stamp with the written date of his naturalization."

"Well?"

"No American passport has ever had that," retorted H.M, leering at Alvarez, "and none ever will. No such passport was ever issued from Washington or any consulate. 'Collier' is a fake. So Duroc got on the cable and even the phone. We'd been neglecting the American end, because all Collier's and Iron Chest's dirty work had come from Europe. But we got back replies from several cities as well as the FBI that nearly burnt the paint off the desk."

During all this Collier, his eyelids dropping, smirked and seemed almost pleased.

"He was born in Russia, all right. Learned his trade as a diamond cutter there, and in Amsterdam. Sneaked into the States; nobody knows how, but it's a big country with a lot of borders. Want to hear why he had to give up prize fighting?"

"Yes," snapped Alvarez.

"He's wanted for murder in Cleveland. But something more fetching – they want him in Chicago for manslaughter, maybe murder. He'd pinched a car and was spotted. He was making a getaway, very fast, when he tried to turn and ran up over the pavement. A little girl was rollin' a hoop near the fence. Good old Collier could have missed her, easily. There were no trees or lamp posts on the outside. But he was feeling . . . well, maybe a little mean. So he ran over her and crushed her and killed her. She was nine years old."

Collier yawned.

"Well, she'll never be ten," he remarked.

There was dead silence, except for a hissing of indrawn breath.

"Pop here," said Collier, putting a toothpick inside his jeering mouth, "give a spiel about my record. That's okay by me. You can't catch me, wise guy. Nobody ever can." His mouth spread wide. "But do I fight, or don't I?"

"You fight," snapped Alvarez. He pointed to the corner between the two sideboards, at the further angle of the carpet. "There's your corner." Then he pointed to the angle between the broad open space and the pigeonholes of folded material. "There is yours, Mr. Bentley."

Bill took up a pair of boxing gloves as Collier turned towards him. One glove smacked Collier full in the face, and broke the toothpick so that Collier flung it out.

"As *Mr.* Collier would say," rattled Alvarez, "we have no seconds, no water bottles, above all no mouthpieces. We have not even a referee . . ."

"Oh, yes, you have," thundered H.M. H.M. yanked off his jacket, unloosed his tie, and pitched both over the edge of the ring. "I'm your referee, and don't think I'm not!"

"Good!" said Alvarez.

Though Collier's thick body did not move, his wicked low-lidded gaze was fixed on Bill.

"You're a amachoor, kid," he said. "I can smell 'em. I'm

gonna take you apart." His rasping tenor grew gentle. "But I'm a good-hearted joe, see? Don't blame me when I break your jaw or split your cheek or put your eyesight so's nobody can fix it. Blame wise guy."

"Turn round," ordered Alvarez.

Collier's eyes moved back. The boxing gloves lay at his feet. In his good right hand Alvarez held the Colt, with its one bullet; in his left hand he held with difficulty the heavy, cocked Webley.

"One final warning," he said in a clear but rasping voice. "If at any time you should try to run from the ring and get away, you will be shot through the head. Now I daresay you suppose, as in all things, this is bluff?"

"I told you I don't bluff easy," said Collier, again almost laughing. "Now I ask you—would I get scared about this?"

"Then you must be taught," said Alvarez. He whipped out his right arm and fired.

Again the sharpened *crack* of noise, unnerving, was rolled back and smothered in its echoes. In the mirror of a sideboard, well behind Collier, there jumped the black spot of the bullet hole, surrounded by long cracks where it had drilled cleanly without smashing the whole mirror.

Collier's right hand darted to the right side of his head. He twisted to look over his shoulder. A narrow but thick plume of black hair, shredding in the air with the red roots intermingled, had flown out as the bullet flashed past without even burning the scalp, and hair had now settled gently on the carpet.

Again Alvarez's cold, steady voice jabbed at Collier's nerves.

"Unfortunate," he said, "I had meant to fire at least an inch wider. Whatever my opinion of firearms, my job requires me to be a first-class shot. Of course, I am not as good as Bill."

Dropping the empty Colt, Alvarez shifted into his right hand the heavy, hair-trigger Webley.

"It was I who told you," he said, "that I never bluff and I despise those who do. Now a part of that same final warning. If you strike one foul blow—just one, remember—you will be shot through the body."

Again Alvarez's right arm whipped out.

"Do you want another lesson?" he inquired.

Collier, despite his fury, could not help recoiling.

"Skip it, wise guy," he tried to say nonchalantly. "What if I foul the kid by accident?"

"You will be shot just the same. . . . That is all. We will dispense with any preparatory signal for seconds out of the ring. The rounds will begin, and end, when I call, 'Time.' Mr. Referee! Let them come out of their corners; give them brief instructions. . . . We can begin."

Part of Collier's mind tapped at his small brain, warning him to be prudent. Picking up the gloves, he swung his shoulders as he strolled to his corner between the side-boards. There he took off his coat, his tie, and also his shirt, sweeping aside curios with a crash so that he could put the clothes on the sideboard. He wore no undershirt.

His torso, red-speckled and matted with reddish hair, was rounded and hard without obvious muscles to show his great punching power. As he pulled on the gloves, perhaps that torso was not in as good condition as it appeared under shirt and coat. But he was obviously unbeatable by an amateur; still formidable and still tricky.

Bill, in the other corner, instantly tore off his shirt. He himself had never troubled to wear an undershirt, and he had a belt as Collier had. Bill, not in the least hirsute, showed white and in perfect condition under the Moorish lamp. His legs shook a trifle. As he snugged his hands into the gloves, keeping the thumb well down, he felt faint sweat on the hands.

"Come here, you two!" boomed Sir Henry Merrivale, himself an immense figure of evil, standing in the ring with his hat gone and his bald head shining.

As he waved the contestants together, H.M. glanced across at Alvarez.

"This idea of a boxing ring full of flyin' bullets," he said in a musing tone; "well, now, that's unusual. But I like it, son. Only, for the love of Esau, don't hit young Bentley and don't hit me."

"I promise, sir."

Bill, moving slowly to the middle of the ring, saw Collier loom up in grotesque shape. The thick red-matted torso contrasted with the whitish broad face under dyed hair. As they met in front of H.M., Collier opened wide oyster-coloured eyes tinged with yellow.

"I'm gonna murder you, amachoor," he said, and looked as though he could.

Abruptly all Bill's nervousness vanished. Up to this night, he had not known Collier's entire record. But that was not it. To the astonishment of Collier, who liked to scare people, in Bill's eyes appeared a glint of pure enjoyment.

Then up spoke probably the most unorthodox referee who ever entered a ring.

"Now listen, both of you," said H.M., his fists on his hips. "The Commandant says you've got to fight by American rules instead of International. To me that's eyewash; but do it. That means"—here he turned to Bill—"that practically anything goes, except what I'll tell you. You can punch in the clinches, but only if you've got both hands free. No holdin' with one arm and punchin' with the other fist. No shoving or wrestling; and anybody who hits on the break will get a thick ear from me. What's more, unless you want a swipe over the eye, don't let me see a low blow, a rabbit punch, or a kidney punch. Got that? Right.

"You know the rules about knockdowns, or you wouldn't be here. Neutral corner, and don't come out till I tell you. If somebody's knocked off the carpets, we'll treat it as though he'd been knocked through the ropes.

"Now this skunk," continued H.M., casually jerking his thumb towards Collier, "may try any dirty trick he's used to. Jam the thumb of his glove into your eye, butt his head under your chin or jaw, foul you with outlawed punches . . . well, there are a lot of 'em. But remember, if he does, he'll get a bullet through his guts. So he may be as clean as he's ever been."

Then this curious referee paused to consider, stroking his jaw.

"No, don't shake hands," he added sharply, as Bill made a tentative movement. "I wouldn't have you touch Collier's filthy gloves for a million in cash. That's all! Go to your corners, and come out when the Commandant calls 'Time.' "

Bill turned and ran lightly back. Collier stood for a moment, shoulders quivering.

"Look, Pop," he said. "If you wasn't an old man . . ."

"So?" inquired H.M.

Again Collier hesitated. In his life, he was thinking, he had seen mean-looking guys, ugly-looking guys, murderous-looking guys. But he had seen no pan like the one on this old guy with the bald head, who looked bigger and tougher than a bouncer in a low joint on the lower East Side. Sure he had a belly; but so had the bouncers.

"So?" repeated H.M.

From his hip pocket he drew a broad knife sharpened to a hair line, whetting his thumb on the blade. He looked straight down into Collier's eyes.

Collier, sneering, moved off towards his own corner.

Alvarez, in some fashion holding his left arm crooked in front of him, never raised his eyes from the second hand of his wrist watch. In that deathly quiet you could almost imagine you heard it ticking.

Hurrying back to *his* corner, Bill for some reason was startled to see Paula. It shook his heart, unnerving him a little. Paula could get her shoulders and arms well over the edge of the carpet. She was standing down at the angle, arms stretched out on the carpet, head raised.

Paula's silky hair was still a little disordered. Her eyes showed a film of dried tears. Very carefully she seemed to adjust her lips before she managed to smile.

"Bill," she whispered. "Luck!"

Bill went down on one knee. He picked up Paula's hand, and almost reverently kissed it.

"Don't worry, baggage," he said. "Be all right."

Then he whipped up and round, because of a sound from across the ring. The slight shakiness took Bill's legs again; his body seemed to itch. No spectators would have thought that a fight of this sort could drive Collier into such fury.

"I'm gonna take you apart!" he screeched across the sombre yet vivid colours of the carpet. "And you know why!" He gulped. "Stuck-up Limey. . . . Jeez, how I hate Britishers. All smart guys do! I'm gonna bust your nose with the first punch. I'm gonna slam your kidneys through your back."

Bill's voice, though not loud, carried clearly across the ring.

"Stop your brag," he said. "Let's see you fight."

"*Time,*" snapped Alvarez.

CHAPTER SEVENTEEN

About two minutes before the call of "Time" while H.M. was giving his instructions to the fighters, there were two persons in that underground room who might have cried in their hearts, without speaking a word, "I can't stand this any longer!"

One of them was Paula Bentley, the other was Juan Alvarez.

Alvarez, who twice had suffered a black-out and nearly fallen, let nobody notice it. As H.M. gave the instructions, his sound right hand, balancing the Webley, pushed back the sleeve of his shirt so that he could see the dial of his wrist watch.

Suppose he couldn't see the second hand? But, though his sight was little dimmed, he had no trouble with it. He had almost ceased to feel pain. Everywhere he kept seeing the face of Maureen Holmes. Once, horribly, he imagined she was there.

Alvarez supposed his lung must have been hit, since he kept swallowing with a taste of blood choked down. Yet, every time he looked at H.M., the old boy kept nodding and nodding as though in reassurance.

Paula Bentley, as she listened to those same instructions by H.M., wanted to curl up somewhere in a corner, out of sight, and stifle her ache of misery where she was certain nobody could see her. What rang most clearly in her mind were the words which Collier had used like a simpleton schoolboy: "I'm a good-hearted joe, see? Don't blame me when I break your jaw or split your cheek or put your eyesight . . ." No!

Paula was terrified by Collier, and had been so since she first saw him. In her heart she did not believe Bill could beat him. Now she hurried over to the angle of the carpets that formed Bill's corner. Bill turned away from H.M., and walked back. He stopped as he saw her. They exchanged those few words which so hurt her yet pleased her, especially when Bill kissed her hand like . . . like . . . Never mind. She sensed he was nervous yet with a kind of joy deep in him.

Across the ring Collier screeched out more of those words which so frightened her. Bill replied as Bill. Fortunately, she thought from the sound of the voice, Juan couldn't have been hurt much. Out snapped his strong voice with:

"Time."

She saw Bill at a half-dance, his left glove out, his right well up but unobtrusive near his side. She knew his shoes, rough soles and rough heels, wouldn't slip on that coloured carpet. She wanted to put her head down, and couldn't.

Alvarez, standing at the height of the ring midway at one side, kept his eyes flickering between his wrist watch and the two fighters. He held the Webley half raised in his right hand. He saw the fighters come out with murder in their eyes. The sheer hatred that flowed between them was like a knife flash from each.

Collier, drawing a deep breath into his thick chest, attempted to dance out like his opponent. Only then did he understand, as he should have understood long ago, that whatever springiness he had ever possessed in his legs was now gone. To dance out like that would make him look foolish, and you must never impair the dignity of G.W. Collier.

Instead he prowled out and stalked out, left arm and glove across him at chin height, right hand held dangerously low. They met near the middle of the ring, with H.M. dodging behind them. Bill was always moving, never in the same place. Collier merely stood, pivoting right and left like a heavy gun. Both men's left hands went out together, with a light *whick-whick* of leather against leather, measuring for distance.

Bill darted to the right. He darted back to the left. Then, darting in over Collier's too-low right hand, he drove a hard left hook to the cheekbone and rocked Collier's head. As the glove thudded against the cheekbone, Collier had that old familiar ringing in his head. Infuriated, he fired back his deadliest weapon: the "killer" right cross. But it went so wild that Bill did not even have to slip it. A strange, puzzled look flashed across Collier's eyes.

Is it possible, Alvarez was thinking furiously, he's so conceited he hasn't realized his timing will be badly out? No!

Incredible!

Again Bill lammed Collier with a hard left to the belly, making Collier grunt. But Collier, thinking for himself, decided it was time to quit fooling around. He'd go in and just bust this guy who hadn't even no hair on his chest. Collier lashed out with the one-two: left hook to the head and straight right to the ribs. Both punches seared through Bill's defence, and thudded hard.

"Haah!" grunted Collier, breathing too hard.

He waded in and crowded, throwing every punch he knew in such a fast and murderous flurry of gloves that H.M. had hard work to follow it.

And Bill, against all advice, was furious enough to stand and slug it out with him.

No, no! screamed some noise inside Alvarez's head, as his eyes flickered dully to the watch and up again. But, if you must do it, use your right hand!

Paula, so dazed she was hardly conscious of her actions, hurried round the carpets towards the same side as Alvarez.

In that thumping flurry, with gloves blurred as they moved, Bill was being hurt—badly. Collier's left pounded him under the breastbone dangerously near the solar plexus. Collier's right jolted him hard under the heart. And both punches make you feel as though the innards had been drawn out of you. Though many of the punches flew wild over Bill's shoulders, and he caught more on his elbows or gloves, Collier was hammering and hammering through.

A swinging right opened a small cut over Bill's left eye. Almost instantly, again Collier's deadly right smashed in under the left eye. And again. It would raise a swelling which might well close the eye. Again Collier fired for it, and landed.

Paula could not watch this, especially when it was Bill's blood. She put her face against the carpet.

Your right hand, she was praying without words. Bill! Your right hand!

Step by step Collier drove him back, presumably to send him over the carpet edge with a right cross. Bill—battered, shaky on his legs, wind going—fought back viciously. He hammered Collier's belly with his left, and drove left hooks that made Collier's face swell red. But still, faintly believing he knew his own stamina, he would not throw his right hand.

The stink of sweat, the closeness of Collier's eyes and Collier's arms, revolted him far more than the blood trickling down on his own left eyebrow. Another right thudded under his heart, and he gasped. By the movement of Collier's left shoulder, Bill guessed the man would throw a dummy punch over Bill's shoulder so that Collier could fall into a clinch.

Wedging both gloves against Collier's shoulders, Bill with a heave of sheer main strength flung the man off. Collier staggered back, and almost fell. Swinging to the right, Bill tried to move lightly and easily backwards about four feet inside the line of carpet and towards his own corner.

But Collier, also wheeling, came stalking in. Both gloves moved slowly under his chin, under the leer of his triumphant eyes and mouth. His right cheek, red and swollen, looked at close range as though it might have been split. Yet Bill could not see this, even if it were not for blinding sweat on his own face. Blood slowly spilled on his left eyelid, and he felt the skin stretch underneath it as the swelling rose to close it.

Get ready!

One of Collier's hands telegraphed a straight right to the head. But that was only an old trick. His left hand shot out and a little up, slamming Bill again not far from the solar plexus.

Bill's breath seemed to explode from his mouth; he staggered, and fell on one knee.

Alvarez, trying to steady his uncertain eyesight on the watch, groaned aloud.

Paula, who had her face down on the carpet, opened one eye just before that. Now she buried her face in the carpet.

At least, she was thinking, it'll be over in a moment. He won't be hurt any longer. That's the main thing. And yet . . . if only . . .

She was roused again by the high, giggling sneer which Collier used for a laugh.

"Amachoors," panted Collier, his red chest heaving. "Sure, they wanna go for the head. No body punches. Naw. They . . .

"There's your neutral corner!" roared Sir Henry Merrivale, pointing behind him at the far angle of the carpets at the other side of Collier's own corner. "Do you get back there, or do you wait till Christmas before I begin counting?"

Collier, about to sneer, thought better of it and trotted

back. But he still faced the side of the ring where H.M., bending over Bill on one knee, had begun to count. As he passed Alvarez, Collier was raising and lowering his arms and elbows fowl-fashion.

Good God! thought Alvarez. That swine is arm-weary at the end of the first minute in the first round. His wind is going, too. It can't be possible . . . ?

Paula kept her head raised, looking towards the right where H.M.'s immense behind was exposed as he bent over to count, and Bill was on one knee. H.M. would thunder out the count, with mumbled words between. Paula heard it all.

"One!" roared H.M. "You don't fool me, son. *Two!* What game are you playin', hey? *Three!"*

Bill quietly brought the breath back into his lungs. When he raised his head, H.M. saw that his eyes were both clear, though one was half-closed. He had been badly hurt and he ached, but his stamina remained. With one glove he wiped the blood from his left eye, and wiped the glove on his trousers.

"I'll take six, Maestro," he whispered. "I've taken his best punches. Now wait."

"Four!" The weasel's not struck a foul blow yet. *Five!* Want me to give him half the knife? *Six!* But you don't need . . ."

Bill sprang to his feet, facing round to the other side.

Instantly Collier was moving out, prowling yet hurrying from the other corner.

As Bill passed Paula, he appeared in bad shape. His legs seemed not quite steady. Under the Moorish lamp another bright-red trickle of blood gleamed above his right eyebrow and the yellowish purple bruise beneath was swelling and closing. His torso showed the red splotches of body blows. His left hand hung down, his right barely up. . . .

Collier knew what to do.

"You son of a bitch," he said softly.

And, dropping his left hand, he lunged forward with full power in his right hand against that smear of blood which gleamed over Bill's left eye.

Then it happened all at once, as though Bill had leaped to life.

Bill, slipping under the punch with head and shoulder moving to his right, caught Collier coming in. At the same instant Bill's heavy right fist streaked out and thudded against the unprotected left side of Collier's jaw.

It was the hardest punch of the fight. Collier's legs shook; his head twitched while the film came over his eyes, and his gloves pawed the air. Immediately Bill drove into him with both hands—and made his greatest mistake. Or, at least, the matter is debatable.

Alvarez swore that Bill could have flung the attack to the head with both fists for a quick knockout. H.M. roared back, perhaps with the most reason, that the attack might have begun at the head; then travelled down and up again.

Anyway, Bill did neither. Putting his head down, he flew with both fists for the belly—Collier's weakest spot. The gloves flashed in and out like piston rods, to gruesome and horrible noises spurting from Collier's mouth. Desperately he tried to straighten Bill up with short, chopping uppercuts from beneath.

He failed. Instead of diving into a clinch and holding on, Collier lost his head. All his ringcraft blew to pieces. Instinctively his right hand went up, to crack down on the back of Bill's neck with the forbidden rabbit punch.

Alvarez's right hand, holding the heavy and hair-trigger Webley, moved straight out in aim for Collier's arm.

Then Alvarez fired. It was less a pistol shot than a heavy explosion.

Because the Commandant's eyesight was unsteady, the shot missed Collier's arm. But it would have blown off the forehead of Sir Henry Merrivale if H.M. had not dropped straight down on his face when he saw Alvarez's arm dart out. Collier, terrified and sick and hurt, at last drove his arms though Bill's and locked him in a clinch. The bullet tore open the looking glass, splitting it with cracks in all ways, sending great shards of the mirror crashing and clattering down.

"Break, you two!" yelled H.M., throwing up one hand from his position on the floor. "Break!"

It was unnecessary to tell them this. Collier, badly hurt and arm-weary, wanted a second to breathe. Bill, again wiping the blood from his eye, darted back three paces. But immediately, as H.M. stood up, they flew together.

Collier threw a swinging left, and Bill a straight right. By a fraction of a second Bill's straight right beat Collier to the punch. It broke Collier's nose, squashing it even flatter against the face, as Bill's right arm jerked up and blocked the other's left swing. Bill's own left hooked to the right of Collier's jaw. The man staggered back.

Juan Alvarez spoke out at last.

"Now!" he shouted. *"Get him!"*

Paula Bentley, well beyond Alvarez, seemed the strangest figure of all. When she thought her husband beaten and hurt, she would not cry or say a word. Yet she was now standing wide-eyed, the tears rolling down her face, uttering only incoherent noises, as she saw him go all out for the finish.

Four punches did it, as Bill drove Collier swiftly back towards the other side of the ring, the side with the second sideboard and a window of crimson glass on either side. Seeing that the side of Collier's right cheek was really split open, Bill would not hit it. He fired three battering-ram punches to the belly, and threw the right cross for the last time. Then he jumped aside.

Collier fell straight forward, as a man does when he is badly hurt. Before he fell, his glazing eyes still bulged with hatred and amazement. And hatred was still welling inside him as his heavy body crumpled face down on the carpet. He stirred, fighting in the dream of the knockout. His heavy legs straightened out. His arms and shoulders writhed, instinctively, so that he could roll parallel to the line of the carpet and get up.

But he rolled the wrong way—towards the edge of the carpets. The blood from his nose, a kind of moustache spreading down over his mouth, left a smear on the carpet edge as he turned over. And Collier, the sneer gone from his face, fell heavily between sideboard and carpet pile, and lay still.

Silence.

It seemed to stretch out interminably, while nobody moved or spoke.

"Time!" snapped Alvarez, and carefully lowered his left arm. With the same studious care he pushed on the safety catch of the Webley, and dropped it on the carpeted floor.

Three minutes. All of it, including that space after the knockout, had happened within three minutes.

Bill, mechanically wiping his left eye with his glove, still stood staring dully down over the edge of the carpet. Alvarez, still straight, surreptitiously saluted him with hand to hat brim. If Maureen Holmes had been there, she would understand the one word which H.M. had applied to him in the tailor's shop. Alvarez was of a breed long-lost in time: one contemptuous of wounds, refusing to yield; a fool, perhaps; yet once the most dreaded fighting man on earth—the Conquistador of Spain.

Without fuss, Alvarez carefully began to lower himself from the table.

Bill Bentley turned slowly away from the edge of the carpet, as though musing on some deep problem. He walked back to the middle of the carpet in the same thoughtful mood; then his legs tottered, and he fell flat on his face.

Paula let out a cry. She flung off the woolly tan coat, and in yellow sweater and black slacks she climbed up on the carpet. She tried frantically to turn him over on his back. But Bill was not unconscious; merely exhausted and hurt. Under his own power Bill rolled over, closing his eyes against the light. Paula threw herself on his chest, pouring out words but sobbing so much that not one word in ten was coherent.

"Told you it'd be all right," muttered Bill, patting her back with the underside of a stained glove.

More incoherence.

"Love me, baggage?"

"Mmm." She flung her arms under Bill's neck.

Sir Henry Merrivale, standing well back and brooding darkly on the insult to his dignity when he was forced to fall flat on his corporation, would ordinarily have characterized this scene as nauseatin' lovey-dovey.

But the big room was still silent, even more stuffy with its smell of burnt cordite from gun shots. It was a second before H.M., with his acute hearing, peered round. There was the Moorish arch to the little curving corridor, paved with tiles, through which Alvarez had first appeared.

Through it, on slippers all but noiseless, moved an Arab girl in a grey *jalebah,* its head cloth ending in a flat square top like a mortar board. A fine-spun *yashmak,* with black lace edging, was drawn up under her black liquid eyes. In her hands she carried a silver tray with a very clean brass bowl of hot water, a box of modern surgical gauze, a little box of adhesive tape, bottles from a modern chemist, scissors, cloths, and other objects he did not observe.

Knowing the girl's errand to be merciful, H.M. glanced at the other side of the ring. For the first time H.M. saw that Alvarez had gone from the table. Hurrying across to the other side, he slid down the carpets and stood up.

There sat Alvarez on the floor, his back propped up against the carpet pile, dreamily smoking a cigarette.

H.M. cleared his throat and writhed.

"Now looky here!" began the great man, with somewhat the air of a chastened Donald Duck. "I told you I was an old buffer, didn't I? I couldn't tell you, because I was refereein' the goddamndest prize fight that ever was fought. I kept noddin' across to you, though I expect that didn't mean much. Son, that bullet never touched your lung. If it had, you couldn't possibly have kept speaking out the way you did."

Having unburdened himself, H.M.'s spectacles now grew stern.

"All the same, there's some bad interior bleeding. You're going to a nursing home as soon as I can find a tele— Hoy! Are you paying attention to me? What are you thinking about?"

Alvarez drew deeply at the cigarette, coughed as he let out the smoke, and contemplated smoke.

"I was thinking," he said rather bitterly, "of the Knight of La Mancha. How he dreamed of doing great deeds, yet there was not a person who did not laugh at him."

H.M. looked down sourly.

"So? Then let me ask you a question," said H.M. "On whose side would *you* have been? The silly asses who laughed at him? Or fine and brave old Don Quixote?"

"That is not exactly the point. Even his Dulcinea . . ."

"Well, you're goin' to see yours. For the love of Esau, stop this depression and be human again. . . . Is there anything I can do for you?"

Alvarez's right hand, just carrying the cigarette back to his mouth, stopped in the air.

"Yes," he said, sitting up and remembering. "Thanks to Bill, we have taken Collier without firing a shot. Collier, in his pure conceit, thought the place was full of his men instead of mine. I must find Perez, and I have not as much voice left as you think. Get up on the carpet, please. Shout 'Perez' several times, as loudly as you can. I shall follow in a moment; I must congratulate him."

"You stay where you are, son. Got that?"

Again, despite his corporation, H.M. climbed back again.

Bill lay stretched on his back in the middle of the carpet, one arm over his eyes. Every time he spoke, it seemed that his face swelled or ached; but the body bruises, some of which had seemed not bad at the time, were worse.

As they knelt on either side of him, there was a low-voiced furious argument in French between the Arab girl and Paula, whose purely hysterical jealousy would not let the other touch Bill.

"If you please, madame," begged the Arab girl, speaking French in a low, sweet voice, "I ask only because your own hands tremble badly. Regard them. And now regard this! The cut over the eye is not wide or deep. Regard, now!" Water sloshed. "We sponge it off, like this. We apply a little of antiseptic, so that it will not take harm . . ."

"Ow! Go easy!"

"Ilya will not hurt you, sir." The Arab girl spoke almost perfect French, her *yashmak* moving in and out with the words. Scissors clicked. "Now a small length of adhesive gauze, like this. . . ." *Snip, snip, snip.* "Now there are soothing lotions to draw away pain . . ."

"We-el," Paula conceded, and stood up.

H.M., in excellent voice, had been bellowing, "Perez, Perez," with such hideous noise that it must have reached the street above. Paula, turning round and seeing him, made a beeline to weep on his shoulder.

Now H.M. should have expected this. It always happened to him, even with totally strange females. But again he was caught off-guard.

"Oh, lord love a duck," he moaned, looking to heaven with martyrdom and spreading out both arms to show that he had nothing to do with this. "Oh, my dolly! I'm a flamin' wreck already. My blood pressure is awful. That feller Alvarez deliberately tried to blow off my onion with a Webley .45. I had to flop flat down on my stummick, which is . . . Now, now, my dolly. . . ."

Paula's sobbed words were now at least audible, if somewhat mystifying to an outsider. She said that she was vile, mean, unspeakable. Though Bill *would* wear that horrible long raincoat and conical hat when he tinkered with a car, and *would* shock poor old Mr. St. John by saying that Milton and Trollope and Shaw were awful, she did love him terribly: adding several somewhat embarrassing anecdotes in proof of this. But she, the loathsome, once or twice had disloyal thoughts that he wasn't aggressive enough. And all the time he had been going about knocking out world champions, and outwitting international warmongers, and banging his fist on the table. . . .

Meantime, Alvarez had crawled on his right side across the carpet to Bill. Bill was now sitting up, his head hanging over. The Arab girl had applied healing lotion to his face, and was now applying other lotion to his chest and shoulders.

"Cigarette, Bill?" offered Alvarez, holding out the cigarette and a lighter in his right hand.

"Thanks, old boy."

The Arab girl, taking cigarette and lighter, put the cigarette between his lips, kindled it, and handed back the lighter. Her dark eyes regarded Bill with such obvious admiration that it was as well Paula did not see it.

"It was a great fight, Bill."

"No." Bill, head down, expelled smoke and shook his head. "You know it wasn't. You could have smashed him in thirty seconds."

"All the same," said Alvarez, "I told Maureen this afternoon you could do him in one round."

"Only the bloke's conceit," said Bill, "made him think he could do anybody. He really believed that, and I admit he looked in good training with his coat and shirt on. Then we were hypnotized by that tremendous account by Mark Hammond."

Each time he wished to speak the Arab girl took the cigarette out of his mouth. Bill, unconscious of this, first frowned in suspicion and then smiled.

"Oh, Mark is honest enough," he said, with his head down. "He really believed that any American-trained fighter is dangerous until he's well past seventy. Collier was . . . well, an old stumblebum. He could punch hard for forty-five seconds; then he was finished. Thought at the time his body punches weren't hard. I was wrong."

Bill lifted and inspected his right hand. "This is my only gravedigger. Collier covered his chin too much with his left. Had to make him think I hadn't got anything before I could get it over. Cut it damn fine, at that."

Out from the tiled corridor thudded the heavy boots of a short thick-set man in white helmet and belt; he could be no other than Acting Commandant Perez. Leaping up on the carpet, he circled round and squatted down beside Alvarez.

"Commandant, you were wounded — !" he began in Spanish.

"Never mind. We've had him," retorted Alvarez in French, for the benefit of the others. "The pig Collier now lies on the floor, over there, between the carpets and the sideboard. Mr. Bentley . . ."

A brief, tight-closed smile flashed across Perez's brown face.

"We have seen it," he agreed. "What a box beautiful! But it is as well, M. Alvarez, that already we have found the dummy window."

"What dummy window?"

"Did not Colonel Duroc speak to you of it? Well, no matter. It is *there.*" And the Acting Commandant nodded towards the great arch window of crimson panes, the one to the left of the second sideboard, and over which on a metal rail hung the great wine-dark robes, the gleaming, scimitar scabbard, the dagger in its rough blue sheath, the Moorish war hammer.

"You comprehend," Perez rattled on, "that first we have measured the breadth of the wall. It looks itself out, apparently, on a sunken garden. But no! The wall is too thick. The window on the outside has the catch on the wrong side. There is a space between the walls, by which our man might again have dropped into a sewer and made escape."

Here the Acting Commandant sighed.

"By good fortune," he added, "the window catch on this side is rusted and hard to turn. But that is why we have put a guard." He gestured vaguely behind him, towards the opposite, should it be necessary. "Thanks to the Virgin, we do not need them."

He was interrupted. H.M.'s big voice spoke gently.

"There, now, my dolly," he said gently. "Ain't that better?"

Paula, normal again and furtively drying her tears, was much ashamed of herself as she turned round. The Arab girl instantly ceased to rub lotion against Bill's chest, took the cigarette from his mouth to squash it out on the tray, and gathered up her materials.

"I — I ask your pardon," said Paula in a small voice, her head down. "I am often very stupid."

"Stupid?" echoed the Moorish girl, rapidly putting everything on the tray and casting a covert glance at Bill. "Would that all women, madame, were as stupid as you."

"I am called Paula Bentley." She used French as had the other. "Who are you?"

"I am Ilya," replied the Arab girl bitterly, "the wife of Ali."

A stir went through the group.

"And I am here," she went on, still kneeling, "mainly to minister to this hurt gentleman. But also to plead with you that Ali and his four accomplices may not be tried before the court of Mendoubia. It is a just court, oh, a very just court," she added hastily, and shuddered. "But I plead because they would rather face Shaitan himself.

"I plead thus not because I love Ali—I hate him—but as balm for my own wounds. You—" suddenly she raised her dark eyes to the embarrassed H.M.—"though you would deny it with your dying breath, are much too kind-hearted and you have great influence with the Commissioner. Only four times in his life has Ali set eyes on the man Collier, and never once, I swear, on Iron Chest. I make this plea to you, and I say no more."

Bowing her head, she crossed arms on her breast.

"I dunno what this is all about. But can't you do it?" growled H.M, in his most savage tone.

"The difficulty . . ." began Alvarez. But he was interrupted.

"Look!" snapped the still-squatting Perez, and thrust out his forefinger. "The crimson window. Look here!"

And again they saw the man who called himself Gregor Weehawken Collier.

Collier had roused to his senses quicker than they thought. Though still dizzy, he was firm on his legs and arms. Surreptitiously he had drawn down his coat and shirt from the sideboard, and put them on. With labour he had crawled below the line of the carpets to the proper place beneath that window.

And then, as though by a blast of magic, they saw him standing on the windowsill. His left hand clutched a concealed rod up the side of the window under the robes, and with the right hand he was frantically twisting the rusty brass handle of the window to open it.

"Commandant, there is only one thing to be done," demanded Perez.

"Yes!"

While Collier stood like an immense white slug against the

crimson panes, frantically working at the catch, the Acting Commandant swept his hand backwards, upwards and outwards, towards the left-hand wall behind him.

"Garcia!" he shouted.

In the wall a half-hidden square spy hole swung open on hinges.

Tat-tat-tattattat, began the chatter of an automatic rifle, quivering as it ripped bullets across the room

"Down!" yelled Perez. "Down on your faces, everybody, down!"

Paula went down immediately. So did the Arab girl. Even Sir Henry Merrivale once more suffered insult as he flopped forward on his stomach. But Bill, who was anyway outside the line of fire, merely sat there with shoulders hung forward. Alvarez, on his elbow, and Perez squatting, saw with sick despair that the angle of fire was too wide. Garcia could not twist it back.

The bullets smashed down in a line of vertical gouges in the stone just at the right of the window, puffing out a cloud of plaster dust but breaking only one pane of the window. Collier swung round his blood-stained face, sneered at them, and began to swing back.

Again Perez's hand went out and up, towards the right-hand side of the wall behind him. Another spy hole flashed open.

Tat-tat-tattattattat, clattered the second automatic rifle, in the fury of its ten cartridge clip.

Perez shouted out. At last they had a proper angle, ripping straight to Collier's right side. The impact of the first bullet nearly knocked him from the window. His right hand reached up and gripped the rod above the window, leaving the handle to his left. The robes swung, the sheathed dagger swayed. But the imitation white-gold and brass-studded scimitar sheath, swinging wildly, banged against the window and flew backwards into the room, landing on the carpet.

Collier's very clothes seemed to flap and fly in the wind of bullets, not to mention what seeped out from them. The last of the bullets came within an inch of Bill's head.

But Collier had now wrenched open the handle with his left hand, kicking the window wide.

Up went Perez's hand, above his head, while he shouted another unintelligible name.

Tat-tat-tattattat, spurted out the rattle of the third automatic rifle, joined again by the first with a fresh clip. The Moorish hammer seemed to jump out from the rail, and by blind chance landed across the scimitar scabbard. To the staring eyes of Alvarez, a gleaming pattern of hammer and sickle appeared on the carpet.

Tat-tat-tattattat. . . Two lines of fire converged to the right of Collier's back.

In dying agony, releasing the rail with his right hand, Collier gave a terrific spring backwards from the windowsill. He landed heavily, face up, on the carpet. His blood flowed out and over the hammer-and-sickle design as he twitched once and forever lay still.

CHAPTER EIGHTEEN

The morning air, heavy and sunny, lay as bland as Parisian air over Tangier.

"You mean, Sir Henry, that there will be something *worse?*"

"Oh, my wench, much worse. Unless I'm wrong, the biggest blowup is going to come tonight. See how frank I am?"

"Then there's a catch in it," declared Maureen Holmes. "Please, what could possibly happen, with Collier dead and nothing important in his papers about him or even Iron Chest?"

"Aren't you forgetting," said H.M., speaking carefully, "the person called Iron Chest?"

Abruptly he craned round to look through the large plate glass and make sure that his sedan chair with the bearers remained safely inside. In the street they had caught the curiosity of so large and fascinated a crowd that a tactful policeman suggested the change.

H.M., to tell the truth, had no idea where he was.

He knew he sat at an iron table, under the awning, of a *terrasse,* in a great, spacious, pleasant square which might have resembled a square in a large French provincial city if most of the buildings had not been white or dun-coloured instead of grey. Three tree-lined streets swept down into it; three more ascended it. Towards H.M.'s right and across the street some self-important building squatted in cool complacence behind a clipped lawn with an outer fringe of trees.

H.M., however, knew only that he was sitting at the little round table, with three cups of black coffee. Across from him sat Maureen Holmes, in a violet frock and dark violet-coloured shoes. Her pale complexion drew colour from the sun, so that the green eyes and black hair had a new warmth. Across from her sat Paula, considering her a trifle over-dressed; Paula wore her usual white sleeveless silk frock, and bright sandals.

Both of them sheered away from the subject of Iron Chest.

"Last night . . ." Paula began hesitantly.

"Paula, it must have been *horrible,*" said Maureen, putting her hand gently on Paula's shoulder. "I couldn't have stood it, I know. All those bullets . . ."

"Oh, I didn't mind the bullets so much." Paula raised one eyebrow reflectively. "In fact, I rather liked them, though nothing could have induced me to look at Collier's body afterwards." She shuddered. "No, I meant the fight. With that horrible, gross, hairy red robot hitting Bill." Paula spoke with her usual candour. "When Bill threw a right cross and knocked Collier silly, I had hysterics and made a dreadful show of myself. I'm sure I can't think why."

"But it was only natural," protested Maureen. "How is Bill now?"

"Oh, not bad. He's at the hotel. He can move about, of course. But he did get a little punishment. He prefers to lie in bed and read *Zadig.*" Paula yawned, the lids of her eyes drooping. "You know, it's a hot morning. I think I shall go back and turn in myself."

"Juan," said Maureen, regarding her clasped hands, "was rather wonderful too, wasn't he?"

"Yes, dear. Silly-wonderful. Like both of them. And yet," said Paula thoughtfully, "that's how I should prefer them to be. How is Juan now?"

Maureen cast her eyes up to the sky in unembarrassed joy, before consulting a wrist watch.

"In fifteen minutes more," she said, "I'm going out to Dr. MacPhail's nursing home to see Juan. Don't you *love* Dr. MacPhail?"

"Love him?" repeated the literal-minded Paula. "Well, no. He's awfully nice, of course . . ."

"I mean," Maureen added rapidly, "He's got a head like a respectable Caesar. Didn't the old Romans paint their busts to make them lifelike?"

"Sure," growled H.M. sourly, "and a well-painted bust now . . ."

Maureen did not even hear him.

"I mean," she continued, "paint in blue eyes, and ruddy cheeks, and a little fair hair. That's Dr. MacPhail, except you haven't got the twinkle in his eyes or the competence of his manner. He won't let me see Juan too often. He says it's bad chemistry."

"H'm," agreed Paula, enlightened.

"And Juan isn't really hurt too badly," explained Maureen, "except that he didn't get attention soon enough for his chest wound. Dr. MacPhail puts all the blame on Sir Henry."

H.M.'s face turned the colour of a ripe eggplant.

"That's fine," he addressed the square in general. "That's the horn o' gratitude overflowing on my noodle with flowers and honey. If anything goes right, it's luck. If anything goes wrong, it's me. Burn my aunt's britches, that's done it."

Both girls, conscience-stricken, turned towards him. For a horrible instant H.M. really feared that both would make a fuss over him in public. But he glared at them, so like a lion over its haunch of meat, that both remained in their chairs.

"Who's done all the work in this case, hey?" he demanded. Putting down his Churchillian bowler hat, he dramatically opened the side of his coat, showing an inside pocket bulging with papers.

"Y'know," he added, his mood changing, "at the end of this month there'll be a bill for cables, sent by me, that'll stagger even Duroc. Here's one I got yesterday, and forgot even to tell the colonel. It's about the big girl from Madrid."

"What big girl from Madrid?" asked Paula, with faint interest.

"I'm telling you. There once was a . . . No, curse it, you'll have me on limericks again! But can't you remember evidence, when you hear it? There was a big, powerful woman who tried to grab the famous iron chest from the real, solid gold Iron Chest himself."

"Yes!" agreed Maureen, the contents of whose notebook remained in her hand.

"Well, she didn't touch it. That was some time ago. When he was about to fire, she now says she wriggled her hips like some *danseuse*. Only, instead of wriggling 'em to the left, she wriggled 'em to the right and got a bullet there. The point is—she now swears, unconfirmed by Madrid police, she saw Iron Chest's face. He was bald and had a moustache."

"Bald? Moustache?" Maureen and Paula exclaimed together.

"And here's another cable," H.M. continued in his martyr's tone, "about a policeman who every month is getting a payment as much . . . Bah!" he snorted, stuffing back both cables. "What do I get for all my concentrated work, hey?"

"But, according to the notes I put down," protested Maureen, "Iron Chest always wore a hat. How could the Spanish woman tell he was bald?"

For answer H.M. clapped on the bowler, and leered.

"Look, my wench. Couldn't you tell I hadn't got any fur on my onion? Except, of course—" Again he leered, and looked crafty.

Paula's voice was so demure that H.M. saw no trap.

"By the way, they *did* capture that man Ali and his four accomplices?"

"They did, my dolly. Oh, excepting the one your husband knocked dead as a mackerel out of an orange tree. Y'see, I understand this Mendoubia business now. The Mendoubia, or whatever you want to call it, is the Arab court. If an Arab is nabbed, he's questioned by the ordinary Tangier police. But, if they've accumulated enough evidence against him, they're bound to hand him over to the Mendoubia for trial. The Mendoubia is a just court, as that poor little Arab girl said last night. But its quality of mercy is strained pretty awful. They'd rather face this feller whose name I won't pronounce, because I'm sure to get it wrong; anyway, he's the devil."

Here H.M.'s countenance assumed a stern, austere look, like that of an English judge considering the judicial procedure of other countries.

"Y'see, my dolly, I'm awful afraid—in the near future, maybe—there's going to be hokey-pokey in this city."

"Dear Sir Henry," murmured Paula, putting her elbows on the table and gazing into his eyes. "Do tell me. Especially about the poor Arab girl."

H.M. shook his head darkly.

"Duroc says the Mendoubia is very anxious to interview an Arab crook they call the Father of Evil. Well! The Tangier police have spotted him, and they're ready to pounce. It wouldn't surprise me if Duroc made a little deal, an honest deal, though, with the head of the Mendoubia. In return for his handin' over the Father of Evil, they'd give Ali and company a light sentence. Of course that poor innocent girl would go free immediately, the only provision being' that she never saw Ali again. D'ye follow me, my dolly?"

"Definitely," said Paula.

She exchanged glances with Maureen.

"H'm," said Paula thoughtfully.

"Really, Sir Henry," burst out Maureen, with all her directness. "You said the stories about all these awful women were all a pack of lies! And at your age, too!"

"We-el, after all," smiled the broad-minded Paula, "why not?"

"I dunno what you're talkin' about," stormed H.M., giving them a look of awed astonishment which would have deceived his own mother. He became tragic again. "I go through life as good as gold, trying to be a big bulb in a naughty world. But if ever there's the least hokey-pokey, they say, 'That's the old man again.' "

"But isn't it? I mean—isn't it really?" asked Maureen in all seriousness.

"No. I'm a poor defenceless old man. They lead me about. I don't even know where I'm going, much less where I've been. Curse it, I don't even know where we are now!" He half stood up, craned his neck, and glared. "Where are we, anyway?"

"But this is the Place de France," said Paula.

"The . . . what?"

"Yes, didn't you know? That smug-looking building over there is the French Consulate."

A look of pure evil gleamed in the eyes of one who had been so saintly.

"This is the square," said H.M., "that nobody's ever able to cross, under any circumstances whatever?"

"Well . . . I never thought much about it, until you began going on last night. But it's true."

"Hem," said the great man, settling his hat and buttoning his coat. "Back in a moment."

With a look of great innocence, his corporation marching before him, he made his way out among the tables to stand on the edge of the terrain. No motor car, not even a bicycle, moved in the drowsiness and glittering tree-heat of the Place de France.

On the metal cleats of the pedestrian crossing at the Boulevard Pasteur, a traffic policeman drowsed with a whistle in his mount. Two business-men were arguing their way down the rue du Fez into the square. A haughty French nursemaid was pushing a perambulator along the pavement past the consulate. H.M., considering, decided that the longest and best course was to walk obliquely across to the swing doors of the Cintra Bar far away.

"Hem," he repeated. And, at his lordly pigeon-toed stride, arms hooked at his sides, H.M. stepped out and began to cross the Place de France.

Considering the horror of this, it can only be conjectured that any witnesses were too paralyzed by its awfulness to move.

The traffic policeman, eyes flashing open, had the whistle in his mouth but stood petrified with the breath stuck in his throat. The haughty French maid, opening eyes of horror, let the pram get away from her and had to run for it. A slightly drunk law clerk, just emerging from the Cintra, put both hands over his eyes and bolted back inside.

Paula later declared that H.M. would have got fully half-way across—he was near it—if he had not been unintentionally betrayed by a waiter from their own café. The waiter came tearing out of the door with a tray of coffee cups and coffee glasses. He broke the spell by seeing the terrible sight and falling flat amid a crash of crockery and glass.

And then the cataract came down at Lodore.

If H.M. imagined he had heard many police whistles that night when they attempted to catch Collier in the rue Waller, he would have abandoned the thought now. The noise of police whistles seemed to deaden the brain. Policemen, springing up out of nowhere—there seemed to be at least fifty of them—poured across the square and surrounded the culprit.

They shouted, blew their whistles, waved their arms, or did all three, amid a roar in three languages. H.M. was also seen to be waving his hands, bellowing back in English and French. It is a curious fact that the two business-men, who had been descending the rue du Fez, turned and ran hard the other way. H.M. had now produced some bluish object, and was pointing to its unmentionable photograph. The tumult subsided to dead silence, except for one deep, stately voice in French.

"Here veritably," it intoned, "we have the old goodman himself."

Every policeman stood back and saluted. A whistle blew. Immediately they formed two lines in military formation, with H.M. in the middle of the front rank like their officer, and marched him back straight to the café from which he had started.

H.M., not at all displeased, gave a slight hem and turned round. He lifted his hand in salute.

Every man, palm outwards and together, saluted in reply.

"Well, now, thank'ee," said H.M., deeply gratified. "You boys like a drink?"

They would have filled the whole café. Smilingly, declining in three languages because they were on duty, they melted away. H.M. sat down in his old chair, to a spatter of applause from nearby tables.

Paula, doubled up with joy, could not speak. Maureen was genuinely worried.

"What was it?" she asked.

"It was a swindle, like everything else." H.M. now spoke sourly. "No law of Charlemagne; no secret society; not one lightning bolt. But look there!"

He extended his hand, moving it slowly round in a circle.

"Rue Ensenar, boulevard Pasteur," he said, "rue des . . . I forget that one, rue du Fez, rue Belgique, rue du Statut. When the full tide of cars comes whistlin' down the up streets, and even jumps up from the down streets, to cross that square is the shortest way to the Pearly Gates. Cor, can't I believe it! Even for the drivers, I expect they've got to have a wrecking car and an ambulance standin' by. But why *now?* Burn it, there's not a car in sight. There's not . . ."

Down the rue Belgique a pink Buick shot like a demented rocket, screeching at the slight turn as it plunged into the boulevard Pasteur. The traffic policeman, by mere whim, had just elected to blow his whistle and extend his truncheon to stop traffic.

How the Buick did it, without knocking the policeman into a popcorn machine fifteen feet away, is a miracle known only to its makers. Its brakes screamed; they expected it almost to stand up on its haunches, but it stopped. Out of one window appeared the large hat and flowing moustachios of a very fat Italian.

"Scusa," sighed the driver, in the liquid tongue of Dante.

The policeman, quite undisturbed, looked slowly and carefully out over a great square where not even a dog stirred. He blew his whistle, and signalled on the pink Buick, which instantly tore into top gear and shot like a rocket down the boulevard Pasteur.

H.M. pounded his fist on the table.

"They're all crackers, I tell you!" he insisted. "I knew it

before; now I can prove it. Why am I messing about with Charlemagne and thunderbolts when there's real work for me? For instance, now. Yesterday, in my noble costume, I was rowed out in the harbour . . ."

Maureen's curiosity had grown frantic.

"That's the second time I've heard you mention rowing out in the harbour," she protested. "What does it mean?"

"Ho," said H.M., and shut up one eye.

"He is without doubt," murmured Paula in a detached voice, "the most exasperating man I ever met. That Arab girl will poison him, Maureen; you mark my words." But Paula could not keep her detachment. "There's nothing in the harbour," she added, "except a very small cargo and passenger ship, the *Valencia,* I think. Bill and I saw it from the mint-tea tower night before last. And the next boat from Gib isn't due until . . ."

"Stop a bit!" soothed H.M. "What you've got to understand . . ."

At this point a heavy, thick-bodied woman in shiny black, her face daubed with powder, mascara, and lipstick like fly paper, sat down on the edge of H.M's chair, attempted by swinging her posterior to make room, and screamed deafeningly in his ear.

"Ha ha ha," coyly shrieked Ilone Scherbatsky. "You must be ze beeg droonkard! But you iss an Anglich lord and I vish to spik to you."

Now there are times which cannot be glossed over by the chronicler, when the behaviour of Sir Henry Merrivale must be considered as no less than deplorable. To certain ladies, even if in somewhat unorthodox fashion, he can be gallantry itself. To other ladies, those whom he considers unfeminine, his conduct cannot too deeply be lamented.

Thus, rising up slightly, H.M. swung his own mighty posterior slightly to the right for purchase and then swung it to the left like a battering ram. It caught Ilone Scherbatsky on the thigh, sending her flying from the chair and landing in a seated position beside the table.

Here H.M. bent down malignant spectacles.

"You smackin' well *are* ze damn nuisance," he stated clearly. "But you are not ze R-r-ussian countess and burn me if I vish to spik to you. Now sling your hook."

Ilone, who had always been treated with deep deference in the main because of her money, was so astounded and infuriated that she merely sat where she landed. Today she wore a black hat bearing the figure of a large white dummy cockatoo, from whose red beak dangled a tiny bell. It tinkled with each wave of agitation.

"Mark," she gasped. "You vill lift me from 'ere! Alzo you get me a chair."

None had noticed her approach, or that of Hammond. Hammond, in a very conservative brown suit and brown hat, was not now surrounded by an aura of gin. His fastidious mouth looked grim. With another powerful heave of his slender-looking shoulders, he set Ilone on her feet.

"I greatly fear," he said, "that all the chairs are occupied."

"Then get me one from one of zees . . . zees – " Her contemptuous look swept round.

"One day, Ilone," said Hammond politely, "your reputation for good nature will vanish too, and then nobody will tolerate you."

But Ilone had heard nothing. Suddenly observing Paula and Maureen, she screamed again, hurled out her arms, and pounced for both to give a lipsticky kiss.

"No, dear," said Paula in a dangerously gentle voice.

It must be repeated that Ilone Scherbatsky was no fool. She paused, bewildered. She did not know that the easygoing Paula, who had spoken only pleasant things of her, had heard from Bill through Colonel Duroc through H.M. of certain words in a tailor's shop yesterday.

Here Paula moved her arms and shoulders in a way which electrified several men on the pavement. Her imitation of Ilone was almost perfect.

"Ah, zis Bill!" cried Paula, with gestures. "He is Anglich. He is not *amoureux*. Ven 'e teach me ze pistol shoot, he do not visper pretty compliments to me; he do not touch me here, and here, and here."

Paula's normal voice returned. "And at target practice, too. Good heavens, who would? Why not at Alpine climbing?"

"Assez, assez!" screamed Ilone, holding out one hand tragically. "I forgive you. Hélas! I forgive everybody. Zat is my veakness. Besides, you are Anglich and all Anglich is cold."

"Do you think so, really?" sweetly inquired Paula, with a curious curl of her lips. Then her tone changed again. "Ah, *un Francais! Quel amant!* Always he look round for ze voomans in company! He do not go to clubs and get dronk, no! He is not com-for-*table* with his own sex. . . . If I had a husband who never wanted to go to his club and get drunk with his male friends," burst out Paula, who was English to the core, "I'd pretty well know all he was good for! What do you know of real love, you old harpy?"

"I forgive you!" repeated Ilone. "Zat is my veakness. I am a R-ru-us—" Here she stopped, remembered something, and looked at the glowering H.M. "Zis big droonkard has called me vat I am not! I ask heem—vy?"

Hammond, trying to shush her, gave Ilone an angry look. But both regarded H.M. in an odd way, as though they had some vague memory of having seen him somewhere before. They did not recognize that forgotten holy man, Hassan-el-Mulik.

"I am insult!" persisted Ilone. "Vy you say zat?"

"Ma'am," glared H.M, "your accent is so polyglot and generally messed up that it's hard to tell what you originally were. You interchange *v*'s and *w*'s in just the wrong places. No French person, in spite of all fiction, ever has or ever will say 'ze' or 'zat.' No, the sound is like 'de' or 'dat.' But the Teutonic peoples give you 'ze' and 'zat.' So do lots of Russians. You might even be Russian, though I think you're from Hungary."

"I am ze Countess Scherbatsky, vife of ze Count Scherbatsky!"

"Well, you may be," said H.M. "But in an awful dull novel, by an awful dull writer named Tolstoi—its called *Anna Karenina*—there's a very aristocratic old gal named the 'Princess Scherbatsky.' Maybe the author just invented her; maybe your husband stuck his birth in a fine old line. Or maybe Mark Twain opened Burke's Peerage and found the Duke of Bilgewater. Like to make a little bet?"

Ilone, merely livid and speechless, did not even make a gesture.

"I knew it," whispered Paula. "I told Bill the title was a fake."

"For many years," Hammond remarked gloomily, "I have been wondering when somebody would spot that. Though I can't agree with your poor view of Tolstoi," he glanced at Ilone, "I'm afraid the lady is in one of her less malleable moods. Shall I get you a taxi, Ilone?"

Ilone paid no attention. She was dancing with both feet on

the pavement in time to the bell on her hat, while she advanced her face menacingly towards H.M's.

"I moost g-know vat go on!" she shrieked. "I must be *au fait—vous avez compris?* — or I die. Yes, I die. Here! I learn only"—for enlightenment it must be remembered that you cannot strike a match in Tangier without someone learning of it—"zat Bill Bentley has knock out Collier in ze firs' round, and afterwards zey shoot Collier full of bullets." She thrust out her face towards H.M. "Now you tell me—vat else is zere to learn?"

"Ma'am," said H.M., sticking his unmentionable face almost in her face, "I wouldn't tell you if you did die on the pavement. There's a very pleasin' spot just there," he added hopefully.

"No?" shrieked Ilone, drawing up and back dramatically. "Zen I tell you vat *you* do not know! Yes! It is a rumour which run ze streets of all Tangier. Iron Chest, zis criminal, is in fact a vooman!"

"What on earth . . ." began Maureen, her green eyes wide-open. But Paula, her good humour restored, merely giggled and shushed her.

"A *vooman?*" yelled Ilone—and made her great dramatic gesture.

Leaping sideways out into the road, flinging up her arm like the Statue of Liberty, and shouting, "Taxi," Ilone was nearly murdered by a Citroen taxi which sprang straight at her and all but ran her down. At the same moment they heard the rattling and grinding of a jeep dashing full speed down the rue Belgique; they watched it crash into a turn.

Ilone leaped into the cab. Only by inches did the jeep avoid smashing against the back of the Citroen, which shot off down the rue du Statut. Still there was a general impression that the jeep meant to proceed straight into the café, except that its magnificent reeling turn brought it up full sideways to the curb. Hammond walked away in another direction, seeking gin.

Out of the jeep, with strutting majesty and the driver behind him, stepped Colonel Duroc.

He did not speak, though his eye indicated that he might have everybody present hanged at any moment. Strutting over to the table of Sir Henry Merrivale, he murmured into H.M.'s ear.

"Enough!" he said. "Now we will have the lunch and make

the conference. You whisper. You hint. You shake. But this night, I ask, what is to happen?"

H.M. suddenly yanked down the Colonel's head so that nobody heard his whisper in reply.

"Maybe not much," he said. "But Iron Chest, the real Iron Chest in person, will try to crack Bernstein and Company tonight."

At this point, both Paula and Maureen made their excuses to leave. H.M. and the Colonel adjourned to the restaurant Ciro in the rue Raphael nearby, for a lunch which lasted over four hours.

And then the shadows lengthened down from the Old Mountain, over an ancient and half-dry river, up and down again over ridges of Franco-Spanish villas, and presently became greyish-blue even in the winking lamps of Tangier.

H.M., at his lunch conference, had outlined to the Colonel exactly one-half—no more—of the plan he had in mind. Determined to be the Old Maestro if it choked him, he meant to execute the remainder himself. Only two questions, repeated endlessly, hammered on at the argument.

"Then you will swear this is to happen?" inquired Duroc, tapping the table.

"No, no, no! Nobody can do that. It may be tonight, or tomorrow, or a week after Whitsun. All I'm doing is gamblin' on Iron Chest's character for tonight. What's bothering you?"

Duroc, his tufted eyebrows drawn down over blue penetrating eyes, looked suspicious.

"I tell you in frankness," he said. "I fear the hoke-poke."

"What d'y mean, the . . . Oh, I see." H.M. scowled. "Y'know, Colonel, you honestly do speak very good English."

"Un petit peu, peut-être," replied the well-gratified Colonel, turning out his wrist in a deprecating way. "I have been much with the British Army as with the Belgian. The best I know of English is too indecent to speak. But also I read your great poets, Ben Shakespeare and the rest."

"What I mean," persisted the purist H.M, "is that just lately you've been using some awful English phrases; and curse me," he added, completely baffled, "if I can tell where you got 'em."

"You do not know, by burn?" asked the astounded Colonel. "Well, no matter then. But I repeat: I have heard too

much of this Chief Inspector Masters. Always you try to do him in the eye. I ask myself: do you wish to do *me* in the eye too, Cain and Abel?"

"Look here," said H.M. "When you and your crowd raided a certain place in the block of flats at 40-bis Marshan last night, did you get a hatful of diamonds or not? You did! Did your coppers shoot Collier as dead as a doornail? They did! And"—H.M. reached for a handful of newspapers from the nearest table—"are they whoopin' you up as a detective like Lecoq and Rouletabille and Arsène Lupin rolled into one? Honest, now, would I do you in the eye?"

"We-el," deprecated the other, his chest swelling nevertheless. "Come! When you tell me of the vanish tricks, and I myself deduce who is the real criminal . . . Stop! Enough. We try your scheme."

Thus they had left the restaurant, Colonel Duroc in his jeep to set the wires humming, H.M. (strangely) on foot for another mysterious errand into the Kasbah and elsewhere. So the shadows gathered, strengthening, down from the Old Mountain, turning to greyish-blue and then to purplish-black.

The electric lamps of the New Town grew harder and brighter against it; the maps of the Old Town, from electric to tallow, crept out and up their snaky hill. The Little Socco woke up and spiritually began to dance. Behind discreet curtains, roulette wheels prepared to hum and cards to slide smoothly from the shoe. Manslaughter was being prepared in the Place de France.

But it was not until a little past ten o'clock—they had allowed a later hour for the appearance of Iron Chest—that Sir Henry Merrivale lumbered down the rue du Statut from the Place de France.

Though H.M. has no nerves to speak of, he was playing a dangerous game and he knew it. Once or twice he growled to himself. He passed the middle slope of the descending street, all white fronts with separated gilded letters, with the Minzeh Hotel now on his right and the premises of Messrs. Cook on his left.

He did not alter his step, on the left-hand pavement, until he neared the scene of their first adventure. The directions being reversed, the rue du Midi lay to the left with the bank at the corner; on his right the steps and incline down into the rue Waller. At the corner was the one dim street lamp, intensifying shadow beyond.

At a curious waddle he crossed the rue du Midi, sensing two skulkers in a doorway on the other side. At his left, beyond two doors, he saw the now very dark alley at the side of Bernstein et Cie. Across the two glass-fronted windows of the jeweller's, the folding steel network was closed and heavily locked, as H.M. discovered by twisting the lock.

He drifted only a few feet farther on, glancing into the black dusty window across which ran the enamelled letters, "Louisa Bonomi: Masks and Costumes," in two languages.

Pure grotesqueness looked him in the face, and ran through his mind. Seen closely, a half-circle of masks swung across the inside of the window. They were of *papier-mâché* or rubber, painted or unpainted, all with blank eyes or sometimes gaping mouths. Long curls of hair hung between them: Just behind them stood the dummy figure of a policeman and the dummy figure of the Moslem devil.

Putting out his hand, making sure the door was locked as it should be, H.M. turned and stood a few steps back towards the jeweller's. He was a dim shape in his black alpaca suit and bowler. Another dark shape in civilian clothes, squat and thick, loomed up beside him.

"I have you, then, old joker," familiarly chuckled Acting Commandant Perez in French. "S-sst, all goes well?"

"All goes well, my assassin," agreed H.M.

"Now tell me," whispered Perez, nodding across the street, "is he in truth a man of yours, as he says?"

H.M. had seen, but not chosen to notice. Lounging against the wall on a sort of cat-walk pavement past the wall of a closed shop, there stood a lean, wild figure possibly intended to represent a Spaniard as conceived in the nightmare mind of Hollywood. In his hands, with long powerful fingers, he held a guitar. He wore an immense flopping hat, and tight-fitting red trousers with pearl buttons encased the long legs.

"He is silent now," continued Perez. "But for half an hour and more he screeches hideously at singing, and he is the original murderer of a guitar. Who is he?"

In partial answer, the very tall and lean man ripped his hand across the strings. Out poured the voice, strong yet hoarse and melancholy, of one who has not seen his homeland for twenty-five years.

Tyke me back to dear old blighty,
Put me on the tryne for London Town . . .

"Not so loud," H.M. called across the road. The voice dropped to a melancholy yowl.

"I used to know the type," continued H.M. in French. "I have found him here in a bar. He was once the fastest sprinter in the Kensington Light Infantry Territorials."

"Ah, my old fox," chuckled Perez. "Good."

"Very sure, my green pig," H.M. assured him. "I figure to myself, now, what you were thinking. When the dead Collier has tried to rob this jeweller, on the roof opposite sits a fat Italian with a guitar. You have wondered to yourself whether the loud singing and playing would conceal the noise of an electric drill?"

"It is not for nothing," growled Perez, "they call you the old goodman."

"Yet one remembers," said H.M., "that, when the alarm of burglars begins, this Italian has dropped his guitar and smashed. No, my cauliflower! No accomplice would have been so surprised he dropped his guitar. That man was what he pretended to be. My man across the street is there to watch and be ready to run. Where now is the Colonel?"

"By here," muttered Perez, and they turned into the dark alley.

"Yours was good advice," Perez continued. "There are two of our best men across the street. Sergeant Garcia and I are at the back of this alley. The Colonel is inside the office of the safe with Sergeant Bonfleur. Fewer watchers, but better placed, so you said once. Good!"

Perez tapped—two long, two short knocks—at the side door of Bernstein et Cie.

It is a sober fact that a bead of sweat ran down from inside H.M's bowler hat, and trickled across his face.

He knew now that what he expected was going to happen, and happen within a few minutes. But he could not tell when, in this few minutes. He must not waste too much time, yet . . .

"Enter," said Colonel Duroc in French. H.M. lumbered in, while the Acting Commandant moved on to the back of the alley.

H.M. closed the solid door. It was not quite darkness, in which he could vaguely see the forms of Colonel Duroc and another man.

"By blue," softly swore the Colonel, "this time I cannot see how Iron Chest has any chance whatever. Look there!"

The beam of a torch hooded in tissue paper moved across the room up the surface of the untouched, untouchable surface of the safe. H.M. stood with his back to the door, which was ordinarily secured by a heavy spring lock, a bolt, and a key. H.M. tapped the door.

"Do you leave this door unlocked?" he asked.

"Of course!" gritted back the Colonel. Without sound, after his magician's tactics as related elsewhere, H.M. eased the key out of the door and palmed it in his right hand. Then he began slowly to open the door.

"Where are you going?" asked the startled and alarmed Colonel.

"S-sst! One goes for a little promenade. One will take care."

"Be sure!" hissed Duroc. "The Sultan's diamonds, uninsured, are in that safe as a trap. If Iron Chest creeps into the safe, if anything should go wrong, we are armed to the eyebrows and we shoot."

Another bead of sweat ran down under H.M.'s hat. Soon now, very soon . . .

Slipping out of the door, H.M. closed it and for a moment stood casually with his back to it. From the rear of the alley, of course, Perez and Garcia could dimly see him silhouetted against faint light from the street. Hands behind his back, H.M.'s right hand slipped the key into the lock from outside. Without any noise even when the key turned, he locked it from outside and pocketed the key.

Stealthily he crept to the mouth of the alley, turned round and to the left, and began to edge back up the rue du Statut with one hand trailing over the folding steel work across the front of the jeweller's store. It was silent except for noise and movement in the Grand Socco at the end of the street.

Not minutes, now. How many seconds?

Across the street, from the Cockney in disguise, voice and guitar were homesick with an old song:

We are Fred Karno's army,

The ragtime in-fan-tree,
We cannot fight, we cannot march,
What goddam use are we?

Then it happened.

A considerable distance away but seeming nearer, and from the harbour, a broad flare of yellow-white light sprang high above all Tangier. The immense crash of the explosion, as the little cargo and passenger ship *Valencia* blew to pieces without a soul aboard, stunned even those who were used to high explosive in earlier days.

Sir Henry Merrivale threw out his arm towards his confederate across the street. The Cockney, crying out in fluent Spanish that he had just seen a man with an iron chest rushing up from the Grand Socco, himself raced down. Hair-trigger emotions leaped too soon. Out from one doorway shot two men, flying after the Cockney. Out from the alley flashed Perez and Garcia, also running hard in the same wrong direction.

H.M., now at the door of the mask and costume shop, whipped out another key and put it into the lock. This duplicate key he had cut from a mould taken yesterday and secretly, on a piece of soap, while he and good Señora Bonomi debated his costume as Hassan-el-Mulik.

Twisting the key, opening the door creakily, H.M. closed it behind him. The shop, with a faint glow that showed white and ghastly mask faces, was densely full of smoke with a bitter tang in it; smoke from a smaller explosion designed to be covered by the first. In it glimmered an electric torch.

"That's enough, Iron Chest," H.M. declared. "Now come out from behind that smoke. Hurry!"

The torch winked.

"I was afraid of this," said a familiar voice.

And, ducking through the smoke, coughing, but with hands raised and left eye still battered, stood up the figure of Bill Bentley.

For a moment they stared at each other, while Bill kept the light on the floor.

"What's the matter with you?" he asked, holding out his hands as though for handcuffs.

"Well, what's the matter with *you?*" said H.M. in a kind of muffled bellow. "I'm not here to arrest you or capture you. I'm here to get you away, out of Tangier and into a safe place for good. Yes, yes, don't tell me; your wife didn't know one single thing about your career as Iron Chest; but I told her and she adores you for it. The special plane's ready for both of you. Now follow me and run like blazes!"

CHAPTER NINETEEN

Two days later, at ten o'clock in the morning, an awning was lowered over the red tiles and marble balustrade of the terrace outside Colonel Duroc's house on the Old Mountain.

It protected those on the terrace from a white, burning sun, unusual so early in the year. The only occupant, at the moment, was Colonel Duroc in uniform, but without a cap, pacing backwards and forwards with short, fussy steps.

It is regrettable that the Colonel, a genuinely good-hearted man, should so often have had to appear in this chronicle in a state of gibbering rage. But facts cannot be helped; and, after all, he had been dealing with H.M. On his head each short white hair seemed to quiver like some wire connected with the electric chair. Though his face was not quite purple, it was near enough.

Stopping his pacing, he swung again towards the front door and for the third time yelled for the fat'ma, whose padded slippers brought her forth again.

"This viper—!" roared the Colonel. Then, with much dignity, he clamped himself hard. You must not speak thus before servants, especially Arab servants. "Is Sir Henry Merrivale not even awake yet?"

The fat'ma gave him a reproachful look.

"The goodman," she corrected, "still snores in healthy slumber."

Colonel Duroc put his hands over his eyes.

"Now harken unto me," he continued in Arabic, "for this time I swear it by Allah. If this *goodman* is not present, here on this balcony, within ten minutes of the clock, I will strangle you with my own hands."

The Colonel glanced round. Against the back wall now stood a long swing, of green-and-white striped padding, hung on a steel framework and with a small awning of its own. Up to it was pressed the round wicker table.

"He may have his breakfast there," added the Colonel. "Should we have in the house any large quantities of arsenic, or other poison sufficiently painful, you will pour it liberally over his food."

Though the fat'ma gave him another injured glance as she moved, it is a fact that within at least ten minutes the viper in question stood on the balcony. Sir Henry Merrivale, freshly shaven, had a look of pure serenity on his face. He still wore carpet slippers, pyjamas and dressing gown, the latter two being of such hideous intertwined colours that Duroc could not decide which was worse.

"Morning, Colonel," said H.M. serenely. He inflated his chest and hammered his fist on it.

Colonel Duroc deliberately turned his back and folded his arms.

The fat'ma rolled out the tea wagon, piled with a breakfast of two hard-boiled eggs, huge slices of ham together with those red sausages which seem to come from heaven rather than Italy, well-buttered toast, a large silver coffee pot with milk jug and all the accessories.

Indicating that H.M. was to sit down on the swing, which he did, his collation was placed on the table piece by piece over a smooth linen cloth.

"Thank'ee, ma'am," said H.M. "This is downright handsome, this is."

The fat'ma, showing all her gold fillings in a smile, reverently bowed backwards out of his presence. With immense satisfaction H.M. picked up the coffee pot in one hand, the milk jug in the other, and poured both. Then, after a long pull at the coffee, he set down the cup.

"Nice weather we're havin'," he volunteered.

The Colonel, back towards him, did not comment.

"I say, Colonel," observed H.M., mildly bothered, "somehow I sense a distinctly chilly feeling in the atmosphere. What have *I* done?"

Duroc, completely staggered, spun round and let go in English.

"What have you done?" he demanded, as though this question had been put to him by ancient Latouche or more modern Jack the Ripper.

"Uh-huh. That's right."

"Villain! Serpent! Traitor!" began Duroc, in the best Chamber-of-Deputies style. But again he recovered himself for a statement of dignity. "All well, I tell you. This Bill Bentley, this Iron Chest—and also his poor innocent wife, who will regret this to the bitterest of her dying day—you have arranged for them to escape to a country in East Africa from which there is *no* extradition by *any* country. And this so-innocent-looking Bentley is an impostor and a thief and a murderer!"

H.M. took up a knife and neatly decapitated the top of a hard-boiled egg.

"Well . . . now," he said. "Tell me, Colonel: just how many murders has Bentley committed?"

There was a silence.

The Colonel opened his mouth, but shut it again. He glanced over towards one of the wicker chairs, on which were piled high his thick *dossiers*.

"Can you think of one, son?" asked H.M.

But Duroc shot out his forefinger.

"Actually, no! The policeman in Brussels, understood, did not die. He is not even insane, since he has only that small loss of memory about the shooting. But what of intention, old hound fox? He fires almost straight into Emil Leurant's forehead, eh?" jeered the Colonel. "That is good, eh? And why does he do it?"

"Because," replied H.M., "for the first and only time in his life—in Brussels on May 5, last year in '49—he completely lost his head. You know why. But it nearly sent Bentley out of his mind. He's been brooding about it ever since."

"He regrets this, eh? Pah! I present you with the nuts!"

"Stop a bit," muttered H.M., groping in the pockets of his dressing gown. "I forgot to show you that cablegram, the latest news from Brussels . . ."

"What cablegram?" demanded the Colonel.

"Well, it was from the Brussels police. Since three weeks after that shootin' of the policeman, Emil Leurant has been receiving a pension. It's paid monthly, through so many banks that the police can't or don't want to trace it . . ."

"What is this?"

"I'm tellin' you. The pension to that policeman is the same as the salary of the Commissioner of Police at Brussels. If you don't believe me, I can show you the cable."

Colonel Duroc twitched a handkerchief out of his sleeve, mopped his forehead, and replaced the handkerchief.

"But now I have you, old *farceur!"* he snapped. "There was a big woman in Madrid. She had tried to rush at him, and Bentley or Iron Chest has deliberately shoot against her hip . . ."

"Not according to her own testimony, he didn't," said H.M. "Lord love a duck! I forgot to show you—"

"Not another cable? No, no, no!"

"But it is. Madrid police. Upstairs in my inside coat pocket. The woman herself says she swung her big hip the wrong way when she should have swung in the proper way. And Bentley, an A-1 crack shot who was trying to miss her as he always did, couldn't help her swinging straight into the bullet when it was too late."

Colonel Duroc looked dazed.

"It seem to me," he cried, "that you would defend this man as well as help him. All well; he is not a murderer. But you cannot deny he is a burglar and a mean thief!"

H.M. considered for a moment, his breakfast forgotten.

"Y'know, Colonel, you can deduce well enough on hard facts. But you can't see motives, or understand plain, ordinary, human beings."

"Then I pray explain me!"

"Bill Bentley," H.M. went on thoughtfully, "was the only real sportsman of a criminal, if you can call him a criminal at all, . . ."

"Quoi!"

". . . I ever met in my life. That's why he and Alvarez got on so well. If you'd seen his face, when Alvarez called him 'sportsman' just before the fight with Collier . . . Never mind, you weren't there. But let's see, now—whom did Bentley rob?"

"Who he rob?"

"You yourself told me," continued H.M., "he never once cracked a private house. In other words, he never took a penny from anyone who could even remotely be affected by losin' it. What did he crack? *Only* big firms of jewellers and rich small banks, which—d'ye see?— were bound to be heavily protected by insurance. Ever think of that?"

"But, whoever shall lose, it is against the law!"

"Oh, absolutely," agreed H.M., leaning lazily back in the swing. Again that expression of serenity stole across his face. "It's against the law. It's shockin'. Big companies oughtn't ever to be nicked like that, ought they? And yet somehow, me being an old sinner, it fails to curdle my blood. It's too much like doin' down the bookies or the income tax. All three of 'em fair game."

There was a silence, while H.M.'s voice seemed to thicken.

"And now," he said, "would you like to hear the real, personal, human-being reason why I wanted Bentley to escape?"

"Yes," snapped the Colonel, his face empurpling again. "If you can."

Whereupon, deplorable to relate, H.M.'s temper blew to pieces with a bang. He surged up, amid a heavy rattle of dishes.

"It was because I like both of 'em," he roared. "That's all; that's enough. Especially I liked that little gal Paula. *You* talk about 'regrets' and 'dyin' days.' Cor! Before I'd let 'em break that gal's heart by arresting her husband, I'd have upset the government of hell and kicked Satan off the smoky throne! Don't come any moralist nonsense over me; it won't go down. Don't try any blatter about 'law' or 'justice'; we both know they don't exist, unless we go out and get 'em for ourselves. Now stick that where you like, but don't forget it!"

Colonel Duroc moistened dry lips. Several changes of colour had come over his face during H.M.'s outburst.

"You would break any law," he muttered, very slowly. "for the sake of friendship . . ."

His voice trailed away. He turned his back and walked to the balustrade, where he looked down over the ridges of Tangier. Beside him on the balustrade stood a marble urn frothing over more heavily with darkening purple blossom. Colonel Duroc tore off an edge of blossom and fretted it. He glanced sideways at the marble nymph.

H.M., whose temper had subsided and who looked a bit sheepish, spoke just the same.

"You'd have done the same thing, Colonel," he said quietly, "if you'd known the characters of the people. What's more, from what I guess of your life, you've done it yourself more than once."

"Pah!" said the Colonel without turning round. But he did not deny the statement.

Meantime, H.M. rediscovered his breakfast. Ham, toast, sausages were wolfed down as well as the smallest scraping of egg. He was sitting back drinking coffee before the Colonel spoke again. Duroc seemed to address an oration to the ridges of Tangier.

"I should have been warned," he declared passionately. "Do not I know already this man's record in America? By burn, it is *'orr*-ible! He steal evidence from the police. Into clink he has thrown the Mayor of Riddleburg. And New York! They chase him up Lexington Avenue in his night shirt, with police shooting at him with pistols. He blackmail Commissioner Finnegan . . ."

"Oh, son, I was only gettin' justice."

The Colonel sighed, whipped round on his heel, and marched back to H.M.

"My friend," he said in a new and different voice, "in my official position I cannot approve your lunatic notion of law. But never think I do not understand."

And he thrust out his hand. H.M. shook it heartily; then, as at their first meeting on this balcony, they were both strongly embarrassed. The usual way out was not available. Unless they were a couple of topers, they could not shout for a bottle of whisky at breakfast time. But it was the Colonel who found inspiration.

"Listen" he urged. "I am acquainted with all the facts, yes. But, if I do not see the people, I do not understand at all. Will you begin at the beginning, and tell me the whole story again; also how you pluck out clues where I see no clues?"

"I second that motion," exclaimed Maureen Holmes, hurrying on to the terrace.

Maureen, her dark-green frock a contrast to her green eyes, looked happy and healthy, yet, with her romantic mind, unhappy too.

"I know some things," she said. "I know Paula and Bill had to go away." She swallowed. "But how did Iron Chest vanish out of a street in Brussels? How did Iron Chest make diamonds and the chest disappear, when I was there? . . . It's over an hour before I can see Juan."

Maureen sat down. Colonel Duroc drew up a chair.

"Proceed," said the Colonel.

"All right," agreed H.M, inhaling smoke complacently. "I'll begin at the very start, when I arrive in the plane with this stubborn, insultin' wench here—*shut up*—and neither of us had ever heard of Iron Chest. The Colonel was bein' as crafty as Machiavelli and Tom Sawyer put together. While he was putting up a welcome for me as the mighty boozer and wencher, which the same I am not—*shut up*—he was luring me out to this house so that he could apply soft words and get me into this mess. Alvarez himself had to act like the Mystery Man from Indianapolis.

"Well, Paula Bentley was there, to represent her husband from the British Consulate. In all innocence she made a remark. I'll tell you what it was." H.M.'s prodigious memory could reach back and grip the smallest detail. "She said, 'They're always sending poor Bill to some dreadful place all over the world to write a report about mud or bananas or machinery or something.' And, 'Of course Bill returned only three days ago.'

"Now two facts—that her husband was doin' a lot of travelling, and that Lisbon is an airport centre for Western Europe—didn't register in my onion at all. Why should they?

"Or another point, after, hem, my noble welcome at the airport. Paula ran off and phoned her husband I was here. I know now—from what she told me herself—she told him she could easily tell where we were going: to this house. Remember, she told Alvarez out loud when he was cavortin' that car on one wheel; Paula said *she'd* tell us where we were goin', if Alvarez didn't; and she said she knew it all the time when we got here. But again, why should it make me wonder?

"As a result, here we landed and you know the rest, outwardly. Even the Old Man's mild temper was goaded by the barefaced, low-minded insults of a person whom I'm not goin' to name, except that she'll look terrible if she doesn't powder the left side of her nose. . . ."

Maureen groaned.

"Oh, please," she begged. "I knew you could solve the mystery. You've done it. But you were so overbearing, so insufferable . . ."

"Me?"

". . . That I had to challenge you. I—I'm awfully sorry. I know your outward attitude towards women is all a fake," said Maureen sweetly, lifting her chin and looking him in the eyes, "and I'm not afraid of you. Except sometimes, maybe," she added hastily. "But"—her gaze drifted away again—"if anybody had taken your bet about Iron Chest, you'd have lost it. You didn't nail him in forty-eight hours. No, wait! Please, I apologize."

"Cease and desist this argument," snapped Colonel Duroc. "Enough, now, continue!"

"Honestly sorry," said Maureen, looking down. "I rather love the old son of a—gun."

"Hem!" said H.M., gratified and emitting poisonous smoke. "Now listen carefully, because we're coming to the one key that unlocks nearly every mystery in the case.

"On this balcony, with the wench taking notes, the Colonel begins to tell me about—so he says—a vicious, mean-minded murderer. Oh, my eye! Even before he described that business at Brussels, there were flames crawlin' up my collar at the general information. What struck me most was this: on every one of his burglaries, this unknown man had carried a chest made of iron, one foot deep and wide by two feet long, weighing forty pounds or maybe more. . . . Cor!

"That sent me into a minor fit, as maybe you both noticed. Questions and answers went buzzin' through my head so fast after I told this wench to write it down, that I stumbled on the real answer almost before I realized it. *Why* did he do that?

"Stop a bit—what had I already heard? Out of a number of burglaries not a soul could give any description of this feller. Nor a soul could describe his face, his clothes, anything, even though some of 'em, many, as I later learned must have got close to him. Why couldn't they describe him?

"Got it! Or maybe. Because that big, glimmerin' iron chest, with a frieze of monkeys' heads, would rivet everybody's eyes. It would hypnotize 'em away from noticing anything else. They wouldn't be looking for a man, but an iron chest. It would be the best possible misdirection. It would be the best possible disguise, except that . . .

"No. Won't do. Unless the feller really is scatty, he won't lug about a weight like that just as a disguise. It'd be simpler to stick a mask on his face. No, no! That's out too, unless . . ."

H.M.'s big voice trailed away. He let a cloud of smoke drift up.

"That was the point, if you remember, where I said, 'I want more information. Though it's just possible that . . .'

"I didn't finish. Because the real, honest-Injun explanation dropped on my cokernut like a horseshoe.

"Suppose the iron chest wasn't really made of iron? Suppose it was made of heavy cardboard on a slim wooden frame? Suppose it could be folded together flat, like a lot of boxes? Suppose it had been painted, by a first-class still-life artist, to look exactly like iron under a dull light?"

Again there was a pause. H.M.'s head stuck out like an ogre's from under the swing awning, and his voice was like the ogre's.

"Why, then," he leered, *"it would serve a double purpose. It would fix attention on the chest, not the man, especially if he carried it as though it were very heavy; you've seen the same thing done in comedy. Second, purpose? If he ever got into a tight corner, it could immediately be folded flat—one foot wide, two feet long, with a hook—and be hidden inside the back of a loose topcoat."*

Colonel Duroc smiled sourly.

"Well," said H.M. in his normal voice, "that was the idea that bumped me. I told you to go on, Colonel, but it was rustlin' and buzzin' round in what you might call a bothered way while you told me about the jewel robbery and shooting and vanishing trick in Brussels."

"Wait," protested Maureen. "This won't do."

"Ho?"

"The policeman who was shot and recovered from it . . . He touched the chest; in fact, he gripped it on each side with his arms over and under! He can testify it *must* have been made of iron."

"Oh, no, he can't," said H.M. "Lord love a duck, but that was the very thing that stumped and sugared me while the Colonel here was telling the story. Until I suddenly remembered—" Here he looked sternly at Maureen. "Got that notebook of yours?"

"I—I'm afraid I lost it," she answered, lowering her defences. "So much has been happening—"

"We-el, never mind. I'll try to quote from memory, my wench."

"Are you being nice to me again?" Maureen asked quickly and hopefully.

"Curse it, I've never been anything else. But will you lemme get at this?

"All right," continued H.M. "The Colonel here told me just what you've said: that this copper, Emil Leurant, remembered getting a good grip on the chest and then seeing the burglar's face before the shot was fired. But, says Leurant, he can't remember anything about the face.

"Right! That seemed to stymie everything, including the vanishing. But, not ten seconds afterwards, the Colonel said: 'Thus the policeman, Emil Leurant, is fairly clear up to the time he saw the iron chest; and at once the man fired.' Whoa! Oi! That's a clear contradiction. Will you explain, Colonel?"

Colonel Duroc inclined his head.

"You see, Mademoiselle Maureen," he said, "Emil Leurant honestly believes to this day he touched iron. But he did not. He thinks so because he has *seen* the chest, and heard so much about it. The contradiction, which myself I do not perceive until this old pirate pointed it out, is that these things do not happen in what you call slow motion. Leurant dives for the chest; Bentley fires. Zip! At once! Like that! And Leurant cannot really remember touching the chest or seeing the man's face."

"And so, towards the end of the story," continued Sir Henry Merrivale, "my cokernut was hit again. Two apparent contradictions made one real truth. The 'iron' chest really was painted cardboard on a wooden frame, ready to be folded up. D'ye have a clear picture of what happened in that quiet, dim-lit little street, with the trees on each side?

"Bentley is in mid-career as Iron Chest. He steps out of the jeweller's. The copper leaps and for the first time somebody *touches* that chest. That's why Bentley goes completely loony and fires. Then he's in even worse a trap. People will come running from a street of lighted cafés nearby.

"What he did would take much less than the few seconds he needed. His diamond loot's in his pocket. He steps into the heavy shadow under a tree, he flattens out that cardboard chest with its hook at the narrow end, he whips off his jacket . . .

"No," H.M. corrected himself. "I had to stop there. The ordinary suit coat fits too closely to hide the bulk of that cardboard, if it's slung from the collar down the back. Iron Chest has to be wearing a loose coat of some kind. And yet everybody swears it's a very warm night; it couldn't be an overcoat or a topcoat. The only thing left would be one of those long Continental raincoats. So," said H.M. simply, "I asked the Colonel whether there'd been any rain that night. He said there had, but for some reason you both seemed to think I was ready for the loony bin myself."

"True, true," said the scowling Colonel. "And just before that, you might remind Miss Holmes . . ."

"Haah," agreed H.M., again leering at Maureen. "Just before that, speaking of Iron Chest, the Colonel had said, 'All, of course, have read about him in the newspapers.' I told you to write that down, because it was very important. You glared at me; just glared."

"I didn't glare! I didn't! I only thou—"

"Never mind," said H.M. with hurt dignity. "But it was important. Because, as I keep stressing, the iron chest was the whole point. When those people poured across from both sides into the street, they were like the policeman—they looked for an iron chest. Whoever carried the chest, they reasoned accordin' to their lights, must be the criminal, because he couldn't get rid of it. He was stuck with that weight. He couldn't chuck it over a fence, or hide it, or do anything with it. But all Bentley did, as I told you, was step behind a tree and in a matter of seconds hide a piece of cardboard. They saw him, all right; he mixed and mingled with 'em; but his hands were empty and nobody noticed him.

"And that's the very simple secret of every apparent 'vanishing' in the whole business. Have you got it now, my wench?"

Maureen nodded. "Yes, but how . . ."

"Be quiet and you'll hear. Immediately afterwards, when the Colonel began to tell me about that affair in Paris, we heard a very old car come bumping and rattling up the road. That car conked out for good in the garage. But in it was a tall young feller, with wide shoulders, wearing a conical straw hat and exactly the sort of grey raincoat I'd been thinkin' about. Cor, didn't my eyes begin to bulge!"

"I told poor Juan," interrupted Maureen, "about that very raincoat, the following afternoon."

"And," grunted H.M., "the little gal herself—Paula, I mean— burbled about how ridiculous that raincoat was when she was cryin' on my shoulder after the Bentley-Collier fight. But never mind that. . . . We're speakin' of Bentley's arrival here in the dead car.

"The little gal had already gone. But *I* insisted, remember, that this Bentley should sit down and hear the readin' of all the evidence against Iron Chest. Occasionally I'd chuck a casual question at him, mostly about himself or his background. Neither of you two can remember, because he never troubled to conceal anything. But I'll bet he's more than once talked about his background with his wife.

"His old man had started him in life as an electrical engineer, because Bill thought that meant nothing but tinkerin' with gadgets. He loved tinkering with gadgets, such as that car. An electric safe drill would have been nuts to him . . ."

"Quoi?" demanded Colonel Duroc, galvanized.

"That's the slang English," said H.M. "It means he'd have loved it and liked to use it. Now stop interrupting me! But Bentley found electrical engineering was more than he thought. So he dropped it and took up painting. Though he couldn't paint figures for nuts . . . easy, Colonel . . . he was first-class at still life. He could have made and painted that 'iron' chest as easy as winking. Finally, he'd done a great deal of travelling, and his base *must* have been Lisbon."

Colonel Duroc rose to his feet, bowed formally, and sat down again.

"You note, Miss Holmes," he said, "that this old *coquin* has not solve your mystery within forty-eight hours. He has solve it within forty-eight minutes."

"No, no, no!" protested H.M., who was so serious that he did not even bask in a compliment. "That was only a mild indication. Listen. . . .

"While we sat here on this balcony with Bentley, I kept watchin' him. He was good-natured and easygoing; no sham about that. But also his brain could move like lightening while he seemed to be slow-moving. In the boxing match he showed both his brain and his body could move together so fast it blurred your eyesight. But never mind that, now.

"At the same time he was sittin' here, you, Colonel, were pouring out the whole story of Iron Chest's career. Originally I swallowed your version of him as a vicious-minded murderer, who'd bash even if he didn't manage to kill.

"But what did the Colonel tell me? In twelve spectacular burglaries, Iron Chest has been seen in public, and people have rushed straight for him, at least nine times. Nine times! Furthermore, he's fired from one to a number of shots at 'em.

"That, of course, was to keep anybody from touching the imitation chest. But a fusillade like that! You'd think that the rottenest shot, who was mean-souled and vicious, must have got at least half of 'em at close range through the head or body. Burn me, anybody must have! *And yet not one of 'em is touched, even by bullets that come close, except a fat Spanish gal who swung her hip the wrong way by accident and the Brussels policeman.* D'ye see? That's where—as I said later—I revised my estimate of matters. This rain of bullets that miss is too much. Iron Chest is really a top-notch crack shot, so afraid of even wounding anybody that he fires a deliberate near-miss even when he's in danger. And, I learned later that same evening, Bill Bentley was the best pistol shot in Tangier.

"It was on that same night, too," H.M. went on earnestly, "that the first actual evidence began to show. Bentley and Collier were partners. Bentley allowed Collier, though Bentley was worried about it, to try that first burglary at Bernstein's. But . . ."

"Please," exclaimed Maureen, "I *must* ask a question or burst!"

When the ogre looked at her, Maureen used all her considerable femininity when she returned the look; and the ogre was as wax.

"I can understand," said Maureen, again imitating Paula by leaning back and crossing her knees, "how Bill could have prowled all over Western Europe—Amsterdam, Brussels, Paris, Rome, Madrid, Lisbon—but no farther, because he hadn't time and he had a real consular mission somewhere else. He could leave here with his own passport. He had to, because everybody knew him . . ."

"That's not bad, my wench!" said H.M., watching her shining eyes as her mind groped. "But, when he got to Lisbon, what would he do?"

"He'd pick up his burglar's kit and cardboard iron chest," Maureen rushed on rapidly, her eyes fixed and wide, "at . . . at Lisbon, of course! He'd hide them there each time, because he had to start from Lisbon wherever he went. And he'd start from Lisbon . . . yes, with a fake passport." Her face and inspiration fell. "But where would he get a fake passport?"

"From good old Ali," said H.M., regarding her like a schoolmaster with a favourite pupil. "You weren't there, but the Colonel was, when I said the first question I asked Ali in my interview was whether he could get me a fake passport. That was so simple . . . Cor!

"No," H.M. hastened to add, "Bentley never did meet Ali, or any of the gang. Bentley did it through Collier. He sent a photograph with a fine wig and a toothbrush moustache. 'Course, Bentley's fake passport would be English, his profession written in as . . ."

Maureen stretched out both hands to him.

"Locksmith!" she cried. "Just as Collier did once. Then Iron Chest could go through the customs anywhere, explain all his burgling kit and even the drill, and point to 'locksmith' on his passport. The iron chest, which seemed to be the biggest problem, was really the easiest. He could wrap up the chest, flattened, in a brown-paper parcel, and stick it at the back of the trunk. Even if a customs inspector wanted it opened, he could have tacked a painting of his own over the frame. It was easy!"

Up to this point H.M., the schoolmaster, had listened complacently while Maureen's imagination confirmed things that Bill Bentley had told him before Bill and Paula departed hastily in the special plane. Now an evil look showed on H.M.'s face as he remembered. Maureen's guesses were partly from real evidence, but partly from information received. *He* was the one for analysis and deduction. He was the old man.

"Hoy," he said sternly.

"I was only thinking . . . yes, Sir Henry?"

"You said you wanted to ask a question. All you've done is gone on gibberin' like Cassandra. What's your question? Then *I'm* tellin' this story."

"I'm afraid it will have to be two questions now."

"Then fire away! Let's hear 'em."

"It's true, isn't it, that Bill Bentley left all his Iron Chest gear—disguise, passport, burglar's kit, imitation chest, and so on—in Lisbon somewhere? He never brought them to Tangier?"

"That's right. He was too well known here; it was too dangerous. Suppose somebody spotted 'em at the British Consulate? Or in his hotel room; his wife, for instance? No, he never brought anything here."

"Then," blurted Maureen, her face white with concentration, "Collier must have carried at least the burglar's kit and the imitation chest through the customs here. But it wasn't an ordinary customs inspection. Colonel Duroc, the whole French customs force and Tangier police. They didn't merely inspect. They measured and weighed and opened and tore things to pieces. That's my question. How, *how* could Collier bring those things through the customs without being caught?"

"Collier didn't bring 'em," replied H.M. woodenly.

"But someone must have brought them. . . . Who did?"

"I did," answered H.M.

"What?"

"Oh, my wench!" said H.M. dismally. "It's the only possible solution. Swing your mind back again to the afternoon we arrived. We were both given diplomatic immunity from having our luggage searched. Don't you remember how they whisked out two trunks and hand luggage, and piled it into a little luggage van that followed us down here? That van was driven by the looniest of all loony chauffeurs in Tangier; and it gave me a blood pressure that might make me die even yet." H.M. brooded darkly. "Whoopin' out in a field," he added, "and then chargin' back to nearly smack the stern off our car. Cor!"

"You mean this man Collier put the stuff in your trunk before the Lisbon plane left for Tangier?"

"Uh-huh."

"But wouldn't that have been dangerous?"

"No, not much. You can deduce what happened from the facts. Remember, Bentley had returned to Tangier only a few days. Collier was still in Lisbon. On March 31, one day before our plane left, Colonel Duroc set off a whole blast of skyrockets from every newspaper here. They shouted that the One and Only Bacchus, the Lead-Kindly-Light of All Wenchers, would arrive next day by the nine-thirty plane; and that this Wonder Boy would be given an official reception.

"What follows? Bill Bentley, who was in the Consular, knew perfectly smacking well what an official reception meant. Among other things, it meant that the visitin' Stuffed Owl and anybody with him would be allowed immunity from luggage search.

"Then what would Bentley naturally do? He'd phone Collier in Lisbon, and tell him to put the dibs inside my trunk. Collier must have howled with joy, because he'd expected it to be harder to smuggle 'em into Tangier.

"After you've weighed in a trunk at a big airport, it's hoicked away. It stands for a while, with a lot of other trunks or luggage, before they shove it on the plane. Each brand of modern trunk, and there aren't so very many brands, has its own key pattern; you can accumulate a whole string of duplicates. Bently and Collier, in their work both had sets of duplicates.

"So Collier, while the trunk was alone with the others,

simply walked up and unlocked what was presumably his own trunk. Into it he put the burglar's kit and the imitation chest flattened out. He locked the trunk and walked away. I've done the same thing myself and nobody noticed. Only it did happen to be my own trunk."

Here H.M., fiendish glee in his face, rubbed his hands together.

"So again," he went on, "we come back to our arrival here, and that luggage van tearin' after us. You'd gone for a walk," he looked at Maureen, "but the Colonel and I heard the van come bumpin' into the garage under this balcony. We even heard the servants carrying up the luggage to the bedroom on the floor above.

"Now again I want you to remember the arrival of Bentley, *in that roomy raincoat,* as he drives up and the car, or so he says, drops dead. I want you to see a piece of smilin' effrontery that was done smack under our eyes, and we didn't see it!"

"Effrontery?" repeated Maureen.

"Yes. Now what was the very first thing Bentley did, after he said his car had died?"

"But he didn't do anything. . . . Wait! Well, he only ran upstairs to telephone for a taxi. The phone is upstairs."

"Right. But on that same floor just above, as the Colonel pointed out when we arrived and as I've indicated just now, what else was there?"

"Our bedrooms. With the luggage!" Enlightenment struck Maureen's eyes. "But you can't mean Bill possibly—"

"Oh, yes. He made a genuine phone call for a taxi. But also he had to hurry, in case somebody wanted to unpack. He had the few seconds necessary to go to my bedroom, open the trunk with his own duplicate key, take out the dibs, and lock the trunk again. Whereupon, if it please you, my fatheads, he hung the flattened chest from its hook to the back of his jacket inside the raincoat. The wrapped-up cloth kit of burglar's tools, which isn't so very long or thick after all, also went inside his raincoat, propped up along his side, with his hand supporting it through his side pocket. And in this he casually strolled downstairs.

"But that wasn't all, not by a jugful! Y'see, he couldn't get into the taxi and drive away in full view of all of us, including the taxi driver. If he did, he'd have to sit down on that cardboard and light wood imitation chest, and he'd smash it to blazes. He had to wait until it was dark enough so that he could unhook it and sling it out sideways in the taxi.

"So for two mortal hours, while the taxi driver went to sleep, he stayed there leaning or lounging against the balustrade with all the stuff in his raincoat, while he talked amiably about the adventures of Iron Chest, or Collier's arrival. Mind you, I already *suspected* the bloke. But I never dreamed he'd have the colossal, star-gazin' cheek to do that, especially as I didn't think until later about the dibs being in my own trunk. I can still see Bentley's face, solid and innocent looking, but with the straight sardonic wit at the corners of his eyes.

"When it was gettin' dark enough, he gave us kind of a stumblin' farewell. I'd already suggested taking him in with us, to keep an eye on him. But he got into the taxi with his goods, and sailed away: first to hand the stuff to Collier, then to meet his wife—who, by the way, had said she was supposed to meet *him*."

"Well done!" Maureen blurted out involuntarily.

"Pah!" snorted Colonel Duroc. "Goose me, no!"

H.M. silenced both with a malignant look.

"Back we come," he said, "to that fatal first night, the night of the burglary at Bernstein's, when I was sure Bentley was our man. By the way, does anybody here know a Turk named Abdul Yussuf?"

Duroc merely grunted. Maureen declared a firm negative.

"Well, you don't have to." H.M. sounded comfortable. "He's only a piece of background; what's important, in its own way, is his evidence. As I say, he's a Turk who always wears an Arab *jalebah* with full-peaked hood. He's got a licence to keep a garden to drink mint tea on the top of an old tower near the joining of the Mediterranean and the harbour."

"I remember," said Maureen. "Paula told me."

"Yes. She and Bill had gone for a swim. Afterwards they

decided—it was still early—to drink mint tea on top of this tower. The old boy in the *jalebah,* who was drowsin' near the door speaks English better than I do. He thought their conversation was sinister, and reported it to the nearest police station. They wrote it down, but nobody thought it was very sinister. It was only revealing.

"Bill talked a lot about Iron Chest: mainly telling what I've just told you, about what happened to us here, but omitting all reference to his tricks with burgling kits or fake chests. The little gal, Paula, kept insisting he was worried about money.

"And so he was, but not in the way she thought. His motive for playing Iron Chest, though he never admitted being Iron Chest except to me, he never made much of a secret; it was public property; certainly he told it to Paula. It was, simply, to retire—to get away from grinds and settle among books.

"But now he was worried. He had a tidy little fortune in new, cut, salable diamonds which couldn't be recognized, as well as untraceable cash. Did he need that last raid against the Sultan's diamonds? Soon he'd retire. Remember, we saw only the froth on top of his mind. But he'd have to tell Paula soon. If somebody had written down his real thoughts fairly, it might have run something like this: *He did not want to tell her the truth as yet, thought there was no reason why he should not have done so. . . . He searched his mind for some excuse which, while convincing, should also sound true.* He found it, of course, in spoutin' all that hocus-pocus about capturing Iron Chest and gathering the reward, which he never meant. But let's go on to the time when he takes a roundabout way and idles the car past Bernstein's in the rue du Statut.

"Y'know, his arrival on the scene seemed *too* pat. A little *too* closely timed. Before the Colonel and I could tumble out that side door together, with the door lamp burning, there was Bentley smack in the middle of things without our knowing how he'd got there.

"He went whizzin' past us for a clean tackle. Of course, Collier had messed up everything by not studying the premises closely enough beforehand—Iron Chest always studied 'em—and Collier needed help. To give him help, Bentley must also establish an alibi for himself.

"Maybe my eye was becomin' too jaundiced. But, of all the rugger tackles I ever saw, that was the rummiest. He had a straight chance for both knees, not even a hand-off to stop him . . ."

"Hand-off?" repeated Maureen.

"In American football, which is a good deal like rugger, you'd call it a stiff arm."

"Oh. But please go on."

"But his left arm goes up for the iron chest. If he really thinks it's iron, that's an impossible move. I think that's where he probably whispers, 'Don't worry, this is Bill; kick your leg free.' Bill himself later realized how fishy his behaviour had looked, and admitted he ought to have tried a clean tackle. But he still tried to defend himself, with this: 'But the damned iron was polished; kind of a film on it, like polished steel; my fingers slipped on it, and down I went.'

"Lord love a duck, that tore it!

"Unless every combination of probabilities had gone wrong, that chest wasn't made of iron. He was lying. Now I had to get real evidence.

"Of course I never had any plan for catching Iron Chest, not a concrete one such as I mentioned in the Parade Bar; I was speaking in front of Bentley, and fishing. And you'll understand how Collier 'disappeared' from the rue Waller. For a time Collier lost his head about that chest, and didn't know what to do with it. The wild stamping and neighing of horses in those stables gave the tip-off. If Collier simply folded up the chest, shoved it under straw along the wall, and then flopped down like a toper, rolled over and played drunk, nobody would notice him—and nobody did—because he didn't have the iron chest and couldn't have concealed it. I might add that both Paula and Bill Bentley had a narrow escape; Collier couldn't shoot for beans.

"And now," H.M. was still revelling, "we come to the next morning. Both you two—as well as Paula and Alvarez—had your dramatic spat with Collier in the crimson-shuttered flat in Marshan. I s'pose," he looked drowsily at Maureen, "you want to know why Collier rented the flat, and then immediately put that rental advertisement in the

Tangier Gazette?"

"It was a fake," exclaimed Maureen.

H.M. glared her into silence. "But not the kind you're thinkin', my wench. Wherever he went, Collier rented a flat. For two reasons: as a secret meeting place for political purposes, and a hide-out where he could cut the diamonds undisturbed. He shipped his load of Bibles and other gear ahead of him, and wrote the manager of the flats about painting the blinds, enclosing the money to do it.

"But before he leaves Lisbon, what happens? Bentley calls him about planting the tools, etcetera, in *my* luggage, and tells him that he, Collier, is to pull the Bernstein deal. That means, in all probability, he won't be in Tangier any time at all—so what does he do? He cables an advertisement to the *Tangier Gazette* offerin' a sublet. It never entered his head that either Paula or Maureen would be looking for an apartment. Cor! Don't you know he was one surprised blighter when Paula walked in that door!"

"Well, that explains the flat and the crimson blinds," admitted Maureen. *"But how on earth did Collier make the chest and those diamonds disappear?"*

"Whatever you wish, my wench," agreed H.M. magnanimously. "Let's take Paula's own account, after she'd burst in on Collier at that inhuman hour and been locked out again. Outside, fortunately, she met Alvarez. Now follow it: they stayed there, by the time given for talking, at least two minutes. Paula heard noises inside. She couldn't identify them. But you tell me: was it a cold day?"

"In the morning, bitterly cold."

"Right. By the way, was there a fire burning in the living room of Collier's flat?"

"Yes, of course, a comparatively small grate holding a bright coal fire that . . ." Maureen drew a quick breath, and again her eyes widened.

"Now at least three times," said H.M. fiercely, "to the point of the gorge risin', we've heard a description of uncut diamonds. They're smallish, jagged lumps, coloured grey and rough on the surface.

"That's the whole story. Pour your diamonds into the fire, where they'll be covered with greyish ash or coal dust, and they'll be indistinguishable from pieces of unburnt coal. Finally shove in pieces of cardboard, especially with oil paint on 'em, and they'll burn like oil-soaked paper in less than a minute. As for the diamonds—ask any consultant—they won't be harmed or melt in the fire except one so infernally hot it'd have to be ten times fiercer than this."

"But the cardboard! Wouldn't there be ash?"

"Uh-huh, and there was. Ever talk to Alvarez about that? He tramped all over bits of heavy, flaky ash when they'd raked out the fire. That's why his questions were so difficult to answer literally. You were lookin' straight at the stuff, but you never saw it.

"That applies to the great big blazin' clue about the chest. Alvarez saw it; ask him. Or, rather, he was confused and angry, and he wasn't quite sure himself. On the centre table in that room was a tablecloth of very soft velvet. Remember?"

"Well, something about it."

"Now on that table, and for some time after Paula burst in, had been standing what purported to be a heavy iron chest weighing around forty pounds. But on the soft velvet there wasn't any impression, such as would have been made by a genuine chest. There were no marks even from cardboard and light wood strips. The surface wasn't disturbed at all.

"Of course you see what happened. The tenant of a flat like that is supposed to sweep up the ashes of his own fire, put 'em in a little bin, and stick 'em in a service hatch for the porter to carry down to the cellar.

"Me," said, H.M. swelling up his chest and tapping it, "not being there, I couldn't tell you what precautions to take. But, when afterwards I unburdened myself to the Colonel about iron chests, and he began to smash the furniture, he knew what to do. There was a man still left at the flats, the Greek porter, who was quite innocent."

"It is so," interposed Colonel Duroc. "He himself takes the ashes and the 'unburnt coal,' which is diamonds, down in the cellar to the ashes bin, and dump them there. I myself lead a party to trap Iron Chest to come and take them. But he does not. No; Bentley decides to try elsewhere."

H.M. nodded. He took out a cigar, but did not light it.

"And that's nearly all, except for human character—I

mean Bill Bentley's—during that rather rough night in the Kasbah, when Collier died.

" 'Course," sneered H.M., lifting one shoulder delicately, "it wasn't a very rough night. True, some—hem—blighter did polish off a Middle-European sneak thief with a knife in an alley on the way there; but that's got nothing to do with us."

"Ha ha ha," said the Colonel bitterly. "I forget him, yes." His temper foamed. "But this I tell you, Sir Henry. You, who come to detect, are the worst mobster I ever meet. When I find a man's throat slit *so,* and the way his hair has been seized, I know experience when I see it! Good experience, I say."

"Well . . . now," muttered H.M. deprecatingly. "Maybe I had to do something like that in Marseilles once; or two or three times at Port Said' or maybe in Occupied Germany . . ."

"Stop!" cried the Colonel. "In this detective, there is more depravity than any criminal."

"Not in a fair-play deal, son. I hadda risk that rattlesnake's leap before I could grab him by the hair. But, as I was saying, about Bentley. Bentley had got to the point, that night, where he and Collier had got to part brass rags. He was boilin'. Worst of all, Paula had walked instead of Maureen into Collier's parlour. Remember, Collier had seen you and me talkin' together aboard that plane, my wench. He'd seen us go across in official welcome. But he'd seen Paula too, Paula walked into his parlour, and reappeared with the police.

"Bentley was quietly awaiting an opportunity to see Collier face to face, even if Collier betrayed him. Collier had done the one unforgiveable thing. Even though he didn't quite know who Paula was, Collier had threatened to cut Paula's throat; and in Bill's eyes that was like the unforgiveable sin. If any danger threatened that little gal . . ."

Maureen spoke softly without raising her eyes.

"Paula was your darling, too," she stated. "That's mainly why you arranged the getaway. That's really why you called her 'my dolly' and me 'my wench.' "

"Y'know, Colonel," said H.M., "there ought to be a law against women having such long memories about personal trifles."

"I too am married," agreed the Colonel.

"And I'm going to *get* married," cried Maureen, her pale face flushing and her eyes shining. "To Juan, as soon as he gets out of the nursing home."

Leaping to his feet, Colonel Duroc beamed and chuckled all over the place. He fussed over her like an old hen. Only with difficulty was he restrained from shouting for champagne, and his feeling was bitter as regarded H.M.'s disdainful look.

"You," he said witheringly. "You have no heart."

"I do not know," retorted H.M., with a villainous imitation of the Colonel's accent, "which is worse: the sentimentality American—or the sentimentality Belgian."

The Colonel's face turned several colours.

"For the love of Esau," yelled H.M., "be quiet while I finish.

"That night, when Alvarez was going into the Kasbah to take Collier, Bill Bentley was quite willing to go. He tried by every means to stop Paula, but she wouldn't be stopped. Now he had a gun. Collier would have a gun; Collier, who'd streaked back to the Riff Hotel just after he nipped out of the Marshan flat and got back to the Riff Hotel just as the alarm went out, had picked up his Banker's Special as well as other things.

"But watch the time that night, when Bill and Paula and I entered old Ali's house by the front door. We sneaked down the stairs towards the carpet room, and got inside in a line against the wall. Neither of you two happened to be there, but I was and I can vouch for what you've heard.

"If I'd ever had a doubt of Bentley's guilt, that was gone now. Standing on a pile of rugs, with his back to us, you could see only Collier's black hair, and a thick body. Paula has said *she* wasn't sure it was Collier. All the talk had been about a red-haired man; he hadn't dyed his hair black until early afternoon. I wasn't absolutely sure myself.

"But Bentley knew instantly. He knew, even though he was never supposed to have seen Collier before. Even on the night in the alley beside Bernstein's, Bentley was lying on his back trying to look back and up; I can testify he couldn't see Collier. But I repeat—Bentley knew. He slid that Webley revolver out of his pocket, whispering something to the effect he never thought he could shoot a man in the back.

"And he couldn't, though it would mean the end of someone who might betray him. He literally, physically couldn't shoot a man in the back. Then he realized something and whispered it. Collier had a gun too. If he called out to Collier, and waited for him to turn round so that they'd be level for a fair duel—well, that was a sportin' proposition and a straight one. Cor! I'd like to wring the scrawny neck of the red-robed old mummy of a judge who said it wasn't.

"But we were interrupted.

"Collier heard Alvarez coming from the other direction. It happened so quickly that Bill hadn't even time to get ready. Collier, a bad shot, fired twice at Alvarez and missed. When Alvarez contemptuously walked close, Collier scored with one shot in the chest. . . . I'm sorry, my wench. I don't want to . . ."

"It's all right," said Maureen, lowering her eyes but trembling just the same. "I'm the one who's stupid. He's perfectly all right now. But if I'd been there . . . you see?"

"Anyway, he came round to our side of the carpet pile, when Bentley twisted the gun muzzle in the back of his neck. While I was examining him, Bentley backed Collier to the middle of the carpets. Just then I happened to glance up and back; and I saw Collier as well as Bentley when they faced each other.

"Oh, my fatheads! It was a dead giveaway. Collier's eyes opened wide, as they do when you recognize; then narrowed, and gave Bentley a very meaning look from under the eyelids. Collier said something like, 'What do you think *you're* doing?' That emphasis on the 'you' made it clear that Bentley was no stranger to Collier. Oh, Collier knew!

"Bentley said, 'You'll find out,' with just as significant a look. It could mean only he was warning Collier to keep quiet, and not give him away; maybe Bentley was here to help him. Whether Collier believed that or not, he was willing to go with it for a while. He honestly believed, at the time, that Ali's men were covering him and he had nothing to fear.

"Then Bentley had a decision to make. Alvarez was badly smashed up. Alvarez, who'd been humiliated three times by a boxer who he knew couldn't even hurt him, was in sick agony. Alvarez would have given his soul to see that Old Pretender smashed. If you don't think Bentley's reason was a sportsman's, I'll stop just here.

"Bentley offered to fight for three reasons, though he wasn't even sure he could beat Collier. He offered it to avenge his friend, because Collier had threatened Paula's life, and finally . . ."

"Yes?" prompted Maureen.

"He despised the Communist tie-up. Collier was a red-hot party member and Bill despised him for it and his phony fetish of crimson blinds.

"Of all the people in this world, you couldn't have found two people farther apart in character than Bentley and Collier. Just say they differ in everything, and you'll have it. Collier hated Bentley almost as much as Bentley hated Collier. When or where they met isn't important. But he *had* to have a diamond cutter who was crooked. Honest diamond cutters ask questions about where uncut stones come from; and there are very few dishonest ones, 'cause it's just as profitable to be straight.

"For those three reasons. We saw his fine strategy, the risks he took, the way in which he used his head—all Iron Chest's strategy. He was nearly knocked out with a blow to the wind. But he came, and landed that Mary Ann which wrote finis to Collier.

"Collier must have known, when he was being beaten badly, that none of Ali's men could possibly be there; that the police had trapped him and would arrest him. So he'd shout out at the end and denounce Bentley too. Bentley also knew perfectly well, when he threw that final knockout punch, that he himself was done. Once Collier woke up he'd be denounced. So he sat there to take his medicine. All that prevented it was that Collier remained punch-drunk even when he woke up, and all he could think about was gettin' away. So he died against the red window.

"About Bentley's try against Bernstein's, there's not much to tell. That was two nights ago . . ."

"Yes," interrupted Maureen, "and where were you yesterday? A whole day gone, and even the Colonel couldn't find you?"

"Ha ha ha," said Colonel Duroc. "This old evil-doer does not dare to face me. For one part of the day he is seen smoking *keef* on a bench by the beach, and they photograph him. For another . . ."

"That's enough!" snapped H.M., with massive dignity. "Do you want me to tell you the very last incident, or not? From the second day I was convinced—because of Bentley's vanity, his one bad trait; *I* got no vanity—that he was goin' to crack Bernstein's again if it killed him. And he was determined to do it under our very noses. But how? He couldn't tackle the front of that safe; it'd be too well guarded.

"But he might, just might, tackle the back of it. He might scrape away, easily, the wood and plaster at the back of the safe which, remember, is against the wall on that side. He knew that both Bernstein's and Louisa Bonomi's would be closed because it was Sunday. During the day, gettin' a key as I got one, he could use his electric drill to make a hole through the back of the safe, almost through the steel. Then he would return that night and with old-fashioned 'soup,' and enough of it, he would blow an opening *if* only he had an explosion timed to cover its noise. He couldn't use a building; Bentley's not the killing kind.

"But there was an empty ship in the harbour, a little one, nobody aboard except a bribable second officer. He could be bribed to set a time fuse and go ashore, his fuse timed exactly with the one to the safe. Risky, but possible. I'd been thinking from the first that was the only way to do it; but I was awful surprised when it really happened.

"After it was all over, I made Bentley leave the diamonds because they were uninsured; I made him leave his fingerprints and another dummy chest, because I promised to give you evidence. And that's all except one tiny fact. The woman in Madrid thought he was bald when Bentley was wearin' only his moustache and no wig. A service haircut leaves something on your head, yes, but it makes you look bald with a hat on; and Bentley's army haircut messed up everything."

"I am glad he got away," Maureen said. "Bill never killed

anybody, except the knife thrower in the orange tree, Paula told me, in self-defence. He never robbed anybody who couldn't spare it a thousand times over." Maureen's gaze wandered away for a moment and she seemed lost in thought. "There was another man, or perhaps somebody mostly from folklore," she continued dreamily, "who did the same thing. But he's been honoured and loved for nearly eight hundred years. They—they called him Robin Hood."

H.M. regarded her in astonishment.

"But what have I been trying to tell you all this time . . . my dolly?"